"FOUR SCALPS" OFER TAL, MOUNTAIN MAN

TERRY GROSZ

WOLFPACK
PUBLISHING
— EST 2013 —

"Four Scalps" Ofer Tal, Mountain Man
Terry Grosz

Wolfpack Publishing
6032 Wheat Penny Avenue
Las Vegas, NV 89122

Print Edition
Copyright © 2018 Terry Grosz

ISBN: 978-1-64119-331-3

CONTENTS

1. CHAPTER 1 — THE CALL OF THE WILDERNESS   I
2. CHAPTER 2 — THE ODYSSEY BEGINS   43
3. CHAPTER 3 — LEARNING THE "TRADE" ON THE "MUSSELSHELL"   73
4. CHAPTER 4 — THIRTEEN ARROWS, "TWO CROWS" AND "FOUR SCALPS"   97
5. CHAPTER 5 — OF GROS VENTRE, "BUCKSKINS" AND THE "RED HAND"   131
6. CHAPTER 6 — TROUBLE AT FT. MANUEL, THE LEGEND OF "RED HAND" BEGINS   159
7. CHAPTER 7 — THE MUSSELSHELL, OF "BLACKFEET, BUCKSKINS AND BEAR TRAPS"   173
8. CHAPTER 8 — "TRUCE", OF MUSKRATS, MARTEN AND FORT MANUEL   217
9. CHAPTER 9 — TRAPPING ON THE "SMITH", THE DEATH OF "LEARNING BEAR"   249
10. CHAPTER 10 — DEATH ON THE MUSSELSHELL, JACK THORN'S "REWARD"   281
11. CHAPTER 11 — BLACKFEET TROUBLE ON THE "SMITH", RETURN OF "SCAR FACE"   313
12. CHAPTER 12 — A "SIXTH SENSE", BLACKFEET AND "BEAR TRAPS"   337
13. CHAPTER 13 — A MAN CALLED "EUSTACE", TRAPPING THE "ROSEBUD"   369
14. CHAPTER 14 — THE ARIKARA AND GOING HOME   415
15. CHAPTER 15 — THE CALL OF THE WILDERNESS   443

A look at Crossed Arrows   459
About the Author   461

This book is dedicated to my son, Richard Grosz, Resident Agent in Charge for North and South Dakota for the U.S. Fish and Wildlife Service.

Richard's dream career as a federal wildlife officer started when he was just nine years old at Chase Lake in North Dakota while goose hunting with his father, Terry Grosz. Trying to spend time with one of my two sons and still work (which was legal in those days) as a Special Agent with the U.S. Fish and Wildlife Service, I found myself working in on three duck shooters who were illegally killing redhead ducks. Finally contacting my illegal shooters so they could be stopped and apprehended for their shooting violations, I all of a sudden was surprised to have my son come busting through the tules and ream the three illegal duck shooters for killing closed season redhead ducks! When I had left him earlier, he was hunting geese from a pit blind a hundred yards away. Then all of a sudden, here was Rich reaming the illegal shooters, who were in the process of denying to me they were killing redheads. Yet, here was Rich at age nine, who had identified the species of ducks from over one hundred yards away and was now in the process of letting the duck shooters know of their serious waterfowl violations! Later after citing the illegal duck shooters, Richard and I had a 'little talk' about how a law enforcement officer must work, without interference, in order to do his job. As I explained to my son 'the rules of the road' when he was with me in the future, I could see he had an unusual look on his face and that everything I was saying was being committed to 'stone'! And then I thought to myself, "Oh no! I hope he doesn't want to grow up and become an agent like me."

From that day forward, Rich quietly committed his soul and life to protecting those in the world of wildlife who had little or no voice. Years later Richard's peregrinations began. Richard earned a B.A. Degree in Biology and Criminal Justice while attending Metro State College in Denver, in addition to playing basketball under a full scholarship. Then Richard went to Humboldt State College, the finest wildlife management college in the nation, where his dad had earned a B.S. and M.S. in Wildlife Management, and there Richard earned his own M.S. in Natural Resources-Wildlife Management. Upon graduation, he went on to Los Angeles to work for the Service as a Wildlife Inspector, then later to Colorado as a Wildlife Biologist-Refuge Officer on a National Wildlife Refuge, and finally qualified, competed with over 1,000 best-qualified applicants for one of only nine Special Agent positions in the U.S. Fish and Wildlife Service. A position where he was certified Number One on the list of ONLY nine applicants selected nationwide for entry into an elite national cadre of wildlife officers!

Since that day, Richard has spent innumerable thousands of hours enforcing the Service's and various states' wildlife laws, not to mention spending hundreds of further hours training new agent trainees at the national academy in addition to numerous Refuge officers, Bureau of Indian Affairs wildlife officers, State Fish and Game Wardens, and Provincial and Federal Canadian Wildlife Officers. And as a side effort of love, Richard co-authored a highly acclaimed waterfowl identification guide book for professional use as well as for use by sportsmen in the field. In short, Richard has come full circle with the publishing of his own waterfowl I.D. book since that day in North Dakota when he was admonishing three outlaw duck shooters for shooting closed season species.

Now approaching the end of his career as a federal wildlife officer, as his father and having watched him throughout his gifted professional career during my own 32-year parallel career, I have to say, "Well Done, Son! You made your dad proud for all that you did for those 'helpless ones in the World of Wildlife' and for those American People yet to come..."

"FOUR SCALPS" OFER TAL, MOUNTAIN MAN

CHAPTER 1 — THE CALL OF THE WILDERNESS

ZIPPORAH TAL, MATRIARCH OF THE TAL FAMILY, WALKED over to the bottom of the staircase in her large Southern plantation-style home and shouted towards the upper bedrooms, "Boys, it is time to get up. Breakfast is ready. Also, your father wants to talk to all of you regarding an important family matter so hurry up, get dressed, wash up and get down here before all of you get a good dose of my wooden spoon alongside your heads."

Upstairs, 20-year-old Ofer Tal, oldest son of Zipporah and Yossef Tal, stirred and then like a good son, quickly bailed out of bed. Once his bare feet hit the cold wooden floor of his and the other four brothers' designated huge upstairs bedroom, he began rousting the rest of them out of their beds so they would not be late for what sounded like an important breakfast event to come. Especially not late for whatever it was his father wanted to discuss of importance with his five sons. He knew that if his father had something to discuss with his five sons all at the same time, it had to be a very important family issue. That being said, it was best not to leave his father, a very busy horse rancher, waiting for all of his sons to assemble for breakfast over what was to follow.

Moments later, 19-year-old Joshua, 18-year-old Gabriel and Daniel (twins), and 17-year-old Jerimiah scrambled out from their beds, poured water from the pitchers in their bedroom washstands into large wash bowls and quickly cleaned up. Then since it was Gabriel's turn, he took their two "thunder-mugs" downstairs, hustled outside into the cold morning's air and dumped them into the family's nearby three-hole outhouse. Then he brought the thunder-mugs back and left them outside on a bench to be washed out by one of their family's black servants. Following that endeavor, he trotted into the large family kitchen just as Emily, their black house servant, pulled a large tray of biscuits from the oven in their woodstove and placed it on the kitchen table on a hot pad next to a crock of homemade butter and another of homemade apple butter.

Soon heard were the thundering sounds of the four remaining young men stumbling down the stairs to join their brother Gabriel. Then the hungry young men trotted into the kitchen full of great smells of Southern fried ham, fried potatoes sprinkled with onions, freshly baked biscuits, fried hen's eggs on top of a bed of fresh vegetables and coffee filling the air. With a flurry of activity, each of the young men gave Emily, their black cook, a hug out of love for the one who had basically raised them because their mother was so busy with her husband 'hewing out' and establishing their ranch in their earlier 'hardscrabble' days. Then quiet quickly filled the kitchen eating area as the five Tal boys politely took their places at the large table alongside that of their previously seated and patiently waiting mother and father. Seeing that all of his family was assembled and now quietly waiting for him to say the blessing, Yossef did so in Hebrew. Upon finishing, quiet reigned around the breakfast table, save the clanking of knives and forks and the sounds of five always hungry young men dishing up the food and enjoying the hearty breakfast served by Emily, the family cook.

Then shortly thereafter just as the family had finished the main course of their breakfast meal, Emily removed a freshly baked apple pie from the woodstove's oven, cut it into large portions in the 16" pie pan knowing the huge appetite for her homemade pies by the Tal boys, and placed it onto the breakfast table on a trivet. When she did, just as soon as the smell of those freshly baked apples, home churned butter used in making the pie dough, and the heavenly smell of cinnamon graced the air around the table, that was immediately followed by the sounds of 'eating-happiness' from all assembled. Once again just as soon as the freshly made slices of pie hit their plates, many soft sounds were made showing their appreciation over the excellence of the special breakfast food, especially by the boys. Emily's homemade pies had always been the absolute favorite of all of the boys ever since they had been little. In fact, come their birthdays, they always wanted a 'birthday pie' instead of a cake. But the boys also knew pies were never served except during very special occasions, so all of them ate with an ear 'cocked' towards their father to see what was the special occasion this day. Once breakfast was finished and realizing the seriousness of the known subject that was to come and it being 'man talk', Zipporah quietly dismissed herself from the table and left the room. But as she did, her heart hardly dared to beat over knowing what was soon to come possibly involving her five sons and one of the greatest and possibly most dangerous high adventure opportunities to come in their young lives!

Seeing their mother beating a hasty retreat from the kitchen table and their father loading his pipe up with his favorite brand of tobacco, told the boys something very serious was in the wind and about to be discussed. Something was always serious in the wind when their father sat everyone down around the kitchen table and then quietly loaded up his pipe for a smoke just before he said what he had to say. And that seriousness was now reflected in the quiet and rapt attention being paid to their father by five 'silent as sentinels' sons.

"Boys, I came to this part of the country when 'she' and all of her 'subjects' belonged to the King of Spain," quietly said Yossef Tal, Patriarch of the Tal Clan. "When I arrived, this land was full of Indians, grizzly bears, snakes, timber that reached to the clouds in the sky, and was a land fit only for the steadfast of mind, strong of back and those holding a heart full of hope along with a loaded rifle in hand. Over those many early years, your mother and I survived because of my ability as a hunter and trapper, and killer of Indians who tried to take away from us what the King of Spain had awarded to me in the form of a Spanish Land Grant. Your mother and I scratched and fought our ways from living on a wild and deadly land to that which we enjoy to this day of cultivated and cleared land, a ranch and farm of over 1,000 acres, a land tended to by 20 slaves and now graced by a horse herd of over 100 of the area's finest prized buckskin horses." By now, the Tal Boys realized their father had something very important to say because of the way he had prefaced the start of his conversation with the history of the land and the hard work being done by the family. With that realization that something very important was soon to come their ways, none of the boys dared to even deeply breathe, nor did they as they quietly waited for their father's word.

Pausing to now light his pipe and take several long drags on the rich-tasting smoke of Virginia tobacco, Yossef began once again. "Years after your mother and I scratched shit with the chickens to build this place and make it our home, along came you boys. Boys of whom I am very proud of because of your character and accomplishments, as each of you has grown into a fine young man. However, being your father and knowing each of you like the back of my hands, I can see in all of you that you are a lot like me when I was younger, full of adventure and hope for what lies ahead. Especially now that the talk going around on all of the wonders that Captains Lewis and Clark saw and have been talking about as it relates to the unexplored lands lying to our west. Don't think for a moment that I don't see those looks of adventure in all of your eyes when you now look at the far horizons surrounding the land around us, especially those lands lying to our west. I have also heard many of your conversations when you did not know I was listening regarding your desires to give up raising horses and farming this land for exploring what lies over the next horizon for each and every one of you. Especially now after hearing all the Lewis and Clark talk going around. At first I was disappointed over what I was seeing and hearing in each of you because I wanted all of you to follow in my footsteps on our property. Your mother and I have worked hard so you boys could eventually have all of what God and we have provided for all of you so you wouldn't have to work as hard as we had to. But I have now come to the realization that times for all of you have changed with this Lewis and Clark 'thing'. Seeing your looks of new wanderlust upon your faces and overhearing all of you speaking as to becoming part of a more adventurous life out west, I have now come to the realization that you, like me when I was younger, need to go forth and see what lies out there for each and every one of you."

By then with all the talking Yossef was doing, his pipe had gone out so he paused to relight the tobacco. When he did, it now seemed that all of his sons could now take a deep breath as they waited for 'the next shoe to drop' on the direction this one-way conversation was going... "Realizing that all of you must find your own way in this world and that none of you wish to continue just being ranchers and farmers at this time in your lives, your mother and I have decided that all of you need to go forth and see what lies out there on the frontier for the five of you as we once did. This letting the five of you leave we can do because we are now financially sound. That and we have a number of very loyal slaves who have learned the farming and ranching trade from all of us and who will continue serving us well, as we have served and cared for all of them as if they are part of our family. In fact, once this country becomes part of the United States and it soon will, your mother and I plan on making all of our family slaves free once and for all from this ugly thing called "slavery". When we do, we feel they will stay with us and prosper, continuing to work on the farm and help us in the raising of our prize horses and our crops for the good of all," continued Yossef.

By then his previously lit pipe had gone out again and Yossef just laid it down on the table and intently looked at each and every one of his sons to see if he could 'read' on their faces the 'tone and tenor' of what they were thinking about what he was proposing. Seeing that each son was still very closely watching him for what he further had to say and with obvious looks of expectation over what was to come, he smiled and continued. Yossef continued because he could see in each of his son's faces that he had correctly 'read' them and their desires to go forth and see what the world had waiting out there for each of them. Especially with all of this exciting Lewis and Clark talk going around. With that fatherly read 'under his belt', he continued. "All of you over the years have become excellent horsemen and knowledgeable and accomplished in the care of your animals. Additionally, what I have taught all of you about living on the frontier, the use and care of firearms, how to accurately shoot and not waste any powder or shot, seems to have 'taken hold' as well. Lastly, all of you over the years have developed into excellent hunters and trackers of man and beast. Something that I feel will be needed if one is to experience what lies out there on the largely unexplored frontier and survive all of its fortitudes."

Yossef, seeing his sons watching him and carefully listening to what he had to say now even more closely than ever, rose from the table, walked over and removed an earthenware jug from the family 'pie safe'. Returning to the kitchen table, he sat it down alongside him with a heavy 'thump'. When he did, Emily, quietly looking on from the cooking area of the family kitchen, dutifully brought forth six glasses and set them down by the jug and then melted off into other parts of the kitchen doing what she did best. However, she knew and loved her master very much because he had been so kind to her and the rest of her family. As such, she made sure she watched over him like a hungry 'hawk does a field mouse' and tended to his every need. This that morning she did in particular, because she innately figured what Yossef had to say to his sons could possibly not only be life-changing to them but to the entire family...

Taking the jug of "Moonshine" in hand, Yossef poured himself half a glassful of the amber-colored liquid and then 'thumped' the cork back into the neck of the jug. Taking a deep drink like what he had to say next would come out more smoothly if he prefaced it with the smoothness of locally produced West Tennessee Moonshine, he continued. "As all of you know, when I came into the wilderness of this land, I quickly fell in love with it and what it had to offer. With the development of this farm and ranch, it has been some time since I could now call this land "Wilderness". However as all of you have seen me and heard me speak, men who enter the life experiences of wilderness cling to it forever afterwards. That has been the case with me and I have already seen some of this in all of you as well when it comes to your intense love for this land. That love is in each of you because most men have an element of the aboriginal life in their being from the life and times in which their ancestors lived. That and I have seen over the years to making sure what you lacked in the love of the land was carefully instilled in each of you. It is because of what I see in each of you today, namely a restlessness that never seems to be even partially quenched unless you are hunting, trapping or exploring in what we have left of the wilderness around our home, that we are having this talk this morning. That being said, that causes me to realize it is time for me to directly address this important family decision regarding your futures. Futures if I have my way, involving the five of you staying together as family as you seek your life's destinies. Just so all of you clearly understand, there is death at every turn in the trail of life and all of us must die. But it is how we die and what we leave behind which are important."

With those words, Yossef paused as if gathering up enough courage for what he was about to propose knowing the potential lethalities that could be associated with his decision making regarding his namesakes. Taking up a deep breath that was audible, Yossef continued saying, "Boys, all of you are old enough now to strike out on your own if that is what all of you would like to do! You have worked hard bringing this farm and horse ranch to life and it will always be here for all of you if you choose to return after going the way I am about to suggest. This I am about to do because all of you have a wanderlust that needs to be quenched and one that cannot be addressed while you are here on this piece of now tamed property doing what others can do."

Feeling his heart beating from within knowing what was coming next, Yossef took another deeper than usual drink of his Moonshine and then said, "Four days ago, I ran across an old friend, namely Manuel Lisa whom I call the "Spaniard". He owns a large emporium in St. Louis and is a pioneer in this area and an American fur trader in the western fur fields around us. He is known for gaining a great deal of experience when it came to dealing with all of our local Indian tribes, especially when it came to supplying them with the white man's goods in exchange for their deerskins, buffalo robes, bearskins and beaver pelts. Now I have known and dealt with Lisa over the last six years and he is a damn good businessman. He recently had a chance to meet with the great explorers Lewis and Clark after they returned from exploring the Far West all the way out to the

Pacific Ocean. Apparently, Clark told Lisa that just about every waterway along their travels across the frontier was literally crawling with hordes of beaver. So much so, that oftentimes when his men were hungry and needed something to eat and in order to save powder and shot, all they had to do was get a club and club the beaver to death, they were so plentiful! Being that wearing a beaver hat is all the rage in the eastern United States and in parts of Europe, Lisa, the exceptional businessman that he is, sees great economic opportunity in all of those beaver 'trappings' if one was able to take advantage of such opportunities and bring them to market in marketable quantities."

Pausing now in his excitement over the information he harbored, Yossef took a deep breath and then continued. "With the information Lisa recently received from Clark, he is planning on taking a large group of men and several keelboats up the Missouri River into the frontier. There he plans on building a trading post so he can trade the white man's goods for the beaver riches found in that area with the local tribes of Indians before any other fur trader can get there and take advantage of such riches. Now having been Lisa's friend and doing ranch business with him over the years, I have found him to be very bold when it comes to enterprise, persistent in purpose and one who possesses a boundless level of energy. Not only that, he is a man of great ability and thoroughly experienced from his many years of trading with our local Indians, understands their cultures and is intensely active in his everyday work. Hell, he will outwork most men many years his junior. Knowing his being such a good businessman and all, I can see why he was quick to grasp the importance of Clark's information concerning the vast fur resources out on the frontier. Again knowing him like I do and if I were a betting man, he will be quick to invest and reap his share of those beaver fur profits just waiting to be harvested out there on the frontier by men of enterprise and daring."

Then looking intently at his sons regarding the information

he had just shared and seeing his sons intently looking back at him, Yossef said, "My friend the Spaniard, intends to form a fur brigade from the common men living in the area and move up the Missouri this spring. He knows the work ethic of you boys and has asked me if any of you might be interested in going with him to eventually become "Mountain Men" fur trappers, seeing some of the beauty in the mostly unexplored country and taking part in the adventures it might offer. There I have said it! If you boys want to join up with Lisa, leave for the fur trapping adventures out on the dangerous frontier with the "Sons of the Prairies", grizzly bears and the like, and see what that side of life has to offer, now is your chance. And your mother and I have discussed such endeavors and would fully support and bless any efforts that any of you would show an interest in so doing. But as I said earlier, your mother and I hope the five of you stick together if you decide to invest your time and the future of your lives in such a risky venture out on the frontier."

For the longest moment in time, Ofer and his brothers just looked at each other with big grins splashed all over their faces. For years, Ofer's brothers more than he, had wanted to partake of such adventures out on the frontier but out of family loyalty, they had pushed such desires and dreams to the backs of their minds. Now Ofer and his brothers could hardly believe what they were hearing... Seeing those surprising and pleased looks on his sons' faces and knowing his boys like he said earlier, "like the back of his hand", Yossef realized no one knew his sons better than he upon seeing those glimmers of adventures now crossing their faces and in their eyes...

"Father," said Ofer, "we too have heard those stories told by Lewis and Clark from all of our friends and neighbors. We have also heard that the Spaniard is thinking about forming a fur brigade from local area folks and traveling up the Missouri into the frontier, setting up a trading post and trading with those Indians like he has for years with our local Indians. My brothers more than me have talked about joining up with the Spaniard and seeing what kind of adventure that would bring us, as well as making our own fortunes in the fur trade and 'not just on the backs of you and mother'. However, I have counseled that we take that kind of talk no further because I am concerned over what would happen to you and mother if we were all to up and leave the two of you alone to manage the entire farm, ranch and our prized herd of buckskin horses."

Yossef just smiled when he heard what Ofer had to say and saw the looks of agreement on the rest of his sons' faces over Ofer's words and what he had just said. "With all of you leaving, that will be no problem," said Yossef. "As all of you know, I have been grooming several of our slaves in the art of managing our property, realizing all of you might leave someday, and Absalom and Jericho are now showing great promise. So with that in mind, if you boys wish to hook up with Lisa, I suggest that you do so as soon as you can. The last he told me was that he was going to arrange for two keelboats to go up the Missouri loaded with goods and supplies for several years, along with about 50-60 men. He figured he would need that many men because they will be needed to tow the keelboats upstream, as well as having enough men to provide protection going through Indian lands for such a large herd of horses and mules trailing the slow-moving river craft. Additionally, they will be traveling through several Indian tribes' lands who do not like the white man. So you can see the need for that many men. But I wouldn't dally around if I were you boys. Lisa should be able to fill his needs for men rather easily because so many are out of work in this area, so I suggest you boys saddle up your horses, head over to St. Louis and talk it over with him to see if he still needs the five of you to go along as part of his fur brigade up the Missouri River."

Then Yossef pulled the cork from his jug of Moonshine, poured each of the glasses in front of him half full for his sons and then without pause, filled his to the brim over the destiny he had just set into motion for his five beloved sons... Then with glasses in hand, father and sons proposed a toast to what lay ahead in each of their lives. As they did, Yossef also said a short silent prayer to the good Lord above for the safe return of his sons, and a request for the 'assignment' of a guardian angel to each young man about to embark on such a dangerous adventure in their journeys of life... Zipporah, standing silently behind a partially open doorway listening to the 'man talk' and the decisions made, felt tears of concern welling up inside her and then rolling off her cheeks and dotting the front of her dress, because mothers always seemed to know what time and subsequent trials life would ultimately bring...

Shortly thereafter, the Tal Brothers mounted their riding horses and sped off to nearby St. Louis. There they met with Manuel Lisa and made their desires known that they wished to accompany him and the rest of the members of the fur brigade into the Upper Missouri wilderness. Lisa, aware of the Tals' reputations as skilled horsemen, riflemen and excellent work ethics, quickly placed the five brothers in charge of moving his horse and mule herd along on the bank of the Missouri and Yellowstone Rivers as the slow-moving keelboats proceeded alongside. This he did because he was aware they would be going through hostile Indian country and needed someone who was very dependable when it came to protecting the very valuable horse and mule herd. In their further discussions regarding the meeting place and date of departure, the Tal Brothers discovered that Lisa had already signed on as brigade hunters and trappers George Droullard, John Potts, Peter Wiser, and Jan "Bear Trap" Driessen. All four men were from the original Lewis and Clark Expedition, who knew much of the country into which Lisa wanted to explore, were encouraging Lisa to move even further west, build his trading post and from there, send out teams of trappers to trap beaver in the heart of the Crow, Blackfeet and

Gros Ventre Indian country surrounding his newly constructed fort and trading post.

Since Lisa planned on leaving in the late spring which was fast approaching, the Tal Brothers headed home and began making plans for their upcoming adventure of a lifetime. Upon hearing of their acceptance into the upcoming Lisa expedition, Yossef set to with his sons in making what he felt were the needed preparations from the ranch's resources. First Yossef selected for each son a good riding horse and a spare in case one was injured or stolen. Then Yossef made sure each son also had two extra packhorses for a total of 20 beautifully marked buckskin horses in the Tal Brothers' pack string. Then it was off to the ranch's blacksmith shop where all of the horses were shod with new shoes for the long and rugged adventure lying ahead of his sons. At that time the ranch's blacksmith also made a second set of individualized horseshoes for each horse and included a set of farrier tools to be included in the boys' inventory since Gabriel had been trained as and was also a skilled farrier. Then Yossef had the boys go to their own supply barn and had the local hands responsible for its operation and management make packsaddles and panniers for the packhorses (Author's Note: A pannier is a wicker or canvas basket carried on either or both sides of a pack animal, used to haul provisions, traps, beaver pelts, boned-out buffalo or elk meat and the like). The ranch's leather shop and saddlery also included an inventory of leather strapping of various sizes, extra buckles, spurs and bits so the boys could make repairs while afield when no ready supplies were available as replacements.

For the next week under the exceptional tutelage of Emily the family's cook, the boys learned the correct way to cook with cast iron implements, how to cook and bake with Dutch ovens, and cooked all of the family's meals as well as those for all of their slaves in order to gain the necessary experience, practice and acumen. This the boys found especially important because each was a large-in-size man and an "eager eater" when it came to mealtimes. During that same time period, Emily made sure the boys learned how to make what they could expect to eat while out on the frontier, the proper amounts and kinds of spices to use with different foods, and the care of their valuable cast iron frying pans, Dutch ovens and bean pots. As it turned out, Gabriel and Daniel were the best cooks among the boys and were so chosen to perform those duties once afield and working as part of a beaver trapping team out on the frontier.

Then it was off to Lisa's emporium in St. Louis where the Tal Brothers went shopping for the firearms they figured they would be best served. However, never having been around the larger and more dangerous species of big game out on the frontier to any degree, the Tal Brothers' 'greenness' showed through as they stood in front of the rifle section of Lisa's emporium. There they stood for the longest time guessing as to what to select that matched their needs out on the frontier. There Yossef's short and silent prayer that the good Lord would assign a 'guardian angel' to watch over his sons was answered... Standing off to one side of the firearms section stood a craggy-looking man dressed from head to toe in heavily beaded buckskins showing much wear, smelling strongly of sweat and wood smoke. That man's dark eyes quickly surveyed the scene of the five men unknown to him hesitating in obvious inexperience in front of the vast assortment of rifles nestled along a long wall in Lisa's emporium. As it turned out, the lithe and bronzed older-looking buckskin-covered man who had obviously spent many a day out in the prairie and mountains' sun's rays and winds happened to be there as well on a mission. As it turned out, the man in buckskins just so happened to be in the same building helping Lisa select and assemble what the rest of his men would need in the way of a year's supply of provisions while out on the frontier building his new fort and trading post as well as trapping beaver. That and what the Indians preferred in the way of white man's goods when they traded in their furs at the soon to be constructed Fort Manuel trading post.

Overhearing the conversations of the five men talking about firearms purchases, the man dressed from head to toe in buckskins realized the men had recently been hired by Manuel Lisa to be part of the forthcoming fur brigade heading for the upper reaches of the Missouri River. Also realizing those five obvious "greenhorns" would soon be part of a contingent of men moving into the oftentimes dangerous and unforgiving frontier along with him, figured they would be better served if he lent some of his expertise gained while out on the frontier when it came to firearms selections. With those observations, the man in buckskins began moving towards the obviously undecided men. "Excuse me, Gentlemen, but I couldn't help but overhearing your conversations on what type of rifles should be chosen for your coming expedition into the upper reaches of the Missouri with Manuel Lisa. Let me introduce myself. My name is Jan "Bear Trap" Driessen, late of the Captains Lewis and Clark Expedition to the Pacific waters and return. In the years I spent afield with the Captains and my previous years' experience as an independent trapper on the northern prairies, I have developed a certain degree of knowledge and expertise as to what you fellas will be more than likely facing once you are out into the wilderness. If 'you be so kind', I have lived out on the frontier among the critters and the primitives, I will also be working for Manuel Lisa as one of his guides on the upcoming adventure, and we more than likely will be mates once this expedition gets underway. So if you would allow me, let me make some 'smoke pole' acquisition suggestions, especially as it relates to caliber, style, make and model."

Then without further ado or awaiting the surprised men's reactions to the arrival of a total stranger in among their midst, Bear Trap instructed the Tal Brothers that their lighter caliber and longer-barreled rifles they were currently carrying would not do while out on the frontier. Then he provided further insight into the problems that occurred with longer-barreled rifles that were clumsy to handle while riding through dense timber atop a horse, easy to bend their barrels when hitting trees, and difficult to quickly reload while on horseback. That statement of experience was followed with further suggestions in procuring shorter-barreled rifles, so riding through heavy timber would not be such a problem as was that of a longer-barreled rifle. That would be especially so when riding fast through dense stands of timber attempting to escape from an Indian attack or that of a grizzly bear. Additionally, Bear Trap advised the wood on their Pennsylvania rifles was a softer wood made many times from maple, whereby the "Mountain Rifle" carried by experienced "Mountain Men" was made from a harder wood like black walnut. And with the advantage of a harder wood used on a rifle faced with heavy and rugged use, it was less apt to suffer broken or cracked stocks or wrists. Then the obviously experienced "Mountain Man" guided the Tal Brothers towards the heavier caliber rifles which he advised were needed to bring down larger, more aggressive species of big game animals like buffalo, moose, grizzly bears and elk. He also advised that it was better to 'blow an Indian from his saddle' than to shoot him with a lighter caliber bullet and then have him still attack the 'shooter's person'! Lastly the brothers were instructed to purchase among the many rifles on display what was then known as a U.S. flintlock rifle, Model 1803 with a 34" barrel, which was quality made, of heavier construction, shot a larger ball and was one of the most reliable weapons of the day for frontier use.

Following those sets of guidances, the Tal Brothers without further questions among themselves and 'being of means', each purchased two Model 1803 rifles of .52 caliber, along with the necessary extra ramrods, smaller-sized powder horns to load the striker boxes on their flintlocks, larger-sized powder horns to hold the heavier grained powder necessary for the barrels of the rifles and pistols, several hundred flints, boxes of oiled patches (increased long range accuracy and reduced black powder fouling), bullet molds, wipers or gun worms, ball screws, extra lock parts and tools for repairing their new rifles and pistols. This they did at Bear Trap's suggestion advising trouble out on the frontier usually came in 'doubles or triples'. That being said and only carrying a single shot rifle, carrying a second rifle with a second shot in a packhorse's pannier could be a lifesaver many times when confronted by man or beast. Then Bear Trap advised the brothers that if they had the money, they would be wise in purchasing at least one pistol apiece, preferably two. In so doing, Bear Trap suggested a single barreled, smooth bore of the 'horse pistol' or "Dragoon" type of the same caliber of the rifles they had just selected. That way they could either shoot buck or ball in the defense of their lives and being of the same caliber, could interchangeably shoot the same sized ball. That use of dual weaponry he advised because according to his experiences most Indian attacks usually involved superior numbers of attackers. And since most "Men of the Mountains" only had one rifle and a single shot at that, one tended to get overrun by Indian attackers under those circumstances and killed, unless they had extra backup firepower like that from a pistol or two normally carried in their waist sash.

With that additional frontier firearms information, Ofer walked over to the display case holding pistols and saw to it that all the brothers 'being of means' were instructed to purchase two pistols each and then at Bear Trap's earlier suggestion, made sure they were .52 caliber like that of their rifles so both would be compatible and fire the same balls. Hearing Ofer's suggestion, his brothers kind of smirked since all of them were excellent rifle shooters and throughout their lifetimes had never needed a second shot. However, Ofer's quiet but serious and cold look back at his brothers upon hearing their questioning reactions to his 'two-gun' suggestion, foretold of his mind set when it came to being under attack from superior forces and making sure he would be the one to survive, not his attacker. That look of seriousness also appeared to be 'seconded' by that coming from Bear Trap. With those looks from the now obvious leader of the Tal Clan and believable guidance from the buckskin-covered, weathered-looking frontiersman, double pistols were immediately procured without further ado... Then with a polite dismissal of his person, his work now being done with the greenhorns, the very believable buckskin-clad person who had introduced himself as Jan "Bear Trap" Driessen, disappeared among Lisa's emporium's storage shelves and display counters almost ghost-like, like a man on a mission. When Bear Trap walked away, Ofer noticed that the frontiersman walked in his moccasins in such a quiet manner that he never made a sound. In fact, Bear Trap walked as quietly as a 'mouse pissin' on a ball of cotton' to Ofer's way of thinking...

Standing there a little in shock over the almost magic-like appearance of a stranger, his powerful and common sense advice and his just as fast disappearance, the Tal Brothers stood there quietly with newly ready to purchase rifles and pistols in hand and arm. Then a company Clerk appeared and relieved the brothers of their new firearms and accessories, placed them on a push cart and then asked, "Will there be anything else?" With that question, the brothers looked over at Ofer, the leader of the group, only to find that he had now also disappeared! Looking all around in surprise, the brothers could see neither 'hide nor hair' of Ofer in the warehouse. He had flat disappeared just as silently as had the man with the strange name of Bear Trap!

Then moments later Ofer appeared once again from among the many aisles in the emporium trailing Manuel Lisa and Bear Trap Driessen in his 'wake'! When everyone was all together moments later Ofer said, "I have an idea. As such I have asked Manuel to listen to what I have to propose and depending upon his answer, we can continue shopping for our needs or we can purchase what we have already selected in the way of firearms and associated equipment and then head home." Hearing no dissent from Lisa and Bear Trap but seeing questioning looks on everyone else's face over what he was trying to do, Ofer continued on with his frontier 'shopping' plan proposal. When he did, the rest of his brothers quickly realized why he should now be looked upon as their leader because of the wisdom now soon to be expressed.

"I would like to suggest, if Manuel is in agreement, that we five brothers shop for and purchase what Bear Trap feels and suggests we will need as trappers for a year in that part of the back country where we are going. I suggest that because firstly while here at Manuel's emporium, we will have an excellent selection of good close at hand goods of every kind. Secondly as father has taught us, we always need to keep a sharp eye tuned for a bargain where we can save some money. And thirdly, Bear Trap just came from an expedition lasting for over a year in the back country without the chance of supply. Who better to ask what we would need for a year of living in the back country than one who just did as we are soon expecting to do? Now correct me if I am wrong, Mr. Lisa. Once we get up on the Upper Missouri, the goods that you propose to bring along for all of your men on your keelboats for use in the back country will then be sold at a higher price than the same item would be priced here in St. Louis, to offset the potential dangers and the losses in transport of the goods such a distance through Indian country. Is that right?" asked Ofer.

Manuel Lisa just looked long and hard at Ofer and then smiled over the young man's keen business perception. "Yes, Ofer, that is correct. To offset my risks and initial investments in goods, it will be necessary to sell my goods at much higher prices once we get my new trading post constructed and begin supplying my trappers and the Indians who come to trade and sell their furs as well."

"That being said," said Ofer, "then it would be cheaper and make better sense if we purchased what the five of us would need for a year of beaver trapping afield here this day at your emporium. Now here is the second part of my suggestion and a request. Would you allow Bear Trap here to assist us in our purchases for this coming year afield? Because since we don't have any idea on what our needs will be out on the frontier, his help would be invaluable. If we could work that arrangement out, we would be willing to purchase a year's supplies here at your emporium and if you would allow us to do so, I am prepared to pay for all of those supplies here today in Spanish silver dollars. Additionally, I am prepared to pay you for hauling those supplies up to your new trading post on your keelboats in Spanish silver as well," concluded Ofer with a knowing smile, signifying that if Lisa went for that deal, he had just monetarily 'cut a fat hog in the ass' by saving himself and his brothers a bucket load of money!

For the longest moment in time, Manuel Lisa just closely examined Ofer's face while he mulled the proposition over in his mind for any signs of weakness in the deal just proposed. Lisa already had figured that once up at his new fort, he would be charging his trappers anywhere from 700-1,000% profit for his goods sold over what it would have cost them to purchase those same items in St. Louis! This he knew he would have to do just to offset the risks he was taking moving those goods up the dangerous sandbar and snag-infested Missouri River in his keelboats. Then he had to take into consideration the risks he was taking going through the territories of the many times dangerous Arikara, Sioux, Assiniboine and Mandan Indians.

Quickly figuring that he had a good deal in the making, Lisa smiled over the proposal Ofer had just made. *Ofer's father, Yossef, had taught his oldest son well,* he thought with a smile. By making such a deal, Ofer and his brothers would save many hundreds of dollars by buying from his emporium this date instead of buying the same needed supplies months later after the trading post had been constructed and they were ready to go afield. Then there was the offer of payment in hard cash, namely Spanish silver dollars if he was to consummate the deal offered by Ofer. Lisa, being the outstanding and shrewd businessman that he was, found the lure of a deal consummated with hard currency in the present, was not one to let such an offer slide away from his hands...

"Yes, Ofer, you have a deal. However, I will hold you to another $100 in those Spanish silver dollars for the transport of your goods upriver in my keelboats, and another $5 in silver for the use of my employee, Mr. Driessen here, for one day's service in the selecting of the goods you and your brothers will need for the coming fall and spring trapping season once at my new trading post," concluded Lisa with a well and hard-earned smile over a business deal soundly consummated to his way of thinking. Upon hearing the sealing of the 'shopping deal', the brothers began talking excitedly among themselves over what was to come.

(Author's Note: The transfer of the Louisiana lands from Spain to France in 1800-03, and to the United States by purchase from France in 1803, doubled the size of the United States! However, the still fledgling United States was still in the infancy of infrastructure development during those days and as a result, the U.S. Mint at Philadelphia was unable to expeditiously furnish 'coin of the realm' to all corners of the new country. Hence the use of Spanish silver dollars as a medium of exchange was continued for a number of years in the new states created from the old Spanish holdings in the United States, until the U.S. Mint could furnish adequate supplies of American 'coins of the realm' to the far western portions of the new nation.)

With a much-satisfied Manuel Lisa heading back into the

bowels of his emporium shortly thereafter to keep working on his newest business venture on the Upper Missouri, Bear Trap turned and facing Ofer said, "Where do you want to start in your provisioning venture, Ofer?"

Pleased with the business deal just struck with Lisa, Ofer turned to Bear Trap saying, "I need you to seek out what might be the provisions needed by me and my brothers for the fall and spring trapping seasons once we arrive up on the Upper Missouri River trapping grounds. Since we have never been in such a venture, we must trust your knowledge and experience to seek out and provide us those provisions we would need for surviving a year out on the frontier beaver trapping. The only thing I might add is that we five all have different tastes. So as you make selections for us, we will chime in every now and then if we need you to add something that suits our tastes, or let you know that which we do not like so it is not purchased. If that is satisfactory with you then it will be satisfactory with the five of us as well. Oh, also, all of us are big eaters and woe to our chosen cook if he is unable to provide the right kind and amount of 'grub' while afield. So make your selections of needed items wisely, especially food items, making sure the amounts selected are on the heavier side instead of the lighter side so that none of us ever goes hungry."

"Alright," said Bear Trap, "but before we start, all of you need to realize that the love of adventure is natural to the heart of every Mountain Man. Keep that thought in mind because it is that which led him into the wilderness and for many of his kind keeps him there, either living or with his bones bleaching out in the sun... Enchantment with the land and its adventures is a hard aboriginal love that is seldom shaken. So all of you need to be aware of the lure of such enchantments and their sometimes deadly side. Now with those thoughts in mind, are all of you sure you want to risk that venture into the unknown and if so, want me to commence with what I feel the five of you eager eaters will need to keep all of your 'slats greased'? But before you answer, all of you need to know that the frontier is the very essence of opportunity, however the frontier is not for the faint of heart!" Nothing but silence and big grins of greenhorn anticipation greeted Bear Trap's rather heady and deep statements regarding the frontier's enchantments and its potentially deadly sides...

With his words of adventure and destiny still hanging heavy in the air, Bear Trap turned and with the five Tal Brothers in tow, headed into the bowels of the well-stocked emporium to gather forth the provisions he felt would be needed by Lisa's soon to be newest fur trappers for the coming fall and spring beaver trapping seasons somewhere in the interior waters on the Upper Missouri. Led by Bear Trap, followed by older brother Ofer and natural leader of the group, the six men walked deeply into the bowels of the emporium's warehouse to start making their selections of their needed provisions. There they hooked up with one of Manuel's company Clerks coming their way to help keep track of the provisions to be selected. Following that, Bear Trap and his charges began the process of selecting enough provisions for the five of them to last for the better part of a year while beaver trapping out on the frontier.

Right off, Bear Trap led the brothers over to that portion of the warehouse holding all of the shooting accessories. There without hesitation based on previous years' experience living out on the frontier, only now based on the anticipated needs of five men, Bear Trap selected six eight-pound, sheet lead-corked, airtight containers holding four pounds each of DuPont's Best FFg powder to be used in their large bore rifles and pistols the Tals had selected earlier. Then Bear Trap walked over to another bin and selected an additional 20 one-pound metal tins of DuPont's Best FFg powder which were easier to carry in one's 'possibles' bag on a daily basis, and another 20 one-pound tins of DuPont's Best FFFFg powder for the priming mechanisms (striker pans) for their flintlock rifles and pistols. When Bear

Trap had selected so many tins of powder, the Tal Brothers collectively gave him the uninformed looks of "why so much powder, we all are very good shooters and were raised not to waste our powder?" Turning, Bear Trap said, "The country the five of you will more than likely be trapping belongs to the fierce Blackfeet and Gros Ventre Indian Nations. Experience has shown they are a proud and warlike people and not inclined to welcome any American white man in their beaver trapping or buffalo hunting country. Plus, the Hudson's Bay Fur Company's British agents keeps them groups of Indians stirred up against the white trappers because they want all the beavers and other furbearers for themselves. That being the case, I would not want to be the one losing my life in a confrontation with them because I was short of powder. Additionally, the five of you will be making your living working around every kind of condition involving water. Falling into such waters will be a way of life and as such, water is the death of black powder. Therefore, by selecting sealed tins of black powder, you are making sure no matter what, 'you are keeping your powder dry' and yourselves alive if called upon to use it. Lastly, by selecting these sealed canisters of powder that are made of soft lead, you can then smelt them down when they are empty and use that lead in casting new balls for your rifles or pistols." Those previous questioning looks from the five brothers quickly disappeared upon hearing those words of frontier survival wisdom and just a damn good dose of common sense.

Moving next over to a wooden pallet stacked high with numerous "lead pigs", Bear Trap pulled out 50 pounds of the soft metal pigs (bars) and handed them to the now two company Clerks trailing the men as they made their numerous selections of provisions from the warehouse shelves and pallets. Then moving over to a number of wooden bins holding precast lead balls of different sizes, Bear Trap had the two company Clerks remove 400 of the precast .52 caliber balls which would fit the

Tal Brothers' just-selected rifles and pistols and had them bagged in canvas sacks. Once again Bear Trap received several looks from the brothers as to why so many precast lead balls, since they had just set aside 50 pounds of lead pigs to be eventually used in the making of bullets. Bear Trap quickly eliminated such looks with the explanation, "It will be some time before any of you have time to cast your own bullets from the lead pigs previously set aside for purchase. Best you have a supply of 'shooting' material on hand just in case the need arises when we begin moving north through those many hundreds of miles through Indian country." With that explanation, the questioning looks once again quickly disappeared.

Next Bear Trap walked over to another pallet holding a heap of cast iron smelting kettles and when he did, he selected and handed three of them to the Clerks servicing the men. Turning once again, Bear Trap said, "You will need three in case during the lead pig smelting process you somehow break one because they are made from soft cast iron, you have a horse wreck and one is broken in transit, someone loses one, or one is stolen from your cabin by Indians when you are absent. If any of that happens, you will still have extras, which you will need in order to survive the land's dangers." By now, most questioning looks had quietly disappeared from all of the brothers' faces and one could tell they were now carefully looking on at all of the purchases as if attempting to learn why each and every purchase was made, based on Bear Trap's vast experience. That made Bear Trap happy because he could see that the Tal Brothers were now slowly turning into 'thinking' Mountain Men before his eyes. Additionally, Bear Trap could see that the brothers were beginning to realize that where they were going to trap beaver may mean they were going to have to fight their ways in and out in order to be successful and make a go of it, as they learned what it meant to become and survive living the hard life of a Mountain Man...

Then Ofer broke the mood in the selections of provisions with a question that even surprised his brothers. "Bear Trap, how come you have such a moniker?"

Bear Trap paused in his 'shopping efforts' for the Tals, turned and quietly faced Ofer for his response to his seemingly innocent question as to why one's strange 'frontier handle'. A seemingly innocent question asked but in that day and age culturally, one did not usually pry into another man's personal background. For a moment Bear Trap quietly examined the asker of such a personal question and then realizing the man's innocence in doing the asking, said, "Some years back while beaver trapping with my kid brother we got separated while checking and setting our traps. I later found him or what was left of him where a grizzly bear had sneaked up behind him while he was setting a trap, killed and ate most of him. Ever since that day out of revenge, I always carry four huge toothed grizzly bear traps with me and whenever I run across a bear den, I set all of those traps in front of that den in such a way the bear has to walk over one or several of them in order to leave that den. The next day, I check my traps, kill the grizzly bear caught in them, skin him out if he is in his 'prime' and sell the bearskin at the nearest trading post. I never pass up the opportunity to trap and kill every grizzly bear I run across in memory of the last of my living kin, as well as eating the meat from the same. My kid brother didn't deserve to be stalked from behind, killed and eaten. To date, I have trapped and killed 58 grizzly bears and will continue doing so 'till my dying day'. That grizzly bear deprived me of living a life with the last of my kin and now I deprive those bears from living with theirs as well. Other trappers have seen what I diligently do every time the opportunity arises and upon seeing such behavior over the following years and bear trapping events, have given me that moniker."

That question was never again asked of Bear Trap when the brothers saw a number of tears dropping from the man's eyes and making dark blotches on the front of his tan-colored buckskin shirt even after all those years after the event of his brother's untimely death...

Quickly turning away after he had explained as to why the strange moniker, Bear Trap headed for a long log bin filled to overflowing with a number of different-sized animal traps. There without further discussion, he pulled from the bin 30 St. Louis-style beaver traps and handed the weighty five-pound traps to the now three company Clerks in attendance. Turning, Bear Trap said, "Normally each beaver trapper only has use for 6-8 beaver traps. That is because they are heavy to tote around at five pounds each, they are very expensive and lastly, a good beaver trapper can catch 5-6 beaver each day with just that small number of traps. Then with that catch of beaver, the work really starts. Those beaver are usually skinned on-site unless you are low on meat, then they make for good eats. After being skinned, one visits a willow patch and cuts a mess of green willow limbs which are used to 'hoop' the beaver skins once they have been defatted and de-fleshed later that same day. Then the hooped skins are set out along one's cabin walls in order to dry or up onto the roof in good weather and once dried, for the most part they are bug proof. Then once a trapper has a mess of dried beaver skins, they are removed from the willow hoops, folded with the fur side in and made into bundles of about 60 beaver pelts to a bundle. Since each pelt weighs about 1½ pounds, 60 pelts will make up a bundle of furs weighing about 90 pounds, which is just a good load for a packhorse to carry on a side. So with 30 traps, even if we lose a few or some are stolen by Indians or fellow outlaw trappers, you five should have enough traps to make a very successful living as trappers."

Then Bear Trap walked over to another long line of log bins holding other various-sized animal traps, from those used to trap marten all the way up to the giant, wicked-looking toothed grizzly bear traps. Stopping, he said, "However, you do need ten of these Newhouse No. 14 wolf traps. Once you fellows freeze out and can no longer trap beaver because the ice is too thick to easily trap through, you pull your beaver traps and then you can begin trapping wolves. That way your winter will be free from beaver trapping to hunt buffalo for fresh meat and trap wolves, which will in turn bring you fellows a pretty penny when you bring those pelts into the fort or a trading post for sale come summertime. Now an old trapper's trick is to go forth and hunt buffalo in wolf country during the winter months. You then take the best parts from a buffalo just killed for your eats and then using the rest of the buffalo's carcass, set your wolf traps around it. Wolves it seems are always hungry come wintertime and if you are careful and clever in your wolf sets because those animals are so damned cagy and smart, you will soon have a mess of dried wolf pelts for sale as well come summertime. However, just remember wolves are very smart, ruthless and like you, are meat eaters. When running a wolf trap line always watch your backsides because if you don't, you will discover that sometimes wolves in the wintertime are not too fussy as to which kind of meat they eat..."

Moving on to another section of the warehouse, Bear Trap caught himself grinning over what he was doing. Here he was, shopping for five 'green as a gourd' and soon to become Mountain Men trappers for Manuel Lisa. With that thought in mind, he sensed just how important it was for their eventual success and survival that he make his selections of the provisions for the five brothers well. Little did he at that moment in time realize just how important his thoroughness was soon to become...

Arriving at the next provision section in Lisa's warehouse, Bear Trap turned and said, "Who is the best cook among the five of you, or who among you has been designated to be the camp's cook?" With that question hanging in the air, Daniel and Gabriel both raised their hands like two kids in "Miss Maude's" third grade classroom needing to be excused so they could go to the bathroom… "Good," said Bear Trap, acknowledging the two men so designated as the group's cooks. "Now watch what I am doing and listen to why I am doing what I am doing. Let me start with the cooking implements. "Dutch oven" biscuits are a must for anyone living in the back country if they can afford hauling around such a large and weighty cast iron implement. That would be especially so with the Dutch oven biscuits for such a large group as you five 'eager eaters' are concerned. Not so much for Dutch oven biscuits if there were just one or two of you because of the size and weight of a good 'Dutch'. But where there are the five of you and with adequate numbers of packhorses, Dutch ovens are a must in my estimation. Now I don't know if any of you have ever used a Dutch oven and if you haven't, I will teach the two of you how to do so on our trip north into the Upper Missouri country. Fact is, when I get through learning the two of you, you will be able to make what I call "lip smackin'" biscuits!"

"First and foremost the five of you should have at least three Dutch ovens in your cookery. I say three because it seems in every camp, someone drops and cracks an oven, cold creek water is accidently spilled into a hot Dutch breaking it, or inevitably one will be broken in a horse wreck when you are packing into or out of country. So stick with three "Dutches", especially if you folks take a liking to my brand of Dutch oven biscuits which I will soon be cooking for all of you once we are out on the trail. Make sure if you are inclined to go this way that you purchase three of the 16" category so you can make adequate numbers of biscuits. Plus, one can make one hell of a 'mulligan' stew with a 16" Dutch. And with five of you reported chowhounds, that will more than fit the bill for providing a huge 'rib-sticking' supper at the end of a long day. If you do, you will thank me for making you purchase three of them. Now, cast iron requires a very special kind of breaking in before it can be used, and I will teach the two of you how to do that as well with bear oil while along on the trail. Next you five are going to need two large cast iron bean pots, three three-legged, 16" cast iron frying pans, three sets of hanging rods so you can hang your cooking implements over the open fire, and at least ten cooking steels so you can roast skewered meat over an open flame," continued Bear Trap, like a man who had more than lived through the life and times of being a "Man of the Mountains" and knew what was needed for one's survival while living out on the frontier.

As Bear Trap continued moving along the well-stocked cooking implement sections of the emporium, he talked and explained as he went in such a rapid-fire manner that soon Gabriel and Daniel's heads just spun from receiving so much very useful information! Next to be handed to the three Clerks in attendance were two sheet iron kettles, two two-gallon coffee pots, and an assortment of metal coffee cups, drinking cups, plates, knives, eating forks, serving forks, eating spoons, and serving spoons for ten people! When Bear Trap selected a number of items for ten people and only five were in the Tal party, all five brothers got a bad case of the questioning 'big eye' once again, figuring Bear Trap had just gone off the 'deep end'! "Whoa! Why eating utensils for ten people when we are only five in number?" asked Ofer, still trying to remain dollar conscious even though he had brought more than enough money to pay for any selections made.

"Ofer, over the years I have discovered that many a time friendly Indians or lost trappers have wandered into my camp-site during mealtime. A good Christian man never turns anyone away from a warm campfire or offering that someone something hot to eat when out on the frontier. To turn anyone away is bad manners and a slight that will turn many an Indian against you for such a rude show of bad behavior. Best to have enough eating items to go around in case uninvited guests show up for what smells good in your cooking pot," said Bear Trap with a big grin. As Bear Trap attempted in his 'shopping' to explain to the five greenhorns his hows and whys of reckoning regarding his selections, he began really enjoying not only the innocence of the Tal Clan but their friendly company, always interested attitudes and learning looks upon their faces, as well as intelligent questions asked...

Quickly moving over to the next section of shelved items in the emporium, Bear Trap paused, turned and looking at his five wide-eyed followers over the fast pace of selections, asked, "Who among the five of you is a builder in the group?" Looking all around the brothers when that question was asked, Joshua finally slowly raised his hand. "Good," said Bear Trap, "the five of you are going to need a place to stay. Many trappers just use an Indian tipi or a dugout in which to live throughout the year. However, where Lisa is planning on taking all of us, we will find ourselves in the northern latitudes just below the country of Canada. Never having lived there, I suspect living there in the winter months will be a lot like the winters I suffered through while trapping out on the Northern Plains. That being said plus the need for protection against any attacks from the fierce Blackfeet or Gros Ventre whose country you will more than likely find yourselves living in, you five best figure on building a 'hell-for-stout' log cabin. That way you will have a structure that will keep you warm in the winter months as well as provide some cover in case you are ever attacked by them damn Blackfeet or Gros Ventre. Additionally, you will need to develop water sources for drinking and watering your horses, cut and split firewood, cut logs for your cabin, build tables and chairs for inside use when winter sets in, have tools to build a horse corral or split open a buffalo's rib cage when out hunting for camp meat."

With those thoughts of eventual needs in the Tal Group's mind, Bear Trap quietly moved closer to the tools and implements section in the warehouse and stood there for a few minutes casting his eyes upon what was available. Then he beckoned over the three now sweating profusely company Clerks as he and Joshua began selecting what tools they figured would be needed, and then they handed the Clerks those implements and tools just as fast as they could. As they did, Ofer was amazed over just how fast and 'cat-like' the man in buckskins moved! Then looking over at his brothers, Ofer could see nothing but amazement in their eyes over Bear Trap and his thoroughness in methodically selecting what the five of them would need to survive for a year in the wilderness. Amazement, especially in light of never having met them prior to that day! Soon Bear Trap and Joshua had selected two square-nosed shovels, a 4'-long bucking saw, three smaller hand axes, three larger chopping, 'felling' and limbing broad axes, six sharpening files, two heavy duty hammers, a 25-pound keg of spikes, a ten-pound keg of nails, a rip saw, an adz, gimlets, augers, a longer 'drag' blade, a 20' logging chain with couplings, and a six-pound maul for wood splitting.

With those selections out of the way, Bear Trap scuttled over to the next section in the warehouse and upon arrival, got a serious look on his face. At first glance, it was apparent that Bear Trap did not approve of the quality of the items he was looking at as he stood there examining the offered selections. Then all of a sudden he said, "THERE THEY ARE!" Picking up his pace in excitement, Bear Trap walked over and pointing to a section of knives on display said, "Look at that bunch of knives over there, Boys! Those are the kinds of knives you will need to carry and use every day while out on the frontier. Those are some of the best butcher and scalper knives made from the finest Sheffield steel the English have to offer. Remember, Boys, a trapper always has a need for a good knife or knives that are style-wise country made, heavy enough for chopping, yet small enough to be used as a 'scalper' or general purpose knife. Those Thomas Wilson knives we are looking at are some of the best knives ever made. I am going to pick you out a number of those knives namely for skinning, butchering and what I call cooking knives. Good knives of this quality are essential to a trapper and if the truth be known, equally as valuable to any Indian worth his 'salt' as well." With that and much evident enthusiasm, Bear Trap gathered up a number of fleshing, butchering, sheath and general purpose knives for the group to use. Then Bear Trap spotted another shelf holding a number of specialty knives. "Well, 'lookee-here'! I am also going to grab-up three of this type of knife for you fellas. You will need to have Lisa's blacksmith, once we get the fort built and he has a place to work, to grind these three knives so the bevel is only on one side of the knife 'specially for the purpose of safely skinning out the beaver the five of you will eventually be catching. That way with that type of blade configuration, that will reduce the danger of 'holing' the fresh pelts, which if done will reduce the value of such pelts once you are back at the fort and selling them." With that, Bear Trap gathered up three of those specialty knives he felt should be re-ground, as well as three butcher's steels and four specialty whetstones to be used in keeping the edges on those knives when in general use.

Following that bit of 'shopping' and at Bear Trap's request, a Clerk led the men over to the extensive clothing and blankets section of Lisa's warehouse. At that section of the warehouse, Bear Trap picked out ten 2½-point blankets at $7 each; 20 good quality horse blankets after asking the men how many horses they would be using, at $6 each; ten heavy woolen capotes after having each man try on his own capote for proper fit for use in extreme winter weather, at $5 each; blue cloth at $4 a yard for clothing repairs on the English quality of goods; and five heavy woolen blankets for more clothing repairs or as use for extra coverage around one's shoulders during the extreme winter weather expected to be found in the northern latitudes in which the brothers would be expected to work. Then turning, Bear Trap said, "Once you get situated on your fall and spring beaver trapping grounds, you men can kill some buffalo, tan their hides into buffalo robes and use them as your extra coverage around your shoulders instead of this 'store-bought' stuff. They will last one hell of a lot longer and are better suited for that purpose than what I just selected. Just make sure that when you do, shoot only bull buffalo in the wintertime for your robes because their hides are thicker than that of a cow buffalo and will last longer. Then observing several piles of buffalo hides and robes, Bear Trap, without another word, headed their way. There after sorting through the mound of tanned buffalo hides, Bear Trap selected five of the biggest, thickest and best looking. Turning, Bear Trap instructed the Clerks to individually wrap each buffalo hide selected so they could be packed on a packhorse for the long trip north. Then turning and facing the Tals, said, "I selected those five buffalo hides so that each of you could have adequate ground cover upon which to throw your sleeping blankets at the end of each day's travel to the Upper Missouri. That way, you won't have to air out your sleeping blankets each day because of the ground's cold, filth and dampness."

Then heading off to another bin full of clothing goods, Bear Trap selected a dozen pair of heavy woolen socks for each of the brothers and made sure they fit before keeping what he had selected. Those selections were followed with the selection of two pair of heavy gloves that fit each of the brothers and heavy duty woven woolen hats for each man. Bear Trap then surprised the brothers with his next selections. Walking over to two huge bins holding tanned buckskin items, he made the brothers strip down to their 'bare-nakedness' below their belts and select two pairs of breechclouts and leggings that fit each man. Then observing that each of the Tals was looking at him like a robin would look at a nearby worm over 'those' selections, Bear Trap broke out into loud laughter! When finished with his mirth over the surprised looks on the five men's faces over the breechclouts and leggings selections, he advised that everyone doing any trapping wore such items to avoid getting their much warmer woolen pants soaking wet when setting traps or retrieving dead beaver hanging in those traps. He also advised that each man should be skilled in trapping beaver since if any of them were killed, others could take their place and the group could continue their survival and economy while beaver trapping. Those chilling words brought the Tal Brothers back to earth with the realization this 'shopping trip' Bear Trap had been ordered by Lisa to take them on in order to prepare them for what was yet to come, was something more than just that which met the eye...

Then Bear Trap had each brother select out and make sure of the fit, two "linsey-woolsey" shirts. The Tal Brothers, from their experiences living and working on their farm and working horse ranch, knew that English-made shirts had a poor reputation for lasting very long under hard usage. Bear Trap just grinned over the Tal Brothers' questioning looks regarding such questionable selections saying, "Those shirts will be worn during the summer months when the wearing of buckskin shirts will be too hot to wear. However, those same shirts will be worn underneath your buckskins during the winter months for the extra warmth they will provide." Those explanations quickly dispersed the brothers' earlier looks of shirt selection disapproval. Following those selections, Bear Trap walked over to a shelf holding a wide selection of wide brimmed hats. There he instructed the brothers to find one that fit so their eyes could be shaded while out under the oftentimes intense prairie or high mountain sun. That done, they moved to the next bin full of wearing apparel. There Bear Trap had all of the men select a heavy fur hat with ear flaps which would be needed for the colder weather yet to come in the northern latitudes, especially when winter trapping wolves. Then for the next 20 minutes, the brothers sat around a large bin holding hundreds of pairs of summer (lighter made) and winter moccasins (heavier made from bull buffalo which had thicker hides), trying them on until each man had two well-fitting pairs of each.

Once again at Bear Trap's request, a Clerk led the men over to another section of Lisa's huge emporium warehouse. Remembering that Daniel and Gabriel were the Tal Brothers' designated cooks, Bear Trap 'scooped up' the two 'quiet as a mouse pissin' on a ball of cotton' brothers. Realizing those two brothers knew everyone in their group's likes and dislikes, the three men went shopping in a 'different direction'. There the three men began the serious business of making provision selections that would have to last the five brothers for almost a year while out on the frontier without any chance of re-provisioning many of the basic necessaries. A detail that they had to get right or starvation would become a distinct possibility and 'friend' or at the very least, suffering a year of want for many things except for that of just meat, which they would find a-plenty on the frontier...

With the weightiness of their decisions now hanging heavily over the three men, the process of amassing the right kinds of food and amounts for a year's living in the back country without any hope of re-supply, the men with much deliberateness intently began making their selections. Moving slowly along the various bins of supplies, the three men conferred constantly as they made their selections, and the three company Clerks began moving from bin to bin retrieving those items set off to one side and identified as necessary for their upcoming adventure of a lifetime out on the frontier as soon to be five newly minted Mountain Men. Again, aware of the brothers' likes and dislikes, 60 pounds of brown sugar cones were selected for the men's coffee and cooked items, at $1 per pound; 150 pounds of green coffee beans (had to be roasted in the bottom of a Dutch oven before being boiled) were selected at $1.25 per pound; 200 pounds of flour (biscuit, Dutch oven pie makings); 120 pounds of rice; 120 pounds of pinto beans; 40 pounds of dried raisins at $1.25 per pound; two one-gallon jugs of honey; three one-gallon jugs of bear grease (cooking base used when making biscuits or pie dough in a Dutch oven); 20 one-pound tins of dried yeast for making biscuits; two ten-pound sacks of dried apple slices; six kegs of Fourth Proof rum (flat kegs made for easier packing on packhorses); two ten-pound sacks of hard candy (all the Tal Brothers had a sweet tooth); 75 pounds of salt; 40 pounds of black pepper; 40 pounds of white pepper; and 20 pounds of red pepper flakes (suggested by Bear Trap for fur trappers who sometimes had their bowels impacted from eating so much meat in their diets. He figured out loud that a goodly dose of red pepper flakes never 'missed' when it came to moving impacted bowels); other favored spices like Zipporah, their beloved mother, and Emily, their black family cook, had used during special occasions like cinnamon and nutmeg; and on it went for the better part of an hour making food provision selections enough to last five, still growing young men for a year...

Letting the three Clerks take a 'blow' while the six men moved over to several other accessory bins, Bear Trap instructed the brothers on other necessary items they would need, but many times were often overlooked due to lack of expertise, expense or just pure damn neglect and ignorance on the part of the one doing the selecting. Following that obvious verbal lesson from Bear Trap, additional selections of items were made to round out what the men figured they might need while out on the frontier. Once again, the three harried Clerks were kept busy scurrying back and forth with selected items being laid out onto the 'buy pile'. Once again with Bear Trap providing guidance to the brothers like he was 'kind of like one of their own', the men selected several sets of steel moccasin awls because they were easily lost and much needed for repairs of clothing, footwear or damaged human flesh; needles and spools of thread for clothing repair; spools of fine wire for repairing cracked gunstocks; iron buckles; extra leather strapping for repairing packsaddles and panniers; a 100' spool of cotton lead rope; two dozen fire starting steels (easily lost or broken); washing soap; shaving soap and extra razors. (Author's Note: Contrary to popular belief, most Mountain Men shaved. Shaved because there was a head lice epidemic in the general population in those days and by shaving, that kept the head lice habitat on one's body somewhat to a minimum.) Nearing the end of what they figured could be needed items and almost as an afterthought, several tins of bag balm used to treat pack and saddle sores on animals and minor injuries on humans; six heavy duty whetstones to keep edges on axes and shovels; and finally 12 'carrots' of James River chewing and smoking tobacco were selected. (Author's Note: Tobacco in those days in order to facilitate easy measurement for valuation and safe travel when packed in horse or mule packs, was tightly rolled and wrapped with a heavy twine until the lump of tobacco resembled that of a large carrot weighing about three pounds. Hence the terminology of the day, when referring to the heavily wrapped with twine lump or 'carrot' of tobacco.)

Since the men had previously selected all they figured they would need in the way of firearms and accessories, Ofer instructed the Clerks to gather up all of their supplies, place them in a secure place within Lisa's warehouse and figure up what was owed. As the Clerks, Bear Trap and all of the rest of his brothers except for Gabriel and Ofer began that chore, Ofer and "Gabe" headed out to where their riding and packhorses were tied off in front of the warehouse. Once there, Ofer and Gabe removed four heavy saddlebags from their riding horses and re-entered the warehouse. There the Senior Clerk had figured what was owed and had sent for Manuel Lisa so he could approve of the rather large sale and collect what he had coming. When Lisa arrived from where he had been working in the mercantile section of his emporium and was apprised of the amount owed by the Tals, he never even blinked. "Ofer, the bill comes to $570.50 for the goods and supplies. Another $100 for my keelboat shipping costs of all of those supplies to the drop-off point along the Upper Missouri, and another $5 for the services Bear Trap rendered this day in assisting you folks in procuring what he figured you all would need for a year of trapping afield during the coming fall and spring beaver trapping season. And if I remember our previous deal correctly, that amount was to be paid for in full with Spanish silver dollars at the day of the sale," quietly advised Lisa.

(Author's Note: With the addition of George Drouillard and eventually John Colter to the Lisa 'team' who 'had been there', they collectively managed to convince Lisa to travel further southwest on the Yellowstone River rather than just constructing his fort somewhere along the Upper Missouri. They had convinced Lisa that the greatest beaver trappings were further west and his best option was to travel further inland off the Missouri River and down onto the Yellowstone. Then somewhere along the Yellowstone, construct his fort and trading post in the heart of beaver trapping country and that of the Crow Indian Nation, who were considered great trappers and suppliers of furs, hides, bear rugs and other peltries in their own right, which Lisa eventually did adjacent the Bighorn River.)

Without a word, Ofer swung his two heavy saddlebags full of Spanish silver dollars up onto an available counter and without a word, began counting out $675.50 in gleaming piles (for many a common worker in that day and age, $675.50 was over a year's wages!). When finished, he had considerably lightened the four saddlebags previously laid out onto the counter. However as he did, he couldn't help but seeing the glint in Manuel Lisa's eyes as the piles of gleaming Spanish silver dollars grew and grew. Yes, his father had been correct in his assessment that Manuel Lisa was a hard-dealing and driven businessman, who no matter what, was going to get his share of any available riches come 'hell or high water'... But Ofer was pleased over the deal he had made with Lisa as well. Had he waited until the new fort had been built and then purchased his provisions at that time from Lisa, he would have had to pay a lot more because of what was to later become known among the fur trapping community as "Mountain Prices". Mountain Prices that ran anywhere from 700-1,000% more for those same goods over what they would have cost if they had been purchased in St. Louis! With those thoughts in mind, if Ofer could have looked in a mirror at that moment in time, he would have seen a glint in his eyes as well over the deal he himself had just successfully brokered and carried out...

Thanking Bear Trap for his very able-bodied assistance and Lisa for the deal just negotiated, the Tal Brothers headed for their small mountain of supplies just purchased so they could take some of them back to their ranch in preparation for the trip into the Upper Missouri that was soon to come. A trip that was soon to come because Lisa had advised he was almost finished with the trip's final supply and transportation arrangements as well as the number of men needed to carry off such a mission. Then Lisa advised the Tal Brothers they were to meet him and the rest of the fur brigade two weeks hence for their trip into the unknown on the Upper Missouri...

Moments later found the Tals digging through their stacks of supplies and retrieving all of their rifles, pistols, some tins of rifle and striker powders, and a number of firearms-related accessories along with their buffalo hide ground covers and some bedding items. This they did so they could take such items back to their ranch, clean and test fire all of them, and then have the family's leather smiths fashion the appropriate rifle slings, construct personalized 'possibles' bags for each brother and assemble each brother's bedroll for travel. Then two weeks hence would find the Tals totally outfitted and ready for their trip and adventure of a lifetime into the western wilds of the new frontier. Something that all of the brothers had secretly hoped for and now their wildest dreams were about to come true.

As to be expected, the remaining two weeks before departure up along the mighty Missouri flew by as the brothers continued making all of their final preparations. Being good sons, the first thing they did was quietly get all of the ranch and farm hands together over a couple of jugs of good West Tennessee Moonshine behind one of their horse barns without Yossef's knowledge. There the boys served their family ranch and farm hands liberal amounts of the liquid Ofer often described as being "as smooth as a schoolmarm's thigh". Those farm and ranch hands realizing something important was 'stirring in the wind' and being very respectful of the family that had treated them so kindly, took nary a drink but just politely held their glasses untouched until they heard what was 'coming their way that would impact their lives and those of their families' from the brothers…

Seeing how quiet the group of hired hands and in reality friends the boys had grown up with over the years had gotten, and then sensing they all were fearing the sale of the family ranch and farm to another master, Ofer just smiled thankfully over the assembled men's family show of loyalty! "There is no use of me beating around the bush," said Ofer. "Father has released us boys to go forth and seek out our fortunes in the undeveloped western frontier as fur trappers. That is something my brothers and I have always wanted to do but out of love for our parents, have never allowed ourselves to do anything more than just dream about doing such a possibly wild and dangerous thing. Recently, Father, sensing the wanderlust in all of his sons, sat all of us down and in essence, released all five of us to go forth into this adventure of a lifetime with his trusted friend Manuel Lisa, and get it out of our systems if it was at all possible."

Letting those words sink into the assembled ranch and farm hands for a moment upon hearing a murmur of 'gasps' surging through the crowd of men, Ofer then continued. "At first, none of us dared to leave our beloved Mother and Father and all of you and your families. But then my brothers and I realized that all of you and your families are and always have been part of our family. And that if we were to leave as we have always wanted to do to seek our fortunes of life, now is the time. Now is the time because all of you have faithfully been doing most of the work on the ranch and farm and will continue to do so even in our absence until we return from the frontier. Realizing that, my brothers and I also realize all of you will continue taking care of our beloved parents while we are absent the farm and ranch." Now Ofer could see his farm and ranch hand friends beginning to relax a bit, now that they could see no dark clouds of their sales to other landowners on the horizon and so much so, a few of them now began happily drinking the glasses of Moonshine they were holding in their hands. Happy over what he was seeing and now sensing in the air, Ofer continued. "Father tells us boys that Absalom and Jericho are doing very well as our new farm and ranch managers and he expects they will continue doing so. Father also advises that all of you have been doing very well and that all of your families are prospering and happy to be living with and as part of our family. Knowing that and not expecting anything to change other than all of you and your family members will soon be granted the status of "Freedmen" just as soon as "Upper Louisiana" becomes part of the United States, as it is rumored, my brothers and I feel we can now follow those desires we have only dared to dream about. So my 'Brothers', drink up because we have two gallons of first class Moonshine to polish off before Yossef finds all of us behind the barn having a good time and 'grumbles' us." With those words, a shout went up and hardly a glass remained holding any whiskey as the men pushed and shoved around Gabriel and Daniel happily pouring and filling many extended empty glasses in cele-bration... Before that day was done, two additional gallons of West Tennessee Moonshine had been retrieved from the cool of the nearby 'spring house' and drained of every drop as well. Suffice to say, not much more got done on the farm or ranch that fine day and Yossef did not find out...

CHAPTER 2 — THE ODYSSEY BEGINS

THE PUNGENT SMELL OF FRESH HORSE MANURE AND methane gasses from impatient horses being previously 'grained' rose into the warming Missouri morning air in the front yard of Yossef Tal's plantation house. Creating those unique smells were 20 beautifully matched, high-spirited and impatient buckskin riding and packhorses sensing the excitement heralding the coming of a new dawn in a very important day in the lives of the Tal Brothers. Family ranch and farm hands finally completed the saddling and packing of such a magnificent string of classically bred and matched horses and then stood waiting to provide any other needed assistance. Finally the front screen door swung open and out walked Yossef Tal followed by his wife of many years, Zipporah. Both husband and wife had seen and lived on the frontier when it was younger, dangerous and yet full of hope and promise. Full of hope and promise just like the new day they now found themselves facing. Through many years of hard work, Yossef and Zipporah had wrung and wrested forth from the harsh Upper Louisiana lands what was in that day and age a spectacularly successful farm and horse ranch. In that long process, Yossef and Zipporah had also raised five sons and lost two daughters to the fierce demands made of those young settlers who had found the courage and had challenged life on the frontier. Today they were about to do so once again, only this time, by allowing their five sons as they themselves had once done, to 'walk' among the many unknown challenges called 'life on the far western frontier and wilderness', in the year of our Lord, 1807...

Streaming out that same front door following their parents were five stout young men, dressed from head to toe in clothing of the time found out on the frontier, from their wide brimmed hats and their flintlock rifles carried in hand, down to their newly moccasin-covered feet. As a matter of course, the men shook the work-roughened hand of their father without saying a word because none needed to be said and then one by one, the boys turned and stood in line from the oldest to the youngest, to say their 'Good-byes' to their much-loved mother. A mother whose face was now showing 'strains' of fearful emotion, realizing she may never again see any or all of her sons once they had disappeared into the largely unexplored wilderness further to the west! Her sons in turn showed no outside emotions even through their insides were roiling around like a 'stomped-on great horned owl' over the events at hand. They too realized they may never see their mother alive again after facing the unknowns out on western frontier as they were soon to do and discover...

Then the five young men mounted up onto their individually hand-picked riding horses, tipped their hands to the brims of their hats towards their mother out of love and respect, let their eyes briefly meet those of their father out of deep respect, and each riding one horse and trailing three fully loaded packhorses then slowly streamed out from the front yard of their home of many years and into an unknown but hoped-for future holding its 'many faces' of destiny.

Meanwhile back on the family's front porch off to one side politely stood a middle-aged black woman, family cook and faithful servant to the Tal family ever since she had been purchased 'off the block' in the streets of New Orleans years earlier for $200. There Emily stood silently with tears in her eyes as she watched the five sons she had in large part raised and nursed through thick and thin during their many good and bad times, slowly ride out of sight. Turning, she walked back into the house's kitchen so she could begin the breakfast meal cleanup with a smile on her face. A smile on her face because before the boys had left and during private moments, each had gathered her up into their strong arms and had whirled her around and around until she had them put her down, all done in a sign of deep love and respect only found between that of a 'son' and that of a 'second mother'...

By late afternoon, the Tal Brothers had arrived at the "Jumping Off" location so designated earlier by Manuel Lisa, as to where all the fur brigade members were to assemble next to his two fully loaded keelboats quietly anchored in the Missouri River. Upon seeing the two keelboats, the Tals just sat there on their horses marveling at what they were seeing. Both keelboats appeared to be about 65' in length, possessing about an 18' beam and a 6'-deep hold. About their decks were scattered numerous boxes and crates of provisions and atop each boat's cabin at the bow and stern of the deckhouse stood ominous looking swivel guns. Shaking their heads in awe, the brothers turned their horses and rode into a camp full of 60+ rough-looking men and a rather large herd of horses and mules quietly grazing on the nearby prairie. Finding Manuel Lisa, he in turn guided the Tal Brothers and their horse herd of riding and pack animals to a quiet spot under some cottonwood trees along the river. There he had the brothers pitch their camp and advised they were to be prepared to get underway at daylight the following morning. Lisa, in his typically highly organized and somewhat frantic manner, instructed and reminded the boys they were assigned to protect and herd along his valuable horse and mule herd once underway. They were to do so by slowly paralleling the daily progress of his two keelboats being dragged or poled along the Missouri River by crews of 20 men each. As such, the Tals were to be under the direct leadership and command of Jan "Bear Trap" Driessen of Lewis and Clark Expedition fame. The Brothers' protection duties additionally included selecting suitable safe nightly camping spots along the river, setting up the evening campsite and having a freshly killed buffalo roasting over the campfire waiting to feed the hardworking boat crews for supper each evening, as well as providing nightly horse and mule herd protection and picket duties.

With those instructions laid out, off Lisa 'whirled' into more organizational work dedicated to having his brigade ready by the following morning for departure on a roughly 2,000-mile trip into the largely unexplored Upper Missouri River frontier lying to their north. A departure and trip that would take his fur brigade through seven different Indian nations, several of which were openly hostile towards white men. The rest of that evening went by in a blur as the brothers made their camp, hobbled their 20 horses in order to keep them apart from the rest of Lisa's horse and mule herd, made their supper and conferred with Bear Trap as to what he individually expected from each of them on the dangerous journey lying ahead.

Because of the Tal Brothers' skills as expert horsemen and excellent rifle and pistol shooters, plus having a reputation of being the type of men who always remained composed under the most demanding of circumstances, Bear Trap assigned them to be the ones acting as outriders on the trip protecting Lisa's valuable horse and mule herd from theft by roving bands of Indians. Protecting a valuable horse and mule herd along the way which eventually would be 'doled' out to Lisa's fur trappers once up onto the trapping grounds located in the vast Indian country surrounding the mighty Missouri River after the trading post had been built and the men were ready to go forth as fur trappers.

It seemed Ofer's head had just laid down against his saddle being used as a pillow when a swivel cannon from one of the anchored keelboats out in the Missouri River was fired right at daylight announcing the day's events had now started for the brigade's epic trip into the frontier. Soon the air around the huge campsite was filled with the many sounds of men meeting the day, the haze of smoke from the many cooking fires and a light cloud of dust in the air, as Lisa's milling horse and mule herd along with the Tals' was rounded up, packed and prepared for a long day along the trail.

Within an hour, another swivel cannon was fired from one of the anchored keelboats and moments later, the two boats were released from their moorings to the grunting and singing choruses of groups of 20 men each slowly "cordelling" (pulling) the boats upriver with long ropes. However, within the hour as the 1807 spring Missouri air had warmed, all good-natured singing initially heard had stopped and the only sounds heard were of struggling pulling men grunting against the weight of the keelboats and steady pull of the Missouri River's currents against their keels. Trailing along the river's bank 'and in witness', could be seen a large horse and mule herd being slowly driven alongside that of the slow upstream progress being made by that of the keelboats. Thusly went that first day and more of the same for the next two weeks without real interruption, as keelboats and herds of horses and mules 'mirrored' each other's steady upriver progress. However, as the boats, livestock and men made progress upriver, it was witnessed by thousands of the beasts of the plains and the local Indians' 'bread basket', the many herds of buffalo.

Then several hours before the end of each long day, a hunting party was dispatched from the livestock herders who forged ahead, located a safe and suitable keelboat anchorage for the evening and sleeping location for the crew's nightly stop. There they killed a cow buffalo from one of the many nearby and constant herds dotting the prairie, butchered out the same and had it roasting over the fur brigade's central fire for the hungry and hardworking men toiling and pulling the heavily loaded keelboats slowly upstream. This monotony of routine was the constant of everyday toil until the group of men and keelboats reached where the Platte River joined the mighty Missouri River.

Just as the keelboats were ready to swing to shore and anchor for that day's evening rest and supper, a shout was heard from the man in the bow of the lead keelboat. Standing in the bow looking for hidden sandbars, floating dead buffalo, uprooted cottonwood trees and other navigational dangers, the man on lookout pointed ahead in the river to a small floating figure of a man coming downstream in a cottonwood dugout canoe! Soon the trapper in the canoe had anchored ashore alongside the lead keelboat and within moments, was in intense and yet friendly conference with Manuel Lisa, the leader of the northward proceeding expedition. While that conference was ongoing, the rest of the men dismounted from their horses or walked back from the upriver shore after laying down their ropes used to tow the keelboats. There they headed for the great smelling and welcome campfires now roasting huge slabs of buffalo meat, along with the great smell of Dutch oven biscuits and coffee being made ready for the hungry and hardworking men using their backs and muscle to haul the heavy boats upstream.

By the end of suppertime, the mystery of the lone Mountain Man figure floating down the Missouri all by himself had been solved and the spread of such identity information whipped through the men like a prairie wildfire! The men learned that the lone Mountain Man figure was none other than a man named "John Colter". The one and same man who had participated in the Lewis and Clark Core of Discovery Expedition that had gone all the way to the Pacific Ocean and had just recently returned after several years of absence. The one and same man who had been released by Lewis and Clark at the end of their expedition to return to the wilds as a Mountain Man fur trapper. Also as the rest of the men soon discovered, John Colter was a close friend of George Drouillard, John Potts, Peter Wiser and Jan "Bear Trap" Driessen, men who also had participated in the Lewis and Clark Expedition and were currently accompanying the Lisa Expedition as "St. Louis Missouri Fur Company" guides, hunters and trappers! Then even more encouraging news from the Lisa and Colter meeting spread throughout the supper gathering of soon to be fur trappers like a cloud of migrating bees moving across the countryside looking for a new home!

John Colter had just spent the better part of a year in the same country Lisa was hoping in which to build his fort and trading post for the fur commerce it would generate by trading with the local Indians! According to Colter, the country, especially that area further to the southwest of the Upper Missouri along the Yellowstone River was so full of beaver, that it was not unusual 'to just walk up to them and club them to death'! (Author's Note: John Colter was known as a storyteller and according to history and other fur trapper friends, he could 'spin a yarn' with the best of them. Especially when Colter, the first white man to visit current-day Yellowstone National Park, told stories about the boiling pools of water and the ground that emitted smoke and steam...) Then it was discovered that Lisa had convinced Colter to turn back around and accompany the expedition as a company "Engagé" and work as a guide for the betterment of the fur trade that was to follow with the Indians living in the area of the soon to be built fort and trading post!

With Colter now acting as a guide, especially being armed with further information regarding the trapping along the Yellowstone River lying further to the south and west, Lisa once again took to the Missouri with his two heavily loaded keelboats heading upstream, mirrored by his huge horse and pack herd trailing alongside the boats' slow moving progress. For the next three weeks after leaving the friendly territory of the Omaha Indians, Lisa and company now tread upon the lands of the much-vaunted Sioux Indians. As it turned out, those following days of travel proved to be an informational and cultural windfall for Ofer. Bear Trap, taking a real liking to Ofer, took the interested young man under his wing and began teaching him what he knew about the Indian tribes, their culture, language, superstitions, and even sign language from what he had learned as a young trapper in the northern prairie areas. Since Lisa's northward progress on the Missouri found little in the way of distractions with the Sioux other than a few trading sessions where numerous gifts were presented to the various chiefs which allowed for safe passage, Ofer took the opportunity daily to learn everything he could from the well-traveled and culturally adroit Bear Trap. And as Bear Trap continued his teachings, he quickly discovered that his student was an extremely quick and excellent learner...

However, weeks later once Lisa had left the territory of the mighty Sioux and ventured into the area of the historically troublesome Arikara Indian villages located along the middle Missouri, trouble came with a capital "T". As Lisa's expedition continued further northward on the Missouri, it became more and more obvious that trouble with the historically treacherous Arikara was brewing. As the keelboats labored along, many times the river channels led the men pulling the boats right along the shores occupied by the curious, troublesome and more often than not, dangerous Arikara. Oftentimes incursions were made by the Arikara in attempts to spook the trailing horse and mule herds as if to separate out individual stock animals and run off with those as valuable prizes. Such actions required extreme diligence by those protecting Lisa's livestock with a many times obvious show of armed force. That due diligence was often applied into the night hours with extra outriders being required in order to preclude Arikara night raids into the valuable horse and mule herds as well. Those same kinds of harassing tactics also befell those hardworking men pulling the keelboats upstream as they moved closer to the Arikara villages lying right along the river. Oftentimes the men riding on the keelboats and those manning the boats's swivel guns were required to present a show of force of many armed men or the obvious loading of the boats' swivel guns in order to drive away the overly aggressive and many times troublesome Indians riding along the shorelines harassing the men pulling the keelboats.

Finally one morning just below one of the lower Arikara Indian fortified villages lining the close at hand Missouri, the Indians made much show of blocking the river off from any further upriver travel! Not wanting to antagonize the Indians any further and recognizing that attempting to force travel upriver would lead to bloodshed, Lisa held up the keelboats' progress and bravely went ashore with gifts to show courage and placate the aggressive Arikara. Those gifts were happily accepted but the aggressiveness continued, requiring Lisa to finally make a grand show of force with all of his men arming themselves and standing guard, along with the loading of the swivel guns as a show of force in order to do battle if necessary. That show of force finally forced the Arikara to back down from their aggressive actions and soon the boatmen and their horse herds were once again allowed to pass unmolested. However, Lisa being the businessman that he was, recognized that to lower his guard even 'one whit' would probably cause him to lose his valuable horse and mule herd as well as all of his supplies carried on the two keelboats! Thereafter until far away from the village forts occupied by the Arikara along the Missouri, Lisa kept his guard up along with preparations to defend what was his at the ready and in plain view at all hours of the day and night.

Several more days of travel away from the Arikara Indian villages then brought an unexpected surprise from Indians who were many miles away from their home territory in what is today northeastern Montana. Rolling out his men for another day of toil up the Missouri, Lisa found his little group of adventurers confronted by several thousand fierce-looking Assiniboine Indians! Once again fierce gestures from the Indians indicated a battle was soon to be forthcoming! Lisa, not to be deterred, had his men load their rifles and the swivel cannons on the keelboats and then fire over the huge gathering crowd of madly gesturing Indians. When he did with such a show of force, the shocked and surprised Indians retreated and when they cautiously returned, they were more subdued. It was then that Lisa, ever the businessman and courageous adventurer to a fault, went ashore with many gifts including some rifles for the Indian chiefs. That initial show of force and then his courage in wisely confronting the Assiniboine with many gifts convinced the Indians that his small force was to be reckoned with and with that, they were allowed to safely pass on their journey.

However, with danger close at hand or not, the affable Bear Trap kept up his cultural lessons with a very interested Ofer Tal, who continued proving to be a very good student. Soon Ofer was 'fluent' in the use of sign language practiced by many tribal members of the "Sons of the Prairies", as well as being able to passably speak the language of the Blackfeet. The Blackfeet occupied many of the lands north along the Yellowstone instead of the Upper Missouri where Lisa, under John Colter's prompting, was now ultimately heading. Additionally, Bear Trap who had taken almost a 'father-son' liking to Ofer, continued his tribal cultural lessons on his quick learning protégé. Lessons that were particularly directed at understanding what was said, how it was said and behavioral quirks exhibited by many of the "Sons of the Prairies", especially when the events being confronted were under some forms of duress or danger.

During many of those daylong teaching sessions, as Bear Trap directed the safe movement of Lisa's horse and mule herd, Ofer found he was becoming more and more interested in what was being taught by his very frontier knowledgeable friend. Ofer also realized that those teachings he was more than absorbing would more than likely save his life or that of his brothers someday. Brothers that heretofore had little or no interest in what Ofer was learning. They, to a brother, were only interested at seeing what was over the next ridge and when they could begin beaver trapping, make their fortunes and then return home so they could show their father the successes they had singularly accomplished... Deciding to confront his brothers regarding their 'laid-back' attitudes when it came to learning more about the Indian cultures surrounding them, Ofer made plans to get them more intensely involved in the Native American learning process as well, or else! This he felt he had to do in order for them to appreciate Bear Trap's words of warning received back at Lisa's warehouse on the frontier and how deadly a mistress 'she' could be to the faint of heart, unprepared or unwary...

The following evening as Daniel and Gabriel were cooking the brothers' supper, Ofer sat on his saddle which he had placed around the campfire as a seat and was waiting for the right time when all of the brothers were present so he could broach the subject of learning more about their surroundings and those of the native peoples. It was about then that Ofer could hear all kinds of excited yelling and hollering coming from the far end of their campsite! Fearing a night attack by Indians, Ofer hurriedly rose from sitting upon his saddle and made ready with his rifle as Gabriel and Daniel just stood there in wonderment with their 'thumbs in their ears' over all of the yelling now rapidly spreading across the campsite.

Then as the sounds of yelling rippling across the campsite were getting closer and closer, Ofer still could not see in the darkness and dim lights from the many campfires what all the consternation was about. He didn't have long to wait... "Ka-thump—Ka-thump—KA-THUMP—KA-THUMP—BLOOM—BLAM—KER-RASH" went a bull buffalo in full charge right through the camp of Lisa's men! As it just so happened, the maddened bull charged right through Ofer's campsite, bowling over Gabriel and sending Daniel sprawling over the now 'flying' coffee pot, Dutch oven full of biscuits and three-legged frying pan sitting on a bed of coals cooking buffalo steaks! That was when the sound of Ofer's rifle being discharged into the side of the head of the hard-charging buffalo sent it sprawling several yards away into the brothers' sleeping area! When it did, it blew bloody snot from its nostrils and buffalo 'dump' from its hind end upon feeling the impact of the heavy .52 caliber bullet fired from such close range! That resulted in flying dirt and spewing blood from its now Ofer-inflicted mortal wound being spread all over the men's bedding! Gabriel and Daniel, now keenly aware of the danger, jumped up and took off running into the darkness without their rifles in hand and their 'thumbs still stuck in their ears' in total non-preparation for what had just occurred, even after hearing the charging beast so close at hand and coming their way...

Upon Gabriel and Daniel's embarrassed return to their cooking station, they found a terribly bent out of shape coffee pot, a badly cracked open and now useless Dutch oven, and a stepped-on by a one-ton bull buffalo, three-legged frying pan now busted in half and of no further use as well. Disgusted over his brothers' lack of awareness upon hearing the charging buffalo coming their way and their immediate reaction of running away like frightened children with 'their thumbs in their ears', Ofer just shook his head in disgust. That evening, the Tal Brothers' supper consisted of very tough roasted meat from a one-ton old bull buffalo removed from its hind end as it lay dead in their now stink-covered sleeping blankets. *It was as Bear Trap had suggested many days earlier that when shopping for provisions, make sure one has enough cooking implements just in case some are broken along the way into or out from the trapping grounds,* thought Ofer, as he looked at the destroyed cooking implements lying in among the dying embers of their cooking fire... Then he remembered his original mission of warning his brothers about learning as much as they could about their new 'home' and its many beasts and people surrounding them... That night as all of the brothers lay in their blood-soaked and stinking sleeping furs, Ofer hoped it was a lesson of life out on the frontier well learned by his brothers...

Weeks later without any further Indian problems, the Lisa expedition reached the junction where the Yellowstone River entered the Missouri. Lisa had originally planned on establishing his new fort and trading post at the confluence of those two major rivers. However, having spent many evenings with John Colter among his tales of 'ungodly' numbers of beaver fur riches that lay further ahead on the Yellowstone River to their southwest near the Rocky Mountains, and the friendly Crow Indian trade that would soon become readily available if they continued further in that direction, Lisa, being the businessman and adventurer that he was, fell under those 'spells'. After lying up at the mouth of the Yellowstone so the men could rest for two days and knowing the work that still lay ahead, Lisa and company then turned their eyes to the southwest and once again began the laborious process of navigating their two keelboats up the Yellowstone and trailing the horse and mule herd in the direction set by John Colter who had trapped beaver in that very area just a year before.

For the next 20 days, Lisa and company navigated their keelboats past snags, hidden sandbars, gravel bars and down narrow channels until according to John Colter, they had reached the mouth of the Bighorn River flowing into the Yellowstone from the southwest. There being deep in Crow Indian country, Indians who were friendly to the whites and their fur trappers,

Colter advocated in that immediate location Lisa should build his fort. Anchoring the keelboats along the shoreline and setting up their base camp at the confluence of the Bighorn River where it entered the Yellowstone, Lisa and Colter set about looking for the right location upon which to build his new Fort Manuel and his new St. Louis Missouri Fur Company trading post. Within the hour, Lisa and Colter had decided the best location for his new fort and trading post should be where the Bighorn flowed into the Yellowstone, on the right bank of each. That in the men's minds was the best defensive position in case they were attacked by the fierce Blackfeet, always troublesome Gros Ventre and Assiniboine Indians located further north, would be above the high water marks of both rivers, was near ample grazing for the horse and mule herds and immediately adjacent a dense stand of pine and Douglas fir trees, making construction of the new fort much easier. (Author's Note: Modern-day archeologists have been unable to exactly pinpoint the location of Manuel's original fort and trading post on the confluence of where the Bighorn River joins the Yellowstone. However, Manuel Lisa is still credited with building the very first American structure and trading post on the upper river systems in the modern-day State of Montana.)

Up on the landward side of the Yellowstone was constructed a temporary base camp for the men to use until the fort could be constructed. Then as George Drouillard and John Potts, designated hunters of the group left the following morning to kill buffalo for camp meat for the Lisa men, Peter Wiser and John Colter assisted Lisa in laying out the outside measurements for the new fort's walls. With Fort Manuel's outside measurements laid out, the Lisa men began unloading the fort's building implements from the keelboats. Following that, two logging crews were designated and immediately the 'forest crews' began felling timber, cutting the logs to length and using horse and mule teams, began hauling the precut logs to the fort's construction site. In the meantime, the building crew assigned to construct the fort began digging the holes for placement of the log palisades, placing them 2-3' into the ground and then banking the earth around the logs' bases once they were installed. Soon a rectangular fort began taking shape as 16'-high log palisades formed the fort's outer walls. Then four feet below the top of the palisade was constructed a plank walkway for guards to patrol. From there, they could remain on the lookout for any signs of danger from outside the fort's walls or could easily observe arriving fur trappers or Indians coming in to sell their furs and trade.

After several weeks of hard labor by the 60+ men of Lisa's St. Louis Missouri Fur Company brigade, the outer walls of the fort were up, construction had begun on the buildings within the walls of the fort, a haying crew had set to mowing and gathering in the winter hay stores needed for the horse herd, and a series of corrals were being built adjacent the fort so the livestock could be easily protected from grizzly bear and Indian attacks. Additionally, Drouillard and Potts had managed not only to fully supply the 60+ men at the fort with daily meat rations, but had brought in extra buffalo meat that was in the process of being made into huge stores of jerky for winter use by the fort's inhabitants as well as for sale to Indian traders.

Then one evening after the group had feasted on roasted buffalo steaks, Dutch oven biscuits, coffee and a pot of spiced-up beans, Lisa walked over to Ofer, tapped him on his shoulder and with a nod of his head signifying they needed to talk away from the rest of the group, walked off a short distance away. Minutes later the Tal Brothers found themselves quietly standing in the company of Lisa, Bear Trap Driessen, George Drouillard and John Colter.

Once all of the above men were assembled, Lisa began by saying, "Gentlemen, Fort Manuel is well on its way to completion. The men are settling into their duties but we are 'burning daylight' when it comes to why we originally came to this area. The fall beaver trapping season will soon be upon us and I have yet to grade or purchase a single beaver although according to Colter here, this country is full of the furry rodents just waiting to be caught. With that in mind, here is what I am proposing be done. You Tal Brothers are already outfitted for the fall and spring beaver trapping seasons since you purchased those goods needed back in St. Louis before the start of this trip. Your provisions are just waiting on one of my keelboats to be unloaded, packed upon your beautiful buckskin packhorses and headed out to the beaver trapping grounds. But as I see it, there is just one small problem. None of you Tal Brothers have ever trapped a beaver, much less correctly skinned and hooped one. Here is what I propose to all of you since my friend Bear Trap here has already accepted this proposal should all of you accept. I propose you Tal Brothers and Bear Trap team up and form one of my trapping teams. Bear Trap here is a skilled and experienced trapper. That and you five boys have a reputation for being hard workers and quick learners. To my way of thinking, that is a 'sure-fire' plan for success with him teaching the lot of you and then you six going forth and trapping the beaver. Additionally, with the six of you working together, it would be foolish for any hostiles to try attacking the lot of you with any chance of success with your proven reputations and skills as shooters and the firepower you men could represent if attacked."

Then Lisa seemed to run down on what he had to say, but just for a moment. Finally getting his 'wind' he commenced once again with just as much energy as he previously had by saying, "I also have another plan that fits in with my first one. I propose sending George Drouillard and John Colter with the six of you onto the beaver trapping grounds, that is if you Tal Brothers accept my proposal. Colter here tells me of an almost magical place just north of here that he previously trapped that he calls the "Musselshell". Apparently, that watered area has such huge numbers of beaver that it is all one can do just to keep his traps empty there are so many beaver abounding about. Colter here also tells me however, that that magical trapping area is in the heart of Blackfeet country and the only safe way to trap that area is by sending in a large party of trappers who can easily defend themselves if attacked. I figure with the Tal group of six men and with Colter and Drouillard joining in as well for a time, that is one hell of a plan for success against attack. By doing it that way, I can send up a safe and sound party of knowledgeable trappers with Bear Trap leading the way, having John Colter showing the lot of you the exact location of such magical trapping grounds, and then all of you men working together getting a cabin built and a horse corral constructed. The way I figure it with the fall trapping season close at hand, you eight men should be able to find a good location in which to build a cabin with Colter leading the way. Then once you are set with your cabin built and by having Colter showing all of you the location of this Musselshell area, you Tals and Bear Trap will be set. Then I am having Colter and Drouillard leaving the six of you to fend for yourselves after the camp work is done, because I want them to forge out, meet other Indian tribes, teach them the proper way to trap beaver with my traps, and let them know the location of the trading post I am setting up so they will come and trade with us. Lastly, by then once all the construction work is done here at the fort, I will be able to send out a number of other trapping parties as well this fall and still have enough men to be able to man the fort so we can have a thriving business and yet protect ourselves as well. There, I have said what I wanted to say. What do any of you have to say about what I have proposed here this evening?" asked Lisa with a 'gleam' of excitement in the sound of his voice and an anticipatory sparkle in his eyes...

With Lisa's proposal laid out for all to mull over, Ofer quickly looked over at the faces of his brothers illuminated by the light of the campfire. Knowing his brothers the way he did, he could see nothing but eagerness to get underway as was just outlined by Lisa. Ofer also felt the same way and turning to Lisa said, "We Tal Brothers are in agreement with what you have proposed here this evening with only one question 'hanging fire'. When would you want us to up and leave for this 'beaver-magical' Musselshell area? I ask that because it will take a few days to unload all of Bear Trap's and our provisions and get all of that packed onto our packhorses and ready for travel."

"The fall beaver trapping season will soon be upon us. The beaver are still shedding a lot of their excess fur and will continue doing so until the weather turns colder sometime after the month of September. After that, their fur will become valuable once again and all of you should be out and about trapping. Knowing that and the distance all of you will have to travel just to get to this Musselshell country, get acquainted with the area to be trapped and then build your cabin, horse corral and any other structures you might want before the arrival of the winter snows, tells me the sooner you leave the better," said Lisa.

Looking over at Bear Trap, Colter and Drouillard to see if he could figure out what they were thinking, Ofer could see nothing but grins of concurrence over Lisa's proposal. It was obvious to Ofer's way of thinking that the old timers in the group of men assembled were not fort builders, but anxious to be a-foot or on horseback in the back country doing what they did best, namely exploring and seeing what lay in their next beaver trap or what lay over the next ridge! Then Bear Trap spoke up saying, "I can be ready to go and be out of here in one day." With those words, Colter and Drouillard nodded their heads in the affirmative and quickly seconded an early departure date with big grins of anticipation as well. When Lisa looked over at Ofer realizing he was the natural leader for his group of brothers, Ofer said, "We are new to the game of correctly packing our horses. I figure we can be ready to go by day two after we get the word."

"Then it is done," said Lisa. "I can have the keelboat men unload all of you Tal Brothers' provisions tomorrow and with some extra help from my crew, can have all of your packs packed and ready to go except for loading upon your packhorses by sundown tomorrow. The following morning with all of the men helping, we can have all of you remaining men provisioned up, packed and ready to go right after sunup," said Lisa with just a touch of excitement now sounding in his voice as well.

Two days hence found Colter in the lead with his riding and four heavily packed packhorses since he knew where they needed to go. Following him was Drouillard on his riding horse trailing four heavily loaded packhorses as well. Then came the Tal Brothers on their long livestock string of 20 buckskins of riding and heavily loaded packhorses. Last in the caravan of trappers heading out from Lisa's base camp rode Bear Trap on his riding horse trailed by four heavily loaded packhorses as well. Of note was the placement of four large toothed grizzly bear traps carried on top of Bear Trap's last two packhorses in his string. It was obvious from seeing such monster-sized traps that Bear Trap still had a score to settle with 'Mr. Grizzly Bear' for previously killing and eating his younger brother and only surviving kin some years earlier...

For the next six days while heading in a slightly northwesterly direction, Colter led the long fur caravan without incident. Throughout the trip, the men passed through herd after herd of buffalo, elk and antelope, all interspersed throughout the numerous lowlands and rolling hills now being traveled. Each night the men feasted upon a freshly killed buffalo cow for their supper and not one time were any bands of Indians in evidence. However, there were many signs of unshod horse tracks throughout the area traveled and several times the men rode upon signs where a buffalo hunt had recently been held by the "Sons of the Prairies". But true to Colter's frontier knowledge and abilities, he never once waivered in the direction in which he was heading or lacking in his enthusiasm for return to the familiar beaver trapping country to which he was heading. Watching Colter so he could learn from the man's actions, Ofer came to realize in John there was truly a Man of the Mountains and he would remain so until his dying day... (Author's Note: John Colter, famous Mountain Man and sterling member of the Lewis and Clark historic expedition, died in either 1812 or 1813 (exact date unknown), not from being killed by the Indians or the British in the War of 1812, where he fought as a private in the American Army, but from jaundice. Jaundice from increased amounts of bilirubin, a byproduct of the breakdown and destruction of the red blood cells in the liver which caused his death. He is buried in Miller's Landing in Missouri, instead of in his beloved mountains on the frontier.)

By the early afternoon on the sixth day of travel, Colter had slowed the procession of fur trappers and their horses to a slow walk as he continued closely examining a series of long ridges 'bleeding' eastward leading down to the narrow waters of what he called the Musselshell. Finally approaching another heavily in evidence beaver stream angling into the Musselshell from the northwest, Colter held up his arm and stopped the men's caravan of horses. Sitting there on his horse looking over the area where the stream he called "Box Elder Creek" entered into the Musselshell from the northwest, Colter pointed towards a small box canyon to the west saying, "There! There is where we should build our cabin and horse corral. By so doing, we will be out of the worst winter weather coming out from the northwest, there is plenty of water and graze for the horses, the campsite will be out of sight from casual passersby and all of you men would be plenty close to some of the best beaver trapping in this here country. Lastly, over there in that stand of timber will be enough logs in which to build the new cabin and has firewood a-plenty to satisfy the need for such come the winter months."

As Colter laid out his suggestions for a cabin site, the rest of the men moved their pack strings closer to him so they could hear what he had to say and let their eyes do the 'walking', as the famed frontiersman laid out his plans for Bear Trap and the Tal Brothers' new homesite. Turning around in his saddle, Colter said, "Well, what do you guys think? Is that a good plan or not?"

Moving his horse string up even closer to where Colter sat upon his horse, Bear Trap said, "That is pretty damn good-looking country in which to set our roots down, build a cabin and work out from if we are going to be trapping all of that country to the east of us. What do you think, Ofer?" asked Bear Trap, as he continued looking over the proposed homesite once again, looking for any flaws in its choice as a new homesite.

"You know what you are looking for far better than my brothers and me since this is new to us. I say we go with what you and Colter have selected, get to it and get out of these damn hard saddles for a change and give our sore knees a rest from being so confined in the stirrups such as they are," said Ofer with a smile.

Twenty minutes later, the pack strings of men had moved even further into several lines of conifers adjacent a number of groves of aspens and cottonwoods. There they soon found them-selves unpacking all of the packs from their packhorses. Finding suitable shade under the grove of cottonwoods and out of sight, the men laid out their packs in such a manner they provided some cover from any kind of attacks from the 'locals' should they occur and from being rained upon by the usual afternoon thunderstorms. Then their horses were hobbled and let out to graze, roll around after their days of hauling heavy loads upon their tired backs and water in a nearby stream running out from the head of the draw in the small box canyon they had selected as their new homesite.

Following those actions, with rifles in hand, the men surveyed the area on foot and decided on the location of their soon to be built cabin. As Colter and Bear Trap 'walked off' the dimensions of their new home, Daniel and Gabriel, now well-practiced as designated camp cooks, grabbed several square-nosed shovels from the packs and began digging out an outdoor cooking site next to the proposed cabin site. As they did, the rest of the men scurried about in the aspen and cottonwood groves, picking up armloads of firewood and brought it over to where Gabriel and Daniel were 'lining out' their outdoor firepit and soon to be permanent outside cooking area. Then under the directions from Gabriel and Daniel, the rest of the men began bringing over the cooking irons, pots, pans, Dutch ovens and such, and laid them out so the two cooks could arrange the cooking area and their cooking implements the way they wanted it done.

As the 'cooks' puttered around and then built a fire in their newly dug firepit so they could have some coals ready to cook by, the rest of the men with rifles still in han, walked back to where their packs had been unloaded and positioned as a defensive ring in case they were surprise attacked. There they began laying out their sleeping furs and blankets under the trees' leafy canopies. That chore finished somewhat later, Colter and Drouillard mounted up on their riding horses and went forth to see if they could kill a deer for supper. With that, Ofer and Bear Trap strung out a rope line in among the nearby cottonwood grove. That they did so when the horses were brought back in for the night, there they would be tied to the new makeshift 'picket line' where the men would be sleeping for the extra protection that offered from grizzly bear attack or Indians trying to steal any of their horses. While those two men strung the 'picket-line', Joshua and Jerimiah with rifles in hand went out to the pasture area where most of the horses were happily grazing free from their saddles and heavily loaded packs. There they set up where they could watch over their livestock to avoid any kind of surprise theft from Indians or attacks from hungry grizzly bears that might be wandering around in the vicinity of the trappers' new homesite.

About then the sound of a single rifle shot was heard by the men back in camp out near where Box Elder Creek ran into the Musselshell. Half an hour later, a shout from below the new campsite revealed Colter riding his horse and Drouillard leading his riding horse into camp with a fat mule deer doe slung over its saddle. Somewhat later as Daniel and Gabriel gutted and skinned out the fat doe and began boning out its meat for supper, Ofer, Bear Trap, Drouillard and Colter ambled over to the ring of packs and began unloading the single buck saw, long-handled felling and limbing axes and a logging chain to be used in dragging by horse the freshly cut logs down to the new cabin site come the following day.

The following morning after the men had shaved, washed up, tended to their calls of nature and finished their breakfasts of coffee, Dutch oven biscuits and roasted deer meat, they headed into the adjacent hills holding the stands of pine and Douglas fir trees. This the men did because quickly building a cabin was of prime importance. Was of prime importance because winter was on its way, the fall beaver trapping season was just around the corner, the men needed to get their packs full of provisions out of the weather, and Colter and Drouillard were still obligated to Lisa to move on and meet other local Indian tribes. After those two men met the various bands of Indians, they were to teach them how to trap beaver using steel traps brought along to be distributed as gifts and inform them of the new trading post located and open for business near the mouth of the Bighorn and Yellowstone Rivers. It was there that Lisa hoped to part the Indians from their trapped furs in exchange for those much-coveted white man's provisions and implements such as firearms, knives, traps, powder, lead, metal cooking kettles and the like.

For the next two weeks, the eight men labored from daylight until dark in felling green timber, cutting those logs to size, hauling them down to the cabin site with horse teams and constructing a large cabin suitable to serve the needs of Bear Trap and the five Tal Brothers for the coming year. Once that major chore was completed, all of the packs and provisions were moved inside the cabin's protective walls and under its roof to protect their valuable contents from the weather's elements, possible destruction from the rodents and porcupines and theft from wandering Indians. Then the men turned their labors to building a 'hell-for-stout' corral for their horse herd of 25 animals belonging to Bear Trap and the Tals. Once that chore was completed, the men turned to constructing two meat poles to hang their freshly killed game above the reaches of hungry critters such as the local black and grizzly bears, hauled in a huge supply of dry, dead, insect-killed and lightning-struck timber for their winter wood supply, as well as built several stout meat smoking racks adjacent their cabin so the men could make jerky for use while out along the trail.

Then while Drouillard and Colter were still available as willing hands, the eight men rode forth one morning and killed six cow buffalo from a small herd feeding nearby. There they butchered out the six animals where they fell and loaded the meat into the packhorses' panniers and brought it back to their campsite. Then as Daniel and Gabriel prepared the men's supper for the evening meal, the remaining six men cut the huge cache of buffalo meat into thin strips and soon the meat smoking racks hung heavy with fresh buffalo meat being smoked and on its way to becoming jerky. Three days later with their saddlebags bulging full of freshly made buffalo jerky, Bear Trap and the Tal Brothers bid farewell to John Colter and George Drouillard as they headed north and west on their 'Lisa assignment' of meeting other Indian tribes, teaching them how to trap beaver the white man's way and acquaint them as to the advantages in commerce when trading at the new trading post near the mouth of the Bighorn River.

As to that 'meet-greet-teach' endeavor, Colter and Drouillard were only partially successful. The Crow, Salish and Shoshoni were all too happy to enter into trade with Lisa at Manuel's fort and trading post. However, the Blackfeet and Gros Ventre were bitter enemies with the Crow, Lisa's main Indian trading partners. Soon a bitter divide and long-term hatred developed between those Indians, the whites in the fort and the friendly Crow, Salish and Shoshoni. A bitter hatred ensued because Lisa traded guns back to the Crow for their furs, a tribe who hated the Blackfeet and as a result, the Crow with the white man's firearms now dominated the Blackfeet in subsequent tribal warfare. Dominated the Blackfeet in warfare because Lisa did not trust the Blackfeet and would not trade firearms with them, which resulted for a time in which the Crow totally dominated the Blackfeet in their tribal conflicts. As a result of this balance of power shift between the Crow and Blackfeet, the Blackfeet began trading with the British of the Hudson's Bay Fur Company in Canada and during the subsequent War of 1812 between the British and the United States, caused economic consternation with Lisa's fur trading operations. Additionally, the Hudson's Bay Fur Company's British operatives whipped the Blackfeet and Gros Ventre into such hatred of the white man that many an American trapper died because of such subsequent hostile Indian actions. This the British did in order to control the trapping operations so they could enjoy the economic fruits of the North American fur trade over that of their American rivals.

However those subsequent problems aside and with the fall beaver trapping season rapidly approaching, Bear Trap and the Tal Brothers redoubled their efforts in preparation for the events to come. There they cut out a portion of a wall and built a fireplace at one end of their cabin. Once that necessary work was accomplished, they made indoor tables and chairs for when the weather turner bitter, constructed sleeping structures so the men would not have to sleep on the rough-hewn and cold timber floor of their cabin, and cut and stacked wood inside and out for when winter weather came. Lastly, they covered their front and side windows with thin, transparent, undressed deer-skins. Deerskins so treated admitted sufficient light, yet excluded most cold, rain and snow.

Then in a fit of civility because he had stepped in various men's droppings scattered around while working about their new cabin, Ofer got an idea that would solve the surprise messes found occasionally underfoot and brought into their new cabin. Engaging the assistance of his youngest brother Jerimiah, the two men built a hewn-flat log bench over the latrine opening so no one would be inadvertently stepping in each other's waste currently scattered about. **Little did Ofer realize such an act of civility would end in disaster...**

With the mornings now arriving with a nip in the air, the men dragged out all of their 30 beaver traps, laid them up onto the smoking racks and commenced smoking them using rotten cottonwood as a smoking agent (creates the most smoke) in order to remove all of the man smells. (Author's Note: Most beaver trappers of the day seldom used more than 6-8 traps per day. St. Louis-style beaver traps, a favorite, weighed about five pounds each including their respective chains. Therefore, weight was an issue when carrying them about, as was their expense, at around $9 per trap at Mountain Prices. Lastly, in the day when numbers of beaver were extremely plentiful throughout the Rocky Mountains and immediately adjacent watered areas, a good trapper could catch a beaver in every set! Then the freshly trapped beaver had to be skinned, defatted and hooped daily to avoid bloating and spoilage which caused the fur to slip. There-fore, 6-8 trapped beaver a day was just about a handful for any single trapper to catch and properly care for. However, to avoid the chance of loss, theft or breakage, most beaver trappers always carried around ten or more traps because they could not be easily replaced while they were afield.)

Moving their efforts back inside their new cabin and in the faint light allowed from their deerskin windows aided by several beeswax candles, the men using their indoor fireplace melted a number of their pigs of lead and cast a mound of rifle and pistol balls for the coming trapping and hunting seasons. Bullet casting labors completed, Ofer then put a keen edge to everyone's knives, disassembled all of their firearms and cleaned out the black powder fouling and leading. Then he reassembled the same and made sure all were functioning perfectly. Following that, the men refilled all of their powder horns with fresh powder, placed new flints, fire steels (easily lost or broken), 100 soft lead .52 caliber balls (could be used in their rifles or pistols), and greased bullet patches (use of greased patches reduced black powder fouling and barrel leading which increased range and accuracy) into their 'possibles' bags for use while out on the trail.

The following day the men rode down to several large willow patches and cut 30 4'-long dry wooden poles for use as their anchor poles as per instructions from skilled beaver trapper, Bear Trap. (Author's Note: Dry poles, not green poles, were cut and used as anchor poles to be attached to the chain ring on the end of a beaver trap's chain. If green anchor poles were used, sometimes a trapped beaver would attempt to cut himself loose by chewing through a green and more supple anchor pole. Seldom did a trapped beaver attempt to chew through a trap's old and dry anchor pole.) Upon returning to their campsite with the 30 dry wood anchor poles, the men loaded them into several panniers in preparation for their first day's fall beaver trapping operations. Then into another pannier went their 30 folded beaver traps, several small hammers to be used in driving the anchor poles into the bottom of the beaver's pond, a small one-pound hand ax, a roll of twine to be used to tie the trap's end of the chain ring to the anchor pole, a shovel and several bottles of castoreum they had purchased from Lisa back in St. Louis to be used as a lure for a beaver to the trap. (Author's Note: Castoreum is an oily liquid removed from the rear leg glands on a beaver. The smell of castoreum is not readily discernible to humans but is picked up by a beaver's sensitive nose at a distance. The beaver being highly territorial will readily swim to the smell of castoreum from that of another beaver to investigate who is in his territory. During the breeding season, that smell of castoreum is especially compelling to a beaver. For that reason, castoreum was used as a very effective lure and attractant in order to facilitate the trapping of beaver.)

Come the first of October, Bear Trap and the Tal Brothers ventured forth so they could more closely look over the beaver trapping grounds available to them along the much-vaunted by John Colter, Musselshell. That entire day the men spent surveying the beaver activity and evidence along the riverine Musselshell waterways looking for the exact spot in which they wished to initiate their fall beaver trapping season. As they did, since none of the Tal Brothers had ever trapped beaver before, they listened intently to Bear Trap as he provided information on what to look for in discerning what would be the best beaver trapping area in which to launch their fall beaver trapping season. Finally deciding they would start their fall beaver trapping season where Box Elder Creek entered the Musselshell, the men turned their riding horses for home with much anticipation for the following day's endeavors to come. That evening as Daniel and Gabriel prepared the men's celebratory supper of roasted buffalo hump ribs, Dutch oven biscuits, beans, coffee and several cups of rum, the men sat around the evening's outdoor fire on their sitting logs and discussed the coming day's events with much anticipation. Then out came a 'carrot' of tobacco and between the sweet smell of smoke from their clay pipes and the smoothness of the rum, the men felt right at home in the wilderness that evening around the campfire with their life's selection of endeavors lying before them.

Since none of the Tal Brothers had ever trapped a beaver, it had been decided that Bear Trap would be the group's primary beaver trapper. However, he would be assisted by Ofer and before all was said and done, everyone would learn the trade of beaver trapping and the preparation of the pelts into dried 'Plus' (pronounced 'plews', which was a first class adult beaver pelt roughly worth about $6 in the early stages of the fur trapping and trade industry). That they did in case someone was injured or killed and the group still needed to be able to carry on so they could survive as Mountain Men fur trappers...

CHAPTER 3 — LEARNING THE "TRADE" ON THE "MUSSELSHELL"

SINCE BEAR TRAP HAD BEEN DESIGNATED THE GROUP'S MAIN trapper because of his previous beaver trapping experiences on the northern prairies, he took the lead the following morning as the six trappers left their Musselshell campsite at dawn right after breakfast. Following Bear Trap rode Ofer, who being the oldest of the Tal Brothers, had been designated Bear Trap's immediate assistant on the initial trapping endeavors. Following that initial training of Ofer in the 'how to' of the beaver trapping trade, Bear Trap had counseled that everyone else in the party should learn the Mountain Man trade of beaver trapping to ensure survival of the group as trappers in case if any of them were killed, drowned or frozen to death. Trailing in behind those two leaders came Daniel and Gabriel leading two pack-horses carrying panniers loaded with all of the equipment and wooden anchor poles the trappers would need for the day. Lastly, behind the caravan of trappers rode Joshua and Jerimiah to provide protection in case the trappers were attacked from the rear by hostile Blackfeet or Gros Ventre Indians as they went about the business of trapping on the nearby Musselshell.

Upon leaving their campsite, Ofer, ever the one to learn new things, kept a close watch on Bear Trap and everything that he did in order to learn the techniques commonly exercised by an experienced Mountain Man. It didn't take Ofer but just a few minutes of riding alongside Bear Trap to begin learning numerous frontier survival lessons. Right off the bat, Ofer observed that Bear Trap took advantage of the best line of the country to follow, avoiding gullies, canyons and broken ground which might have otherwise impeded his advance or provided the very distinct possibility of crippling up his very valuable mode of transportation, namely his specially trained riding horse... By the second half-hour of travel, Ofer got his next lesson in Mountain Man survival techniques while working deep in hostile Indian country. All of a sudden, Bear Trap reined up and just quietly sat there in his saddle looking off at a distant series of hills. Ofer, ever the good student, said nothing but looked in the same direction Bear Trap was looking in the hopes of spotting what had caught what he now considered his mentor's eyes. Then Ofer saw what looked like two distant but distinct figures on horseback quietly observing the line of trappers heading down into the creek bottom holding the Musselshell's beaver-laden waters. For the longest time the trappers just sat there watching the two figures of distant mounted riders carefully watching the line of fur trappers and their horseflesh moving towards the Musselshell. Then in the blink of an eye, the two figures of the "Sons of the Prairies" had melted off into the vastness of the wilderness like they had never been there in the first place. For the longest time, Bear Trap continued sitting there on his horse watching the distant ridgeline as if to ascertain the direction the 'figures' were subsequently heading and who they might be, friend or foe...

Finally turning in his saddle, Bear Trap quietly said, "You just got a good example of what I call the 'lynx eyes' of Indians. They saw us before we ever saw them. Always remember, Ofer, out here, the 'War-Hoop', flying bullets or speeding arrows, especially in Blackfoot country as we now occupy, are usually the first intimations of danger. And in most cases, especially if one is not alert, the last things one remembers while he is here on this good earth. But that is part of the love of adventure that is so natural to the heart and mind of every Mountain Man. That is also what leads him into the wilderness and many times keeps him there, more often as not ending up as 'bear scat' left out on the prairie or as bleaching bones on a hillside with an arrow sticking through the remains of his rib cage..."

Then without another word since none were needed, Bear Trap headed his horse down the side of the Musselshell stream bank and drew him up next to a large patch of willows. Dismounting, Bear Trap walked back to the two packhorses being led by Gabriel and Daniel and began stripping off his buckskin pants and regular pair of moccasins. Then reaching into one of the packhorse's panniers, he withdrew a set of breechclouts, buckskin leggings and heavy duty moccasins that had been purchased back in St. Louis at Manuel Lisa's emporium. Soon he was dressed in what he considered his trapping paraphernalia and then looked over at Ofer still sitting there on his horse looking on like 'a robin does to a worm'. "Best get down and get dressed if you intend to work with me trapping beaver," said Bear Trap, as he headed for another pannier looking for a beaver trap, hatchet, wooden anchor pole and a small corked bottle of castoreum. Then he patiently waited for Ofer to dress accordingly, grab up some of the same gear that Bear Trap was holding and then slowly followed him along the Musselshell as Bear Trap intently examined the muddy stream bank along the way, looking for evidence of an area of fresh beaver use as evidenced by numerous tracks in the mud.

In the meantime and without being told, Gabriel and Daniel led their two packhorses and Ofer and Bear Trap's riding horses, as they followed along the two Mountain Man trappers walking along the Musselshell examining the stream bank before them for fresh beaver sign. Collaterally, Jerimiah and Joshua slowly rode along behind the contingent of trappers on their horses. This they did from their horses on the high ground, watching all around the men as they did for any signs of danger, especially now that they were deep into hostile Blackfeet Indian territory. And now even more so since they had been seen earlier by the two distant Indian riders sitting on their horses, obviously quietly watching the trappers with more than a normal interest.

About that moment in time, Bear Trap called Ofer over to where he was standing and pointed downward to a well-used beaver slide area in the soft mud as it entered the Musselshell's waters. A slide area that was dotted with numerous tracks of the large rodent they were seeking indented into the muddy bank. "Here is what we are looking for, Ofer. Where there is a much-used slide area like this one, that is a good place to set a trap. Here, let me show you how it is done once you have located a good solid spot on the bottom of the pond onto which to place your trap, then locate it right next to the slide area. And remember, these slide areas are what they are using to drag freshly cut branches and limbs back into the deeper waters. Like I said earlier, it is important to look for a good solid piece of ground onto which to place this here trap. Notice that I have already set this here trap ready to spring shut before I get into this damn cold water. That way, all I have to do is carefully lay it down on the solid piece of ground that I just selected, so the trap will snap upward the right way when a beaver steps into it. In so doing, I make sure the trap is placed under only about four inches of water. Then watch this trick my beaver-trapping mentor taught me back on the northern prairies," continued Bear Trap, as he swirled the water with his hand carefully over and around the previously placed trap until it was covered and out of sight with just a slight film of muddy water. "When you do this, make sure it is covered with just a slight film of muddy water and not gobs of mud or loose sticks. If you do otherwise it might just screw up the trap by not allowing it to completely close and allow the animal to escape when it steps onto the trap's pan and springs the jaws of the trap shut upon its foot or feet," continued Bear Trap, as he looked intently into Ofer's eyes making sure the instructions he had just provided had sufficiently registered with his trainee.

"Now comes the important part! Notice how carefully, without moving my now set trap, I walk out into the deeper water until I reach the end of the trap's chain. When you do this, make sure you do not jerk your trap off the solid piece of ground upon which it is setting covered with a slight film of muddy water. Because if you move the trap and the muddy film covering the trap is disturbed exposing the trap, the arriving beaver may see it and not step onto it. Now, throw me that dried wooden anchor stick. As I explained to you earlier when we were cutting these from that willow patch, I only use a dried wooden stick as my anchor pole. I do so because as I have learned, a beaver once trapped will oftentimes chew through a fresh green anchor pole whereas if a dried stick is used, it will not. And keep in mind, if the beaver chews through your anchor pole, he will swim off with your trap to someplace he considers safe, chew off his foot and you will lose your valuable trap and the critter! Remember, we learned back in St. Louis that once Lisa was at his new fort, he was going to charge his trappers $9 per beaver trap. That means you will need 1½ adult beaver skins to purchase another trap at Mountain Prices for every one lost, so we sure as hell don't want to lose any of them! Also, if you don't place your anchor pole in deep enough water, the beaver, if he can get his feet upon the muddy bottom after being trapped, may damn well chew off his foot. He then will escape and there goes your pelt and all of your hard work!"

Bear Trap, then careful not to drag or disturb the previously set trap, passed his wooden anchor pole through the steel ring on the end of the trap's chain and then placed the end of the anchor pole and the trap's ring on the bottom of the pond. Then taking his smaller hand ax, Bear Trap carefully drove the anchor pole deeply into the bottom of the pond. However when he did, he made sure he left several feet of the pole sticking up from the muddy bottom so it could be easily seen when checking one's traps. Removing the twine previously tied around his wrist taken from a small spool in the pannier, Bear Trap then made sure the steel ring on the end of the trap's chain was tightly tied to the wooden anchor pole. That way, if the trapped beaver somehow dragged the anchor pole out from the bottom of the pond, the weight of the five-pound trap would still drag the beaver's head under water and drown him. Later under such circumstances, when looking for the beaver trap, it would be discovered still tied to a floating anchor pole out in the pond's waters and could be recovered without the loss of a valuable and irreplaceable trap while afield and away from the nearness of a trading post or active Rendezvous site.

(Author's Note: The Author in college as a Wildlife Student took a parasitology class, since his Master's Thesis required him to identify the parasites in his thesis animal of study, namely the Pacific White-winged Scoter (sea duck). As part of the parasitology lab project requiring collection and identification of a large number of parasites from a number of different animal species, the Author ran a beaver trap line to collect that species' unique fur and intestinal parasites. In so doing, the Author in one of his trips caught a 109-pound beaver! In the days of the fur trappers of old, that would have produced what they classified as a "Blanket Sized" skin and an extremely valuable beaver pelt! Hence, one of the many reasons for a trapper having such a stout, four-foot anchor pole deeply anchored at the end of one's beaver trap chain.)

Finished with the mechanical trap setting process, Bear Trap walked back to where he had set his trap in the shallow water near the fresh beaver slide near the willows, took out his sheath knife and cut off a nearby green willow twig about two feet in length. He then peeled off all of the green bark with the blade of his knife so any nearby beaver would not attempt to eat the freshly cut twig. Bear Trap then had Ofer hand him the corked bottle of castoreum that he had been carrying. Removing the cork, Bear Trap dipped one end of the shaved twig into the end of the bottle of castoreum, an oily liquid derived from the caster glands removed from the back legs of a beaver. He then stuck one end of the willow twig into the soft mud of the stream bank and adjusted the other end of the twig with the castoreum on the end of it, so it hung diagonally over the water about four inches high over the trap lying directly underneath just inches under the water's surface.

Then Bear Trap saw Ofer's questioning looks on his face over what he had just done. "Ofer, beaver are very territorial, especially during their breeding season. If any beaver passing this way smells the scent of an unfamiliar beaver in his territory, it will stop everything it is currently doing and will come right over to investigate this new smell from another beaver. When it does, he will swim right up to the end of that stick I just dipped into that bottle of castoreum, and stand up in the bottom of the shallow water so he can reach up and pull the end of the stick over to his nose for a closer smell. When he drops his feet in order to stand, reach up and smell the end of that stick, his feet will land in the pan of the trap. When that occurs, the trap will spring shut and we will then have a beaver with one or both hind feet caught in the trap. When that happens, the beaver will swim away in a panic from where the trap just closed on either one or both of his feet and swim out into what he thinks is the safety of the deeper water. However, the now trapped beaver can only swim out to the end of the six-foot length of the trap's chain and no further because the end of the trap's chain is still anchored to your anchor pole! There swimming at the end of the trap's chain in panic, the beaver will continue hanging there as he tries swimming away from whatever has a hold of him because the anchor pole is holding him swimming in place. Soon the five-pound weight of the trap and chain will cause the beaver to become exhausted and with his head being dragged underwater the whole time, cause him to drown. When we return, if we have set the trap just right, we should have a $6 beaver at today's prices drowned and hanging dead in the trap. So ends your first beaver trapping lesson and in case I am unable to trap for whatever reason in the future, it will then be up to you and your brothers to continue with what I am showing you, so you can carry the fortunes of the group instead of just me being the main trapper," said Bear Trap with a big and well-satisfied grin over his lesson just rendered unto his subject.

By around two o'clock in the afternoon, with Bear Trap teaching each of the brothers in turn the beaver trapping techniques in the cold waters of the Musselshell, they had managed to set all 30 of their beaver traps in the rodent-rich 'magic waters' so described and previously shown to them by John Colter, the much-experienced and traveled Mountain Man. Then Bear Trap surprised the Tal Brothers by teaching them another beaver trapping trick of the trade. Instead of riding back to their campsite straightaway, Bear Trap had the brothers slowly backtrack themselves along their morning's trap line checking their morning's previously set traps. When they did, the Tal Brothers discovered they had already caught 14 beaver in their traps set earlier in the day!

With that 'discovery', the Tal Brothers then discovered that their workday as trappers had just begun! Making each brother then wade out and retrieve every one of the now dead beaver hanging in their traps, Bear Trap then began his third set of lessons of the day behind their trap setting lessons and the checking of their previously set traps later that same day. With that third lesson came the oily and stinky business of properly skinning out each beaver once removed from their traps on-site and in so doing, done in such a manner that the pelt paid off in its highest value when sold to a fur buyer.

Standing there on the stream bank with the first trapped beaver in hand, Bear Trap gathered the Tal Brothers around him saying, "Since all of you need to know how to properly skin out a beaver and since none of you have ever done so previously, let me show you how it is to be done. Do it otherwise and it will cost us big money when we get back to Lisa's fort and his graders and sorters take over." With those words of caution, Bear Trap grabbed up a 90-pound beaver just retrieved from a trap and laid it out onto a nearby grassy stream bank on its back. Then he took out one of his specially ground Thomas Wilson knives with a bevel only on just one side. A knife blade discovery that Bear Trap had made early on in life as a trapper, especially when one had icy cold hands from so much water immersion, which reduced fur cutting mistakes. Then looking over at the brothers gathered around him to make sure they were keenly watching his every move, Bear Trap said, "There is a right and wrong way to do this beaver skinning thing. I will show all of you the way I want it done, and the way the old trapper who taught me how to properly skin a beaver did it. Now watch carefully how I slit the skin on this here beaver down the entire length of the center of the animal's belly. That cut made and done, I will now make transverse cuts along the inside of each of the beaver's legs and then I am going to cut off each of the animal's feet. OK, now I am going to cut off the tail and toss it into a pannier because once roasted, they are a real treat because of their fatty content and unique flavor. Try to remember that little tip of the trade. The colder it gets the more fat we will need in our diets in order to keep our body heat up and keep from freezing. I tell all of you this because as all of you will soon discover, buckskin clothing alone will not keep you very warm. So in addition to other layers of clothing, you will need to eat meals that are high in fat content in order to keep warm. And over the years, I have found that eating some fatty beaver tails will aid you in being able to stay warmer and stave off the cold more easily. And as most of you know, riding a horse in winter weather is a cold proposition. Since we will be retrieving our trapped beaver every day in these here cold waters, waters that will only get colder as our trapping season progresses into the winter months, we need to remember to keep a mess of fatty beaver tails on hand for roasting and eating. By so doing, that will help in keeping us warmer during all of the cold water immersions we are facing in this damn cold trade we find ourselves in. Besides, the tail's outer skin makes for a quick and easily made knife sheath if one is in the need for one." Then Bear Trap paused and looking up once again at the brothers who appeared to be hanging onto his every word, continued saying, "Additionally, beaver meat is a real treat. What say all of you that I introduce you to a roasted beaver supper tonight once we are all back at our campsite?"

Only hearing utter silence over the thoughts of eating a rodent from those 'unwashed' who had never eaten such a critter, Bear Trap smiled inwardly and then kept going with his beaver skinning lesson already knowing what the answer to his beaver eating question was soon going to be... "Next watch carefully as I skin this critter and all of you are to do so carefully, because once again cut through the side of a beaver pelt other than alongside its edges when we 'hoop' them and for every such cut in the wrong place, it is a dollar off the value of your pelt! Also, a beaver has a very heavy fat layer between his body and the skin. That fat layer is what allows him to live and swim around in such cold waters, even comfortably swimming in the frigid waters once under the ice. Again, using one of my specialty knives with the bevel only on one side, I am going to carefully remove the skin from this here beaver's carcass and when done with that field work, will toss this pelt into the pannier for transport back to our cabin. As for the extra beaver carcasses we do not need or want for food, they are to be left out here for the critters to eat. That is done because we do not need a small mountain of rotting beaver carcasses stacked up back at our cabin as an open invite for every black bear, grizzly and gray wolf to come calling for a free meal. That happens and all of us will sooner or later experience a violent run-in with such hungry and many times mean-assed critters, as will our horses in a corral. So unless we need several beaver carcasses for our supper, they will remain out here in the wilds for the meat-eating critters to enjoy. Now, let's continue checking the rest of our traps and each and every one of you give it a go as I have just shown you in the proper techniques to use when carefully skinning out a beaver."

Once all 14 freshly caught beaver had been skinned out, the men under Bear Trap's careful guidance and tutelage moved off and began cutting fresh green willow limbs to be used in the 'hooping' process lessons soon to come. Those green limbs in turn were also stuffed into the packhorses' panniers along with the fresh beaver carcasses. Then with more work yet to be done on the fresh beaver pelts, the trappers mounted up and headed for home. But not before Bear Trap, the consummate Mountain Man, kept a 'peeled' eye on the far ridges and examined the surrounding forests looking for a repeat view of the two mystery riders he had seen earlier at the start of the men's day. Mystery riders who very well may have been watching the obvious white men fur trappers with devious thoughts of either attacking them later down the line or locating their cabin and stealing their valuable horses and provisions. This careful watching of every type of vegetative cover from whence an ambush might come was soon adopted by the rest of the Tal Brothers, who were eagerly learning from one of the best.

Later back at their camp while Daniel and Gabriel began preparations for the men's supper, Bear Trap lined out for Ofer,

Joshua and Jerimiah the proper defatting, stretching and hooping techniques on the beaver pelts taken earlier that day. Once Bear Trap was satisfied the three men had the proper pelting techniques down pat after watching him set the example, he headed outside to give Gabriel and Daniel a hand in the proper roasting procedures when it came to beaver tails and the three fresh carcasses they had brought home so the Tal Brothers could experience proper Mountain Man fare. But not before he had carefully instructed the three 'hooping' men back in the cabin how and where to carefully make the slits around the edges of a fresh beaver pelt and how to properly hoop each one with their freshly cut willow limbs and pieces of cut twine. That evening after all 14 beaver pelts had been carefully defatted, hooped and set out to dry (reduced bug infestations and facilitated transport to Fort Manuel), the six men feasted on freshly roasted beaver tails and carcasses, bean pot beans, Dutch oven biscuits and coffee... When finished with their 'rodent' suppers, the Tal Brothers pronounced their first eating experience when it came to such kinds of dinners as 'top drawer'. They even admitted later while sitting around the campfire that such suppers in the future would be most welcome...

For the rest of that month, the daily beaver trapping regimen became the same. An early morning's breakfast of roasted venison or buffalo meat, Dutch oven biscuits and coffee, checking the trap line with Bear Trap and Ofer as the group's main trappers, resetting or moving traps, and constantly adjusting the trap line's location as the beaver became quickly trapped out. Then a daily return to a willow patch for more hooping material, de-fleshing and defatting of fresh beaver pelts so they could dry when hooped with green willow limbs, almost the same supper nightly as they had for breakfast and then tiredly off to bed to await the next day's activities. Fortunately for the trappers deep in the country of the white man-hostile Blackfeet and just as deadly Gros Ventre Indians, hardly 'hide nor hair' of an Indian was seen after that first day of trapping. However, that issue of dangerous discovery not occurring by the dreaded Blackfeet whose home territory the trappers trapped within was soon to change...

Sensing the arrival of daylight in his 'biological clock', Daniel quietly slipped out from his sleeping furs so he would not awaken the rest of the sleeping men, hurriedly dressed and grabbing his ever-handy rifle, quietly opened the cabin's door and carefully looked about. This Daniel did as a matter of frontier habit, quietly standing in the open doorway first and looking all around for any signs of danger from either man or beast near at hand. Not seeing or sensing any sign of danger, Daniel exited the cabin and headed for the outdoor fire's stacked woodpile in order to start a fire and begin the daily making of coals so there could be Dutch oven biscuits for breakfast for the men. Taking one more look all around for any sign of danger in the morning's early light, Daniel laid his rifle down against a close at hand sitting log, picked up an ax and began splitting a 'round' of pine so he could have some kindling with which to start a fire. Starting the wood splitting process, Daniel stood the half-round of wood he was working on upright and swung the ax downward to split the chunk of wood into smaller pieces so he could make an easier starting fire.

WHANG went the metallic sound of the head of the ax as it glanced off an unseen knot and sailed its bladed edge directly into Daniel's shin! "YEOOW!" yelled Daniel, as the ax's sharp blade sliced through the leg's flesh and then firmly embedded itself into the bone of his shin! Within seconds of Daniel screaming out in pain when the head of the ax embedded itself deeply into the bone of his shin, the cabin door exploded open and was instantly filled with half-dressed fur trappers each sporting their rifles held at the ready looking for any signs of danger that had brought forth Daniel's scream of pain! Then seeing his younger brother wildly rolling around on the ground by the firepit with an obvious ax head embedded into his lower leg, Ofer threw all caution to the wind, ran from the cabin, jumped over a near at hand sitting log by the firepit and knelt by his obviously in pain brother. Arriving at his brother's side, Ofer immediately felt his brother's hands reaching out and grabbing him as he writhed around on the ground in intense bone pain from his self-inflected wound!

"Daniel, how the hell did this happen?" shouted Ofer, as he hurriedly laid down his rifle and grabbed his brother's wildly outstretched and thrashing around hands!

"THE AX, THE AX!" screamed out Daniel in intense pain, as he now held the head of the ax in his hands with all kinds of blood spurting through his fingers from the badly wounded leg!

Looking down and without thinking, Ofer instinctively reached down, grabbed the end of the ax's handle and quickly shoved it downward to spring the blade back out from the lower leg bone!

"YEOOW!" screamed Daniel, as the ax's blade broke loose from the shinbone! Immediately, even more bright red blood flowed from the gaping wound as Bear Trap now on the scene, whipped off his buckskin shirt and seeing the extent of the problem, wrapped a sleeve of that shirt around Daniel's leg wound to stem the flow of blood. Then grabbing Ofer's hands and directing them to apply pressure on Bear Trap's shirt sleeve wrapped around the damaged leg, he leapt up and trotted for the front door of the cabin. Moments later, Bear Trap returned from the cabin carrying a small bolt of gray cloth normally used to repair clothing and a tin of bag balm. Right behind him trotted Gabriel after seeing the problem with Daniel's leg, carrying Ofer's sewing kit. By now, Joshua had arrived on the bloody scene carrying a bucket full of water from the stream near the horse corral. With Bear Trap and Gabriel lifting Daniel up, they carried him over to a nearby sitting log and carefully sat the much in pain brother down. As they did, Ofer knelt next to a whimpering in pain Daniel, cut off a swatch of gray cloth from the bolt with his sheath knife and began stemming the flow of blood from the damaged leg. Then a just-soaked cloth rag from the horse bucket was applied to the damaged leg and soon the cold compresses began stemming the blood flow but only slightly. Then with a cupful of rum in hand, Jerimiah handed it to Daniel for the painful drama that he knew was soon to come to his much in pain brother. Soon after Daniel had quickly drained his cup of rum, Ofer had a small fire started with his fire steel in the firepit and was holding a needle's point over the small flame. Moments later with leather sewing needle and twine in hand, the wet compress was removed from Daniel's wounded leg. An ugly blue, black and purple six-inch gash into the flesh and bone was revealed in the morning's sunlight to the eyes of the concerned onlooking fur trappers! Trappers who were all looking on with concern for their companion, yet out of developing frontier experience, occasionally all of whom looked up and around their campsite for any signs of danger coming from another quarter with their rifles still in hand...

Without a word, Ofer gently grabbed up Daniel's leg and looking over at Bear Trap and Jerimiah in such a manner that the two men looking at him realized what he wanted, knowingly reached down and held Daniel still by his shoulders for what was soon to painfully come. Seeing his younger brother restrained by Bear Trap and Jerimiah, Ofer splashed some rum from another hastily filled cup over the ax's ugly and still bleeding wound! When he did, Daniel lurched upwards into the arms of Bear Trap and Jerimiah in intense pain but uttered not a word! Seeing his brother under good physical control, Ofer gently wiped the excess rum and blood from the wound and then without hesitation and before Daniel could gather up any defensive thoughts, plunged the needle and thread through the now inflamed leg tissue and began sewing the gash shut as more blood flowed through his fingers making holding the needle and thread difficult. When the needle first plunged through the two adjoining badly damaged flaps of leg tissue, Daniel once again lunged upwards into the strong restraining arms of Bear Trap and Jerimiah but only uttered a low groan of pain. Ofer, now beginning to sweat under the stress of what he had to do, kept going and in so doing, made sure his drops of sweat were not dropping into the still bloody and partially open wound creating further issues...

Soon the deed was done and in the process, Daniel had drained the second cup of rum or at least what was left of it after much of its contents had been splashed over the open wound before the 'frontier doctoring' had begun. Suffice to say, Gabriel did all of the morning's cooking that day as Daniel just quietly sat on his sitting log by the fire and continued rocking back and forth in quiet but intense pain. Pain created by the slip of the blade of the damn sharp ax upon hitting a hard pine knot and sending that blade glancing off into Daniel's shinbone! Later that morning because he could not mount his horse or suffer the intense pain of having his damaged leg hanging down and banging around in the stirrups, Daniel stayed back at the campsite quietly nursing his third cup of the fiery rum and keeping the fire going while the rest of the men headed off to tend their active trap line. But as Daniel sat there in pain on his sitting log, Ofer was aware that smoke from their campfire sometimes attracted unwanted guests, amd had placed his brother's rifle alongside his sitting log, along with two fully loaded pistols with buck and ball just in case Daniel suffered a visit from any Indians. Shortly after their breakfast, the trappers, having a long trap line to tend, waved their 'Good-byes' to Daniel as they slowly streamed out from their campsite.

Long about late afternoon, Daniel feeling the urge to take care of an urgent call of nature, using the barrel of his rifle as a handhold and its stock as a rest upon the ground, he staggered behind the men's cabin towards the latrine. A now very well-used latrine that Ofer had ordered constructed after stepping several times in previously deposited waste near their cabin, and tiring of such experiences made what he considered a civil change in the campsite. However, as Daniel dropped his buckskin pants and placed his bottom over the cleverly constructed log bench set-up which allowed the user to comfortably take a dump, he did not look down into the hole. Did not look down and realize that something had discovered the well-used latrine and had cleaned and eaten out from the bore-hole all the waste that had been previously deposited by the large numbers of trappers using the structure...

Daniel, about ten minutes into his 'call of nature' and because his pain-filled mind was dulled by three cups of rum, DID NOT HEAR WHAT WAS COMING UP BEHIND HIM! SENSING A DIFFERENCE THAT MORNING AT THE LATRINE, A HUGE BOAR GRIZZLY BEAR UPON APPROACHING THE LOG SITTING AREA HABITUATED TO THE FOOD SOURCE LYING BELOW, STOPPED AND REALIZED THERE WAS NOW SOMETHING SITTING ON THE BENCH LOG AT THE EDGE OF THE LATRINE! HOWEVER, IN ADDITION TO THE FAMILIAR SMELLS OF THE USUAL FOOD SOURCE THAT LAY BELOW IN THE OPEN PIT, THE BEAR ALSO SMELLED FRESH BLOOD! IN AN INSTANT THE BEAR LUNGED FORWARD THE LAST FEW FEET TOWARDS THE LATRINE, GRABBED THE UNAWARE OBJECT SITTING ON THE LOG SEAT SMELLING OF FRESH BLOOD AND SUGAR-SWEET RUM, AND CRUNCHED DOWN UPON THE UNMOVING OBJECT'S HEAD IN A KILLING BITE! DANIEL DIED INSTANTLY IN THE GREAT BEAR'S JAWS BECAUSE OF A CRUSHED SKULL...

Throughout the morning, the team of trappers found for some reason almost every one of their previously set traps contained a dead beaver! Then on their way back along their previously set trap line, the trappers discovered another 12 dead beaver hanging in their traps, or a total of 40 beaver being caught for their day's efforts in their newest trap line, a new daily record! Catching so many beaver that day and after skinning out such a number and paying several visits to adjacent willow patches gathering up several panniers full of willow limbs, the tired trappers headed for home. However, their day was not yet done. On the way back come late afternoon, Ofer shot a huge cow elk because they were low on camp meat. Then as Ofer watched the cow elk buckle from being hit with the .52 caliber ball, he immediately felt a physical twinge within his body that was not 'of this world'! He then stood stock-still as he recognized the twinge inside of him as that of his old and familiar sixth sense that always seemed to dog him in times heralding impending danger or trouble! A sixth sense that he had inherited from his mother, Zipporah, who was also dogged by such internal happenings when her maternal instincts 'told' her that something bad was about to happen to someone in her family... Standing there and now hurriedly reloading his rifle as he worriedly looked all around remembering what Bear Trap had told him about Indians' 'lynx eyes' and their ability to be upon you many times before they were even seen as were their arrows or bullets, he redoubled his 'speed' reloading efforts! That Bear Trap teaching about the 'lynx eyes' and the realization of being deep in the country of the dreaded Blackfeet, caused him to continue looking concernedly all around for the danger his sixth sense 'was now more than warning him about' as he continued until he had finished his reloading drill!

Ofer's strange physical reactions after making such a clean-killing shot on the cow elk all of a sudden drew all the rest of the trappers' rapt attentions! Then Bear Trap realizing something had 'set' Ofer to acting all strange-like began looking all around as well, figuring Ofer's lone shot may have attracted a number of curious Indians and he had seen some. By now, all of the trappers' senses were on high alert as they all began keying off of Ofer's strange actions!

Then Bear Trap quietly said to Ofer, "What the hell is the matter? What do you see, Ofer, that has you all wound up and acting all strange-like?"

"I don't know! But my sixth sense is roiling around inside me and when that happens from my past experiences, something bad is about to happen or there is danger close at hand," said Ofer, as he continued looking all around once again for what he figured was a close at hand and unseen Indian menace.

Finally after everyone looked all around for what Ofer figured were close at hand Indians and not seeing any, the group of men slowly settled down. However, that did not allow for Ofer's sixth sense to do so. Finally, Ofer and company set aside their 'high alert' status and began butchering out Ofer's cow elk before she started to bloat and ruin the meat. Later by the time the elk had been butchered out and her meat supplies loaded into the almost full panniers, the sun was setting low in the sky to the west. Then once again, the trappers formed up into a protective caravan and headed for their campsite, some great cow elk meat-eating during a much anticipated supper, and then some well-deserved rest after they had defatted, fleshed out and hooped all 40 of their monster catch of freshly caught beaver.

Rounding the turn into the draw heading up to the trappers' cabin, the men did not see their ax-wounded brother on his sitting log by the fire. In fact, there was no evidence of a recent fire either. And once again, Ofer's sixth sense was flitting around inside of his body big time! Figuring Daniel had slipped back into his sleeping furs in order to get his damaged leg laid out straight in order to reduce the pain, the men continued riding into their cabin site. There they quietly unpacked all of their horses and let them out to graze so they did not wake Daniel up if he was sleeping inside their cabin. In addition, the rest of their horse herd was released from the corral so they could graze and water as well. Then as Gabriel, now the camp's lone cook headed for the firepit to get a fire going and begin making some Dutch oven biscuit mix so it could rise, the rest of the men hoisted the elk quarters up onto their meat pole so it could begin cooling and glazing out. Then the four panniers were hauled over to the front of the cabin so they could be more easily unloaded in preparation for the defatting and hooping duties to follow. It was then that Ofer went into the cabin in order to check on the wellness of his younger brother. Within moments, Ofer emerged from the cabin with a look of worry spreading all over his face saying, "Do any of you see Daniel? He is nowhere in our cabin!"

It was then that the men suspected something was bad-wrong and immediately began a search of the immediate area! It was then that Jerimiah discovered Daniel's partially eaten remains back by the latrine! His shout brought the rest of the men running to the area of the latrine and within moments, the story of the disaster became abundantly clear to all. From all of the tracks around the latrine, it soon became obvious that Daniel had gone to the latrine to go to the bathroom, only to be ambushed from behind by a hungry grizzly bear who had probably been attracted to the latrine's interesting smelling contents and quite possibly to Daniel's still oozing and bloody leg wound. The extent of the disaster was quite clear. Daniel's blood was everywhere all around the latrine signifying a savage and surprising attack from behind! All that remained was a partially crushed and eaten head, two uneaten hands, part of a pelvis and two bloodied leg bones from below the knees, as well as his two uneaten feet! Everything else had been consumed by the big bear! A bear later determined from its huge footprints by a deadly quiet Bear Trap to be a large male grizzly probably exceeding 1,000 pounds in weight!

(Author's Note: In the 1990's, one of the Author's Montana agents assisted a Park Ranger investigating the grizzly bear attack and death of a female back country hiker in Glacier

National Park, who had been hiking alone without a warning bell on her person or carrying a can of bear spray. Subsequent investigation of the attack scene revealed blood everywhere and that the bear had eaten everything of the female hiker except a partially crushed and eaten head, two uneaten bony hands, a partially consumed pelvis, two uneaten and bony feet, and her two bony legs with the flesh unconsumed below the knees. Hence the Author's rather realistic and descriptive account of a grizzly bear killing and consumption of a human when it came to describing Daniel's demise and partially eaten remains.)

By now the sun was setting in the west and it was apparent that to try and track the large bear at that time in the afternoon would be pure folly. The trappers, in great mental agony over the loss of one of their own, decided they would begin tracking the bear right at daylight, track it to its den where it would be sleeping off its big meal and destroy it! Then Bear Trap interceded in the angry and shocked conversation being held among the brothers regarding their planned revenge of the great bear saying, "No, that we will not do. We caught 40 beaver this day and I expect in this new trapping area we just established that our catch tomorrow will be just as large. It will not do for us to leave a large number of dead beaver hanging in our traps tomorrow for the predators to have at, as well as to court discovery by any Blackfeet Indians wandering by and seeing that there are active American beaver trappers in the area. No, tomorrow you four brothers are going to run our trap line and return with our hard-earned catch. In the meantime, all of you know what the grizzly bear did to my last of kin which is just like what happened to Daniel. Tomorrow, I will take my four grizzly bear traps, track this bastard down and once again extract my revenge for what this species did to the last of my kind and my friend Daniel. Then when trapped and hanging in the traps, I will return the next day and finish what needs doing for Daniel's sake and mine. Ofer, you know what to do and it will be up to you to take the lead to see that our group continues with our beaver trapping successes. Then when all of you return tomorrow night, I hopefully will have word on where this killer went and where I set my traps. Then the next day, since I will have set my traps at his den's entrance and the bear will have to walk over them to get a drink after his big meal of Daniel, I will have him. Then I will finish the job as you men continue running our trap line. At the end of the day when I kill this bastard, I will bring back that bear's head and hide, or die trying. Now, I know just how everyone feels over the loss of our 'brother' Daniel. But we now have 40 fresh pelts to defat and hoop, so I suggest we get at it and take our frustrations out on those pelts knowing the day following that the bear will get his due come 'hell or high water.'"

As to be understood, there was a great sadness hanging over the remaining five trappers even in light of one of their most successful days trapping. However, the volume of work required in defatting and hooping 40 beaver took most of the night and into the early morning hours. Suffice to say, the next morning's breakfast was a couple of cups of rum each and then the men parted company as had been decided the evening before. As planned, Ofer, no longer feeling what his 'right on the money' now quiet sixth sense had to say from the day before, led the trapping party out and sure as Bear Trap had predicted, the new area being trapped along Box Elder Creek produced another 31 beaver before the day was done! Arriving back at their campsite, Ofer and his brothers were greeted with a roaring outside fire and a happy Bear Trap on his sitting log with a cup of rum in hand. After the men had dismounted with the good beaver trapping successes reported to Bear Trap, he also had good information for the brothers. He had tracked the great bear to its den about a mile distant from the trappers' camp. The den was located in a bluff of rocks and Bear Trap was able to place all four of his giant bear traps in such a manner that the bear would have to walk over one or all of them just to exit its den! As such, knowing the bear would have to go to water after consuming such a big meal as a human being, he was confident the following day would result in the great bear's demise and both he and the brothers could then take solace in the fact that Daniel would be the bear's last meal, ever!

That evening, Gabriel began preparations for the men's supper after recovering Daniel's remains and burying them alongside their cabin under a large rock pile so no other critters could dig his remains up and eat them. The men had been so distraught over finding the remains of Daniel the day before that they in their sadness, shock and haste to get at their mess of pelts, had forgotten to bury their brother. Gabriel saw to it that the task of burying of his brother was sadly completed. Once again that evening, the trappers' rum supply took a 'hit' as the men celebrated the memory of their brother and the need for something to lay their feelings to rest, knowing what was coming on the morrow along their new trap line in the way of work. The next morning after breakfast and feeding and watering their horse herd, Ofer and company took off to run their very active trap line, and Bear Trap went forth to put the finishing touches on his mission of revenge and subsequent destruction of the man-killing grizzly bear for the sake of his brother and fellow trapper and friend Daniel.

That evening, Bear Trap never returned...

CHAPTER 4 — THIRTEEN ARROWS, "TWO CROWS" AND "FOUR SCALPS"

WAY BEFORE DAYLIGHT OFER WAS UP AND HAD THEIR outside fire going just in case Bear Trap was on his way back and needed some light to guide him back to the cabin. Come daylight, Bear Trap had yet to return so Ofer got his tired brothers out from their sleeping furs, had them wash up, shave and finally seated around their roaring campfire. As Gabriel hustled around the fire preparing the brothers their breakfast, Ofer said, "Well, Bear Trap did not show himself this morning and my sixth sense and I fear the worst. I suspect that the bear he went after reversed his fortunes and took out Bear Trap instead of the other way around. Hell, even his horse did not return to the corral, so I fear the very worst for our friend Bear Trap. On top of that, we have just set out our new trap line in beaver-rich country along Box Elder Creek and because of our trapping successes, we cannot just up and leave it unattended and our caught beaver hanging in the traps while we go looking for Bear Trap. So here is what I suggest we do. Joshua, since you are the next oldest, you and the rest of the brothers are to continue running our trap line like nothing is out of the ordinary. I expect

Gabriel and Jerimiah to do the actual trapping and skinning of anything we catch and you, Joshua, to remain seated on your horse so there is ample protection and early warning of any sign of danger for those along the water doing the trapping. You three are to run the trap line just like Bear Trap taught us and once finished, get your tail-ends back here to our cabin for the defatting and hooping duties to follow, so we don't lose any of our valuable pelts due to spoilage."

Ofer then paused as if further gathering his thoughts since he was now the leader of the group of brothers until Bear Trap returned or... Then Ofer began once again, saying, "I will be leaving you, my brothers, this morning to go out and see if I can discover what has happened to Bear Trap. I will be taking one of our packhorses along with some supplies so if it takes me several days to backtrack Bear Trap, I can do so. In the meantime all of you are to stick together, continue running our trap line and remain ever alert so you do not fall into any kind of a trap set by the Blackfeet. Now if I do not return in ten days, all of you are to pack up our camp and return to Fort Manuel. It would not do for mother and father to lose all of their sons to the harshness of this land. If returning to Fort Manuel is in the cards, I suggest all of you who remain board the first keelboat leaving Fort Manuel on the spring's high waters. Then once back in St. Louis, head home back to mother and father so they will at least have a few of their sons around for the later years in their lives. Now, how about some of those Dutch oven biscuits, Gabriel?" said Ofer with his characteristic grin, all the while trying to allay his brothers' concerns over what had happened to their friend Bear Trap, as well as what lay ahead for Ofer in his hunt for his friend and mentor.

Later that morning as the rest of his brothers headed out to run their trap line, Ofer sat on his horse trailing a packhorse and quietly watched them leave. Then being the excellent tracker that he was, he began following the hoofprints of Bear Trap's riding and packhorse left from the day before. For about the next six hours or so, Ofer slowly trailed Bear Trap's horses' hoofprints up into the nearby mountains. As he did, he also carefully watched around him and on his back trail for any signs of Blackfeet Indians trailing him or his horses as Bear Trap had always taught him to do.

By early afternoon on that first day, Ofer had discovered why Bear Trap had not returned to their camp. Riding up into the bluff of rocks Bear Trap had described days earlier as to where he had tracked the killer grizzly bear, Ofer discovered the remains of a grisly scene... Below the bluff of rocks at a cave's entrance lay a dead and partially skinned-out monster in size grizzly bear. Off to one side lay four giant bear traps that from the damage on the bear's right front and left rear legs had done their job in catching the killer just as Bear Trap had predicted. Then all the tracks around the remains of the bear's carcass were those from Bear Trap's big feet AND A NUMBER OF SMALLER MOCCASIN FOOTPRINTS MADE BY AT LEAST FOUR INDIANS! However, there was no sign of Bear Trap or any sign of a human struggle... That told Ofer that apparently his friend Bear Trap must have been surprised and taken captive by the Indians!

Standing there with his rifle held at the ready, Ofer's now Bear Trap-trained senses scanned the surrounding hillside and fringes of timber looking for any signs of immediate danger. As he did, he also realized his sixth sense was once again quietly making its presence known that some sort of danger was in the air! Seeing nothing in the way of danger close at hand, Ofer relaxed a bit and then went back to his tracking techniques as taught to him by Bear Trap during their previous months together. As it turned out, Bear Trap had been a good teacher and Ofer a great student. Soon Ofer was on the trail of eight horses, six of which were unshod, all heading further up into the surrounding high timber country. Ofer deduced the eight sets of horses' tracks represented those from four Indian riders, those from Bear Trap's riding and packhorse and two extra sets of tracks, probably from the Indians' packhorses. But surprisingly, the tracks were leading away from where Ofer knew was the heart of the Blackfoot Nation and were leading towards the northeast, or that of the territory of the dreaded Gros Ventre Indians!

One day later of hard but slow and careful tracking, because he only had his one set of eyes watching out for danger, found Ofer himself deep into heavy timber just at sundown. Getting ready to dismount for the night because the day's reduced light made tracking difficult, Ofer froze in mid-dismount! Once again, Ofer found himself utilizing all of his Bear Trap-taught senses when he found himself scenting the faint smell of wood smoke in the cool evening air! Quietly taking in great 'draughts' of the night's air through his nose, the faint smell of burning pinewood 'told' his nose he was close to his mystery quarry! Finishing his dismount, Ofer tied off his two horses so they would not wind the quarry's horses if nearby, and give away his presence with an untimely 'recognition of the smell of another horse' whinny. As he did, he once again felt his sixth sense making its 'presence of danger' feelings known in a less than gentle fashion... About half an hour later in the now gathering darkness found Ofer silently looking into the flickering light of a small campfire from a short distance away. At first he saw nothing or any sign of human movement, just the flickering light from a small campfire like that an Indian would make to avoid detection.

Then all of a sudden emerging from the darkness and inside that camp illuminated by the campfire's flickering light, Ofer could make out the figures of four Indians whose dress and garb he did not recognize as to their tribal affiliations! But that made no difference because at the outside edge of their campfire's flickering light from where the Indians had just emerged he now could faintly see three human figures tied to individual trees! And one of those figures at the very edge of the light from the Indians' campfire appeared to be that of his dear friend Bear Trap! Moving in even closer towards the flickering campfire after once again checking the priming on his rifle and two pistols, Ofer paused. He then realized there were four Indians in evidence around the campfire and he only had three shots in his rifle and two pistols… Then without hesitation, Ofer reached behind him and felt the reassuring handle of his ever-sharp tomahawk. It was at that very moment in time that Ofer felt a physical and emotional change rippling through his body like that of a revelation. He realized he was soon to face a possible deadly life-changing situation that possibly required him to not only take a human life, but four! He had never been faced with such a situation like this before but for some strange reason, he felt a calmness overcoming his 'person'. He then realized he would do what he had to do in order to save his friend's life and not be looking back with remorse at any such violent actions that it would take to do so! It was at that very moment in time that Ofer Tal changed from a privileged country boy once living in the land mass of Upper Louisiana to that of a Mountain Man in the land of the largely unexplored and many times violent western frontier. A Mountain Man who was always more than ready to get back to the forests, mountains and prairies where conventionalities never stood in his way… Quietly cocking his rifle and two pistols against his soft buckskin shirt in order to mask the unnatural metallic clicking sounds they made going to 'full cock', Ofer took a deep breath to calm his rapidly beating heart and then began slowly and quietly approaching the activity around the Indians' campfire. That he did, walking silently in his moccasins like an Indian would do, as Bear Trap had previously taught him to do under like circumstances. As he got closer and closer to the four unaware Indians facing away from his approach, Ofer's sixth sense was now more than ever making its presence known that danger and death were in the air! However, little did he realize whose death was in the air...

Holding his rifle at the ready, Ofer silently slipped right into the Indians' campsite as they squatted busily eating their supper as they faced their fire. For what seemed like the longest moment in time, no one took notice of the buckskin-clad Mountain Man standing just in the ring of light from the four Indians' campfire with his rifle held at the ready! That and possessing a look on his face indicating there would soon be four more candidates ready to meet the rest of their tribal ancestors, the "Cloud People" in the "Upper World"...

All of a sudden, the closest Indian to where Ofer was quietly standing realized there was an unknown man standing close behind where he was sitting and eating! Turning and looking up in surprise and seeing an armed Mountain Man standing there with a look upon his face 'that said it all', that Indian jumped to his feet! As he did, he quickly withdrew his sheath knife and died where he stood when Ofer's heavy rifle barrel came crashing down upon his skull, immediately crushing it! Jerking out his almost-stuck rifle barrel from that now dead Indian's crushed skull as he dropped to the ground from the deadly violent impact, Ofer shot the next Indian quickly rising to his feet in alarm in the face! That shot was taken at such close-in range that the flame from the discharging rifle burned the dead man's face black in an instant as he fell away and into the nearby fire! Dropping his rifle straightaway and quickly whipping out a pistol in each hand from his sash, Ofer shot the next rising Indian from his sitting position around their campfire square in the throat! The impact of that large .52 caliber ball striking the man from just three feet away hurled him into his last living partner now starting to rise from his sitting position around the campfire and as he did, started to sing his 'death song' as he rose to meet the danger at hand or "The Great Spirit", whoever came first...

Shucking off his now falling partner, the last living Indian drew his sheath knife and slashed it across Ofer's extended left arm still holding the just-fired pistol! Ofer hardly felt that knife's blade slashing clear to the bone on his left forearm, as the blast from his second and last loaded pistol fired from just two feet away with his right hand blew most of that knife-wielding Indian's face into such a pulpy mess that even his beloved mother would not have been able to recognize him! Then it was all over except for the sound of the crackling wood fire and the nervous shuffling of the surprised horses' hooves tied off on a nearby rope picket line when they began hearing the close at hand shooting and then smelling the scent of fresh blood. Then almost mechanically as Bear Trap had always taught the Tal Brothers, "Soon as you shoot, get to quickly reloading because you may have need for more firepower in the next moment in time," which Ofer began rapidly accomplishing, madly bleeding left forearm notwithstanding.

As Ofer hurriedly reloaded his rifle and both pistols, his eyes were quickly sweeping the entire Indians' campsite looking for any other signs of danger he may have missed once the shooting started and he was totally distracted. Seeing none, now reloaded and both pistols back under his sash, he took out his sheath knife and cut off a swatch of cloth from the nearest dead Indian's buckskin shirt. Then using his teeth as an 'assist', tied off that 'swatch' of buckskin shirt from the dead Indian around his bleeding forearm to slow the flow of blood from his knife wound. That accomplished for now, Ofer's eyes quickly swept the campsite once again looking for any other signs of danger. As he did, he once again observed what appeared to be two young Indian men tied to trees and hanging face forward in their ropes like they were unconscious. From all appearances, both young Indian men had been badly beaten and abused. Neither young man appeared to be conscious but just hung forward over their ropes, dripping blood onto the ground from their heads from what had to be previous brutal beatings by the four now dead Indians! Then Ofer's eyes turned to the very edge of the light from the campfire where his friend Bear Trap appeared to be tied up to a tree as well. When he did, what he saw almost made his heart skip a beat, as he drew in a sharp breath in the abject realization of what he was seeing and the instant misery of the moment!

Hanging in his ropes, his friend Bear Trap did not appear to be moving! Trotting over to where Bear Trap hung face forward in his ropes, Ofer's heart froze over what he saw once he got closer! There hung Bear Trap alright, but sticking out from his chest and stomach area were the shafts from 13 arrows! Arrows apparently shot from just feet away into the helpless man hanging in his ropes and driven deeply into his torso and vital organs! Arrows that obviously had been shot into his body from close range as he stood helplessly tied to his tree by the three now dead Indians lying around on the ground and the one lying across the Indians' campfire smoking away... Upon seeing such barbarity, Ofer's senses shuddered and then he went cold as ice as did his heart! Without a word and now understanding what his earlier sixth sense had been 'telling' him once he saw Bear Trap hanging dead after being 'arrowed' while helplessly roped against the tree, Ofer determinedly walked back to the four dead Indians he had just killed with narrowed, hatred-filled eyes! It was just as Bear Trap had told all of the brothers back at Lisa's warehouse at the start of their procuring of provisions for their trip out onto the frontier as new fur trappers. "The frontier is not for the faint of heart," had said Bear Trap, as he tried to inform the five greenhorns looking at their first trip out into the largely unexplored and sometimes violent frontier as to the reality they might face... As it now stood, Ofer's heart was not faint, but cold in the realization of what he now faced as a Mountain Man and how he would face it in the future...

Walking back to the campfire with a determination of soul he had never felt before this moment in time, Ofer first removed the dead Indian, who upon being shot had fallen into the fire and was 'cooking' and 'smoking' away. Then without one ounce of remorse, humanity or hesitation, Ofer laid down his now reloaded rifle, removed his sheath knife and totally scalped the partially cooked Indian! Then without any further hesitation, Ofer visited the remaining three dead Indians and totally scalped off every bit of hair from their skulls as well! By now, Ofer's hands were totally running with not only his own blood from his forearm wound but from the blood when he had savagely removed all four of the Indians' ENTIRE heads of hair! Then without hesitation, Ofer gathered up the four bloody hairpieces still dripping blood, walked over to the horses' picket line and firmly tied off each Indian's scalp into each Indian horse's mane. Then taking his bloody hands, Ofer made sure his bloody hand-print was imprinted firmly high up onto each Indian's horse's neck next to each tied-off scalp! Then he untied each Indian's horse with the bloody Indian's scalp tied firmly into its mane and a bloody handprint on the side of the animal's neck as a warning to the always superstitious Indians. He then slapped each horse on its ass so it would head for wherever its original 'home' was back in the Indian band's horse herd as a dire warn-ing! Then having run out of scalps, Ofer just planted a bloody red handprint on the necks of the Indians' two remaining horses and turned them loose as well. That he did remembering what Bear Trap had previously taught him culturally about different Indians' beliefs and superstitions, especially as they related to their dead compatriots missing any of their body parts, LIKE A FULL SCALP! Superstitions about the fact that if an Indian was missing any body parts as a result of dying in battle, he would wander forever in the "Upper World", never able to enter the "Happy Hunting Ground" with the rest of his "Cloud People"...

Then without any feelings of remorse over his savage behav-ior, done so especially in light of what those four Indians had done to his friend and mentor, Bear Trap, Ofer wiped his bloody hands off on the dead Indians' clothing. But not having any water to wash off his bloody hands, Ofer just ignored the residual blood-red coloring as he walked over to the two young Indian men apparently still alive and hanging from the trees where they had been tied up earlier by the now four dead Indians. There he untied the two young men and gently carried them individually over to the fire where they could warm up and recover from their shock of capture and subsequent savage beatings. In order to make room for the two young men around the fire's circle of warmth, Ofer just dragged the four Indian bodies off a short distance. There he left the four bodies where they fell in the forest for any hungry critter to find and feed upon, which was just another superstitious disgrace among many Indian tribes...

Finally, the two young Indian men came around to their senses and for several long moments they appeared mentally confused over the fact that they had gone from four Indian captors to that of being captured by a fierce-looking Mountain Man with hands all covered with blood... Then when they had come completely around whereby they seemed to be of fit mind even though their bodies were wracked in pain from being previously brutally beaten by their four Indian captors, Ofer 'spoke' to the young men. This he did through the universal talk of the Plains Indians, namely in 'sign language'. As the two young Indian men now ate ravenously of the four dead Indians' supper, they signed back to Ofer between gulping down their food saying, "They were from a small band of Crow Indians who had been almost totally wiped out, including their parents, by a larger band of Gros Ventre. Then the attacking Gros Ventre had split up, leaving the two young Crow men and brothers to the four Gros Ventre Indians Ofer had just killed, to be sold to the Assiniboine Indians as slaves." Then the two young Crow teenagers began crying realizing they had no family or clan members to return to and that they were now homeless and in the hands of a savage Mountain Man! It took a few moments for Ofer to get the two young men to settle down and that was only accomplished when he informed them that they were not his slaves but free to go as they pleased. He further advised that he had only come to rescue his friend, the white man the 'bad Indians' had previously captured as he was skinning out a dead bear and had subsequently been savagely killed in their camp. But since he had been too late and the four Gros Ventre had slaughtered his friend by shooting him full of arrows where he had been tied to a tree, after burying him he was going to return to his brothers and fellow trappers in order to continue trapping beaver in a place several days' ride from their current location. Then not knowing why he said what he was about to say, Ofer informed the two young men they could return with him and live among him and his brothers if they wished.

Without responding to what Ofer had just said, suddenly the two boys looked over at Ofer's still blood-covered hands and vaguely remembered him placing his bloody hand on each Indian's horse as a warning with the scalp attached before he sent the horse free. With those remembrances in mind, the two Indian boys began talking almost reverently among themselves in their native Crow tongue... Ofer finally got the two boys to quit talking in their native language, and asked them to return to sign so he could understand what they were so amazed or excited about in their discussions. In so doing, he wondered if he had offended the two young men with his offer for them if they wanted, to return with him to his brother trappers and live with them since they now had nobody to return to. That was when the older of the two boys, named "Black Eagle", told Ofer that he was a great man and warrior. That he, Black Eagle, and his younger brother, "Little Raven", had been pretending that they were not aware of what was going on when tied to the trees in order to avoid further beatings from their Gros Ventre captors or the Mountain Man. Black Eagle further stated that they had then seen Ofer all by himself slay and then scalp the four great Gros Ventre warriors! Then they had observed him attaching those scalps to each Indian's horse's mane and placing a bloody handprint on each horse's neck as a warning. Silent until then, all of a sudden Little Raven chimed in 'talking' rapidly in sign saying, "We both feel that you are a great warrior as well, and 'Thank You' for saving us from a fate worse than death by being sold to our enemies the wicked Assiniboine as slaves. We both have decided that a great warrior such as yourself needs to have a powerful name that matches the might of your spirit and speaks to your powers of bravery. My brother and I will now 'name' you, as our Crow culture requires of any great warrior. We have decided that your new name according to our Crow traditions shall be "Four Scalps," and we would like to go with Four Scalps wherever he goes and live as his brothers since you have saved us from death."

Ofer just smiled over the Indian name the boys had just given him and what they had said about living with him and being his 'brother'. Then after looking down at his bloody hands and looking over at the pile of dead Gros Ventre, each with their ENTIRE heads of hair removed and now attached to their long-gone horses as a deadly reminder to any other Gros Ventre, he just smiled again. But in the back of his mind, a now changed forever Ofer Tal realized he now truly was a Mountain Man in all of its aspects and had earned a moniker, as had happened to his dear and now long-gone friend, Jan "Bear Trap" Driessen, namely that of Four Scalps... A moniker now attached to him that no other trapper would have to ask about like he had done with his friend when asking about his odd name of Bear Trap.

That evening, Ofer, Black Eagle and Little Raven feasted on the remains of the now dead Gros Ventre Indians' supper and then quietly slept 'like dead men' in the dead Indians' sleeping furs because all three were so emotionally exhausted. The next morning, since the three men did not have any shovels, they located a crevice in a rocky bluff not far from the Gros Ventre campsite and buried Bear Trap therein under a huge mound of packed-in boulders, so the wolves and grizzly bears would not be able to dig up and eat Jan "Bear Trap" Driessen, the last of his family and kind... But before 'walking away' from his dear friend and mentor's body, Ofer said a final farewell and prayer in Hebrew as the two young Crow men quietly looked on. Seeing the reverence in Ofer's eyes as he said his 'quiet' words, followed by the upwelling of tears before he turned away after saying some white man's words they did not understand, Black Eagle realized for the first time that a truly great Mountain Man must now be lying underneath the boulders. Sensing the importance of the man underneath the boulders to the Mountain Man they had named Four Scalps who had just bravely rescued both him and his brother, Black Eagle said a short prayer on the dead Mountain Man's behalf to The Great Spirit as well... As for the four Gros Ventre, Black Eagle and Little Raven were happy the dead were left where they fell for the critters of the forest upon which to happily feast and desecrate. As for the four Gros Ventre horses released carrying the scalps of their owners tied into their manes with an ominous bloody red handprint on each horse's neck and their two other horses with just the bloody handprint on their necks, only two managed to find their ways back to the horse herd at their original Gros Ventre encampment a number of miles away.

When they did, great consternation ran through the Gros Ventre encampment when the horses were recognized as belonging to their fellow tribal members and much quiet discussion was held over the significance of the scalps being attached and the meaning of the ominous bloody handprint on each horse's neck... The Gros Ventre Medicine Man in camp determined the scalps had been put there as a warning by the 'evil spirits'. Those two horses were never ever ridden again by any Gros Ventre tribal member from that band and were left to live out their remaining days as 'death horses'... As for the scalps, they were left to rot where they had been tied until they fell off and eventually became part of the soil... But the memory of what the Gros Ventre had seen plastered on the side of the horse's necks and the rotting scalps was not lost on the members of their band...

Then mounting Black Eagle on Bear Trap's riding horse and Little Raven on his packhorse, Ofer and company walked back into the deep timber where he had left his riding and pack-horse tied up the evening before. Recovering those horses, the three men rode the long way back to Ofer's campsite located near the Musselshell. When they did, Ofer's packhorse's pannier carried all of the dead Gros Ventre's rifles, sheath knives and tomahawks, as well as Bear Trap's firearms and the four giant grizzly bear traps... Little did Ofer realize that the day was coming when Black Eagle and Little Raven would themselves be carrying those very same Gros Ventre weapons acquired by the one they now reverently and with great honor, chose to be associated with, serve and now proudly called Four Scalps...

That afternoon as Joshua led his little fur caravan followed by his brothers Gabriel and Jerimiah rounded the finger of trees below their campsite and upon looking up at their cabin, imme-diately stopped! There by their outdoor firepit sat three men tending a fire! Then when one of the men by the firepit, upon seeing the fur trappers rounding the finger of trees below their camp, stood up and waved, Jerimiah then recognized the figure of his long-absent brother Ofer! With a "WHOOP" and a "YELL", the fur caravan broke into a gallop and stormed into their camp-site in a cloud of 'happy' dust! Immediately all three brothers bailed off their horses and ran happily into Ofer's welcoming arms! For the longest time there was much joy, laughter and backslapping going on, until Gabriel realized there were two obvious Indian strangers quietly standing by the sitting logs and none of them was their long-lost member and dear friend Bear Trap...

Then the men's conversations just exploded as Ofer was deluged with question after question as to what had happened and where was their friend Bear Trap. Ofer finally got everyone calmed down and began explaining what he had discovered and what had happened. Then all of a sudden he realized he had not introduced Black Eagle and Little Raven to his brothers so he turned and by sign and spoken word, introduced the two 'strangers' to his three brothers. After those introductions were done, the questions just flew once again as to needing more details on the previous day's events and the two young Indians in their camp.

With that, Ofer sat everyone down on the sitting logs positioned around the fire and in great detail explained what had happened over the last few days. When he had finished, there was a great silence around the campfire. Silence out of respect for a lost friend and leader and his untimely death. Then even more silence followed over what was to become of their little group of fur trappers seemingly getting smaller and smaller in number by each day in light of the deaths of Daniel and Bear Trap. After hearing the particulars of the battle with the now four dead Indians, even more intense silence over the savage and surprising way their normally gentle and older brother had lethally and surprisingly addressed the problem with the four Gros Ventre... Not so much judgment over what Ofer had done but the savage manner in which he had done it. A side of Ofer none of the brothers had ever witnessed before but as each of them had quickly deduced, Ofer was a changed man. It was very obvious to all the brothers that Ofer had become very circumspect and serious about not only his life but that of life out on the frontier...

Then 'out of the blue', Ofer brought up the current situation and homelessness issue regarding the two young Crow men now quietly sitting around their campfire and what was to become of them. What happened next made Ofer's heart swell with pride over his remaining three brothers' reactions to the new situation now facing them as a diminished family clan of trappers with the loss of their brother Daniel and great friend Bear Trap. "Hell," said Gabriel, "we are down by two members in this camp and if Black Eagle and Little Raven have nowhere else to go and wish to join us in our fur trapping adventures until if and when they can rejoin their own people, why can't they become part of the 'Tal Brothers'?" That question was immediately seconded by Joshua and Jerimiah in a heartbeat! "Yeah, why not?" was their joint and immediate reply to Ofer, as if he was the hurdle in having Black Eagle and Little Raven joining in with the remaining Tal Brothers.

Ofer just smiled saying, "For the last two days of our travels back to this campsite, the three of us have been talking back and forth in sign. In those discussions, Black Eagle and Little Raven have advised me that they have nowhere else to go since their entire band was wiped out by the Gros Ventre. When I told them about what we are doing and the rest of you three back at camp, their eyes lit up and I could tell they were more than interested in joining our group. Other than a language barrier for now since none of us speak the Crow lingo, thanks to Bear Trap teaching me sign, I can speak to the two of them in sign and we can all manage until they learn English. They have nothing left but their memories and the clothing they are wearing, so it will be up to us to support them but they are willing to join us and work alongside of the four of us, so I say let us give it a try. In the meantime, it will be up to all of us teaching them English. Additionally, they can have Bear Trap's horses to ride, we can eventually arm them with the weapons I took off the dead Gros Ventre and they can have Daniel and Bear Trap's places in the cabin as well as their sleeping furs. As for any profits the bunch of us make, we can all share. Come to think of it knowing them as well as I now do, I think Daniel and Bear Trap, if they were alive, would go along with including these two into our clan as well," continued Ofer.

Then later as Gabriel and Little Raven began working together as the camp's designated cooks fixing supper, Ofer, Joshua, Black Eagle and Jerimiah began the defatting and hooping the 25 fresh beaver pelts the trappers had just brought in from their trap line that day. In a surprising move, Black Eagle did not consider the defatting and hooping of the beaver skins women's work, having done some of the same back in his band as a trapper before it was wiped out. Additionally as a trapper, he had experienced trapping beaver, muskrat, river otter and wolves before his family's destruction as well. That evening after a heavy supper of roasted buffalo, Dutch oven biscuits, coffee and a cooked rice dish loaded with plumped raisins and brown sugar, the group relaxed around the campfire. As they did in the light from their campfire, Ofer provided instructions to Black Eagle and Little Raven in sign as to the proper use, maintenance and care of a rifle. Additionally, the two young Crow men being the same size as Daniel were given his clothing that had been left back in the cabin. Lastly, Ofer dug into the group's supplies and produced a 'scalper' or general purpose sheath knife for Black Eagle and Little Raven each as their own. By now, both young men were so surprised and amazed over the treatment they were receiving from the group, that Black Eagle being the older brother felt he, not having any kind of a gift to give in return as their culture required, quietly stood up in order to get the group's attention. When he did, the men around the campfire grew quiet and facing Ofer, Black Eagle began 'talking' in sign. He said, "He and his brother appreciated being taken in by the other white men and most of all having Four Scalps rescuing them from their historical enemies, the Gros Ventre." Then tears welled up in Black Eagle's eyes and finally working his way through the emotion said, "My culture requires that when the gift of life is given, that it in some form be given back in return to the one who has saved such a life. Since Four Scalps gave my brother and me our lives back, we will give them in return anytime it is necessary to protect him and our new brothers. So understand that Black Eagle and Little Raven now consider themselves to be blood brothers to Four Scalps and his kind for as long at the great herds of buffalo roam our lands." Then like most Indians who have just had their say, he sat back down and looked straight ahead as more tears from the emotion of the moment welled up in his eyes... With that, Ofer got up from his sitting log, walked over to Black Eagle and gave him a hug. Then still holding Black Eagle in his right arm, gestured with his left and soon had it filled with Little Raven as well. Soon without asking and in total silence, the entire group of men had soon fallen into each other's arms out of relief for Ofer's safe return, the emotion of the moment having recently lost a brother and great friend, and now having gained two more 'brothers'. Fallen into each other's arms full well realizing the brotherhood shared by one and all was a most important facet of life while living out on the frontier, a theme espoused by Bear Trap many times before his death. That being that in the brotherhood of man on the frontier, all were equal and shared the toil and dangers of the day and the rest of the night with their 'fellows'. Without another word or action, the men quietly adjourned to their sleeping furs in the cabin and bid the rest of that evening and special emotional moment in time, adieu.

For the rest of that month, the new 'Tal Brothers' found life's events passing like a 'dust devil' out on the hot summer prairie. Ofer spent time while not trapping beaver working with Black Eagle and Little Raven teaching them the finer points, use and maintenance of firearms. As it turned out, since neither young man had ever used or possessed a rifle or pistol, they had developed no bad habits in their use. That plus Ofer being an exacting teacher when it came to the use and maintenance of firearms because sometimes lives depended upon that degree of excellence, both young men soon developed into fine if not outstanding shooters. True to form, both young men were provided with their choice of firearms that had been taken from the four dead Gros Ventre that had initially captured them. Additionally, Ofer saw to it that both Black Eagle and Little Raven were provided all of the needed accessories such as powder horns, 'possibles' bags, fire steels, worms, bullet screws, tins of 'striker' and barrel powder, extra balls and the like.

Gabriel and Little Raven, being about the same age and temperament, soon became like biological brothers in just about everything they did together, including cooking! Little Raven took to cooking and eating like there was no tomorrow and soon became Daniel's 'replacement' as one of the camp cooks. Little Raven soon discovered that what had been considered 'women's work' back in his band before they were all killed, had its advantages in the white trappers' camp. Advantages like always being able to sample the cooking to make sure it was done, and many times getting to not only eat first but getting the choice cuts as well since he and Gabriel had done all of the work in the cooking...

Joshua on the other hand, took both Big Eagle and Little Raven under his care and soon the three of them were making winter clothing for the two indigent Crow brothers. So much so from the ready supply of tanned animal skins and bolts of cloth kept for clothing repairs, Black Eagle and Little Raven soon became the best dressed among the 'Tal Brothers'. That was especially so when it came to wearing new and still clean buckskins. Buckskins that were clear of camp smoke, animal grease from being wiped with one's hands across the front of the shirts, sweat and blood spatters from the frequent butchering out of large game animals like buffalo, moose, elk, and bighorn sheep for camp meat...

Jerimiah, last but not least, took straight-shooting Black

Eagle under his care and guidance when it came to providing protection to those brothers at the waterside setting the beaver traps and retrieving the beaver carcasses from the traps. There Jerimiah quickly came to recognize the value in his choice in providing protection for the unarmed trappers working the trap line could not have been any better. As Jerimiah quickly came to learn, Black Eagle possessed not only numerous skills just learned in the use of firearms to that inherited from his Indian heritage, namely that of having a great set of 'lynx eyes'. As Jerimiah quickly learned, Black Eagle spotted anything out of place or suspicious long before he ever did…

Lastly, all of the brothers worked on a daily basis teaching Black Eagle and Little Raven how to speak English and they in turn, taught the rest of the brothers how to 'speak and decipher sign' or the 'language of the Plains' as well as the art of tracking… As such, it wasn't long before the entire group was communicating with each other in English, the use of 'sign' or both.

With the advancing season and colder weather approaching, the 'Tals' soon found themselves removing all of their beaver traps just one week before freeze-up. Then taking the time, the 'Tals' headed out onto the nearby prairies, killed and butchered out six cow buffalo for their partial winter meat supply and for making jerky. There the Tal Brothers learned another Indian specialty from the two Crow brothers, namely the eating and enjoyment of fresh buffalo liver taken right from the side of the just killed animal! At first, the Tal Brothers were aghast over what they were seeing when their Crow brethren began slicing open the side of the just killed buffalo and then eating chunks of bloody raw buffalo liver!

However, soon Ofer was coaxed over to the side of the freshly killed buffalo and convinced to try a small slice of raw liver. That Ofer did and soon found he was eagerly eating large chunks of raw liver just like Black Eagle and Little Raven. Soon the rest of the Tal Clan, not to be outdone by their older brother, bailed off their horses and within moments, their faces were also smeared with the fresh blood from the liver just removed from the dead cow and eagerly chewed and swallowed, much to the joy of Black Eagle and Little Raven...

Shortly thereafter, the real work began. Several hours later, all the packhorses' panniers had been filled with slabs of raw buffalo meat and leaving the rest to the critters, the trappers slowly headed for their cabin. Once there as Gabriel and Little Raven began preparing the trappers' supper, the rest of the men hung a number of the buffalo quarters into the fall's air to cool out and glaze on the two meat poles out of the reach of any land predator. However, the Steller's jays, black-billed magpies and Northern chickadees quickly discovered the meat and feasted...

As for the rest of the meat, after Gabriel and Little Raven had removed what they wanted for supper, it was cut into long one-inch-wide thin strips and laid over the smoking racks. Somewhat later, the smoking racks hung heavy with fresh meat strips and soon dense smoke from their mountain mahogany wood began rolling up through the racks and surrounded the fresh meat as the smoking and jerky-making process began.

After supper and still surrounded by hungry clouds of ever-present mosquitoes who had not yet gone to bed for the winter, Ofer brought out a 'carrot' of smoking tobacco and a flat keg of their rum. Soon, the Tal Brothers had introduced Black Eagle and Little Raven to smoking in their pipes some James River smoking tobacco and a cup of rum in celebration of the end of their first fall beaver trapping season. Later, there was also a cup of rum 'tipped' in memory of the two lost friends and family members, Daniel and Bear Trap, just before everyone adjourned for the warmth of their cabin and their sleeping furs...

For the next two weeks, the men stayed busy readying themselves for the winter wolf trapping season and other 'housekeeping' duties. Mounds of firewood were cut and placed next to the outdoor firepit, stacked alongside the front door of the cabin, and brought inside the cabin and stacked near their fireplace. Then for several days, winter clothing was mended or made heavier. Then under the guidance of Little Raven, the trappers were shown how to make heavier winter moccasins with just one cut from the tanned hide of a bull buffalo. Then Joshua saw to it that once again the edges were 'set' to everyone's knives and tomahawks. Then all powder horns were refilled with fresh powder from the sealed lead canisters, and extra bullets and flints were added to everyone's 'possibles' bags by Jerimiah. Following that, Ofer once again disassembled every rifle and pistol, made sure all parts were functional, reamed out the black powder and lead fouling and then had them reassembled. Lastly, Ofer took the time to teach Black Eagle and Little Raven how to melt down some lead pigs and cast .52 caliber balls for all of their rifles and pistols. And as it just so happened, two of the rifles taken from the four scalped Gros Ventre earlier in the year were .52 caliber in size like the rest of the Tals', and those were the two Black Eagle and Little Raven had chosen to carry as their personal weapons. Then everyone pitched in making new knife sheaths from treated beaver tails and rifle scabbards from tanned skins for Black Eagle and Little Raven's horses. Last but not least, the entire group of trappers spent several days folding the fur sides of their beaver skins into each other and with a makeshift 'V-shaped' log press, bundled 90 beaver to a bundle, wrapped each with a tanned deer hide and bound them with deer hide strappings for eventual transport to Fort Manuel by packhorse come summer.

The following evening as Gabriel and Little Riven were preparing the men's supper, Joshua brought the horse herd in from their adjacent meadow and headed them for the corral where they could be kept in better safety. As the horse herd slowly walked by the firepit, Gabriel noticed that one of the horses had a loose shoe. That was brought to Ofer's attention and the next morning all of the men turned out and began examining all of their horses' shoes for tight fits. As it turned out, five of the horses had loose shoes and Gabriel being the only trained farrier in the bunch, went to the cabin and brought forth all of his farrier tools so those horses with loose shoes could be reshod. Then with the rest of the group holding the horses still and with Gabriel teaching Little Raven how to shoe horses, those five horses had their old shoes removed and were fitted with new shoes brought all the way from St. Louis because of the insistence of the Tal Brothers' father Yossef, who was an excellent farrier and knowledgeable horseman.

Seven days later, the first snowstorm of the season laid down a foot of freshly fallen snow. When that event occurred, the outside cooking duties were transferred inside the men's cabin and as Gabriel and Little Raven prepared a large batch of Dutch oven biscuits for the men's breakfast in their fireplace, Ofer went outside and gathered up their 10 Newhouse No. 14 wolf traps from their storage shed. Wolf traps which had been previously smoked on the jerky smoking racks in order to rid them of any suspicious man smells so the normally clever wolves would not be any wiser as to the dangerous man-smelling traps. As he picked up an armload of wolf traps, he all of a sudden realized his sixth sense had set him 'abuzz' the very moment he had picked up the armload of wolf traps! Looking all around quickly for any signs of danger, he saw none. He then trotted over to the horse corral, dropped off his wolf traps and then trotted back to the cabin so he could retrieve his rifle, just in case... However, no danger reared its ugly head and when Gabriel announced breakfast was ready he headed for their kitchen table and thought no more of his sixth sense warnings. After breakfast, the men dressed into their heavier winter clothing, including capotes and buffalo robe capes for the colder weather, saddled up their horses and two packhorses, checked their 'possibles' bags one more time for readiness and headed out into the area of several heavily timbered ridges known to the trappers to be a home range for a rather large pack of gray wolves.

Utilizing a technique taught to the Tal Brothers earlier by Bear Trap, Ofer directed the killing of a cow buffalo from one of the ever-present herds in the area near the ridgeline where the large pack of gray wolves was known to frequent. There after feasting on hot and raw buffalo liver since all the men had had for their breakfast that morning were a few Dutch oven biscuits, the cow was eviscerated. Then Ofer and Jerimiah laid out four of their wolf traps surrounding the now eviscerated buffalo in such a manner that the hungry wolves would not suspect that a man-made danger existed just under the blanket of freshly fallen snows. Then the group moved onto another nearby ridge and repeated the buffalo killing and trap setting process with four more wolf traps. Then understanding the extent of the first wolf pack's home range, the group moved several miles further away and repeated the buffalo killing and eviscerating process once again for their remaining two wolf traps in another wolf pack's home range. By then, Black Eagle and Little Raven wore questioning looks on their faces as to why their brothers were killing perfectly good eating buffalo and letting them lay after opening them up and spreading their intestinal parts all around the wolf traps. Seeing the questioning looks on their faces, Ofer paused and explained to the two young Crow men that by so doing with the dead buffalo, the smell of death would be more pronounced. That being the case and with wolves always hungry for an easy meal, especially during the colder winter weather, hopefully they would wind the dead and now eviscerated buffalo and come over to investigate. Then by so doing, some would hopefully overcome their wariness because of their hunger and end up trapped in the Newhouse No. 14 toothed wolf traps scattered hidden around the gut piles. With those explanations as the men rode along heading for home now that all of their wolf traps had been set, Black Eagle and Little Raven's curious and questioning looks over the wasting of three perfectly good buffalo now appeared to be answered to their satisfaction.

BOOM—BOOM—BOOM—BOOM! went the sounds of four quick shots as the trappers streamed by a covering finger of dense conifers! With the first shot fired, Ofer was spun off his horse and hit the snow-covered ground in a flurry of flying snow. With that, his rifle went cartwheeling through the air as well! Jerimiah, trailing Ofer, had his horse shot out from under him as he also went cartwheeling through the air over the head of his falling horse! However, Jerimiah was lucky because he managed to land on his feet and now obviously alerted, quickly looked around for whoever was shooting at his family group of trappers. As he did, the rest of the men, unhurt from the initial fusillade of shooting near-misses coming from the finger of conifers, slewed to a halt amidst much flying snow and swinging of rifles to face in the direction from whence had come the unobserved danger and sounds of shooting.

There in the timber sat four Indians on their nervous horses, all in the hurry-up process of reloading their rifles after surprising and shooting at the trappers to their front. **BOOM—BOOM—BOOM—BOOM!** replied four quick shots from the now recovering from the surprise, ambushed trappers! In that flurry of return shooting from the trappers, two Indian shooters spun out from their saddles after being solidly hit by the trappers' return fire, as simultaneously two other Indians' horses dropped like stones after being shot out from under their riders! Then as if on command, the four remaining horsed trappers charged towards the Indian shooters with drawn pistols in hand and reins now firmly clasped in their teeth! By now, the remaining two Indians seeing the full charge by the much-aroused trappers and not yet having reloaded their rifles in the face of such a furious attack, jumped off their horses and took off running for their lives down through the finger of dense brush and timber...

Leading the trappers' charge was Black Eagle and Little Raven because they had been the closest in the line of passing trappers to the Indian shooters. Down through the fresh snow charged the four remaining trappers, only to have Gabriel's horse step on a small log hidden under the snow, stumble and then go down hard, tossing Gabriel 'pell-mell' head over heels through the air as his rifle went wildly spinning through the air as well! Just as the remaining three trappers stormed up to where the Indians had fired upon them from their positions in hiding, one Indian, previously wounded in the surprised trappers' initial return fire, staggered to his feet to shoot his horse pistol at the onrushing horsed trappers. When he did, it was only to have his head exploded in a spray of bright red blood and gray matter after being shot in the head by a very determined Jerimiah still standing back where he had hit the ground running after his favorite riding horse had been shot out from under him just moments earlier!

That was when Black Eagle and Little Raven, still leading the remaining charging horsed trappers, sped off down through the conifers and brush on their racing horses after the two remaining and fleeing on foot for their lives, Indians! When they did, the rest of the trappers reined up next to the downed Indians in order to make sure they were dead and of no further threat. As they did, Black Eagle and Little Raven stormed out of sight into the darkened timber hellbent after the two remaining fleeing Indians like the devil was on their tails! Moments later, "Time to say Good-bye", as two rifle shots rang out from deep within the timber and then only silence followed, as the violence directed at the passing trappers from the finger of trees had come to a violent, bloody and deadly end...

Joshua bailed off his horse with pistol in hand and with one shot saw to it that the remaining wounded Indian lying on the ground struggling to get up never saw another sunrise... About then, Jerimiah came down the hill struggling with his brother

Ofer being steadied in his arms. Ofer, who was still groggy after the spill he had taken off his horse and being struck alongside his head by a rifle ball with a still ringing head, was staggering along. When those two arrived at the scene from whence had come the ambush, Ofer frantically looking around said, mindful of the two unexplained shots taken in the timber below them, "Where are Black Eagle and Little Raven?"

In the fury of the moment and the flurry of shots taken, everyone had lost track not only of the time but the whereabouts of Black Eagle and Little Raven... Ofer then said through a still ringing head and narrowed eyes from all the pain his head was causing him, "Joshua and Jerimiah, you two take off after where you last saw Black Eagle and Little Raven heading after those last two ambushing son-of-a-bitches! See if they are alright and if they aren't, see to it that those who have harmed them may never again do so to any of our kind ever again..."

About then, Ofer saw through his narrowed eyes held so in pain from being struck alongside his head, some movement coming their way from deep within the timber. Immediately the trappers went for their pistols once again fearing the two earlier escaping Indians were now returning to finish the battle. Then up from the timber finally rode Black Eagle followed by his brother Little Raven. Both young men appeared from a distance to be alright and that was when Ofer finally relaxed, but just a little. Shortly thereafter, the two brothers rode up to the rest of the men gathered around the two dead Indians lying on the ground by their feet.

That was when Ofer realized what had just happened in the deep timber! Tied to Black Eagle and Little Raven's horses' manes were two very bloody Indian scalps! Then on each young man's horse's neck in plain view was the very distinct fresh and bloody-red handprint... Just like Ofer had done to the four Gros Ventre Indians who had shot his friend Bear Trap full of arrows while tied to a tree and later their horses as a warning to those 'who later saw'... Now, the two young Crow Indian men had done the same thing to the two fleeing Indians they had just killed! Looking up at the two young Crow now warriors, Ofer said, "I take it they did not get away?"

Looking down at his friend from his horse, Black Eagle said in his newly learned English language, "They were Gros Ventre. They will never again ambush and kill our people or abuse my brother and me ever again. We only followed Four Scalps' lead and did what he did to bad Indians..." Ofer found there was no need to say anything more in light of what his two young Crow 'rescues' and 'charges' had done. He was just thankful that his two young men had come back to him alive and well. He was also thankful that his sixth sense naggings of pending danger had since faded away as well...

It was only then that Ofer truly realized he was wounded after seeing all of the rest of the trappers looking strangely at him. Well, that and a head that now seemed to be ready to fall off his shoulders at any moment if the intense ringing sounds in his ears and any painful movement meant anything. Raising his hand to the side of his head, Ofer only then realized his bearskin hat was missing and when he touched his head near his right ear, found that his hand came away sticky with blood and small chunks of tissue! Ofer then realized that he had been hit in his right ear during that first round of ambush-shooting! In fact feeling gently with his fingertips once again, Ofer discovered that only a small part of his right ear flap remained! The rest of his ear, as he subsequently discovered with more feeling around, had been blown off the side of his head from a near fatal head shot! Then he realized that his shirt, full of blood having run furiously down the side of his head, neck and into his chest and shoulder areas under his heavy winter clothing, was now beginning to freeze to his skin and causing him to chill.

About then, Jerimiah returned with Ofer's rifle which had spun out from his hand upon being hit in the ear with a bullet, blown violently out from his saddle and off his horse. Upon closer examination, the rifle's lock was broken and as such, would not fire. Seeing the damage through his pain-narrowed eyelids, the thought quickly crossed his mind of the time back in St. Louis in Manuel Lisa's emporium when Bear Trap had him purchase a number of spare rifle and pistol parts in addition to the tools needed to repair them. This he had done because he had advised Ofer, "Unexpected things happen out on the frontier and one had best be prepared for all of them, including being able to repair your lifelines like your rifles and pistols." With that remembrance sailing through his still spinning head, Ofer realized with a smile that once again his dear friend and fellow Mountain Man, Bear Trap, was still 'speaking' to him from 'wherever' he now was and no matter what he was doing...

After Ofer had been gently helped back into the saddle on his horse and Jerimiah had removed the saddle from his horse which had been killed in the initial shooting from the now dead Gros Ventre and placed on one of the dead Indians' remaining horses and with the ambushers' valuable weapons all collected, down the hill went the trappers. However, this time, Black Eagle with his 'lynx eyes' was in the lead to preclude any more almost deadly surprises from other "Sons of the Prairies".

The way back to camp was without further deadly incident and when the men arrived, they unsaddled all of their horses. Then they hobbled both captured Gros Ventre horses and then let all of their stock out so they could feed and water in their nearby meadow. However, Gabriel and Little Raven accompanied the horse herd out into the meadow and stood guard just in case any other Gros Ventre were in their area and on the prowl for some valuable horseflesh. Then it was into their cabin, a fire was built and a pot of water set on a hanging rod over the fire in the fireplace to boil, while Ofer undressed from his blood-soaked clothing. Then as Joshua rinsed out Ofer's blood-soaked clothing and hung it on a wall peg to dry, Jerimiah got out the needle and thread, several rags and a short time later, the now hot water from the pot on the hanging irons over the fire. Then very carefully, he commenced washing off around the bloody shot-away ear and from around Ofer's head, neck and shoulder areas. Then with a full cup of rum in Ofer's now steady hand, Jerimiah, using his always razor sharp scalper knife, began cutting away the remains of the shot all to hell ear and much of its adjoining damaged tissue that was going to rot away... As he did, only Ofer's wincing and quickly closing eyelids betrayed his pain as Jerimiah's sharp knife did its 'cutting and gutting' duties. Soon all that remained was a madly bleeding stump of a right ear! As Jerimiah was 'cutting and gutting' on the side of Ofer's head, all Ofer could think of besides the burning pain every time the knife lopped off another chunk of still living tissue, was what Bear Trap had once told him. "Ofer," he had said, "the Mountain Man always loves every kind of adventure, be it bad or good. That is what led him to suffer the wilderness and by the hand of God, will keep him there or its memories in his heart forever, no matter the cost..."

Ofer slept sitting up that night in his sleeping furs with his back propped up against the wall of the cabin in order to reduce the amount of bleeding coming from the remainder of his right ear 'stump'. Come morning, another pot of hot water, more washing off of the wet and dried blood, some liberal application of bag balm, another cup of rum and with Jerimiah's keen eye and sure hand, Ofer had the remains of his swollen ear-stump sewn up! Then with Ofer's head partially wrapped in gray cloth and covered partially with his bearskin cap, the men dressed in their heavy clothing and with Jerimiah riding another buckskin horse from their remaining string of valuable animals, the six men ventured forth once again to check their recently set wolf traps.

Somewhat later, they discovered two wolves in their first set, no wolves in their second set and two wolves in their third set.

However, as they rode by the area of the shootout with the four Gros Ventre, they discovered the wolves had fed heavily upon the three dead horses and two dead Indians who had fallen near those horses. With that, four traps were pulled from their second set and placed around the dead horses and two fed-upon Gros Ventre Indians. That they did because knowing once the wolves had fed safely and fully, they would return without suspicion to feed once again in the same setting. Hence the setting of their four wolf traps in and among the partially fed-upon dead horses and Indians. The following morning checking those wolf traps, as was suspected, all four wolf traps held a snarling wolf! And in order to save powder and shot, not bring any further attention to their presence from the "Sons of the Prairies" with the sounds of shooting and not damage the pelts, all four wolves were clubbed to death and skinned on the spot. Thus went the winter without further deadly incident except those occurring to the wolves caught in the deadly traps, rendering out 44 beautifully furred wolves come the end of the wolf trapping season.

Come the first vestiges of spring, both the horse herd and the trappers were more than ready for the thaw, the new nutritious crop of grasses to help fatten up their horses and the spring beaver trapping season to begin. Ofer had high hopes for the coming trapping season after they had caught and pelted out 244 beaver, most in the Made Beaver class (adults in prime condition). John Colter had been right in his assessment of what the Musselshell could produce when it came to trapping beaver. Now the men were facing the time of the year when the beaver, after living under the ice all winter, would be in their best pelage due to all of the cold living under the ice they had undergone.

By that time, Ofer's right ear had pretty much healed up and was passable. It was still somewhat sensitive to the finger-touch and the brim of a hat lying against it, but life was still good and going to get better if what Ofer and the rest were seeing in the number of beaver along the Musselshell was any indication of good things to come. Stepping out from the cabin one morning and after tending to a call of nature but carefully so remembering what had happened to his brother Daniel at the latrine, Ofer took care of business and departed after many backward looks over his shoulder while doing 'his business'. That he did as he worriedly discovered that his sixth sense was slightly acting up once again! Walking over to their little stream, he washed up, shaved and combed his hair. As he did, he could see Little Raven and Gabriel chatting by the outside cooking fire fixing breakfast. THEN OFER DID A DOUBLE TAKE AS HE LOOKED BACK INTO HIS SHAVING MIRROR! For just a split second, Ofer thought he saw another human face peering at him from a long distance away from down in the aspen grove behind him and below the camp! Dropping his razor and hurriedly grabbing up his rifle lying against a nearby tree and whirling around, Ofer saw nothing more of the sort. Then he saw an early nesting pair of black-billed magpies flitting through the aspens carrying sticks to a rather large stick nest nearby. Figuring the 'face' he had just seen for a split second in his shaving mirror was just 'that' of a magpie flitting by, he lowered his rifle and reduced his frontier caution, but just a little. But his sixth sense feeling did not 'lie' down but persisted... For another long moment in time, Ofer kept looking through the wind rustling leaves of the cottonwoods and aspens where he thought he had earlier seen what he thought was a face, one belonging to that of an Indian. He was rewarded with seeing nothing further and then the rumbling from his stomach told him Gabriel and Little Raven had to be close to serving up another great breakfast. With another long look in the area he thought he had seen a face flitting through the trees of an aspen grove, he once again saw a magpie carrying a bill full of dry sticks up to its new nest and then forced himself to relax.

That did it! Gathering up his rifle in the crook of his arm, down he walked to the outdoor firepit, sat down on his sitting log, laid his rifle nearby and had a hot cup of coffee thrust into his extended hand by Little Raven. *God, it was good to be alive in the springtime, living out his dream in the wilderness and having a great cup of coffee in his hand.* For a moment a 'song of a life well lived' spun through his mind and then a sip of the strong 'trapper's style of coffee' brought him back to his reality of life on the sitting log...but that damned nagging sixth sense...

CHAPTER 5 — OF GROS VENTRE, "BUCKSKINS" AND THE "RED HAND"

BLUE SKY AND THE AIR FROM A WARM SPRING MORNING greeted Ofer as he exited the cabin as he usually did with rifle in hand and checked all around looking for any sign of danger from the indigenous people, even though Little Raven and Gabriel were already busily working around their campfire preparing the trappers' breakfast. Breathing in deeply the cool morning's air, something inside him told him today was the day. "Hey, you guys. Make up a big breakfast if you would. I think today all of us need to take a long ride along the southwestern portion of the Musselshell and see how much of the ice from the past winter's freeze-up has broken up and melted away. I say that because I am feeling it is time we need to be out and about spring beaver trapping, and today is as good as any to 'get crackin'' and go take a 'look-see' if we are ice-free."

With a wave of acknowledgment, Gabriel and Little Raven walked over to one of the camp's meat poles, lowered down on a rope a quarter of an elk and with their knives began cutting away a large chunk of a backstrap. Then as Gabriel pulled the elk quarter back up once they were finished so no land-based critter could reach its remains, Little Raven walked back to their log table around the fire with the long chunk of backstrap. Then with his scalper (sheath knife), Little Raven began removing the white scat left on the meat by a number of previously feeding birds while perching on the elk quarter and tossed the tainted scraps of meat covered with bird droppings into their fire. Satisfied that he had removed most of the bird scat remains, Little Raven began cutting off thick steaks from the length of backstrap as per Ofer's request so the men would have a 'meat-hearty' breakfast. And a hearty breakfast they did have later that morning of roasted elk backstrap, Dutch oven biscuits, beans and coffee. As the two 'cooks' put the finishing touches on the trappers' breakfast, Joshua and Jerimiah staggered out from the cabin and headed for the latrine with their rifles in hand. Upon their return, they washed up, shaved and then headed over to the corral to give Ofer a hand in saddling up their riding horses for the day's junket exploring a new portion of the Musselshell checking out the amount of winter ice remaining in its beaver trapping waters. Finished with their saddling-up chores, the men headed for their sitting logs around the fire and had their morning coffee as Little Raven and Gabriel finished dishing up the men's warmed-up metal plates heaped high with roasted elk, biscuits, beans, all followed with more steaming hot cups of coffee. Then for the next few moments there were no sounds heard around the campfire except those made by hungry men as they 'put away the groceries', the sounds of a pine limb crackling fire and a Steller's jay calling out from atop a quarter of elk hanging from a meat pole as it also was also happily enjoying a 'breakfast' of elk fat.

Placing their dirty dishes into the wash water pan warming up next to the fire, Ofer, Joshua, Jerimiah and Black Eagle walked over to their corral, separated out a pair of packhorses, saddled them up with a pair of panniers each, and then commenced loading them with what would be needed for the day's events in case Ofer decided to begin trapping instead of just looking over the watered areas most likely holding colonies of beaver. Somewhat later with Ofer and Joshua in the lead, followed by Little Raven and Gabriel leading the packhorses and trailed by Black Eagle and Jerimiah providing 'rearguard against Indian attack', the men rode down from their campsite and eventually out along the Musselshell. Turning southward, Ofer led the men quietly several miles along the Musselshell until it began heading westerly. Not having previously trapped that area where the Musselshell turned to the west, Ofer began closely looking at the winter ice-free trapping waters for signs of beaver activity. 'Sure as shootin'', Mountain Man John Colter had been 'right as rain' during his earlier discussions with the men regarding the Musselshell's beaver-rich resources. All of the watered ways along and adjacent the Musselshell where Ofer and company had yet to trap, beaver sign in the ways of freshly repaired mud and stick dams, conical houses and freshly used slides was observed to the trained and experienced sets of Mountain Man eyes looking on that morning!

Excited at what he was seeing, Ofer dismounted, handed his reins back to Little Raven and then began rummaging through one of the packhorse's panniers. There he withdrew his old breechclout and a well-used pair of buckskin leggings. Removing his woolen pants and placing them back into a pannier, he dressed in his breechclout and leggings for the multitude of immersions in the cold beaver trapping waters to come. As he did, Joshua mirrored Ofer's actions as he too undressed and then dressed into his breechclout and leggings as well. Then as Jerimiah and Black Eagle took up protective positions near the two trappers atop their horses, Ofer and Joshua gathered up the trapping gear they needed and began slowly walking along the Musselshell looking for fresh beaver sign. Within moments, Ofer began setting his first trap as Joshua 'leapfrogged' Ofer and after walking about 30 yards further down the Musselshell, began setting his first beaver trap as well. For the rest of that morning and into the early afternoon, Ofer and Joshua, after walking about two miles further southwesterly along the Musselshell and into a number of its adjacent watered areas, had managed to set all 30 of their beaver traps.

Following the completions of their trap setting, the six trappers moved into a dense nearby leafing-out aspen grove, dismounted and let their horses feed in among the trees while they rested and ate some buffalo jerky. As they did, Ofer kept having old sixth sense feelings occasionally wash over him for some unknown reason. The same kind of feelings that he had other times in his life when something odd was about to happen to him or those loved ones around him. However, after looking all around his brothers and their surroundings and seeing nothing unusual, he relaxed. In fact, after a hard and cold morning's work in the icy waters setting their beaver traps and now with the warm afternoon's sun warmly filtering through the budding aspens and warming up the men, they began dozing off one by one as their horses fed quietly nearby on the rich spring-sprouting grasses under the aspens.

However, Ofer was still having those almost physical feelings continually washing lightly over him and it was another 30 or so minutes after the rest of the men had dozed off before sleep finally overcame him as well. The next thing Ofer realized was that his eyes were flung wide open as his internal frontier sixth sense had picked up a sign of danger! Without showing any sign of physical movement other than his eyes rolling all around looking for that which had suddenly awakened him, his eyes surprisingly met those of Black Eagle who had been resting nearby looking intently right back at him! Black Eagle had also awakened over some form of danger being in the air and he too was frozen in time and stature, except for that of the quiet movement of his eyes until he had fully deciphered what had awakened the senses in him as well...

Then Ofer and Black Eagle heard a sound that 'froze' the two men's movements even further! Further out onto the prairie along the nearby Musselshell, Ofer heard a horse other than their own 'whinny'! Instantly his hand slowly moved to his nearby rifle as Black Eagle upon hearing the same sound of a nearby horse that had smelled the trappers' horses and had 'whinnied' a recognition call, reached over and quietly shook the leg of his still sleeping brother. After waking his brother, Black Eagle filled his own hands with his rifle as well! Within moments, all of the trappers were wide awake as the alarm was quietly sounded among the men! Lying there in last year's bed of dry leaves in the aspen grove, the trappers continued looking hard in the direction that Ofer was pointing from whence the strange horse had 'whinnied'. As the trappers unlimbered for any action to follow in light of a strange Indian's horse being in the vicinity, they saw nothing and heard nothing more. Then from below a rise further out in the prairie, the men saw an Indian slowly moving into view with rifle in hand with his head down and obviously tracking the fresh shod hoofprints of white men's horses heading for the grove of aspen now occupied by the trappers! And that wasn't all! Behind the hard-tracking Indian hot on the fresh trail of the trappers' horses' hoofprints, quietly rode another six Indians following their tracker and looking all around for any signs of danger as they did!

"GROS VENTRE!" quietly uttered Little Raven through gritted teeth, now that he had seen and identified the oncoming Indians from the clothing they were wearing. With those uttered words of warning, Ofer heard five metallic clicks of flintlock rifles being pulled back into 'full cock' and now ready for firing, followed by a sixth click of Ofer's rifle in suit mere seconds later!

Then all of a sudden, the Gros Ventre Indian on foot doing all of the tracking of the white men's shod horses' hoofprints in the dampened spring prairie soil stopped what he was doing, and began looking hard at the aspen grove he was approaching as if examining it for any signs of movement or danger. From his actions, it was now obvious that the Gros Ventre Indian tracker realized whoever had ridden the obviously white men's shod horses across the prairie had ridden them into the nearby grove of aspens! About then the remaining Gros Ventre Indians on horseback slowly following their tracker, reined up behind the man out in front and then a short 'confab' was held among the seven Gros Ventre now showing signs of intense excitement. Presently after that short discussion among themselves, all the rest of the Indians dismounted and after showing very evident signs of checking their rifles, began sneaking in a line abreast slowly towards the line of aspens into which the suspect white men's horses' hoofprints had mysteriously entered and disappeared into the deep gloom of the aspen grove! The collective looks on the faces of the oncoming Gros Ventre clearly showed that a 'killing' was in the wind and it would not be theirs...

Then those familiar sixth sense inner feelings stirred now more strongly within Ofer once again, taking him back to days earlier when shaving, thinking he had seen an Indian flitting through the aspen grove below their cabin in the mirror! And instead of pursuing the fleeting figure just to make sure over what he had seen or not seen, he had just written it off as that from a nearby nest-building magpie. Written it off thinking he had only seen the movement of a magpie bringing a bill full of sticks to its new nest being built in the aspen grove instead of that of an Indian spying on him and the rest of the men. He then quietly realized that Bear Trap was 'speaking' to him once again about always being ready and suspicious of strange happenings and occurrences while out on the frontier, or otherwise one just might leave his bones bleaching out under the hot prairie sun...

As the seven Gros Ventre Indians slowly continued moving forward towards the aspen grove in a crouched-over position holding their trailing horses' reins in their teeth so their gun hands would be free for any sign of danger they might be facing, they did not seem to realize the steely determination that now might be facing them as well. Steely determination in the hands and minds of six deadly shooters waiting for the Gros Ventre to make the first deadly move, and then may The Great Spirit help those who were about to die...

However, mindful of the possible danger they might be facing, fortified by their 20,000 years of survival heritage surging through their veins, the Gros Ventre, as if on command based on instinct and the possible danger facing them in the aspen grove, split up even further apart so they would not make such easy targets if any shooting was to occur. However that little survival movement on their collective parts of splitting up just executed so brilliantly by the Gros Ventre did not truly amount to a 'pinch of puppy shit' when it came to increasing their chances of survival as they were soon to discover! **BOOM—BOOM—BOOM—BOOM—BOOM—BOOM!** belched the flame, white clouds of black powder smoke rolling out across the prairie and deadly hot lead from the aspen thicket, as the six trappers' flint-locks fired in rapid unison once the line of attacking Indians hove into a deadly killing range! Six speeding .52 caliber lead balls smashed into their targets, tearing entry holes into their bony chests, splattering any organs hit on the way through and then tearing great gaping holes through the backs of the lead balls' intended targets! Instantly, six Indians died before walking another step forward on 'Mother Earth' for their last time... The seventh and remaining living Indian untouched by the white man's speeding hot metal just stood there for a moment in utter shock and confusion after seeing all his compatriots around him dropping to the ground from the violent impacts from the flying lead balls! Then realizing in that instant of his now mortal plight, dropped his unfired rifle, quickly withdrew his tomahawk from behind his back belt sash and loudly singing his death song to The Great Spirit, the seventh Indian charged the still unseen death lying hidden in the aspen grove! Just as the death song-singing Indian reached the very edge of the aspen grove, a single pistol shot was heard and as a white spew of black powder smoke enveloped the attacking Indian's physical body from such close range, a .52 caliber lead ball tore through his chest, ruptured his heart and blew out a rib in his back as it exited!

However when the speeding lead ball exited the now falling dead Indian's back, it proceeded across the prairie as if on its own mission and struck one of the seven trailing Indians' horses in the forehead, dropping it onto the prairie and killing it instantly! With the surprise of the dropping horse among their ranks and the new smell of fresh blood and burned black powder in the air, the remaining six Indian horses bolted, took off running and headed for the safety they knew existed back in a nearby line of aspen trees! When that happened, Ofer got a grisly idea, as he lowered his pistol just used in dispatching the death song-singing, last attacking Indian... As he did, the only sound heard after that was from a nearby black-billed magpie squawking its head off over being disturbed while building its nest in the grove of aspen trees occupied by the six trappers now furiously reloading their rifles in case there were more of the same Gros Ventre just over the rise wanting to die as well...

As all of the trappers finished their reloading drills in case there were additional Gros Ventre just over the next ridgeline on the prairie waiting to attack, Ofer put his grisly just-thought-up plan into action. Turning back towards the rest of the trappers now standing at the ready in case more shooting was called for, Ofer quietly said, "I want the rest of you to head back, check our just set traps for any freshly caught beaver if there are any, skin them and then pull all of our traps. When you get that trap pulling done, head for our cabin by a different route than we initially used in order to throw off any other Indians who might be out looking for the tracks of other American springtime beaver trappers. But before you do, all of you go out and collect up all of those dead Gros Ventre weapons and load them into one of our packhorse's panniers so we can save them. Who knows, we may have need of such firepower in the future. In the meantime since these Indians according to Black Eagle were Gros Ventre, I intend to send another message back to their people because I am getting tired of their random depredations upon us trappers. Send a message because more than likely there will be other Gros Ventre who will come looking for their lost kin who are now lying out there on the prairie in front of us. I am hoping by sending my own personal type of a message, the rest of the superstitious Gros Ventre in the area will understand, back off and leave us alone unless they want to sing their 'death songs' as well. However, Black Eagle, I need your 'lynx eyes' and you are to stay behind with me so you can watch my back as I do what I am about to do." With those words of instruction, Ofer just intently looked at the rest of the men in such a manner that they all knew he was a man on a mission and his motives, whatever they were, were not to be questioned. Especially in light of the fact Ofer was more than likely going to do something that Bear Trap had taught him regarding the Indian culture and their fear of the 'unnatural' and all of its 'evil spirits'...

Ofer waited until the rest of the trappers had mounted up and disappeared over the ridgeline en route their just set trap line in order to check it for beaver and then remove it. Ofer figured that all the unusual shooting would only bring more curious Indians to the scene and that would not do, so it was best to remove their trap line from that new area and leave. That, plus what he was going to do was something he had learned from Bear Trap when he was alive that dwelt with the supernatural as seen through the eyes of many of the indigenous people. Then calmly turning, Ofer said to Black Eagle, "Black Eagle, several of those Gros Ventre horses just ran over into that next grove of aspen over yonder and appeared to stop and begin feeding. I need you to ride over and see if that is the case. If so, bring back what horses you can find. In the meantime, I have work here to do. Now get moving just in case any other Indians heard all of our shooting and decided to come over and investigate."

Realizing something was 'up' and trusting Ofer, Black Eagle set off looking for any remaining Gros Ventre horses to bring back as Ofer had instructed. Ofer just stood there watching the young man he had saved from the Gros Ventre earlier in life ride off out of sight. Then laying his rifle down alongside one of the dead Gros Ventre, he began doing what he felt needed to be done in order to further send a message to 'stay clear' to the wide-ranging and deadly Gros Ventre roaming the area looking for Crow Indians or other American white fur trappers to rob and kill.

Somewhat later, Black Eagle returned with four of the previously spooked-off Gros Ventre horses retrieved feeding near the aspen grove. When he did and upon seeing what Ofer had done, his eyebrows shot up in amazement and then his eyelids narrowed over his eyes with a slight but knowing smile of agreement on his face. Without a word, Ofer with thoroughly bloodied hands, took all seven of the previously removed Gros Ventre bloody scalps and with quiet determination, wove their long braids tightly into the just returned horses' manes! Then soaking his hands once again from on top of each dead Indian's still blood-oozing skulls, made sure a legible bloody red hand-print was firmly imprinted on the side of those horses' necks. Then Ofer removed their bridles and slapped those horses hard on their rumps, sending them sprinting out across the prairie and hopefully heading for the comfort of the Gros Ventre's home band of horses for all to see. Then since there was no nearby source of water, Ofer urinated on his hands in order to wash off all of the blood and wiped them on nearby prairie grasses until all the bloody sign of what he had done was essentially erased from view. Not one time did he say anything to Black Eagle, a deadly enemy of the Gros Ventre, the same tribe who had killed off his family, nor did he have to... Then mounting up on their own riding horses, Ofer and Black Eagle headed back to their cabin via another more circuitous route in an attempt to throw off the trail any other Indians who might be following their shod horses' hoofprints across the prairie. As for the dead Gros Ventre, they were left out on the prairie where they fell for the predators of the land to enjoy. And now that the killing was over, Ofer realized that his sixth sense feelings had once again disappeared. As they rode off, little did Ofer realize the consequences of his scalping and 'red hand' actions...

That evening, Ofer and Black Eagle arrived back at camp before the rest of the group had returned. When the four trappers who had pulled all of their traps returned, they were quietly greeted by Ofer and Black Eagle as if nothing out of the ordinary had occurred. And by looking at Ofer now with stream washed off-fingernails and cleaned hands, nothing out of the ordinary had occurred... After supper that evening and with cups of rum all around, Ofer said, "All of you did a nice job today. I expect the more we roam around trapping beaver in the lands of these hostile Indians, we can expect more of the same as we got today. However, next time there may be more of them than us or they may catch us not looking. With that in mind, Black Eagle and I need to more closely examine the Gros Ventre weapons we seized today after the fight. Five of those rifles appear to be very fine .52 caliber rifles more than likely taken from the hands of dead trappers. So tonight I will tear down all five of those rifles, clean and replace anything that needs replacing from our stock of extra parts, and from now on we will use three packhorses and three sets of panniers when we are out trapping. On the new packhorses' panniers we will start carrying the five extra rifles we took from the field of battle today, as well as those three rifles I took from the Gros Ventre who killed Bear Trap and captured Black Eagle and Little Raven some time back. That way we will have a fighting chance and if we are intercepted by a mess of hostiles, we six will have eight extra rifles in the panniers in addition to the six rifles we normally carry as well as our own pistols. If we need more firepower than that, then we too like that last Gros Ventre we heard today, will be singing our 'death songs'. But that aside, all of us have decided we will work together out here in the wilderness doing what we love, namely trapping beaver, eating buffalo meat and seeing what our God of choice has brought us each and every day in the way of our blessings. Now, Black Eagle and I need to move into the cabin, get our candles lit, and tear down and examine the five rifles we took from the dead Gros Ventre today for any mechanical problems. Then we will clean, reassemble and load them for our use in case of an emergency. The rest of you can also help us by reloading all of our 'possibles' bags, with extra canisters of powder, flints, wads, ball worms and balls for our personal and new guns as well. Then tomorrow, we are heading even further southwest than today to start anew on the Musselshell and see what 'she' has in store for us in the way of beaver trappings and less Gros Ventre. Oh, we also need to defat and hoop the 11 beaver you guys brought in from our last trap line this evening as well." With that, Ofer drained his cup of rum, rose and headed for the cabin to work on the recently acquired Gros Ventre Indian rifles. Taking that as his cue, Black Eagle polished off his cup of rum and headed into the cabin to help Ofer clean and inspect the new rifles as well. Shortly thereafter, the cabin was ablaze in the light of their beeswax candles and the light from the fireplace, as the men tended to the business of survival in a harsh land that was at hand on a daily basis. Two hours later, all that could be heard in the cabin were the sounds of six men sleeping soundly after what was in many instances, just another normal day for the trappers of furbearers in the west's largely unexplored wilderness...

******

Chief "Buffalo Horn" of the Lodge River Band of Gros Ventre, found himself hastily summoned from his tipi by one of his sub-chiefs named "Coyote", early one morning. Minutes later found the chief with others from his tribe standing in and among their band's extensive, loose-roaming horse herd. For the longest time no one spoke after the arrival of their chief, but just quietly watched for his reactions over what he was seeing. Standing there in among the numbers of the feeding band's horses stood one familiar horse with two dried scalps with long braids dangling from its mane into which they had obviously been tied! Gros Ventre Indians, who from recognizing the horse to which the scalps had been attached into its mane, realized that same 'warhorse' belonged to the chief's youngest son! Also in stark evidence was a very distinctive bloody red handprint on each side of the horse's upper neck! A bloody red handprint that the Lodge River Band of Gros Ventre had seen in their horse herd previously from returning horses from other now what they had assumed were also dead members of their band! Chief Buffalo Horn recognizing his son's favorite riding horse and realizing what had more than likely happened to him, remained 'stone-faced' in that recognition but in his heart, a slow burning desire for revenge was now rearing its ugly head for the one responsible for the obvious deaths of the members of their band by the hand of the one his tribe had quietly began calling "Red Hand" or "The Scalper". Calling the one doing the killing Red Hand because of the distinct bloody handprint on horses' necks and The Scalper because of the dried scalps from the horses' owners hanging from their horses' manes as an obvious and deadly warning... And Chief Buffalo Horn and the rest of his onlooking warriors realized that because of the way those scalps had been removed, such scalping had been done by a white man and not at the hand of an Indian!

Later that morning after Buffalo Horn had quietly uttered a command to his sub-chief Coyote, back at the horse herd after viewing the scalps and claret red handprints on the horse's neck, found 12 of his finest warriors heavily armed and quietly standing, waiting as their chief exited his lodge and now sternly faced them. For the longest time, he said nothing as he viewed the well-tested warriors standing before him. Then he quietly began speaking without a single mention of the more than likely loss of his much-prized son to what he felt had to be a nearby American white man fur trapper and demon that his band had twice named as Red Hand or The Scalper. A white man trapper his band had named the killer of their own kind as Red Hand or The Scalper as a result of the recognized dead Gros Ventre Indians' horses from their band returning with such bloody handprints on the sides of their neck and their owner's scalp woven into the horse's mane! "My warriors, for many moons our band has been sending many of our young men south into the territory of the hated Crow looking to count 'coup' for their very first time. Counting 'coup' against the hated Crow and their allies, the hated American white man trappers roaming our rivers and streams taking what The Great Spirit has left for us. This our young men did by killing the hated Crow and white men fur trappers and taking their horses and furs. Then we have been taking those horses and furs and selling them to our white friends, the "Canadians" from the Hudson's Bay Fur Company to the north for more guns and whiskey. By so doing, we now find ourselves facing what must be an evil American white man killing our young men and sending a message back to us on our young men's horses in the form of their scalps and bloody red handprints as a warning. A bloody red handprint and scalp, I suspect, is being placed there on those horses' necks after our young men have been killed in battle by an evil American white man trapper after they tried taking what was his and were not successful."

Pausing and looking over the 12 serious-looking warriors standing before him looking for any signs of weakness and finding none, Chief Buffalo Horn began once again by saying, "I am sending you, some of our most experienced warriors, south into the territory of the hated Crow, looking for this American white man trapper named The Scalper or Red Hand, who I think is dealing death to many of our younger and less-experienced warriors. I am not sure where you will find such a person so named by our people, but our last numbers of young men were heading south to the country of what the American white men call the Musselshell where trappers are trapping our beaver. This our young warriors did in order to find where the trappers were camped, kill them, take their horses and furs and then bring them back. Bring them back so we can sell them and then purchase more firearms from the Canadians since the traders at the new Fort Manuel refuse to sell those weapons to us. Then with those weapons purchased from the white men who call themselves Canadians, we can at least fight off the Crow who are being sold those weapons in great numbers by the white man traders at Fort Manuel, which they use to kill our people. That has got to stop and stop it you will, my finest of warriors."

Later that afternoon, those 12 experienced warriors said 'Good-bye' to their families and then they headed south from their homeland towards the Musselshell to see if they could find the mysterious white man fur trapper they had named Red Hand or The Scalper. A white man fur trapper named Red Hand or The Scalper who was killing their young men and in so doing, kill him and those around him, take all of their horses and furs and then return victorious to the land of the Lodge River Band of Gros Ventre.

******

As Gabriel and Little Raven prepared the men's breakfast the following morning, Ofer and the rest of the trappers saddled their horses and loaded the now three packhorses accordingly, especially the third one with all the captured Gros Ventre's many fully loaded rifles in its panniers. After a hearty breakfast and cleanup, the men trailed out from the cabin in their normal order, turned and began the long ride to the southwest so they could trap out another portion of the Musselshell that they hadn't already trapped and hopefully a section of the waterway not heavily visited by the now much-hated Gros Ventre Indians. Once again on their newest of trap lines, Ofer and Joshua had set their 30 beaver traps and now the trappers were once again resting on a small hill in a grove of aspens so they could watch their back trail, as they let their horses quietly feed and water in and around them.

Thus became the normal routine of the six trappers on the Musselshell until the first of May. Then noticing that a number of the beaver caught were already shedding their heavy winter undercoats of fur, Ofer began contemplating withdrawing all of their beaver traps and preparing for the coming summer's long trip back to Fort Manuel. There to sell their huge accumulations of beaver and wolf furs, resupply, take some time to visit with old friends, let their hair down and not worry about being attacked by Indians, grizzly bears, freezing to death, or suffering injuries from horse wrecks. There they would also visit with other company trappers and make their plans for the location of their coming fall and spring trapping seasons. Then come late September on their new trapping grounds somewhere along the Musselshell further to the southwest where the beaver had not already been trapped out, start all over again with the running of their beaver trap lines.

As their spring beaver trapping season began coming to a close because many of the beaver caught were already beginning to shed their more valuable winter under fur, Ofer sat by the last furs hooped and closely examined them for shedding. They had already caught 244 beaver during the fall trapping season, 44 wolves during the winter wolf trapping season and another 291 spring beaver on the Musselshell and Box Elder Creeks, as well as had hooped and bundled the same. Finished with his examination of the last 23 pelts caught, defatted and hooped, Ofer figured they had one more week at the most to catch Made

Beaver then the best part of the spring fur season was over. Stepping outside the cabin he saw Gabriel and Little Raven trimming the hooves and shoeing for the first time those horses they had captured and kept from some of the Gros Ventre Indians in previous battle, and in so doing he just grinned. Grinned because to his way of thinking, Gabriel and Little Raven had grown so close they might as well be real brothers. Then Ofer yelled for the group to assemble around their campfire.

When everyone had put down what they had been doing and assembled around Ofer where he sat upon his sitting log, he said, "Looking at our last beaver catches, I am beginning to see fur slippage as the spring weather warms up and rolls along. With that in mind, we need to close down our trap line, finish bundling the last of our hooped and dried beaver skins, clean out our camp and head back down to Fort Manuel to sell our furs, relax and celebrate for a change. As near as I can tell, maybe a day or two more of running our trap line and then I say we close her down and make ready to head down to Fort Manuel." Looking around at the faces of the group, Ofer could tell they were more than ready to stop trapping for a bit, return to civilization as they knew it back at Fort Manuel, and just relax without the hard work and danger associated in the great beaver-laden area they had currently chosen to trap. As for Little Raven and Black Eagle, neither knew what Fort Manuel was or what it represented but from the happy looks on everyone else's faces, it must be good. So without knowing what Fort Manuel was all about, they were excited to go and see what those white man times and experiences represented as well.

The following day, Ofer once again led the group of trappers to the southwest where their current trap line was in place. Throughout most of that day, Ofer and Joshua removed another18 beaver from their traps. However as Ofer had feared, the time to best trap beaver had slipped away. Of the 18 adult beaver trapped that day, 14 were already were showing signs of fur slippage and in so doing, would bring a much reduced rate of return once graded and sold at Fort Manuel. Realizing the time had come, Ofer pulled all of the traps that day as Gabriel and Little Raven skinned their catches in the field. However, all was not lost. In celebration of their highly successful trapping season, Ofer had Gabriel select out four of the fattest beaver and save their carcasses for a special 'end of trapping season' supper that evening. He figured with that effort done for the year, they would head home and while Gabriel and Little Raven fixed up a celebratory supper of roasted beaver, Dutch oven biscuits, beans, a pot of cooked rice, raisins and brown sugar and their favorite style of strong coffee, he would drag out one of their last two flat kegs of rum for the group to enjoy as a kind of 'dessert 'for all of the hard work done. Then all of a sudden, Ofer began having those damn nagging sixth sense feelings inside that everything was not all right! But his feelings of something being wrong were faint and he finally wrote them off to being tired and hungry for the supper to come that evening and everything else surrounding the end of a very busy spring trapping season.

Realizing their day was done for the season, the men laughed and teased each other all the way back to their camp, knowing the next few days would be hectic, as they packed up their entire camp and headed for a summer of relaxation at Fort Manuel. Rounding the finger of trees leading up into their camp, the men hooted and hollered as they realized this would be the last such time a trip would be made at this cabin site. Trotting their horses into the cabin's clearing, THE MEN WERE SHOCKED TO DISCOVER THEIR REMAINING BEAUTIFULLY MATCHED BUCKSKIN HORSES AND THEIR NEWEST EXTRA RIDING HORSES WERE ABSENT THEIR CORRAL! THEN LOOKING EVEN MORE CLOSELY, IT BECAME EVIDENT THAT THEIR CABIN HAD BEEN BROKEN INTO AND LOOTED AS WELL!

Grabbing their rifles and quickly dismounting, the men ran

to their cabin expecting maybe a grizzly bear to be the culprit of the missing and run off horses and the broken-into and ransacked cabin. Cautiously approaching the open doorway and peeking into the gloomy cabin's interior looking for a soon to be dead bear, all the men saw was the almost total absence of everything of value! Then Little Raven who had dismounted and run over to the corral, shouted and with that shout, the rest of the men stormed out from the cabin expecting to do battle. It was then that the men learned what Little Raven had discovered. There were moccasin tracks and the signs of unshod Indian horses from at least ten Indians, maybe more, who were the ones that had stolen all of the trappers' valuable buckskin horses! Then a closer subsequent inspection of the cabin revealed that their last tins and keg of gunpowder, all the bundled beaver and wolf pelts, their last kegs of rum, their extra firearms and all of their knives were missing! Then to make matters worse, the Indians who had raided the cabin and taken everything of value had taken the time to take 'dumps' everywhere inside the cabin, including on top of the men's sleeping furs as a sign of disrespect and utter contempt for the American white trappers invading the Indians' home grounds... Quietly standing there and looking around and realizing the depth of what had just happened, Ofer thought back to his earlier in the day, unusual feelings that he had just written off as being tired and hungry. He now realized that even a slight discomfort received from his sixth sense was to be listened to if he and his fellow trappers were to survive...

Now with all laughter and merriment gone, Ofer had the men turn around, mount up and with Black Eagle and Ofer starting to track the moccasin-wearing culprits and shod tracks from the valuable buckskins, the rest of the men fell in behind. When they did, the stone cold silence coming from every man foretold of evil things to come if those who had done the taking were ever caught. With Ofer now tracking from horseback following the stolen horses' metal horseshoe hoofprints, the men fanned out in a defensive posture and rode hard after those who to their way of thinking needed a little fatal adjustment for such thievery.

The 'story' the horses' tracks 'told' was that the thieves riding their unshod horses were pushing the heavily loaded and now very valuable string of pack animals hard away from the area. They had to be figuring that the owners of the stolen goods would immediately be on their trail, so the thieves tarried very little. Finally with the arriving dark that first night of 'hot-on-their-trail' pursuit, found the group of trappers huddled under a mess of conifers gathered around a very small fire so they would not give their pursuit-presence away, eating half-cooked beaver meat. Beaver meat that had been meant for a celebration at the end of a successful beaver trapping season and now was being gagged down half-raw with a lot of 'bile' by the cold, hungry and extremely pissed-off trappers...

Just as soon as tracking could begin once again at daylight the next day and the trappers' outriders could safely watch the backs of their trackers out in front, the men were once again 'horsed' and in hot pursuit. For most of that day of pursuit, the tracks of those being pursued showed once again they were pushing their riding and pack stock very hard and fast to avoid discovery, recapture and recrimination. However, around noon as the trappers pursued the unknown Indian thieves heading almost due north, Ofer came to the realization that they were now heading deeply into the very heart of the land of the deadly Gros Ventre! And in so doing, away from the land of the more friendly Crow Indians! It was also about that time in the day that those being pursued began slowing down and were not pushing their stolen stock as hard, figuring they were now safely away from any form of pursuit. With that discovery, Ofer and the men pushed even harder, hoping their well cared-for riding horses could outlast those belonging to the Indian thieves and in so doing, their overtaking of the thieves would be shortly forthcoming and then there would be hell to pay...

That second night of pursuit, the trappers had nothing to eat and by then, their thoughts of killing those responsible for the problem equaled those of their worst thoughts! Ofer had everyone up way before daylight the next morning because it was so cold and sleep was almost impossible because of the weather change. Additionally, a foot of freshly fallen spring snow only added to the misery of the trappers and the amount of 'bile' each man now possessed, when it came to his thoughts regarding those who were causing the trappers such suffering, was immense and growing by the minute!

Taking the time to attend to a call of nature in order to rid his body from the previous meal of half-raw beaver meat, Ofer at first discovered he was not using all of his senses as Bear Trap had previously taught him when out and about in the wilderness... All of a sudden his previous training kicked in and was rewarded with the very faint smell of pinewood smoke and cooking meat! Pulling up his cold buckskins, Ofer trotted back to the rest of his men who were busy saddling their riding horses and when they saw him coming at a trot with a strange look upon his face, everyone's eyes fixed on him realizing something was afoot! Running up to the tired, wet and cold men, Ofer touched his index finger to the side of his nose 'indicating he wanted the men to smell'. Black Eagle was the first to wind the faint smell that had captured Ofer's senses, which were soon followed by the rest of the men! With that deadly clue now in the air, the men's horses were tied off to the nearby trees, the locks on their guns were closely inspected as were their extra rifles still carried in their third packhorse's pannier, and then gathered up and made ready for battle! With newfound spirits sent soaring over the 'smell' discovery, the men began sneaking through the trees with their rifles held at the ready, all the while utilizing their newly rediscovered and heightened senses to the fullest!

About an hour and a half-mile later of sneaking up into what appeared to be a box canyon in the timber, the men were now more than smelling the welcome smoke of a wood fire and cooking meat! Soon several small plumes of smoke could be seen spiraling into the heavy snow cloud-laden sky from the mystery fires below. Leaving the men huddled under a big Douglas fir tree, Black Eagle and Ofer quietly sneaked the distance down towards the fire. Soon they could see 11 Indians gathered around several roaring fires and hear a lot of 'happy' talk ongoing between the group's members. 'Happy talking' obviously somewhat fueled by the nearby flat rum keg lying near one of the Indians' fires... Then observing the group of Indians eating breakfast consisting of what appeared to be a large portion of spitted venison, Black Eagle was heard to quietly utter in a tone meant for Ofer's ears only, "Gros Ventre!" Then Ofer spied a line of horses picketed off to one side consisting of his valuable buckskins and the Indian horses of unknown lineage. Following those observations, Ofer spied what appeared to be one of his buckskins lying on the ground off to one side in the Indians' campsite. At first he thought the horse was just lying down and then his brow furrowed and a tightness of his lips could be seen developing. Ofer had just realized the Indians below in the camp had apparently selected out one of his valuable buckskins, killed it and were now spitting a large chunk of its hindquarter over the fire for their breakfast! If Ofer's heart needed any further hardening over what had occurred, namely the needless killing of one of his valuable and matched buckskins for breakfast, it turned that which was left of his humanity into that of a stone cold killer for those who richly deserved such treatment! A stone cold killer hellbent on the same level of destruction to the thieves that they had just needlessly accorded to one of his favorite buckskin horses, not to mention jeopardizing the trappers' lives by stealing their frontier 'lifeblood', namely their horses!

Laying those deadly feelings aside for just a moment and having finally figured out the lay of the land as well as a method of attack, Ofer touched Black Eagle's arm to get his attention and then the two of them quietly slipped back to their anxiously awaiting group of trappers. Using a stick in the snow kicked-away soil, Ofer diagrammed the camp's layout and quietly lined every trapper out as to his responsibility when their shooting started. Then the men began silently sneaking through the timber in the sound-deadening fresh snow covering the ground, 'as quietly as falling snowflakes' with a determination as cold as was the killing soon to come! Ofer's attack plan was such that every man of his group would have a tree from which to safely shoot from and a specific target or targets to kill. Yet all would be close enough to the coming action that Ofer's 'unique' command to attack, which would start the final journey of the horse thieves on their ways to meet their own "Cloud People", would be seen and 'make no mistake', clearly understood by all of the trappers!

Sometime later as the 11 Gros Ventre Indians hooped and hollered around their campfire, obviously fired up with liberal doses from the rum keg stolen from Ofer's group of trappers, they neglected in their merriment to see a buckskin-clad trapper all of a sudden materialize from behind a line of trees and boldly walk directly into their midst! Upon all of a sudden seeing the strange Mountain Man right in their camp next to all of them with a distinct look of 'death' spelled clear across his face, caused the stunned and slightly drunken Gros Ventre to just stand there for a second and stare at the suddenly appearing apparition of death from just feet away! Then one large Indian gained his survival senses and made a quick move for his rifle lying against a close at hand stack of firewood. Ofer shot his face clear off when the heavy .52 caliber ball from his rifle struck the man in the side of his head! Then quickly dropping his rifle, Ofer whipped out his two pistols from his waist sash and killed two more Indians standing 'thunderstruck' right next to where he stood! This he did just as those two Indians managed to lay their hands upon their stacked rifles in a final effort to defend themselves from the death they now knew was soon to be on its way from the trapper in their midst! Neither Indian even wiggled after being head shot by Ofer from such a close-in range with a load of 'buck and ball' from his pistols! Then amidst the whistling of a number of rifle balls heading into the ranks and tearing into the flesh of the now madly scrambling Indians for their weapons from the other trappers on the nearby hillside, the killing was over before it had really started and before the Gros Ventre horse thieves could even grab a rifle and fire a single shot...

However, unbeknownst to the trappers now rapidly approaching the Indians' campfires with drawn pistols and extra rifles held at the ready, a Gros Ventre Indian was rising up from tending to a call of nature in the brush a number of feet from the now dead Indian thieves' campfires... As he did, his dark eyes looked on in horror over what had just occurred to his fellow countrymen! He had just seen his two brothers and a number of his friends gunned down in total surprise from a single and then a hidden group of Mountain Men! Then realizing the danger he was facing, that Indian quickly pulled up his buckskins and quietly since he was unarmed, scurried off even deeper into the brush to keep from what had just happened to his friends from happening to him! Finally stopping in his flight behind a large pine tree, "Dark Eyes" took one last look at his dead friends and two brothers. Then he fled deeper into the timber so he could remain hidden, yet still observe what was happening below until the Mountain Men had left the deadly scene. As he did he realized returning to Chief Buffalo Horn with the bad news that his 12 best warriors sent to kill the one trapping on the Musselshell, that his Lodge River Band of Gros Ventre called Red Hand or The Scalper, had in turn been ambushed by some of the white men trappers they had been sent out to rob and kill.

Watching from his place of concealment, Dark Eyes found his heart hardening when he watched one of the trappers riding up on a buckskin stallion and then after dismounting, begin scalping every one of his former victorious party! Then the one doing all of the scalping begin weaving his friends' and brothers' long braids of hair into each of the Indians' horses' manes still tied up at the picket line. In even further horror, he watched the Mountain Man doing all of the scalping of his friends, rubbing his hands on their freshly scalped heads in order to further bloody up his hands! Then that same Mountain Man began slapping his bloody red hands against each of his friends' and brothers' horses before he removed their bridles and slapped them on their rumps, sending them on their ways back to where they came from. He now knew he was looking at the one his people had named Red Hand or The Scalper!

Then horrors of horrors! All of a sudden Red Hand doing all of the scalping and slapping his bloody hand against each horse's neck leaving a bloody handprint before he slapped it on its rump and sent it on its way, REALIZED THERE WAS ONE MORE INDIAN HORSE LEFT AND NO INDIAN'S SCALP TO WEAVE INTO THE HORSE'S MANE! THEN LOOKING AT THE REMAINING INDIAN'S HORSE, NAMELY THE ONE BELONGING TO DARK EYES WHO WAS HIDING ON THE HILLSIDE, REALIZED THAT ONE INDIAN HAD ESCAPED THE KILLING... THEN THE SCALPER BEGAN LOOKING UP INTO THE TIMBER FOR THE ONE INDIAN WHO HAD POSSIBLY ESCAPED BEING KILLED AND ALL OF A SUDDEN, DARK EYES FOUND HIMSELF LOOKING DIRECTLY AT THE INTENSE-LOOKING EYES OF THOSE OF THE SCALPER! It was then that Dark Eyes silently slipped off deeper into the dark timber and once out of sight from those piercing eyes of the one called The Scalper, ran like the wind was at his back and an evil spirit was hot on his trail! As he did, Dark Eyes realized that in the eyes of his people, he would now be treated like a failure and an outcast! Treated so because he and the rest of his band of 12 warriors sent out to kill the Mountain Man called Red Hand or The Scalper by Chief Buffalo Horn had failed! A man he had now seen and could identify by the buck-skin stallion he rode and in person by face recognition, espe-cially since he was missing an ear... Red Hand or The Scalper was indeed a Mountain Man trapper who with others of his kind was trapping beaver on the waters called "The Musselshell" by other white men... That he had finally figured out because they had stolen the horses from the trappers who had a cabin near the Musselshell. And now those trappers had followed them and their stolen horses right to the 12 warriors' camp! But in his mind, he was not through with Red Hand or The Scalper for what he had just done to his two head shot brothers, and the shame he had brought to his name by not being in the actual fight but of taking a dump when the one-sided killing had occurred! As those thoughts ran through his mind, it lent speed to his feet as the now dishonored Gros Ventre, one of the Lodge River Band's 12 best warriors purposely sent to find and kill Red Hand or The Scalper, headed for his distant wintering band's location far to the north. As he did, he once again realized that he and the others had utterly failed partially because of all of the stolen rum they had consumed, but now he at least knew what Red Hand or The Scalper and his horse looked like, and he would find a way to gather other warriors around him to hunt him down and do to him what he had just done to his two brothers and friends...

Not truly aware that one of the Gros Ventre had gotten away just because there was one Indian horse extra, Ofer and company moved carefully into the Indians' main camp and after collecting all of the dead men's weapons, warmed themselves by the two campfires. Later, the men feasted on the remains of one of their fine buckskin horses the Indians had slaughtered for food. And the trappers were glad to have something warm to eat after their days of cold tracking without food while out on the trail of the horse thieves. After breakfast and repacking all of the packhorses with the trappers' stolen goods, the men hiked back to their tied-off horses and several days of travel later arrived back at their campsite. When they did, it was to another surprise! A grizzly bear in the trappers' absence and one that was fresh out from hibernation, had taken up residence in the trappers' cabin! Seven shots later, the great bear lay dead in the front yard of the trappers' cabin and soon its rather stringy meat was being spitted over the men's outdoor cooking fire as the rest of their goods was returned to their cabin. Then they tiredly hobbled their remaining horse herd and released them so they could graze on the newly sprouted rich grasses in their meadow. Within the hour found the tired and emotionally drained trappers sound asleep in their cabin with all the smells left by the grizzly bear, who figured he had found a very nice place to live and made himself right at home, his last...

CHAPTER 6 — TROUBLE AT FT. MANUEL, THE LEGEND OF "RED HAND" BEGINS

FIVE DAYS LATER AFTER LETTING THEIR HORSES GRAZE TO their hearts' content in their nearby meadow, the trappers brought them back into their campsite, curried all of them down, repacked all of their packs and the following morning way before daylight, saddled their riding stock and packed their packs on the packhorses with all of their furs and other property. Then heading out after a breakfast of just buffalo jerky, the men headed their fur caravan due south towards Fort Manuel for the summer fur sales, reprovisioning and get-together. Four days of travel without incident later, Ofer and company rounded a long meadow leading to the fort and then made the short approach into the grounds of Fort Manuel, arriving at the closed gate just minutes later.

There at the fort's massive front gate, Manuel Lisa met Ofer and company with a happy to see them greeting. Then personally remembering Ofer and his group as some of his original trappers, Lisa noticed that they were two men shy from their initial white man complement that had left the newly built fort a year earlier. Lisa's inquiry to Ofer over the missing men was met with the abrupt words, "Grizzly bear got Daniel, Gros Ventre got Bear Trap!" Seeing the look of pain on Ofer's face when he uttered those sad words, Lisa made sure that subject was never broached again in front of the man who had violently lost his brother and a very good friend to what had to be a savage form of death…

"Ofer," exclaimed Lisa quickly changing the subject, "It is good to see all of you once again. And from the looks of your heavily loaded and still great-looking signature buckskin horses, you and the rest of your group did very well. I figured you would do well if the bunch of you listened to what John Colter had to say regarding the good beaver trapping grounds up on the Musselshell and sure as 'God made green apples', it looks like it worked out for you men."

"We did very well with over 500 beaver pelts and in excess of 40 wolf hides as well," said Ofer as he tiredly dismounted, rubbed his sore knees from the long cramped ride in the stirrups, and then shook Manuel Lisa's extended welcoming hand with a tired looking smile upon his face.

"That is great news!" said Lisa. "We just so happen to have a break in trappers returning from the back country today and if you feel up to it, run your stock into the fort and by my graders and sorters, and we can settle up right here and now, and then you and your group can rest up and celebrate inside the safety and confines of our new fort if you choose to do so."

A few minutes later inside Fort Manuel, Ofer and company found themselves surrounded by Lisa's St. Louis Missouri Fur Company sorters and graders unpacking their pack animals, plowing through their bundles of furs, grading, sorting and stacking them accordingly. As they did, Ofer had all of his brothers watch closely and make sure the company men were accurate in their counts and correct in their grading qualities of the furs being unpacked. Soon all 575 beaver furs had been unpacked, sorted out as to size and quality and counted. That was when Ofer was surprised that his Musselshell beaver had graded out to 400 Made Beaver (high quality, adult beaver 'Plus'), and 175 smaller but still high quality 'Plus'! The 44 wolf pelts were all graded out as the highest of quality and color and were stacked off to one side as well. That work done, the Tal Brothers found themselves a surprised $5,387.50 richer! Upon hearing that final tally, the Tal Brothers ended up whooping and jumping around in joy like a bunch of little children! They had received $6 per pound for their 400 Made Beaver, $4.50 a pound for their 175 smaller beaver, and $50 per wolf pelt, for a total of $5,387.50! For all of the misery they had suffered in cold water immersions while trap setting, grizzly bear problems, loss of a brother, freezing weather, horse wrecks, loss of a dear friend in Bear Trap and constant depredations and fights with the far-roving Gros Ventre, they were now rich men! *Their father, Yossef, would have been proud over his sons' accomplishments,* thought Ofer with a tired smile.

Ofer accepted a credit slip from Manuel Lisa's St. Louis Missouri Fur Company for $5,387.50, and the entire group of men happily accepted the offer of staying in the company clerks' barracks while they stayed at the fort during their summer stay. As all of those earlier fur sorting and grading activities swirled around the men's heads, Black Eagle and Little Raven, never having been in a white man's fort and seeing how it operated, found their heads spinning as well. First of all, found their heads spinning in just seeing such a huge man-made structure. Then Black Eagle and Little Raven found even further amazement in seeing so many white men in one place, hearing so much noise as compared to living out in the wilds, and seeing so many new and wondrous things like a working blacksmith's shop! In short, they found their senses overwhelmed as they continued looking 'goggle-eyed' at all of the white man events now swirling and happening around them!

That evening after the Tal Brothers' herd of horses had been hobbled and let out into the fort's nearby heavily guarded pasture to feed and water, they were surprised to find themselves supper guests of Manuel Lisa. There the men found themselves feasting on roasted buffalo, fresh potatoes, carrots and onions from the fort's garden, home-baked loaves of bread, freshly churned butter, chokecherry jam and all the homemade wild plum pies the men could hold! The next morning found all of the men sitting in the communal seven-hole outhouse passing pure streams of diarrhea from all of the rich and unfamiliar food just 'deposited' into their usual 'mostly meat-adjusted intestinal' systems after eating at Lisa's supper table! Additionally, the Tal Brothers, Black Eagle and Little Raven were soon to suffer ailments from the number of men all crowded together with less than clean living habits and conditions in the company clerks' barracks, with more to come on that...

During the next month, Ofer and his group of men mingled with all of the incoming trappers from the back country, as well as the hundreds of Crow Indians coming to the fort on a daily basis to sell their furs and buffalo hides and trade for the white man's much-desired goods. As expected, there was also much celebrating and mingling with old friends around the supper fires of those who were camping outside the fort's protective walls and not living in the company clerks' barracks as were the Tal Brothers, Black Eagle and Little Raven. Especially frequently visited were those friends who had made the original and dangerous trip up the Missouri River in 1807 with Lisa and his two keelboats.

Then one afternoon, three fully loaded keelboats arrived at the fort's boat docks at the mouth of the Bighorn River after struggling up through the summer low water levels of the Missouri River! Those keelboat arrivals with fresh supplies created a mad scramble by every trapper and many Crow Indians and their wives for the new trade goods just arriving. However, since the Tal Brothers had originally accompanied

Lisa upriver in 1807 and had helped in guarding his horse herd while en route, Manuel saw to it that they were given the privilege of being some of the first in line when it came to acquiring the much-needed provisions for another year afield. Once again, after all the supplies had been offloaded into the fort's warehouses from the just-arriving keelboats and as all the hides, pelts, robes and beaver *'Plus'* were being loaded on board the boats for a dangerous return journey to St. Louis through the lands of the dreaded Arikara Indians, the reprovisioning of the trappers for the coming fall and spring trapping seasons began with a rush inside the fort.

Again as the process of reprovisioning began by the various groups of trappers and Indians, Black Eagle and Little Raven were once again amazed over the wealth of white man goods they discovered stored in the warehouses when it came their turn near the front of the line to resupply! When that day of reprovisioning arrived, Ofer had organized his group into the 'shoppers' of needed wares. First because food was so important, Gabriel and Little Raven as the designated camp cooks were at the head of the line. Since the group had all the cooking wares and implements they needed, they concentrated on procuring the needed food and food-related wares. Within an hour, Gabriel and Little Raven had amassed a small mountain of sacks of flour for their daily staple of Dutch oven biscuits, two dozen tins of dried yeast to make the all-important biscuits rise, bags of beans, rice, brown sugar cones, salt, black pepper, white pepper, red pepper flakes, cinnamon, jugs of rendered bear 'leaf-lard' oil (for use in the Dutch ovens), jugs of honey, dried fruit and the most important staple of life to a trapper, 200 pounds of green and dried coffee beans for the making of every trapper's meal staple, coffee.

Then Ofer and Black Eagle saw to it that their much-diminished supplies of lead pigs, tins of powder, flints, greased rags, spare pistol and rifle parts, needles, awls, fire steels, six whetstones, four files, two one-pound axes and one six-pound maul were replaced. As they made their selections, Ofer and Black Eagle, ever mindful of the roving Gros Ventre and the dreaded Blackfoot country they trapped beaver in, made sure there were more than ample supplies for the 'business end' of their rifles and pistols, namely, flints, powder and lead...

Following that, Joshua and Jerimiah made sure the clothing needs for each man were met, including bolts of cloth to repair clothing, new wide brimmed hats for every man, socks, extra leather strapping to replace leather needs on riding and packsaddles, as well as an assortment of horseshoes and horseshoe nails. Lastly, they made sure they procured two 25-pound kegs of nails and spikes so when they built their next cabin come late summer, they would have the right and much-needed building supplies. Lastly, all the men chipped in and purchased new clay pipes to replace the ones that were broken over the last year, a number of 'carrots' of chewing and smoking tobacco and lastly, six flat wooden kegs of rum instead of their usual four.

Then as an afterthought, Ofer purchased two additional .52 caliber horse pistols, one for Black Eagle and the other for Little Raven. That he did because when he passed the pistol display case in the warehouse, something inside him told him to stop and purchase two of the pistols. Having had those kinds of sixth sense feelings before and remembering that every one of them had come to fruition with occasions needing that 'issue' addressed, he did not hesitate with that procurement. Little did Ofer realize that sixth sense-aided purchase would save his life and the lives of others later on down the road in the Blackfoot country in which they lived and trapped furbearers.

Come the 4th of July when the entire fort was celebrating with much eating of roasted buffalo, drinking, fighting, running foot races to see who was the fastest trapper in camp, singing, telling of tall tales, horse races to see who had the fastest horse and other celebrations of such, trouble raised its ugly head that special 'country birthday day' with the Tal Brothers and six company trappers. Standing in line waiting their turn for some freshly roasted buffalo and a cup of free rum courtesy of Manuel Lisa in celebration of his new nation's birthday (Lisa had been a Spanish citizen before the United States had purchased Upper Louisiana), Black Eagle all of a sudden was struck from behind with the butt of a rifle, knocking him stunned to the ground! Ofer standing alongside Black Eagle whirled around when Black Eagle was struck and found that he was looking down the barrel of a rifle being held in the hands of a rough-looking fur trapper with a knife or tomahawk scar running clear across the cheek of his face and a leer of disgust 'spelled' across that scarred face! Feeling his emotions rising up from within, Ofer slowly dropped his right hand towards the butt of one of his pistols in his sash, when Black Eagle's restraining hand reaching up from where he lay on the ground stopped him…

"You have something to say, 'Injun' lover?" rumbled the voice of the rather large man positioning the end of his rifle barrel right in the center of Ofer's face! "If not, I suggest you get that damn stinking, no-account, louse-ridden 'Injun' out of this line because I object to having him standing in front of a real man," rumbled "Scar Face's" voice, as he stared hard at Ofer after seeing him tense up and drop his hand to one of his pistols.

WHUMP! went Gabriel's rifle buttstock into the side of Scar Face's head dropping him to the ground, as **BOOM!** went his rifle which involuntarily went off right next to the side of Ofer's face, dropping him in an instant as a result of being hit in the face with the edge of the force of unburned black powder and flame from the holder's rifle's accidental discharge!

In the next instant, Gabriel, Joshua, Jerimiah, Little Raven and now Black Eagle back up from off the ground after being struck in the head by Scar Face, were swarming over him and the surprising entry of his five fur trapper friends with swinging gun butts, rifle barrels, flashing knives, pistol butts and fists!

Soon, 20 or more other drunken fur trappers standing nearby in the 'free cup of rum line' had joined the brawl just for the 'hell of it', and it took a very angry Manuel Lisa and a half-dozen of his company clerks several minutes to begin breaking up the fight before someone got killed or cut to ribbons!

However, not before Ofer had gotten up off the ground, jerked out his tomahawk and only being able to see out of his left eye, slammed its blade a glancing blow into the bearded jaw of Scar Face, dropping him to the ground under the feet of a number of fighters still going at it on the battlefield next to the rum kegs and roasting buffalo meat...

Finally, not until the fighting trappers were under the leveled rifle barrels of now a dozen stern-faced company clerks did Lisa manage to get control of the brawling men, allowing for a return to a form of 'peace and quiet'. Having been the one doling out the free cups of rum, Lisa had seen the entire fight from its beginning to its finish. Under the command of Lisa, his clerks separated the five fur trappers and the now badly bleeding scar-faced one out from the other general combatants and hell raisers who had just joined into the fight because it was a damn good fight and seemed like the thing to do on such a great day of celebration.

"Dan Wessen (Scar Face), you gather up your five men and I want you off the property of this fort by sundown! I will not tolerate any general fighting or defaming of my Indian clients now or ever! You and your men get your gear together and since you have already purchased your provisions, get off this fort's grounds and from now on, you six are relegated to doing all of your trading and purchasing of provisions from the Hudson's Bay people or their counterparts at the Northwestern Fur Company in Canada, and never again at my fort as long as I am alive! Now, my six clerks will escort you to your camp. See to it that you are packed up and out of here by sundown or I will know the reason why! Now move your miserable damn carcasses or I will order you to be shot where you stand, by damn it!"

With those commands, Scar Face's men hoisted his huge frame up from off the ground where he lay bleeding from Ofer's tomahawk strike and with that, under leveled rifle barrels from the fort's company clerks, the six trappers were escorted back to their campsite and several hours later, were observed slowly moving off to the north and west away from Fort Manuel with their caravan of horses. In the meantime, Lisa saw to it that his personal doctor administered to Ofer's powder-burned face as best as he could. However, there was not much he could do. When Scar Face's rifle had inadvertently discharged alongside Ofer's face after Gabriel had 'buttstocked' his brother's assailant in the head, the bullet had missed, but the right side of Ofer's face had been badly burned by the flame from the end of Scar Face's rifle being fired from such close quarters! Additionally, the flame from that rifle's discharge had burned off the remaining skin on Ofer's partial right ear, causing it to bleed madly! Also, the right side of Ofer's face was badly blistered from the flame, his right eye was swollen closed and all he could hear in his right ear was a loud ringing sound from the rifle's blast! That and a big swatch of his flowing locks had also been burned away from the right side of his head as well. However, he would live and but for Gabriel's timely intervention, he could have suffered a worse fate had Scar Face pulled the trigger when the barrel was directly pointing at Ofer's face, or without warning, stepped forth with his sheath knife or tomahawk and physically attacked Ofer for attempting to intercede on Black Eagle's behalf...

But it was the 4th of July, the United States' birthday and the celebrations went on. However, Ofer's participation in such events was slightly subdued because of all the pain he was suffering from his injuries, that was until he had consumed his fifth cup of rum. Then other than being blinded in one eye and not hearing in one ear, he, along with his brothers and friends made sure the United States' birthday was duly celebrated frontier-style, burned face, closed eye, bleeding right ear, ringing in his ear and loss of hair be damned...

Come the last week in July and now mostly healed up after his altercation with Scar Face, other than an obviously still-blistered right side of his face and a mess of burned-off missing hair, Ofer realized he and his group of trappers were 'burning daylight'. Summer was fast coming to a close, they had to decide where they were going for the fall and spring trapping season, and they had to get there wherever that place would be and build their new cabin before fall trapping was upon them. That evening while sitting around a fire in the fort's courtyard nursing cups of rum, Ofer broached the subject of leaving and then going somewhere in order to continue trapping. Without one word of dissent, all of the men wanted to return to somewhere along the bountiful Musselshell where it had not been trapped out and where they could once again be successful. Ofer suggested that being the case, how about just moving somewhere further along the Musselshell to the southwest from where they had left off late in the spring. Once again, there was no dissent with his suggestion and with that, Ofer suggested they make ready to leave as soon as possible because they had to locate their exact trapping grounds, build a cabin, construct a corral for their horses and set aside a substantial pile of firewood for the coming winter's snowy weather.

With that, Joshua suggested they get all of their horses reshod over the next few days, assemble and fill all of their packs with their new provisions, get all of their visiting done with their friends and then hit the trail for their new trapping grounds along the Musselshell. That was agreed upon and the next day Ofer met with Lisa and settled up with him regarding their purchases. But not before he had visited the fort's warehouse and procured some new pine marten and muskrat traps on a whim. Then with a tally of $1,050.00 in goods purchased, Lisa took back Ofer's credit slip and cut Ofer a St. Louis Missouri Fur Company Letter of Credit for $4,337.50 for the remainder his company owed the trappers, a small fortune in those days. With his group's Letter of Credit in hand and after shaking Lisa's hand and thanking him for allowing the men to bunk in his clerks' barracks, Ofer headed over to the fort's blacksmith to see how the reshoeing process of his horses was progressing. The three blacksmiths were almost done, so Ofer lingered around and visited with one of the other 'smithies' that he knew from the days of 1807, and the original trip into the headwaters of the Missouri and the heralded beaver trapping opportunities that awaited the hardy. When he did, Ofer was surprised when another fur trapper and his Indian partner trailed their pack string right over to where he was sitting visiting with his 'smithy' friend, and then stood there looking at him for a long moment in time.

"Say, I don't mean to intrude in your conversation with your friend here, but is that there big buckskin stallion standing over there your'n?"

"Sure is, Partner. Why do you ask?" said Ofer.

"My partner here is an Assiniboine Indian and caters to what he hears from other Indians and the 'whispers' he hears from others of his kind who are kin of some sort. He spied that big unique-looking buckskin stallion there and I say a magnificent-looking one, if I might be so bold. He is only one of several buck-skins in camp and a bit of a novelty if one was to ask me. I say that because most of us are riding old plugs of some sort just as long as they can get us around. But that horse of your'n stands out like a 'broked thumb'. And that is why I am here askin. "Burned Leg", my Indian partner here, reared back when he saw that horse and you a-sittin here. I don't mean to be so bold but have you been a-tangling with a number of them deadly Gros Ventre as of late? Because if so, you are getting some kind of a reputation and a wild- sounding moniker as a result among a number of the Indian tribes in this here area according to Burned Leg for some things you are being accused of. Seems word has gotten out regarding a white man fur trapper Indian killer, who is scalping everyone he runs across a-botherin' him, ties their scalps into those Indians' horses' manes and sends them a-packing back to their tribe's horse herds with a bloody handprint on each of those horses' necks as some kind of a warning! Pardon my 'nosy' but you don't happen to be that scalping son-of-a-bitch that is scarin' the hell out of most of the Indians in this neck of the woods, be you?"

Upon hearing those words, Ofer just quietly looked back at the old fur trapper asking all of the questions with an all-knowing and quiet look and offered no response to the rather awkward question being asked...

"I knowed it, I knowed it when I saw this big ole buckskin stallion standing here! You ARE THE ONE all the Indians according to ole Burned Leg here, are a-calling "Red Hand"! Calling you Red Hand because you are not only killing them some-bitches off trying to kill you, but sending their horses back with their bloody scalps tied to their manes and with a bloody handprint slapped on their horses' necks. I knowed it once I laid eyes upon you that you had to be that fella scaring the hell out of every Indian from here clear across God's country. Best you be careful there, Young Fella. Iffen them redskin devils ever get a-holt of you when you ain't a-lookin, they will skin you alive and eat your heart and liver from right out of your coolin' carcass. You got more guts than my dear old passed father had in his hog slaughterhouse, if that ain't the truth. Here, let me shake your hand."

With that, the old trapper just reached out and forcefully took Ofer's hand lying on his lap and shook it up and down like a pump handle trying to get water out from a dry well on the desert... Then shaking his head, he turned and said, "Let's go,

Burned Leg, afore this man takes a liken to that ole rag you call a head of hair, removes it and slaps a bloody handprint on that ole nag of your'n," and with that, the old trapper ambled off in the typical trapper's shuffle, shaking his grizzled old head of hair in wonder and talking to himself over having just met a feared legend in the making. As he ambled off, Burned Leg trailing his grizzled old white partner kept looking back at Ofer as if he was worried Red Hand would get up from his chair and come after him...

For the longest time, Ofer just sat there in his chair alongside his old friend the smithy, who had now grown quiet as a 'mouse pissin' on a ball of cotton' over the "Red Hand" revelation about his usually quiet friend, then shaking his head, Ofer rose saying, "See you next time around, Charlie," and ambled off trailing his signature buckskin horse, which according to the old trapper just met and spoken with, indicated to many an Indian that the newest Gros Ventre scalping legend named Red Hand and his unique-looking buckskin horse was in country and 'bad Injuns' best step lively...

CHAPTER 7 — THE MUSSELSHELL, OF "BLACKFEET, BUCKSKINS AND BEAR TRAPS"

FOUR EASY DAYS OF SLOW TRAVEL LATER WITH THE HEAVILY loaded horses found the Tal Brothers camping along the lower Musselshell. There they had stopped, and since none of them had quit scratching and itching ever since leaving Fort Manuel having picked up lice infections from those company clerks also residing in the clerks' barracks, the men set up their camp near a meadow where their horses could 'put on the feed bag'. Then Ofer, using an old remedy taught to him by his nanny and family cook, Emily, had the men bathe in the Musselshell and once ashore and still wet, using their razor-sharp sheath knives or straight razors and shaving soap, shave off all of their body hair that each man could easily reach! Following the naked men was their host of accompanying mosquitoes, as the scratching men returned to their previous night's campfires. There using wetted handfuls of ash from those cold campfires, the men took turns rubbing the ash mixture all over each other's bodies. Then the naked men spent the day continually rubbing even more fresh ash all over their bodies in order to kill off the infestations of body lice and eggs each man had picked up in the clerks' filthy sleeping quarters back at Fort Manuel. As they did, the men also assembled several high wooden racks over the campfires and spent a day heavily smoking up all of their clothing in order to rid themselves of the bothersome parasites contained therein as well. Then it was once again back into the Musselshell and after washing all the ash off, each man using some of their precious shaving soap, shaved once again. (Author's Note: Contrary to historical beliefs, many of the Mountain Men shaved daily because in that day and age the human populace suffered from major infestations of head lice. So to rid themselves of the troublesome pests, many Mountain Men removed as much hair off their bodies as appropriate for that day and age, including shaving, in order to reduce the environment the lice preferred. The bodily application of wood ash and water creating a mild lye concoction was a common frontier infestation treatment when afield by those finding themselves afflicted with such skin parasites.)

As the men tarried along the Musselshell treating their skin infestations, they discovered that a number of their fur trapping brethren from Fort Manuel, upon hearing of the Tal Brothers' earlier trapping successes on the Musselshell, had followed them to those waters hoping for the same trapping successes. Seeing those 'infestations' of their fellow trappers along the close to Fort Manuel parts of the Musselshell, Ofer kept heading his group along that same waterway further to the west for the next six days, until they ran out of trapping competition and found themselves alone in the first range of mountains in what John Colter had told them would be called the "Little Belt Mountains". Mountains that he had also told Ofer's group, "Would be full of Made Beaver at every turn of the stream and in every waterway if they cared to brave the Blackfeet, Gros Ventre and bad winter weather at every turn in the trail to trap it."

Finally satisfied they had left numbers of trapping parties behind them and being a rather large party of trappers capable of taking care of themselves in and among the indigenous peoples like the Blackfeet Indians surrounding his group of trappers, Ofer finally stopped their westward travels into even more mountainous country. That he did because in addition to finding no further competing trappers, every waterway observed seemed to be heavily utilized by beaver. Heavily utilized as was evidenced by numerous fresh mud and stick dams, some over 100' feet in length, beaver ponds in numbers throughout, conical-shaped mud and stick houses in every ponded-up area, and extensive signs of willows, aspens and cottonwoods in different stages of being cut down and in the process of being dragged into the deeper watered areas to be used for the beaver's underwater food caches away from the hungry mouths of the many competing moose observed frequenting the area.

Earlier, as Ofer had led the men deeper and deeper into the area of the Little Belt Mountains he never ceased to be amazed over what he saw! Huge stands of pine, fir and spruce timber covered every ridge top, nook and cranny along the way. Everywhere he looked he saw blue grouse, dainty mule deer, the lordly moose (largest member of the deer family), grand elk with rounded healthy bodies, black and grizzly bears disappearing into the stands of timber upon seeing the oncoming trappers' caravan of horses, nesting eagles along the Musselshell, and beaver, river otter, muskrat and osprey galore!

Rounding a long finger of giant Douglas fir trees, Ofer found that the other side of the huge stand of timber opened up into a huge meadow at the base of a long ridge, bifurcated by a vigorously flowing stream, dumping itself into the nearby Musselshell. There he stopped and just looked the area over approvingly with a now practiced set of frontier eyes, thanks to Bear Trap's earlier teachings. Jerimiah rode up alongside Ofer and like his older brother, just closely looked the area over now spreading out before their eyes. Then Gabriel and Little Raven rode their horses up alongside the now gathering group of men and quietly sat in their saddles looking all around as well. As Black Eagle rode up and stopped alongside the others, he quietly said, "Looks like our new homesite to me."

Ofer just smiled over hearing what Black Eagle had to say. In fact, Ofer had been thinking the very same thought. Then with a moccasin nudge into his horse's flank, Ofer headed his horse and string of pack animals he was trailing over to a stand of aspens on the northern side of the stream running through the meadow and then swung easily out from the saddle. Then upon having his feet touch the ground, Ofer just hung onto the saddle horn for a moment, steadying his legs from the long ride in cramping stirrups which always sored up his knees. Then he said, "You might as well all swing down. I think we have found us a place in which to live and from here, it is an easy ride down to the Musselshell and all of those watered areas in that huge meadow below." (Author's Note: Ofer's choice of a new campsite was near the town of White Sulphur Springs in current-day Montana.)

For the next few minutes the beautiful area just chosen was full of excited talk from all of the fur trappers. Fur trappers happy to be out from their saddles and standing on the ground they would soon occupy for the fall and spring beaver trapping seasons. However, 'all was not biscuits and fur trapper songs.' Standing off in the trees some 100 yards distant stood a surprised Blackfoot warrior in the process of gutting out a mule deer buck he had just shot with his bow and arrow! For the longest time, his dark eyes took in the obvious fur trapper activity to his front next to the stream and an aspen grove. It soon became apparent to him from all of the pack animals being unloaded and the packs being assembled in a defensive ring in the aspens, that the intruders into the land of the fierce Black-feet, home of his forefathers and American fur trappers at that, were there to stay...

Quietly mounting up on his horse, the Blackfoot warrior left his freshly killed buck deer where it fell and quietly picked his way through the timber and out of the area now being noisily occupied by the white men fur trappers. For now, he was too outnumbered by the white men fur trappers to do anything, but he figured he would just wait and see at some later time if they had stayed. If they did and like all fur trappers he had killed and robbed in the past, they would let their guards down when trapping beaver and leave their livestock alone back at their camp. When they did, he figured, along with some of his friends, they would return and help themselves to the trappers' fine-looking buckskin horses and whatever else they found in the cabin soon to be built that they liked. With that, the Blackfoot warrior quietly rode out of sight from the noisy gathering of obviously happy fur trappers in the meadow below. Soon the Blackfoot warrior was out of sight but he had not forgotten...

For the rest of that day, Ofer and company gathered up firewood for their evening campfire, assembled a temporary rope picket line in the aspens to be used by their horses until a permanent corral could be built, hobbled their horses and let them out to feed in the nearby huge meadow so they could get acquainted with their new pastured area. Then with their rifles in hand, began scouting out the area for a potential cabin site, corral, outside firepit and close at hand trees that were stout enough for potential cabin building logs and meat hanging poles.

As they did, Ofer and Black Eagle stumbled across a freshly killed mule deer buck at the edge of their meadow with an arrow sticking into its side behind a front shoulder! Adjusting the rifle in his arms, Ofer, after discovering the freshly killed buck, kept looking all around for the deer's owner. As he did, Black Eagle knelt alongside the dead deer and examined the arrow's shaft. Rising to his feet and with his head down, began obviously tracking the deer's shooter. Moments later he discovered where the shooter of the deer had stood in the shadows of the timber and obviously watched the trappers arriving and begin unloading their packs. Then he discovered where the Indian had tied off his unshod horse, eventually had mounted up after seeing all that he had wanted to see and had ridden off to the north. When Ofer returned from his scouting around, Black Eagle handed Ofer the arrow uttering just one word, "Blackfoot!"

Not to look an opportunity off, Ofer and Black Eagle finished gutting out the freshly killed mule deer and carried it back to where the trappers were setting up their campsite. After an explanation over what and how they had discovered the deer, the rest of the trappers then found their eyes uneasily sweeping the edge of the timber from whence the buck had been discovered. That evening, the trappers kept a peeled eye and lookout for any sign of danger as Gabriel and Little Raven, also not to look a gift horse in the mouth, skinned out and butchered off the meat needed for the trappers' supper that evening. That they did as Joshua and Jerimiah retrieved their single buck saw and ax from one of the packs, cut down a small Douglas fir tree, made a cross member from it, and constructed a meat pole between two stout trees in the grove of aspens nearby where Gabriel and Little Raven had planned on establishing their outdoor firepit and eating site. That way the two camp cooks would always have easy access to the meat pole for their meat supplies when cooking up the trappers' meals in the future.

That afternoon the rest of the men laid out their sleeping furs, dug a conveniently placed trench for their latrine and scouted out their future cabin site. Ofer and Black Eagle took the single buck saw, a felling ax and their rifles and headed off into the nearby timber. Soon they had a large pine tree down and had begun cutting it into six sections to be used as sitting logs for each trapper soon to be placed by their new firepit. Then with a shout, Ofer waved the men to come over and roll the sitting log sections to the place Gabriel and Little Raven had begun setting up their permanent outdoor cooking area. By dusk, the firepit had been dug and a number of the packs holding the cooking implements had been unloaded, which were then hauled over to the cooking site. Once that site was established, the sitting logs were placed accordingly, a pot of beans set off to one side in a bean pot filled with water from the creek so they could soak for the next day's meal, and the cooking irons and hanging rods were in place over the firepit. Shortly thereafter, the air around the campfire smelled heavenly of roasting venison over the fire and baking biscuits in the Dutch ovens. With those smells ranging through the air, that soon found all of the hungry men hanging around the cooks putting the last vestiges of supper together. Then the smell of hot coffee drew the remaining men to the cooking area and soon in the cool of the evening, the only sounds heard were those of hungry men eating. Well, that and the usual hordes of mosquitoes surrounding each smelly trapper and a newly discovered species of bird by the Lewis and Clark Expedition, a Clark's nutcracker (a member of the woodpecker family), hammering away in the top of a distant and dead lightning-struck pine tree, as if welcoming the trappers to their new homesite.

The next 30 or so days leading late into the month of September found the trappers' campsite a whirlwind of activity. After breakfast each morning, Ofer, Black Eagle, Joshua and Jerimiah would take the single buck saw and their axes with rifles in hand and troop off into the stands of timber next to their new campsite. Soon, the mountain air would be ringing with the sounds of a single buck saw and several axes chopping away in the crisp morning air. In the meantime Little Raven and Gabriel would be cleaning up after the breakfast meal, squaring up their cook site, gathering in more firewood, and then taking two teams of horses up into the stands of timber where the other four 'lumberjacks' would be felling, limbing and cutting to lengths the needed logs for the walls and roof of the soon to be built cabin. Then 'teamsters' Little Raven and Gabriel would hook up the horses to the precut logs and haul them down to the cabin site. This they did until it came time to prepare the hard-working men's noonday meal. Stopping with the log hauling, the two would then prepare the 'lumberjacks' their noonday meal and with a shout, bring them off the hillside for lunch. After the noonday meal was over, the men would cease the timber cutting and taking the logs hauled off the mountain all morning long, would then begin notching and assembling the cabin's walls. By day's end, Gabriel and Little Raven would have supper ready for the hardworking men and afterwards, a refreshing bath in the nearby creek, a cup of rum and off to bed would be the 'word of the day' for the tired but pleased with their efforts, men.

The next day's activities would be a repeat of the same until by the end of that second week of work, the cabin's walls, roof and rock, mud and stick chimney were completed. As Gabriel and Little Raven moved all of their packs, sleeping furs, saddles and packsaddles into the cabin for safekeeping and out from under the frequent afternoon thunderstorms, Joshua, the Tal Brothers' best builder, found himself supervising and constructing the front door, front steps, window frames, inside table and chairs, and bedframes so the men would not have to sleep on the cold, slabbed-log wooden floor of the cabin in their sleeping furs but up off the floor.

As for the cabin's roof, it was a nature-made work of art and genius. The log roof started off with heavier logs to be able to carry the overall weight of the roof and heavy winter snows. Then smaller and smaller logs were added in layers until the roof was covered and fortified. Lastly a natural layering of first sage-brush, then grass and then dirt completed the unique roof. By so doing, the roof was stout enough to withstand the heaviest snows, preclude any moisture from seeping into the cabin and lastly, in case of an Indian attack, precluded any 'fire arrows' from igniting the roof and driving the trappers fighting from the inside, outside and into any hostile Indians' fatal field of fire.

As for the windows, another work of art by Joshua was in the offing. After the cabin had been constructed, window openings were then cut into the front and end walls of the cabin. Cut into the front walls so the trappers could control the field of fire to the front of their cabin in the event of frontal attack by the local Blackfeet. As for the window openings cut into the walls at the end of the cabin, they provided a view and field of fire facing the horses' corral, precluding any attacking Indians from easily opening the corral gate and stealing the horses in plain view of the trappers. And once again, the 'windows' were another unique work of frontier art. Joshua, after cutting window openings into the front and end walls of the cabin, then had earlier split several smaller logs into framing material. Then with the window openings framed and nailed in place, they were covered with heavily scraped-thin, almost transparent, undressed mule deerskins, which admitted sufficient light but excluded rain, snow and cold drafts from the outside. Said skins had one end nailed into the top of the frame so they could be rolled up in the summer months to allow cool air into the cabin and then let down once inclement weather was at hand.

Last to be constructed by Joshua were the three front steps and an 8"-thick log front door, built to withstand any entry by fired bullets, arrows or hefty Indians trying to smash the inside latched front door inward. Then installed by popular demand for all of the men were the split log planks constructed to give the men something flat to sit upon while 'taking care of business' over the latrine dug and placed at the back of the cabin and conveniently located downwind...

Then the work really kicked into high gear because of the approaching trapping season rushing their way as the advent and arrival of cold weather began rearing its head on a daily basis. Many dry trees, either insect killed or lightning-struck, were cut down and hauled by horse teams down to the cabin area for the men's winter wood supplies when the snows became too deep for easy woodcutting and hauling. Collaterally, Gabriel and Little Raven built two 'hell-for-stout' meat smoking racks at one end of the cabin so jerky could be made, so the men would have something to eat while out on the trail for extended periods of time. At the same time, Joshua drilled a number of holes in the interior cabin's walls with a hand auger and filled the holes with hand-carved wooden pegs. From those pegs the men could hang their rifles, wet clothing and the like. Joshua additionally drilled out a number of holes in the cabin's rafters and pegged the same so deerskin-filled sacks of jerky could be hung, as well as sacks of dried fruit, rice, beans and spices in order to keep the mice in their cabin at bay. Joshua finally split more logs and made shelves laid over wall pegs to hold other valuable items, like canisters of spices and tins of powder, up off the floor and away from the damp associated with their cabin and the normally present rodents and insects in the cabin.

Then once again, the 'lumberjacks' moved back onto the mountainside and began felling the timber needed to construct a proper corral for their horses. Horses which heretofore had been picketed on a long rope strung through the aspens near the cabin. By late that first afternoon of timber cutting, Ofer and Jerimiah had felled enough smaller trees for their entire corral. Walking back down to camp, they hitched up four of their horses, went back up onto the hillside and began hauling down the needed logs for posts and rails for the horse corral. In the meantime, Black Eagle and Joshua had been digging the needed postholes for the corral posts. When Ofer arrived, out came what remained from their 25-pound keg of nails that had been used in building their cabin. Then as Ofer and Joshua placed the posts in the pre-dug postholes and tamped them in, Black Eagle and Jerimiah cut the rails to proper lengths and began nailing them into place. Come nightfall when the men brought in their hobbled horses from the nearby meadow, the horses had a new 'home'. With that, the rope picket line used to date came down, was rolled up and placed back inside their cabin for future uses.

Needing a break away from 'household' chores, Ofer had the men saddle up one morning and loading four of their buckskins with dual panniers each, headed out down to the nearby valley floor holding numerous herds of feeding buffalo. Six dead cow buffalo later, the mineral-starved men feasted on the fresh raw livers from two of the dead cows. Then getting down to the serious business at hand, butchered out the cows, loaded the panniers full of meat and then happily headed back to their cabin. Once back at their homesite, Gabriel and Little Raven began cooking up the hardworking men's supper. A supper of spitted buffalo over the fire, a potted rice and bean mixture, Dutch oven biscuits, coffee and a previously soaked in water dried fruit mixture, heavily slathered with cinnamon, nutmeg, brown sugar and a stirred-in cup of rum. Then that special treat was slow cooked alongside the campfire so it wouldn't burn. That rounded out the men's special celebratory dinner of almost being ready for their fall beaver trapping season.

As the two camp cooks continued cooking up a meal fit for a frontier king, Ofer, Black Eagle, Jerimiah and Joshua, in a hurry before the buffalo meat in the panniers began spoiling from all the retained body heat, began cutting the chunks of meat into one-inch-wide, thin strips. As they did, Joshua took armloads of the cut-thin meat and hung it over the newly built smoking racks until they literally 'groaned' because of the weight being placed upon them. Then with a good but not too hot fire producing lots of smoke going underneath the fully loaded meat racks, the hungry and bloody men sat down to the prepared supper feast. For the next 20 minutes or so, the only sounds heard were the hungry men making fast of what was set before them before their 'empty stomachs ate the little guts' inside them... Well, that and the constant humming of the clouds of ever-present mosquitoes hovering around the men and sometimes falling into and being trapped in the food on the men's plates. Mosquitoes which soon found themselves many times instead of being dug out from the food on the plate into which they had fallen, just being eaten along with all the rest of the 'grits' by the famished and hardworking men...

Then as the smoking racks and the heavy drying smoke underneath 'worked their magic' on the always great-eating strips of buffalo meat, Ofer brought out one of their kegs of rum and a carrot of tobacco. Soon the men's cups were full of the sweet tasting rum and the air filled with the rich smell of James River tobacco smoke from the clay pipes being stoked fully and smoked. However, it seemed that the hungry clouds of mosquitoes always found a way to bypass the happy clouds of nicotine-laced pipe smoke and find an uncovered piece of skin and then 'have their supper as well'. Shortly thereafter, the men adjourned to their sleeping furs for a night's rest with the exception of Gabriel and Little Raven. For them their evening was just beginning. First they had to wash all of the metal plates, cups and eating utensils from the evening's supper. Then there was fresh water to be hauled for the morrow's rounds of cooking, more firewood to cut in order to keep the campfire going and more mountain mahogany wood to split for the meat smoking fire. Then as Little Raven kept turning the fresh buffalo meat on the racks so it would smoke appropriately, Gabriel made sure the fire underneath the smoking racks did not break out into flame but just smoked so the meat would not be overcooked and ruined as jerky.

Halfway through the night, Gabriel woke up Ofer and Jerimiah, who then spelled the two cooks until daylight was just showing itself in the eastern skies. Then Gabriel and Little Raven were awoken. Once again, they took care of their business at the communal latrine, washed up in the creek and shaved since they now had some daylight in which to see, then off to their duties at the meat pole cutting off chunks of venison and tending to the rest of their duties at the firepit. That Little Raven did, spitting the meat and all, as Gabriel mixed up his biscuit dough with water, flour, a little brown sugar (the men's favorite way of making biscuits) and dried yeast. With that, the bowl full of biscuit dough was set by the fire so it would stay warm but not cook so the yeast would cause the dough to rise. Then later with a dose of bear oil in the bottom of the heated Dutch oven, Gabriel's style of biscuits would soon be on their way. Then into their two-gallon pot of now boiling water hanging on a hanging rod over the fire went several generous handfuls of freshly roasted and just crushed green coffee beans, and soon the aromatic smell of freshly brewing 'trapper's style of coffee' was on its way. Coffee that would be strong enough to stand a mule's shoe up in the metal cup and it would not fall over... Plus, if one was to take his first sip of 'trapper's' coffee with his eyes just half-open, the strength of said coffee would flip one's eyelids wide open and they would stay that way the rest of the day! Then with a yell and a shout, the men retired to their sitting logs and enjoyed a trapper's hot breakfast out on the frontier with its Creator and all of His critters...

The rest of that day was spent tending the smoking fires, removing that meat which was ready and filling tanned deerskin bags with the valuable smoked meat for later use while out on the trail. Then those filled deerskin bags were hung from pegs in the cabin's rafters to avoid rodent damage, and by allowing the air to circulate, kept mold from forming on the jerky. As Gabriel and Little Raven tended to their meat processing details, Ofer, ever mindful of the onrushing fall beaver trapping season, retreated to the cabin and sitting on a new chair made by Joshua by an open window for the needed light, began disassembling all of their extra previously seized rifles taken from dead Indians after battles. This he did making sure of the readiness of all of their mechanical parts, cleaning out all of the black powder and lead fouling and those passing the test were reassembled. Those needing new locks or springs had them replaced and they too were then added to the 'ready for business' stack. Lastly, taking one rifle at a time that was each trapper's personal weapon, Ofer once again thoroughly tore down, inspected, reassembled, cleaned and made sure it was ready for whatever came 'its' way. That day and the next occupied Ofer's time and when completed, the group had 12 rifles in the ready inventory and that of their personal pistols as well. Then the rest of that day, Ofer set a damn sharp edge to everyone's personal blades and that of their tomahawks and straight razors. As he did, Gabriel brought in all of his cooking, scalping and chopping implements asking for them to be sharpened as well, which Ofer did.

The tired men quietly ate their supper that night after two additional weeks of hard duty, making sure they were almost prepared for the start of the fall trapping season which ran from daylight into the late dark of the night. As they did, Ofer made the next day's assignments. Ofer and Black Eagle were to cast a small mountain of bullets for everyone's rifles and pistols. Additionally, they would see to it that everyone's 'possibles' bags were filled and made ready. Joshua and Jerimiah were to assemble and check all of their beaver, wolf, pine marten and muskrat traps, making sure they were operational and smoke all of them in order to get rid of all of the 'man smells'. As for the two cooks, they were responsible to make sure they had all of the cut wood needed for their outside firepit, including cutting and stacking a supply of firewood near the cabin's front door for inside use in the fireplace once winter weather arrived, and see to it the men had good meals. Those assignments made and after a final cup of rum, everyone adjourned to their cabin, the door was locked from the inside and soon the cabin resounded with the sounds of 'tired' men making the most of their downtime.

Two days later, Ofer exited the cabin in the morning with his rifle in hand. Looking all around, he saw the two cooks working around the campfire preparing breakfast and seeing no signs of danger, headed to the latrine. Finished with the business at hand, Ofer washed up over at the creek, shaved and then walked over to the firepit where the cooks were hard at it. Sitting down on his personal sitting log, he soon had a hot cup of coffee thrust into his hand and after taking a sip of the steaming hot liquid said, "Today is the day, Boys. Fix up a lot of grub because it may be a long day afore we are back at this fire come sundown. I think the water is now cold enough that the beaver should be coming into their prime, and I think we should plan on scouting out an area where we want to begin our fall beaver trapping." With those words from the group's leader, both Gabriel and Little Raven just knowingly smiled at each other and picked up their cooking pace so that no time was lost in hitting the trail and doing something they truly loved and enjoyed even more than their cooking duties.

Later that morning found Ofer and Black Eagle leading the way out from camp, followed by Gabriel and Little Raven trailing the three loaded packhorses and Joshua and Jerimiah bringing up the rear of the trappers' caravan providing protection. As per Ofer's earlier instructions, the men now trailed three packhorses instead of the usual two. Ofer's reasoning was that now being deep into the territory of the fierce Blackfoot, he figured if they ever ran into Indian trouble they would have their hands full being faced with superior numbers of attackers. Therefore he had ordered that a third packhorse should be added to their trappers' caravan and in its panniers there would only be the extra rifles they had seized after a number of previous battles with the Gros Ventre for the extra firepower and survival presence it would represent. That way if jumped by superior numbers of Blackfeet in the country they were now trapping, between the extra rifles carried in the third horse's panniers and the battery of weapons they normally carried, they would have a fighting chance at survival. With those preparations in place, Ofer headed the men northwest as they left their campsite and deeper into the Little Belt Mountains as they followed the Musselshell. About a half-hour of travel later found the six men stopped along a rather extensive assortment of likely looking beaver dams, lodges and waterways. Additionally, as they had traversed the Musselshell that morning, they found more than ample evidence of beaver activity throughout its entire length in beaver slides and fresh tree and willow cuttings.

Dismounting, Ofer handed his horse's reins back to Little Raven and then walked back to that man's trailing packhorse. There he changed into his breechclout and buckskin leggings in preparation for the coming cold water immersions into the beaver trapping waters at hand. As he did, Joshua followed suit since he was the group's second designated trapper. Then with traps, wooden anchor poles, wire and hand axes in hand, the two men moved into the first area to be trapped. As they did, Gabriel, handing his horse's reins to Little Raven, followed along the two lead trappers carrying extra anchor poles, a bottle of castoreum and extra traps. As the men doing the trapping moved along the waterways selecting trap sites and setting their traps, Black Eagle and Jerimiah remained horsed and rode along at a short distance away on the lookout for any signs of danger, be it from an irate cow moose with calf lurking in the beaver ponds, hungry grizzly bears looking for an easy meal 'a la trapper' or wandering Blackfeet or Gros Ventre Indians chancing upon the American white men trappers afoot and defenseless. (Author's Note: The Blackfeet and Gros Ventre Indian Nations had little use for the American fur trappers because of Manuel Lisa's weapons trade restrictions. Weapons trade restrictions with those two native peoples because Manuel deemed them treacherous as a people and as a result, refused to sell them firearms. However, Lisa did openly trade such weaponry with the friendly Crow Indians, who as it turned out, were the hated enemy of the Blackfeet and Gros Ventre. The Crow with the white man's weapons were then able to dominate their enemies, the Blackfeet and Gros Ventre, which exacerbated this hatred with Lisa and the rest of the American fur trappers. So as a result, the Blackfeet and Gros

Ventre freely traded with the Canadian Hudson's Bay Fur Company traders, easily acquiring such weapons and whiskey from them with their fur trades. Then with encouragement from the British agents in the Hudson's Bay Fur Company, those two Indian Nations 'went to war' with the American fur trappers, killing and robbing many of them. This open warfare is just one of the many reasons why around 25% of the American fur trappers were killed or disappeared EVERY YEAR during the heyday of the fur trapping industry on the frontier!)

******

Sitting on his horse quietly watching the trappers' caravan leaving their cabin site that morning was "Yellow Wolf" from the Smith River Band of Blackfeet Indians, the very same Indian who had just killed a buck mule deer several months earlier as Ofer and his trappers moved into and selected the very same meadow area for their cabin site near where he had killed his deer. Sitting alongside his friend of many years sat "Bear-Moves-Fast" quietly on his horse as well. Yellow Wolf had remembered the day when the trappers had arrived in the very same area in which he had just killed his mule deer buck. But most importantly, he remembered the string of classic-looking buckskin horses they had trailed into the area as well. Yellow Wolf had vowed he would return someday when the trappers were absent their cabin and steal one or more of their excellent-looking horses and to his way of thinking, today would be a good day to add a buckskin horse or two to his small herd of horses back at his band's winter campsite. Yellow Wolf and Bear-Moves-Fast had been looking for a runaway Salish Indian slave boy earlier, but when they chanced upon the group of trappers leaving the remainder of their horse herd unattended in their corral that morning, that had left a lure and opportunity to gain some high-grade horseflesh that was just too great to pass up.

Checking the direction once again in which the trappers were heading earlier upon leaving their campsite and seeing no sign of them making an early return, Yellow Wolf kicked his horse in its flanks and slowly the two Indian men cautiously headed in the direction of the trappers' horse corral. Then Yellow Wolf got an idea and motioned for Bear-Moves-Fast to stop. Handing his horse's reins to his friend still sitting on his horse, Yellow Wolf quietly laid out his plan, dismounted and then trotted the last 100 yards over to the horse corral holding the remainder of the trappers' valuable buckskin horse herd. The buckskins smelling the unfamiliar Indian smell began nervously milling around in the corral. However, that did not deter Yellow Wolf who quickly pulled a bridle and set of reins from off a nearby corral post, leaped over the corral rails and began moving in and among the trappers' horses looking for the mount he most desired. Finally selecting the horse he wanted, Yellow Wolf quickly cornered the horse against the rails of the corral, slipped in its bridle and then walked that horse over to the corral gate. There he tied up the horse, slipped another bridle and set of reins off a corral post and once again entered the group of nervously milling horses sensing something wrong in having the unknown individual in their corral. Moments later, Yellow Wolf had cornered his second buckskin against the corral rails, bridled it and led it over to the corral gate as well. Then with a cautionary look in the direction the trappers had headed earlier, he opened up the corral gate, exited with the two buckskins, closed the corral gate and then slowly walked the two horses back to his friend in waiting some 100 yards away.

Once back with his patiently waiting friend, Yellow Wolf handed Bear-Moves-Fast a set of reins leading to one of the stolen buckskin horses. Then holding the remaining set of reins leading to the just-stolen buckskin he wanted, Yellow Wolf quickly leapt up into the saddle of his riding horse. Then just as quietly as they had arrived, the two Blackfoot Indians from the Smith River Band trailing the two stolen horses left the area to continue their hunt for the runaway Salish Indian slave boy... By only taking two horses, Yellow Wolf figured the trappers busy with their beaver catches for the day would not miss the two stolen horses in a corral full of like-in-kind horses, allowing for Yellow Wolf and Bear-Moves-Fast time to hunt down the Salish boy they had been tracking and then still make a clean getaway with two valuable and beautiful buckskin riding horses! And in so doing, not only gaining two valuable riding horses without getting caught but being able to count 'coup' against the hated American white man trappers...

******

By early afternoon, Ofer had set their 30th beaver trap near a slide covered with many entry and exit beaver tracks. Then as they usually did, the men headed for a nearby grove of trees where they dismounted and let their horses feed. Breaking out several sticks of buffalo jerky apiece from their saddlebags, the men seated themselves on a mound of dirt in their grove of trees, rested and visited after their morning's spate of hard, wet and cold work. Then with Ofer standing guard, the rest of the men snoozed for about an hour. However during the last of those quiet moments in time, Ofer once again felt his familiar sixth sense stirring from within. But just about then, the rest of his trappers awoke, gathered in their horses and remounted. While that activity was ongoing, that caused Ofer to forget about his sixth sense warnings, slight as they were. He especially forgot those warnings when Gabriel's horse bolted when a startled feeding robin rose from under its nose and in surprise over the closeness of the bird, bucked its rider off. Then with laughter from all the rest of the men over Gabriel's embarrassment over being bucked off, Ofer just wrote off his earlier eerie feelings over the just-happened horse wreck...

Working their ways back along the just set trap line, the men discovered 11 beaver already hanging drowned in their traps. Those were hurriedly skinned by Gabriel and Little Raven and their carcasses left in the area for the predatory critters to find and feast upon. Once the last trap had been checked, Ofer and Joshua removed their wet breechclouts and buckskin leggings and re-dressed into their warmer dryer clothing. Then the trappers headed for the confines of their cabin where the freshly caught beaver could be rid of the remaining meat and fat on their pelts and then hooped for the needed drying process to begin. However, that was not done until the men had stopped along a large patch of willows and cut two panniers full of willow branches suitable for the hooping process to follow for the fresh beaver pelts brought in over the next few days. Later after the trappers' arrival back at their cabin, Gabriel and Little Raven released their horses from the corral so they could feed and water. When they did, the rest of the trappers unloaded their packhorses' panniers so they could begin processing and hooping the fresh pelts. Then Gabriel walked over and removed a number of elk steaks from an elk half hanging on one of their meat poles, while Little Raven began making fires in their firepits with a fire steel so they could have a large amount of fresh hot coals for the biscuit making to come. Then as Gabriel mixed up the biscuit making dough, water and dry yeast, Little Raven set the previously set pot of rice, raisins, brown sugar cones, cinnamon and nutmeg and water cooked in the morning's fire, back near the firepit so it could re-heat for their supper.

Finished with the fresh pelt cleaning and hooping, Ofer exited the cabin, walked over to the stream, washed up and then headed for the outdoor cooking fire. There he began sipping a hot cup of freshly brewed coffee and began visiting with Gabriel and Little Raven over the quality and size of the beaver taken during that day. Then all of a sudden, Ofer dropped his cup of coffee, grabbed up his rifle and began running out into their horse meadow! Realizing something was wrong, Gabriel and Little Raven grabbed up their rifles and began running after Ofer and as they did, began wildly looking all around for any obvious signs of danger that had set Ofer off running into the meadow with their horses!

Following Ofer's lead, Gabriel and Little Raven ran into the center of the quietly feeding horse herd and then stood alongside him looking all around as he was doing for the sign of danger that he must have been seeing. For the longest time, Ofer just looked all around the fringes of timber surrounding the horse meadow as if looking hard for something. Finally Gabriel said, "What the hell are we looking for, Brother?"

"We are missing two of our horses!" said Ofer quietly, as he continued looking all around the edges of the timber surrounding their horse meadow as if looking for either the two strays or their reason why they were absent the horse herd...

With those words, Gabriel then quickly looked over the horse herd counting out loud all the while. "Damn if we aren't!" said Gabriel. Then he counted out loud one more time and came up with the same number of missing horses again! "What the hell happened?" quietly said Gabriel under his breath, as he nervously fingered his rifle as if expecting the reason for the missing horses to come charging out from the timber and attacking the three trappers standing out in the middle of the meadow at any moment.

However, while the two white men looked all around as if expecting an Indian attack at any moment, Little Raven was walking across the horse meadow looking down at the ground all the while. Finally, he waved and yelled at Ofer and Gabriel and beckoned for them to come over to where he was standing. When Ofer and Gabriel arrived over to where Little Raven was standing, he pointed to the ground at a number of horses' hoof-prints saying, "Two horses with iron shoes and two horses with no iron shoes. Two Indians took two of our horses and rode off with them this way," said Little Raven, pointing towards the line of timber lying to their south...

Soon all three men with their rifles held at the ready were

trotting along the four sets of horses' hoofprints with Little Raven in the lead doing the tracking. Finally stopping in the timber and after looking all around, Little Raven returned to Ofer and Gabriel whom he had left at the edge of the timber so they would not mess up the tracks he was following saying, "Two Indians, probably Blackfeet sat here for a while. Probably they sat there watching us leaving this morning when we left to run our trap line. Then they rode their two horses partway across the meadow, stopped and sat there for a while. Then one Indian left where the two horses were left standing and now I need to follow those tracks." With that, Little Raven backtracked himself and then with head down, began tracking some faint moccasin tracks leading towards the horse corral. Moments later he was back at the horse corral and then walking all around inside the corral with his head down obviously looking for something. Finding what he was looking for, he once again began following the mystery tracks from the horse corral all the way back to where he had left Gabriel and Ofer standing quietly watching him with more than just a keen interest.

Stopping a short way from where Ofer and Gabriel stood, Little Raven beckoned the two men over to where he had stopped. When Ofer and Gabriel arrived over to where Little Raven had stopped and were looking at him with questioning eyes, he began speaking through tightened lips. "Two Indians rode their horses this far and then stopped. Then one Indian for some reason dismounted and walked over to our corral. There he went inside, and from the looks of the scattered moccasin prints, he chased the horses all around and finally took two of them. Then he opened up the corral gate, removed two horses and then closed the gate back up. My guess is that he did that so we would not realize what he had done in just taking two of our horses. He then walked them across the meadow, met the other Indian and then the two of them took off with our horses. They did it that way so there would not be lots of suspicious tracks all over the front area of our cabin for us to see and raise an alarm. That way, by the time we discovered we were only short two horses, they would be long gone and by that time, pursuit would be all but hopeless."

With that explanation, Ofer got a strange look upon his face remembering his earlier sixth sense warning back at the aspen grove where they had all rested after setting their morning trap line and then quietly said, "The two of you have some supper that needs cooking. I suggest that you get to it. As for me, I will bring in our horses and then there is something I have to do."

Somewhat later, the horses were back in the corral, Gabriel and Little Raven were tending to their supper making but as they did, their eyes were part of the time watching Ofer over at their supply shed doing something with metal that made 'clanking sounds'... Then without explanation, Ofer walked over to the horse corral, set a shovel alongside the side of a corral rail then returned to their firepit for a cup of coffee without explanation as to what he was doing. About then the rest of the group exited the cabin, washed up after finishing with the beaver pelt processing and then unaware of the losses of two of their prized horses, came over to the firepit and joined the rest of the men not realizing the extent of their loss of valuable horses.

There as Gabriel and Little Raven served all of the men their suppers, Ofer quietly explained to the others what had happened. As he did, Black Eagle and Little Raven quickly noticed a very unusual and steely tone of voice in which Ofer spoke. Consternation among the rest of the men soon followed over the loss of such valuable horses! However, Ofer remained strangely quiet and icy calm as if he had a solution to the problem but wasn't ready to discuss it as of yet. That he subsequently did after the men had finished with their suppers. But not before listening to the rest of the men as they tried among themselves to come up with a solution whereby their remaining horses could be fully protected when they were out trapping.

That and yet they could somehow continue beaver trapping as well, without worrying about further horse loss with their full complement of trappers for the protection against Blackfoot Indian attack that offered. Finally Ofer quietly spoke up after the air around their campfire had been almost turned 'blue' by the men over the problem of future losses of horses and not having any solutions to the problem if they expected to survive as trappers in the wilderness.

"Tomorrow, I, like Little Raven, feel our horse thieves will return for more horses because of today's easy success and maybe this time, they will take all of them. If that were to happen, we would be afoot and in this country, that is akin to a death sentence. Therefore, I have a plan in mind to address this life or death issue. Tonight when it gets dark so no one can see what we are doing, we will remove those horses we need for tomorrow and picket them on a rope picket line outside the corral. Then since we have fed and watered the rest of the horses, I will wire up the corral gate once it gets dark so it can only be opened with difficulty. Then I will put the second part of my plan into action. However, now I suggest we all eat our supper just like we always do and retire to our cabin in case we are being watched by our horse thieves. Then come dark, we picket those horses needed for tomorrow as I have suggested when no one can see what we are doing. After that, I will need a little help when things get dark and quiet down around our cabin like they usually do when all of us 'hit the hay'.

Come darkness and with all their candles blown out in the cabin just like the trappers had gone to sleep, their front door opened up quietly and the trappers streamed out. Joshua and Jerimiah headed for the corral, removed those horses to be ridden and packed the next day and picketed them behind the corral. Leaving the rest of their horses inside the corral, Ofer took some of their gunstock repair wire and wired the corral gate closed so that anyone wanting to remove any more horses would have to work at unwiring the gate first in order to do so. Following that bit of work, Ofer and Little Raven began digging four shallow grave-like holes in front of the corral gate directly near where anyone trying to undo the gate wire would have to stand. Then Ofer and Gabriel headed over to their storage shed and removed four massive in size, chain rattling and metallic 'clanking' sounding 'things'...

Those four 'clanking' sounding 'things' were then laid out in the shallow grave-like places dug into the ground near where the horse corral gate had been wired shut. Then to avoid any more sounds being made outside the trappers' cabin, everyone quietly returned to the cabin and went inside. That was except for Ofer, who quietly remained outside. For the next half-hour or so, Ofer remained outside doing something with a shovel, armloads of straw and a lot of horse manure removed from inside the corral. Then he returned to their cabin and went to sleep without explanation as to what he had been doing. However as he soon discovered lying there in his sleeping furs, his sixth sense had once again returned and when it did that time, he found further sleep hard to come by.

The next morning right at daylight just like clockwork, the trappers were up. Those who had to make a trip to the latrine did so and then shaved and washed up just like they always did. In the meantime, Ofer saddled up all of the horses and pack-horses by himself as if he did not trust the rest of the group to do so. Then as Gabriel and Little Raven put the finishing touches on their breakfast, the rest of the men sat down upon their sitting logs, had some coffee and then when breakfast was ready, everyone ate just like they always did. Finishing their breakfast, the men mounted up like they always did, formed up into a protective caravan and rode out from their campsite heading to the northwest in order to check and run their trap line.

******

Quietly sitting on their horses hidden out of sight in the line of timber sat ten heavily armed Blackfoot warriors from the Smith River Band of Blackfeet Indians! Sitting among the warriors quietly sat the buck hunter who had first observed the trappers entering the area months earlier when they had first arrived, namely Yellow Wolf. However that morning, Yellow Wolf now sat upon an impressive-looking buckskin horse that he had recently stolen from the trappers! Sitting alongside his friend Yellow Wolf sat Bear-Moves-Fast. He too was riding a beautiful buckskin horse that he had recently stolen from the trappers as well. As those ten Blackfoot warriors sat there in the morning's cold in their place of hiding, they all quietly watched the six trappers streaming out from their campsite and heading off to the northwest. Just as they had done the day before when just Yellow Wolf and Bear-Moves-Fast had observed and reported to the assembled group. When they did, all of the warriors looked at each other with knowing grins over what was soon to come once they made sure the trappers were out of sight and working along their distant trap line.

An hour later, the eleventh Blackfoot Indian of the group was seen working his way through the timber towards his ten patiently waiting, sitting upon their horses, compatriots. Riding up to Yellow Wolf, the leader of the group, the arriving Indian with a wide grin on his face advised that the trappers had indeed ridden up along the Musselshell and out of sight heading for their trap line. That meant that the way was now clear to the valuable corral full of beautiful buckskin horses ready for the taking. With that, Yellow Wolf proudly led the way as the now 11 warriors with big grins of expectation on their faces headed for the undefended horse corral and the rest of the trappers' horses which were soon to be their new mounts.

Because there were only seven buckskin horses left in the corral since several had been killed, several stolen and the remainder were being currently ridden and packed by the trappers, Yellow Wolf had decided since he already had one of the beautiful and valuable buckskins, he would let his friends each have those remaining buckskin and Indian horses left in the corral. By so doing, he knew he would gain added stature in the eyes of his tribe as a leading warrior by being so giving and generous. As far as he was concerned, he was more interested in what he could steal from within the trappers' cabin like rifles, knives and rum, than adding another horse to his herd of horses back at his band's winter encampment. So as his ten happy Blackfeet rode up to the corral to select their horses, Yellow Wolf dismounted in front of the cabin and greedily ran up to the cabin's heavy log front door. That he did because he knew once all of his friends had chosen a horse from the corral, they too would come storming into the trappers' cabin to steal what items of value they could steal as well.

Throwing open the heavy log door and standing there in the doorway for a few seconds so his eyes could adjust to the dim light inside the cabin and once they had, inside Yellow Wolf eagerly went. In one corner of the cabin Yellow Wolf saw exactly what he was looking for, namely four rifles leaning against a wall just waiting to be snatched up. Running over to the rifles, he gathered up all four rifles in his arms and then let out a whoop of joy over his valuable find. Then he saw two pistols hanging from a wall peg in the cabin next to the doorway, obviously left there to grab in case someone stormed inside the cabin attacking those trappers inside. Then with difficulty, Yellow Wolf with an even bigger grin, grabbed both pistols and tucked them inside the front of his waist sash.

"YEHEWW—EYIEEE—HEYIIE!" SCREAMED THREE BLACKFEET INDIANS WHEN THEY RAN UP TO THE CORRAL GATE TO BEGIN OPENING IT AND IN THEIR GREED TO CAPTURE A HORSE, HAD BEGUN TUGGING ON IT NOT REALIZING IT HAD BEEN WIRED SHUT. THAT WAS WHEN "CLUMPP—CLUMPP—CLUMPP" BONE AND FLESH-CRUSHING SOUNDS ACCOMPANIED THE

ALMOST SIMULTANEOUS SCREAMS OF ABJECT PAIN ON THE PART OF THE FIRST THREE INDIANS RACING UP TO THE CORRAL GATE TO SELECT OUT THEIR HORSES OF CHOICE! "**EOOHOW!**" WENT A FOURTH SCREAM FROM BEAR-MOVES-FAST! THAT IRONICALLY AS THE JAWS FROM HIS 'NAMESAKE' OF THE FOURTH HIDDEN IRON-TOOTHED GRIZZLY BEAR TRAP JUST STEPPED INTO SLAMMED SHUT, CRUSHING BOTH OF HIS LEG BONES, FLESH AND TENDONS, JUST AS THE REST OF THE BLACKFEET GREEDILY JUMPED OVER THE CORRAL RAILS AFTER A HORSE OF THEIR CHOICE!

In their eagerness to select their choice of valuable buckskin horse now nervously milling within the horse corral upon seeing so many strangers running at them, the first group of quickly dismounting Indians had not observed the slightly altered ground in front of the corral gate covered with straw and horse manure. Running for the corral gate, the first four Indians ran over the four deadly grizzly bear traps once belonging to Bear Trap, and instantly discovered what such traps could do when it came to crushing one's leg bones, muscle and tendons in the blink of an eye and the snap of a trap…

When those four Indians went down screaming in the deadly iron jaws of the well-placed grizzly bear traps, instant pandemonium reigned among the remaining horse thieves now inside the horse corral! Not realizing what had just happened but upon seeing four of their kind in screaming agony because 'something had jumped out from the ground and had grabbed them', the rest of the horse thieves ran around inside the corral in terror afraid to leave!

******

Hearing the terrible screaming coming from the area of the corral, Yellow Wolf dropped all of the rifles and pistols and then ran out from the cabin just in time to see the six fur trappers running through the aspen trees behind the horse corral with rifles in hand, and the looks on their faces said it all! Then as if on cue, all six trappers stopped running at the back side of the horse corral and threw their rifles up to their shoulders. Simultaneously their rifles belched clouds of white black powder smoke that rolled across the horse corral, completely enveloping the remaining totally surprised horse stealing Blackfoot Indians! Between their four compatriots screaming out in abject pain and lying bear-trapped in front of the corral, and the whistling hot lead pouring accurately in the direction of the remaining horse thieves inside the corral, 'hell had no greater fury' than that moment in time! Those remaining six Indians just moments before trying to steal the buckskin horses madly milling around in the corral over all the surprise action, died among the nervous horses' hooves in and among the layer of horse crap in the corral. The four still screaming Blackfeet Indians who had stepped into Bear Trap's four toothed grizzly bear traps cleverly hidden in the ground just in front of the gate leading into the horse's corral by Ofer the night before, continued writhing and screaming in pain with smashed leg bones firmly crushed in the jaws of the huge traps designed to hold monster-sized grizzly bears in check!

Yellow Wolf, emerging from the trappers' cabin and seeing such a scene of carnage among his fellow compatriots, broke from the cabin's doorway and made a run for his stolen buckskin. The buckskin not being used to the smell and actions of the Indian sprinting for him and now all of the close at hand shooting and smells of fresh blood, broke and ran! Six lead .52 caliber balls now being fired from the trappers' pistols simultaneously smashed his lower jaw, broke his left shoulder, shattered a knee and drove two balls deeply into his stomach area rupturing his intestines. As it turned out, Yellow Wolf died in just as much pain as did his four compatriots who had run over the hidden grizzly bear traps, stepped onto the trap's pans and had their legs crushed! Black Eagle and Little Raven, dropping their new pistols, ran forward to the four trapped Indians screaming in pain on the ground and cut their screams short with tomahawk strikes to their heads! In so doing, both Crows had now counted 'coup' on their historical enemies, the Blackfeet.

Then aside from the smell of human urine emitted in their death throes, the acrid smell of freshly fired black powder and stirred-up horse manure dust in the warm fall day by milling horses in the corral, all was quiet. Well, except for the moaning and groaning coming from Yellow Wolf, who soon had his sounds of death near at hand cut short by Black Eagle who cut his throat!

Then after the rest of the trappers had reloaded their weapons as their friend Bear Trap had always counseled, they used the screw clamps to depress the jaws on the grizzly bear traps and removed the leg-trapped dead Indians. As Gabriel rounded up the dead Indians' horses, with the exception of the two previously stolen buckskins by Yellow Wolf and Bear-Moves-Fast, they had the Indians' long-braided scalps now removed by Ofer, woven into their horses' manes. After that chore was accomplished, Ofer slapped his bloodied red-colored hand on each horse's neck holding a scalp woven into its mane, its bridle removed and then with a slap on its rump, sent it back to wherever it came from. With that, the horses took off without any riders and as Ofer hoped, would head back to the familiar Blackfoot band's horse herd from whence they had come. And in so doing, playing on the Indian's culture and superstitions, eliminate future Blackfoot Indian depredations among their own kind and among those of the 'evil white man trappers'! Since Ofer had been doing this to the Gros Ventre, after a fashion that band of Indians stayed away from a number of the hated white man trappers along the Musselshell for fear of being killed, scalped and forced to wander forever in the 'in between world' because their bodies were not complete. Ofer figured 'what was good for the goose was good for the gander' and hoped the much dreaded Blackfeet would get the same message, hoping his scalping and red hand actions would play on their superstitions as well and keep them at bay.

The rest of that afternoon was spent by the trappers dragging the 11 dead Indians' bodies down to the Musselshell and dumping them therein. There they figured since the local grizzly bears seemed to be always frequenting the waterways looking for food, they would find the bodies and make short work of them. That being said, that would reduce any opportunity of their brethren from finding the bodies, blaming the white men trappers in the area and coming looking for them with 'blood in their eyes'. As Ofer finished, he then realized that he no longer had any feeling of his sixth sense roiling around in his body. As for Bear Trap's old grizzly bear traps, they were quietly returned to the trappers' storage shed in case there was ever a need for them again in the future...

Then the men worked until dark running their trap line for that day, removing 18 trapped beaver in the process. This they had to do because they had turned around earlier that morning in order to return and ambush the suspected horse thieves' return for more horses. In the process, they brought four beaver carcasses back with them since the men had not had the time to replenish the meat on their meat poles, which served as their meat staple for their suppers that evening. That and coffee, Dutch oven biscuits and a pot of pinto beans heavily spiced with red pepper flakes to relieve the men's constipation from consuming such a high meat diet. The next morning Gabriel and Little Raven's application of healthy doses of the fiery red pepper flakes did the trick. So much so that the latrine was found to be a favorite gathering place for the entire contingent of the Tal family of fur trappers...

Following breakfast that next morning found the usual beaver trapping contingent traveling along the Musselshell en route their new trap line's location. As usual, Ofer and Joshua did all the beaver removal from the traps once on-site and the placement of traps in new areas in which the beaver had yet to be trapped out. Then still nervous over the previous day's events, instead of lounging around in a grove of trees waiting for their new beaver sets to yield freshly caught beaver and allowing the group to relax, the men returned straightaway to their cabin site. This they did just in case other Blackfeet had heard of the buckskin bonanza at the trappers' cabin and were heading that way as well to cash in on the valuable and easy to steal horseflesh. This change in their routine trapping habits was followed for the next two weeks only to find that they had no new Indian 'takers' when it came to the trappers' uniquely marked buckskin horses or what they had in their cabin in the way of treasures.

******

One afternoon, as Chief Avonaco or "Learning Bear" of the Smith River Band of Blackfeet and his childhood friend Apisi or "Coyote", returned from a deer hunting trip, he observed a gathering of his people around the chief's tipi. Sensing a problem, Chief Learning Bear kicked his warhorse in its flanks and trotted up to the small crowd of people gathered around his tipi. When he did, the crowd respectfully parted allowing him to ride right up to the opening flap in his tipi. Just as soon as he had dismounted, Waupun or "Dawn", his wife ran out from the tipi and into the chief's arms crying. After getting her quieted down, Chief Learning Bear received the bad news of the probable death of his oldest son, Bear-Moves-Fast! Minutes later Chief Learning Bear and his friend Coyote, after learning about what had happened to his son rode out to where his band was keeping their large herd of horses. Off to one side were a number of his warriors gathered around three of the band's horses. Upon his arrival, Chief Learning Bear learned that three horses had returned from a number of his warriors who had ridden south and east toward the water called by the white men trappers, "The

Musselshell". That group of warriors led by Yellow Wolf also included the chief's oldest son named Bear-Moves-Fast, and had ridden into the Musselshell area to steal some beautifully marked buckskin horses when the trappers were away trapping. Horses that had been observed by Yellow Wolf a number of days earlier when he had been hunting in the area. Remembering what he had seen Yellow Wolf and his friend and the chief's son had ridden down to that same place and both of the men had managed to steal two of the trappers' buckskin horses with ease when they were out trapping for the day. Being so successful in stealing just two of the trappers' valuable and uniquely marked buckskin horses, Yellow Wolf and Bear-Moves-Fast had formed a small war party to head south and steal all of the rest of the much-hated white men trappers' horses. That small group of warriors had left days earlier on a quest to steal those specially marked horses and just recently, the small Indian boys responsible for watching over the band's horse herd had observed three riderless horses entering the herd from the south. When those boys had walked over to the three riderless horses entering the band's horse herd, they had discovered that all three animals carried a dried-up Indian's scalp whose long hair had been woven into the mane of each horse! One of those horses was immediately identified as that belonging to Coyote's brother. The brother who had also ridden south on the horse stealing trip with Yellow Wolf and his closest friend, Bear-Moves-Fast, the chief's oldest son! The scalp tied to the mane of Coyote's brother's horse, from the red twine used to tie up his long braids, was identified as that belonging to his youngest brother! Then the group also pointed to the dried bloody handprint on Coyote's brother's horse's neck, the same kind of handprint that had been found on some of their sister tribes' riderless returning horses, the Gros Ventre! In fact, that same kind of dried bloody handprint was found on all three horses' necks that had been ridden south by the band's warriors days earlier on the Musselshell trappers' horse stealing trip that had returned riderless the day the young horse herders had discovered them!

With the recognized bloody red handprint on each horse's neck, the same kind of symbol discovered earlier by an adjacent band of Gros Ventre, a murmur of dread had gone through the crowd gathered around the three returning horses. A murmur of a story told by their sister tribe the Gros Ventre, of an evil spirit that was mysteriously killing their warriors as well. An evil spirit that was tying scalps to horses' manes and then placing a bloody red handprint to the horses' necks before they had been released by those Indians' killers to return back to the horse stealing warriors' band of horses! Fearing the worst, Coyote faced his chief and requested that he be allowed to lead a small band of especially talented warriors to the Musselshell, and see if they could find this trapper or trappers who were killing and scalping the warriors from their sister tribe of Gros Ventre and now from the Smith River Band of Blackfoot.

With a nod of approval, Chief Learning Bear remounted his horse and then rode back to his tipi in an effort to comfort his obviously heartbroken wife over the more than likely loss of their oldest son by the evil spirit that was killing and scalping his bravest warriors, and leaving a red handprint on the rider's horse's neck as an evil warning! Coyote on the other hand with the chief's permission, gathered together his father and remaining two brothers for the trip south in the direction the last group of braves had headed. Early the next morning found Coyote, who was an excellent tracker, backtracking the three riderless horses' hoofprints from where they were seen entering their band's horse herd. From there, the hunt was now on for the evil-spirited, more than likely white man trapper, who was killing and scalping those warriors from his band and their sister tribe band of Gros Ventre... Coyote had decided that he would not rest until he had killed The Scalper of his people and had tied his scalp to his personal horse's mane for all in his band to see what a great warrior he was...

******

Returning back to camp early one afternoon with 17 freshly caught beaver pelts in their horses' panniers, Ofer and company spotted a small herd of buffalo feeding just over a rise. Having such a large number of mostly Made or very large beaver to defat and hoop out and no fresh meat hanging on their meat pole, Ofer made a command decision. Ofer and Black Eagle detached from the group of trappers heading for their cabin and began a short stalk on the small herd of buffalo. A few minutes later, a fat cow buffalo lay cooling out as Ofer and Black Eagle first feasted on some raw buffalo liver and then began butchering out the animal as she lay on the ground. About an hour later, their packhorse had just about all the weight in fresh buffalo meat that she wanted to carry in her two panniers. Then after washing off in a nearby stream their bloody hands and faces still covered with the drying blood from eating the raw liver, the two men mounted up and happily headed for their cabin. Happily did so knowing that night all of the men were going to feast to their hearts' content on freshly roasted buffalo meat.

Riding along side by side and trailing their one heavily loaded packhorse, Ofer all of a sudden stopped and began looking all around like danger was near at hand! Black Eagle, keying off the experienced Mountain Man's defensive actions, quickly grabbed his rifle up off his lap and made ready for any kind of deadly action coming his way. For the longest time, both men just sat there on their horses and looked all around like there was some kind of danger nearby. Then Ofer said, "Black Eagle, I just had one of my almost physical sixth sense feelings 'roll over me' like the rest of our group is in some sort of trouble. Let us pick up our pace and get back to our cabin just as fast as we can, just in case this feeling of mine is for real when it comes to me being thusly concerned."

With those almost overriding concerns raging through the body of Ofer, the men picked up their pace but not so much so that they were not keenly aware of everything going on around them as they hustled their horses along. Both men had spent too many miles riding along on the frontier to let their need for speed override their wilderness sense of caution. That sense for caution regardless of a now-stirring sixth sense was to soon pay itself back in life's big dividends...

Riding up to the finger of trees that fringed the lower end of the meadow leading up to their cabin, Ofer held up his hand to stop. Then almost like an afterthought, he turned his horse away from the trail normally traveled up to their cabin and headed into the dense stand of timber until he, Black Eagle and their horses were well concealed. Bailing off his horse and tying it to a tree along with their packhorse, Ofer turned to beckon for Black Eagle to do the same, only to find himself looking at his dear friend standing there already alongside him. Since no words were needed, both men began sneaking through the dense stand of conifers until they were almost at their horse corral. There Ofer once again held up his hand to 'stop' before they got too close to their horse corral for anyone to discover their presence. That he did because he knew if the horses in the corral spotted either Black Eagle or himself, they would be looking their way with interest. If the horses did that, it would be a dead giveaway to anyone watching that something of interest was there for the horses to act in such a manner. Ofer also realized that would not do if he wanted to sneak up close to the cabin to see if everything was alright. And if everything was alright around the cabin and the rest of his group of brothers and fellow trappers, then maybe his still raging sense of danger would die down and 'let his inner being alone'.

As Black Eagle and Ofer slinked into a position where they

could observe the happenings around their cabin and yet not be observed themselves, they settled in and froze all movement as if death had overtaken the two of them. For the longest time, Ofer and Black Eagle only observed Gabriel and Little Raven working around the firepit. As for Joshua and Jerimiah, they appeared to be in the cabin defatting and hooping the large number of large in size beaver they had just caught that day in a new series of waterways along the Musselshell.

About then Joshua and Jerimiah exited the cabin with coffee cups in hand and headed for the activity ongoing around the firepit. There they paused to visit with Gabriel and Little Raven for a few seconds as they poured themselves fresh cups of coffee. Then the four men began visiting once again as they took a break from the defatting and hooping details and the supper making preparations.

THAT WAS WHEN OFER AND BLACK EAGLE SPOTTED THE DANGER! Not 30 yards in front of the two men they saw movement in the bushes! Soon Ofer and Black Eagle could make out the bodies of four armed Indians slowly crawling inch by inch towards the edge of the brush lining the meadow near the cabin, as they sneaked up on the four men chatting around the firepit! Four trappers who were totally oblivious of any nearby danger! All four Indians were pushing their rifles slowly ahead of them as they crawled, and now even the horses in the corral had spotted them and were intently observing every Indian's movements. Had the four trappers not been so engrossed in their conversations, they too would have observed the corralled horses' unusual interest in something close at hand near their corral, and that would have been occasion for increased alertness as to the danger close at hand on the part of the trappers gathered around the firepit...

SLOWLY, EVER SO SLOWLY, THE FOUR CRAWLING INDIANS STALKING THE FOUR MEN AROUND THE FIREPIT CAREFULLY AROSE FROM THEIR POSITIONS ON

THEIR BELLIES TO KNEELING FIRING POSITIONS AT THE EDGE OF THE BRUSH SHIELDING THEM IN THEIR PLACES OF HIDING! AS THEY DID, THEY SLOWLY RAISED THEIR RIFLES IN UNISON SO AS NOT TO BE NOTICED MAKING ANY SUDDEN MOVEMENTS, LOWERED THEIR HEADS ALONG THOSE RIFLE STOCKS AND TOOK CAREFUL AIM AT THE STILL FOUR UNKNOWING TRAPPERS GATHERED TOGETHER SOME 30 YARDS DISTANT AROUND THE FIREPIT...

ALL OF A SUDDEN, COYOTE AND THE MAN ALONGSIDE OF HIM HAD THEIR HEADS EXPLODED INTO 'PUFFS' OF BRIGHT RED BLOODY SPEW, AS TWO RIFLE SHOTS BOOMED OUT FROM CLOSE BEHIND THEM — **BOOM—BOOM!**

Upon hearing rifle fire so close to them, Gabriel, Little Raven, Joshua and Jerimiah whirled around to face the sounds of danger obviously dangerously close at hand! Out from the edge of the close at hand brush field hiding Ofer and Black Eagle rolled two white clouds of black powder smoke, clouding everything in its path for an instant!

THEN **POW—POW!** WENT TWO QUICK PISTOL SHOTS INTO THE REMAINING TWO KNEELING INDIANS GETTING READY TO SHOOT AND STILL IN SURPRISE OF THE MOMENT OVER HEARING THE TWO QUICK RIFLE SHOTS BEING FIRED FROM JUST FEET BEHIND THEM, AND THEN BEING SPEWED WITH BODILY ESSENCE FROM THEIR TWO NOW DEAD COMPATRIOTS! Both .52 caliber pistol balls churned through the two Indians' backs, mushroomed into their internal organs and then blasted clear through their chests and then blasted into the open air on the other side! Both men instantly were blown forward out onto the open ground by the bullets' impacts, where they could be seen by the four men around the firepit and then did their death quiver as their essence drained from their bodies! By now, the world of the four trappers standing around the firepit was in a whirl and an uproar of surprise over what had just occurred! Then the four trappers quickly went for their rifles, still in shock over what they figured they were being shot at from such close-in range! Then the brush near the horse corral 'exploded' with the bodies of Ofer and Black Eagle lunging forward with upraised tomahawks and then slamming them into the heads of the four Indian ambushers in quick succession making sure the killing was complete. THEN IT WAS ALL OVER EXCEPT FOR STILLING THE TRAPPERS' MADLY BEATING HEARTS, ON BOTH SIDES! Well, that and the further surprise of having the coffee pot on the hanging rod over the fire explode its dark brown contents into the blazing fire, as one of the exiting .52 caliber pistol balls blew through the first Indian and slammed into the coffee pot by accident. That and the other .52 caliber ball exiting its back shot Indian target, rolled across the ground and then stopped at the point of Joshua's moccasin! Then in the following micro-seconds of excitement, Ofer and Black Eagle had to yell at the four trappers drawing down on them in the panic of the moment to avoid joining the four dead Indians on the ground over being accidently shot by their own surprised and now emotion-charged fellow trappers! It took about another five minutes for everyone to completely finally settle down over nearly being killed and by those lucky enough to be on hand to do the killing! Then all kinds of backslapping and "Thank the Good Lord Above" exclamations filled the air over the fact that no one was killed except for those who needed a damn good killing...

Later as Ofer scalped all of the four now dead Indians, the rest of the men assisted by weaving the dead men's scalps in their finally discovered tied-off horses some distance from the trappers' camp, but the bloody handprint slapped on each horse's neck duties fell to its originator... Then once again, all of the horses had their bridles removed so they could more easily feed along the way home and then were released in the hopes they would return to their familiar band of horses back at the Indians' encampment. And in so doing, spook the hell out of the Indians once they saw the scalps and bloody handprint on the necks of the horses from sending such killing parties after the white men trappers in the future. Such scalp and bloody hand displays on the returning horses' necks seemed to have deterred the far-ranging and depredating Gros Ventre, and now Ofer hoped it would work its magic on the tribe of the four dead men just identified by Black Eagle as Blackfeet. Only time would tell as to who was going to last the longest in this deadly game of 'frontier-chance'...

That evening after a supper of roasted buffalo meat, beans, Dutch oven biscuits and coffee produced from their last undamaged coffee pot, as Bear Trap had earlier suggested be purchased way back in St. Louis in case one was destroyed, the men celebrated. Out came a flat wooden rum keg (flat because it packed better on a horse) and needless to say, the rum fairly flowed that evening in the celebration of life... But from now on, the men realized they were the hunted, being now that the Blackfeet realized they were there and realized they had best act accordingly or they would become meals for the critters of the forest as well.

******

Four days after Coyote had assembled a war party consisting of his father, his remaining two brothers and himself and had headed south towards the Musselshell to see if he could find who was doing the killing of the Blackfoot Indian warriors, weaving their scalps into their horses' manes and slapping a bloody red handprint on the necks of the men's horses, a number of warriors approached Chief Learning Bear's tipi. Summoning the chief from within, he soon emerged only to be confronted by four of his serious-looking warriors leading two riderless horses. Chief Learning Bear immediately recognized one of the riderless horses as that being the favorite warhorse of his long-time friend Coyote! Walking over to Coyote's warhorse, the chief observed a recently removed scalp whose long braid had been woven into the horse's mane and was hanging down and slowly twisting in the wind! Then the chief's eyes moved over to that portion of the horse's neck next to its head. There for all to plainly see was the bloody and now familiar smeared handprint on the animal's neck!

For the longest time, the chief just stood there realizing first it had been his son and now his dearest friend and one of his best warriors who had fallen to the 'evil one' doing all of the killing and bloody hand-printing on his warriors' horses' necks. It was now plain to the old chief that The Great Spirit was angry with his 'children', not only the Gros Ventre but the Blackfeet of his Smith River Band as well! With that realization, the highly superstitious chief had one of his warriors go and bring to him the Smith River Band's Medicine Man. Moments later, the Medicine Man arrived and looking in the direction in which his chief was pointing, saw the dried scalp dangling from Coyote's horse's mane and the now much known about among the Gros Ventre and other Blackfeet bands, the characteristic dried bloody red handprint on the horse's neck! The Medicine Man upon seeing the fresh scalp dangling and slowly twisting in the wind just sadly shook his head. Coyote had been the Smith River Band's finest warrior in battle, next to their powerful chief, one of the band's bravest and for many moons the most blessed by The Great Spirit. Now he was gone and with him went his powerful medicine! To the Medicine Man, the loss of the chief's most respected son and now Coyote, the band's most powerful warrior, was clearly an omen that the Smith River Band of Blackfeet had fallen out of favor with The Great Spirit, as had a number of bands of the Gros Ventre.

Turning to the chief, the Medicine Man intently looked right into his dark eyes saying, "The Great Spirit does not favor us for something wrong that we have done. 'Last Moon of the Popping

Trees' when you wanted to attack the winter encampment of the peaceful Salish for the slave peoples it would produce for our band, I, after going through the Sacred Sage Smoke Ceremony, advised you not to do so because of the 'bad signs' that I saw in the smoke. But you listened to your young warriors like Coyote, Yellow Wolf, Bear-Moves-Fast and even your oldest warrior, who counseled for the attack against the peaceful Salish to our west... You finally listened to those young warriors and now they are all gone, apparently killed and scalped by the 'Powerful One' with the scalping knife and bloody hand! After the attack against the Salish, the Gros Ventre for their many attacks against the white men trappers, and now the Blackfoot have suffered at the hand of the unknown Scalper. We gained many slaves and women from that attack on the Salish, but now we have lost a large number of our best warriors whose tipis now wail with the 'Songs of Death' sung by their hungry women and children! To me and the 'Spirits' around me, I have recently felt a coldness of spirit that only comes with the snows. I am afraid unless you do something to appease The Great Spirit, our band will suffer even more at His hands for the misery we brought to the gentle Salish People. An attack against the Salish even after I advised against it and the 'Gods of Smoke' told me only an ill wind bringing death would come from such an action."

As the band's Medicine Man spoke his words to the chief from his heart, Learning Bear's mind was for once truly listening. With a wave of his hand, the chief finally dismissed the Medicine Man because he had heard what he needed to hear. He then dismissed the warriors holding the 'Death Horses' with instructions that never again should any of their band ride those horses so marked for the evil spirits it would bring to the rider. They were to be allowed to run with the herd, but any foals they produced were never to be ridden as well. With that, the great chief went back inside his tipi, sat down next to the fire and had his wife bring him some sage and tobacco so he could perform a sacred ritual he now needed to do... The rest of that afternoon, Chief Learning Bear spoke to the spirits and burned offerings of sage and tobacco. By the end of that day, Chief Learning Bear of the Smith River Band of the Blackfeet had made up his mind as to how he would deal with The Scalper whoever he was, for what he had done to some of his finest warriors, dearest friends and his son...

CHAPTER 8 — "TRUCE", OF MUSKRATS, MARTEN AND FORT MANUEL

FOR THE NEXT MONTH BEFORE FREEZE-UP AND AFTER THE fight with the four Blackfeet, the Tal trappers' campsite was once again a whirlwind of peaceful activity. Winter wood had to be cut and stacked for easy use when the snows became too deep for easy access and woodcutting movement in the Little Belt Mountains. The men's meat poles and smoking racks fairly groaned under the combined weight of buffalo and elk meat, and many an evening found the men defatting and hooping the wealth of beaver skins being taken from the Musselshell on a daily basis. Additionally, bullets for the pistols and rifles were cast nightly until Ofer was satisfied with their reserve supply, and every firearm was once again disassembled, repaired if needed and given a thorough cleaning from the almost constant black powder and lead fouling when in use. Then after supper on many a night, the men were commonly found in their cabin working under the light from their beeswax candles and the light from their indoor fireplace repairing clothing, making new winter moccasins (thicker and heavier-made from bull buffalo hide), and the almost constant bundling of the dried beaver pelts for transport to Fort Manuel come summertime.

Finally came the day when Ofer decided the ice on the waterways was becoming too thick to easily trap for fear of the trappers becoming too cold in the freezing waters for their own safety or having their valuable beaver traps frozen in the mud and lost. With that, their beaver trap line was pulled for the season. However, their work did not stop there. They still had to smoke their muskrat and marten traps, continue bringing in buffalo meat for their meat poles and smoking racks, and constantly cutting and splitting wood on a daily basis. But as they did, the trappers were forever, especially after the fight with the four Blackfeet who had pulled a sneak attack upon their camp earlier in the year, on the lookout for the next signs of danger from the fierce Blackfeet or the ever-wandering and mean as snakes, Gros Ventre. Additionally, every time they ventured forth from the confines of their campsite, they always trailed one extra packhorse above and beyond what they normally needed, carrying two panniers with a number of fully loaded rifles they had acquired in battles with the Blackfeet and Gros Ventre over the many months since they had begun trapping along the beaver-rich Musselshell. Ofer's thinking was with a combination of their personally carried firearms and the extras carried in their reserve panniers, given the opportunity of a fair fight with any group of Indians, they stood half a chance of surviving. And at the very least, if overrun and killed, they would at least give a fair accounting of themselves by making their attackers pay a high price for taking on the six very heavily armed trappers. (Author's Note: Historical records are replete with passages regarding the various Indian tribes' reluctance to do battle unless surprise of attack was on the side of the attacker, they had overwhelming numbers over their enemy, or they were faced with desperation which forced their hand. Additionally, due to their many battles with the white man and among other enemy Indian tribes, deaths resulting from buffalo hunts or with grizzly bears or white man's diseases, male Indian numbers generally remained low among many tribes. Because of those factors, the constant taking of young hostages and raising them as their own to buttress the tribes' numbers of males and careful calculation before going into battle was a common practice in order not to lose large numbers of their fighting men. Hence, many tribes practiced caution against any unnecessary losses. And facing numbers of accurate shooting and heavily armed trappers or in later years the U.S. Army, was not considered wise by most Indian tribes. Even during the Battle of the Little Bighorn, the Indians did not attack until they felt they were cornered and had superior numbers before they did so with several thousand Indians against several hundred of the Seventh Cavalry soldiers!)

******

One morning as Ofer was in the cabin filling his 'possibles' bag with more lead balls and a tin of powder, he heard Gabriel, who was at their outside firepit preparing breakfast for the men because it had yet to snow and the trappers preferred eating outside, yell out, "INDIANS!" Grabbing his rifle from where it lay against the inside cabin wall next to the door for use in emergencies, Ofer streamed outside from the cabin and quickly looked all around for the danger Gabriel had warned about. As he did, Joshua, Jerimiah and Little Raven exiting the cabin at about the same moment in time, did so as well. Black Eagle, detained back at their latrine and upon hearing the warning yell, hurriedly pulled up his buckskin pants, grabbed his nearby rifle and ran for the front of the trappers' cabin as fast as his moccasin feet could carry him! He quickly rounded the side of the cabin and with searching eyes, headed over to join his brothers.

Gabriel, busy checking his baking biscuits in the two Dutch ovens, had his head down and had failed to see the two approaching Indians slowly riding across their horse meadow towards the cabin! But upon looking up moments later, he was startled to see the two Indians now quietly sitting on their horses just 30 or so feet away intently watching him! In fact, they were so close, they could have easily killed him and he would have never even realized what had happened… But their closeness did not stop him from reaching over, grabbing up his rifle lying against a sitting log so he could be ready for any kind of action that followed and swinging it up into a 'ready' defensive position!

Seeing the other men now holding their rifles at the ready and not seeing any dangerous movement by the two Indians, Ofer lowered his rifle and in sign, bid the two silently looking on and stoic-appearing Indians, "Welcome". Then Ofer heard the oncoming Black Eagle running up next to him, stopping and facing the Indians, quietly uttering the dreaded word, "Blackfeet"!

Then for the longest time, the two Indians just stared hard at the assembly of armed trappers and they in turn just stared right back with Indian-experienced frontier 'hardened' eyes. Then Ofer once again signed "Welcome", and that time Chief Learning Bear nodded his head in acknowledgment. Then without warning, Chief Learning Bear quickly dismounted, handed his horse's reins to his son who remained upon his horse and then strode forcefully over to where Ofer quietly stood watching his every oncoming move.

Striding right up to Ofer and then in sign, Chief Learning Bear signed, "Strange White Man, my son and I have ridden for two days following the tracks left by some of my warriors who were heading for the Musselshell looking for a number of white trappers like you and your men. Those horse tracks led directly to your campsite! Those warriors were looking for the one we call The Scalper. This Scalper is a white trapper who has been killing and scalping not only the Blackfeet but some of our brothers the Gros Ventre, now for a number of moons. Then this Scalper who has been killing warriors from both tribes, scalps them, ties their scalps to the manes of their horses and then placing a bloody handprint on our warriors' horses' necks, and allows those horses to return to the horse herds they came from. This I figure The Scalper did so as to warn other warriors not to attempt to steal the white trappers' horses or kill them for trapping in our sacred lands." Then Chief Learning Bear stopped signing and just looked long and hard at Ofer for his reaction as to what had been just signed.

What the great Blackfoot chief saw was only a cold, deadly looking stare coming right back at him from the white man trapper over what had been signed. Chief Learning Bear, a man of many seasons and life's experiences, then realized the look he was getting back from the white man trapper standing in front of him was none other than that coming from the one his people were calling The Scalper! The one and same man who had not only killed one of his sons but his best friend Coyote, as well! With the coming of that realization, the great chief tensed up internally with the emotion suffered over his great losses! However, when he did, he also realized that the steady and intense look in the white man trapper's eyes standing in front of him had just also changed. Especially when he had sensed the understanding and recognition change in the chief, realizing for the first time that he was now facing the very deadly man his tribe called The Scalper! In that very instant when the chief had realized he was facing the killer of his son and best friend, the man standing before him had just slightly altered his hand from that on the wrist of his rifle to that of the butt of the pistol he was wearing in the sash around his waist! It was plain to the great chief that if he let his emotions overcome his common sense and he did something foolish, like trying to kill this man he suspected was The Scalper, he would soon be a dead man! A dead man from a quick pistol shot from the trapper facing him, and would soon join those who had been scalped, had their scalps tied to their horses' manes, a bloody red handprint placed upon his horse's neck and the animal turned loose to return to its familiar herd... But killing such a man was not why he had come to the suspect trappers' cabin and had confronted him. He was here now on a higher calling required by The Great Spirit...

For the longest moment in time, the chief's and Ofer's dark eyes just looked hard at each other in silence and yet in a frontier form of respect. Respect because both in that moment in time had come to the realization and tacit understanding that they were both nothing more than two stars passing each other in the night's sky...soon to burn out and be forgotten!

At that singular moment in time, Chief Learning Bear came to the realization once again that it was HIS people after all who had come to the Musselshell to steal the white man's valuable and life-giving horses and kill those trapping the beaver. Then the chief 'heard' the prophetic words of warning once again from his Medicine Man in the back of his mind and in his heart. He realized his Medicine Man had spoken strong words about The Great Spirit being angry with his people for what they had done to the many white man trappers caught and killed, as well as what they had done to the gentle Salish People living to their west during their earlier winter attack. Lastly, the chief realized that his and that of his present son's mortality were hanging in the balance in front of all the heavily armed and ready to defend what was theirs, trappers. Especially if he tried to avenge his tribe's earlier losses of warriors, paid no heed to the wise words from his Medicine Man, showed his understanding that he was staring at The Scalper and made any foolish killing move now rising up in his heart over the nearness of his tribe's most deadly nemesis...

It was then that the great chief's wisdom came to the forefront of his soul and he found the teachings of The Great Spirit rising up inside of him. Then Chief Learning Bear, still not letting his dark eyes leave those of Ofer, began signing once again. "Brave white man, I am Chief Learning Bear of the Smith River Band of the Blackfeet Nation. I have come to bury the war ax between our people. From now on as long as I am the chief of the Smith River Band of Blackfeet, peace shall reign between my people and those white man fur trappers in my country. That is as long as the white man fur trappers do not fire on us, my people will not fire on them. However, my people will always make war against the hated Crow and those white men residing in the fort called "Manuel" far to our south and east." Then in another surprising move, Chief Learning Bear reached for his sheath knife, quickly drew it and sliced its blade across the palm of his now open hand! Then holding up his bloody hand and extending it towards Ofer, he held it steadily there as it continued dripping blood and as his eyes never left those of Ofer's. Then Ofer heard Black Eagle quietly whisper to him, "Four Scalps, he wants to be your blood brother. That is a great honor! Take your knife, draw it across the palm of your hand and then clasp his hand. By so doing, that makes the two of you blood brothers because of the mixing of the blood from the two of you," continued Black Eagle quietly, as he hardly dared to breathe over the actions now taking place between two deadly enemies!

Without ever letting his eyes leave those of the chief's, Ofer removed his pistol hand from the butt of his pistol, laid his rifle down against a sitting log, pulled out his sheath knife and drew its sharp blade across the palm of his hand without showing any sign of pain as well. Then reaching out, he clasped the extended hand of Chief Learning Bear of the Smith River Band of the Blackfeet Nation, all the while never letting his cold stare leave that of the chief... Little did Ofer realize that when he had reached out to the chief and had clasped his hand in friendship, Black Eagle had tightened his hands around his own rifle just in case the Blackfoot chief, a hated enemy of his Crow People, made any deadly move toward Four Scalps, his dearest of friends, life-giving mentor and father figure.

"BREAKFAST IS READY!" said Gabriel loudly, as he tried to soften the intenseness of the moment. Then turning, he removed the roasting chunks of buffalo meat from the 'iron spitting rods', laid the meat down in a large heated metal bowl so the men could dish out what they wanted, laid out two Dutch ovens' worth of piping hot biscuits on another plate alongside their jug of warmed-up honey, put a ladle into the just removed from the fire pot of beans, and then removed the coffee pot and held it ready to pour into the metal cups for all of the men as a further gesture of friendship between the two groups of men.

All of the trappers and two Indians dismounted or slowly walked over to the sitting logs around the firepit, all the while never taking their eyes off each other! That was except for Jerimiah. Taking his rifle just in case people changed their minds, he headed for the cabin and moments later emerged carrying several swatches of gray cloth and a tin of bag balm. Then walking over to the firepit where everyone else was beginning to eat their breakfast and yet keeping a close and still suspicious eye on each other, he walked over to where Chief Learning Bear was just starting to eat his breakfast with just his uninjured hand. There Jerimiah gestured toward the chief's still bloody hand with a swatch of the gray cloth in one hand and the tin of bag balm in the other. As he did, the chief looked up with a questioning look upon his face. Then Jerimiah slowly took the chief's bloody hand, wiped the blood off and taking some bag balm, gently rubbed its healing jelly into the open knife wound. Then he took the swatch of cloth and gently bound the chief's injured hand. Then walking over to Ofer, he repeated the procedure of caring for the open wound on his hand as well. When he did, no one said anything but the chief noticed the caring from the unknown trapper and smiled his great fullness, as did the chief's son.

Once the uneasy group of men had finished breakfast, the Indians prepared quietly to leave without fanfare. However, before they left, the chief walked over to Ofer and once again the two men exchanged a handshake of 'friendship'. Then the two Indians mounted up and without another word or backward look, rode off in the same direction that they had come from earlier that morning. As they did, Chief Learning Bear remembered his friend and warrior Yellow Wolf on one of his horse stealing trips had returned trailing a beautiful buckskin horse that he had obviously stolen from a fur trapper. Then on another horse stealing trip to the area of the Musselshell, he had ridden that beautiful buckskin. After that trip, Yellow Wolf had failed to return and had been presumed killed by The Scalper! Killed by The Scalper because the other warrior, namely Bear-Moves-Fast, who had ridden with Yellow Wolf on that same trip had another horse, other than the buckskin he had also stolen and ridden earlier that morning, return with his scalp tied into its mane and with a bloody handprint on its neck! Without a word but many thoughts, Chief Learning Bear noticed the trappers had a corral full of beautiful buckskins just like the one Yellow Wolf and Bear-Moves-Fast had stolen on one of their horse stealing trips. It was then that the chief realized he had truly stared into the eyes of the much-dreaded man among his people called The Scalper, and did not have a bloody red handprint on the neck of his horse or his scalp tied into its mane...

******

The next morning after being visited by Chief Learning Bear, the trappers awoke to two feet of snow, sullen, low-lying gray skies, with more snow on the way. Two days later the snows let up in the Little Belt Mountains and the men dug their ways out, as they shoveled a much-needed path to the latrine, the horse corral and their close at hand stacked pile of logs and split cordwood. With the snows came the deep freezing temperatures and soon all the previously open waters in and around the

Musselshell had frozen over with a hard and deep layer of ice, more than ending the fall beaver trapping season.

As Gabriel and Little Raven fixed breakfast in their cabin's fireplace, Ofer had the men dress warmly for the coming day's endeavors. As the men quietly ate their breakfast of biscuits and spitted buffalo, Ofer said, "Today we break out the muskrat traps and go trapping. As my brothers remember back on the farm, Father had me trapping muskrats all months of the year. That was because they always riddled our drainage canals with their digging, causing our levees to leak out our irrigation water and many times, wash out the banks of our canals. So today I am going to show all of you how to trap muskrat. They won't bring more than 25¢ per skin, but it is something to do and will supply us even more money when we get back to Fort Manuel and sell all of our furs this coming summer. Then once we get our muskrat traps set and start catching some 'rats' as they are called, we can take the meat and use it as well as their tails as marten bait once we begin running our marten traps. Additionally, spitted and roasted muskrat is pretty good eating for a change in our diets. So let us finish our breakfast, saddle up our horses and packhorses and get going in trapping some muskrats now that the ice is thick enough to hold our weight."

Later that morning the trappers streamed out from their campsite in two feet of snow. Once again, they trailed three packhorses, with the third packhorse also sporting two panniers carrying a number of rifles taken over the many previous months from the Blackfeet and Gros Ventre in different battles. That they did for the extra protection those extra rifles offered such a small group of men if attacked by superior numbers of Indians. This they also did just in case the 'breakfast' pact or truce they made with Chief Learning Bear failed to 'hold any water' or they ran into any Gros Ventre war parties hunting the much-hated white trappers.

Once out and around the now frozen-over watered areas

around the Musselshell, Ofer showed the men how to recognize a "muskrat push-up". The muskrat push-up being nothing more than a mound of grasses, aquatic plants and plant stems pushed up into a mound over the ice, hiding a breathing hole around the frozen watered areas for muskrat use as they swam and foraged underneath the ice. Upon discovery of such a push-up, a small amount of the plant materials was moved aside near the breathing and exit hole being kept open in the ice. Then a small muskrat trap was placed near the hole in the ice in and among the plant materials. Somewhat later when the muskrat came up through the breathing and exit hole carrying some plant material on which to sit and eat on the ice, it would get caught in the trap and soon the men would have another pelt to sell during the summer when at Fort Manuel. Then throwing the rats into their panniers, they could later be skinned by all the men once off the ice and their carcasses either tossed away for the other critters to eat or retained. Or skinned back at the cabin and the meat and tails used later as lures or bait when they established and ran a marten trap line in the heavy forests. Then once again, the skins could be hooped with the fresh willows, dried and later bundled up and transported to Fort Manuel for sale. For the next two weeks the men ran their muskrat trap lines very successfully, and then Ofer decided it was time to not only set out their wolf traps but establish a marten trap line in the dense forests of the Little Belt Mountains because those animals would now be in their prime as well.

Following breakfast on a later date, the men retrieved their wolf and marten traps and set out heading deeper into the forests above their cabin to the northwest. However, that first morning of travel looking for good wolf trap set sites, the men ran into a party of about 20 Blackfeet Indians! When the two groups of men stumbled onto each other, the vastly outnumbered trappers headed for a dense site of timber, tied off their horses and prepared for battle. Soon the group of Indians cautiously approached the men and when they did, Black Eagle said out loud so all of the rest of the men could hear him, "It's Blackfeet!" Using the pine and fir trees as cover, the men waited for the inevitable since they were so badly outnumbered. As the Indians slowly approached the trappers obviously preparing for battle, their leader stopped and then rode forward a few yards from his cluster of men. He then raised his right arm in the universal sign of peace. Seeing that, Ofer moved away from his group of trappers by a few yards and raised his right arm in the sign of peace to the Indians as well, hoping they had not forgotten the truce pact between Chief Learning Bear and himself. However when he did, he kept his fully cocked rifle at the ready just in case it was a trick meant to lure the trappers into better rifle and arrow range.

With that and a wave of acknowledgment, the Blackfeet Indians whirled their horses around and rode off towards a small herd of buffalo lying to their southeast. Breathing a sigh of relief, Ofer turned and headed back to his unhorsed trappers waiting to see what the outcome would be between the two groups of men. Moments later the Blackfeet rode off out of sight and began killing the buffalo and with that, the trappers led by Ofer mounted up and continued on their way looking for good wolf trapping sites. However, they still kept an eye on their back trail just in case… For the next month and after several more run-ins with other groups of Blackfeet Indians, a simple gesture of peace and both groups proceeded on their ways as if nothing out of the ordinary had occurred. Soon, the trappers began relaxing more and more every time they ran across groups of Blackfeet Indians out riding or hunting in the back country. Chief Learning Bear's word was good and with his truce, fighting with the Blackfeet was just one less thing the trappers had to worry about.

As winter progressed into spring, the men continued running their wolf trap line one day and then their marten trap line the next. Following that, the order would be changed and the wolf trap line would be run one day and the muskrat trap line the next. That was because the wolf pelts being the most valuable of those three species being trapped, that trap line needed to be run daily. By tending the traps in such a manner, hungry wolves would not be eating their own kind found hanging in the trappers' traps if left too long unattended. As for the muskrats, not much ate them hanging in the traps partially concealed in the plant covered push-up except for a few nosy ravens, mink, river otter or wandering coyotes who just happened to be out on the ice and discovered a 'free' trapped muskrat 'dinner'.

Finally with the arrival of spring and the warmer weather, the ice soon left the watered areas of the Musselshell and its surrounding areas. The leaving of the ice allowed for the ending of the muskrat trapping and the arrival of the beaver trappers. Soon Ofer and Joshua were collecting many dead and heavily furred and very prime beaver from their spring set traps. This they did after they had closed down their wolf, marten and muskrat trapping lines in favor of the more productive beaver trap lines. As the beaver trappers collected their bounty from the waterways, Black Eagle and Jerimiah continued providing cover against any types of either animal or human dangers, while Gabriel and Little Raven provided the trapping team support as well as doing all of the beaver skinning on-site. That regimen and allotment of group members led to a very relaxed and efficient beaver trapping operation in light of Chief Learning Bear and Ofer's earlier truce between the Smith River Band of Blackfeet and the trappers.

ZIPP-ZIPP-ZIPP-ZIPP—BOOM! flew a hail of arrows and a speeding rifle ball from ambush right at daylight at the two trappers providing protection to the men below them running the trap line! The rifle ball hit Black Eagle and blew him off his horse, while three of the arrows aimed at Jerimiah missed but the fourth slammed into his torso, clearing him from his saddle as well! **BOOM—BOOM—BOOM!** went one quick and two subsequent rifle shots in the direction of Little Raven and Gabriel at the same time, fired from a grove of aspens alongside the water's edge as they were in the process of skinning out two rather large, over 60 pounds each, beaver! As fortune would have it, one rifle bullet skidded across the back of Gabriel's right hand as he was skinning out his beaver. When that first shot boomed out, its speeding bullet grazed his hand causing him to jump in surprise and pain! That quick reflex action and jump from pain saved his life. For the next bullet coming his way microseconds later meant for his chest, struck the large beaver tossed upwards after the first bullet's impact with his hand caused Gabriel to toss his beaver upward in pain and surprise from that first bullet strike! **SMACK!** went the heavy slug into the thrown upwards beaver carcass as that bullet's impact slammed the beaver's carcass back into Gabriel's chest, knocking him backwards from the impact and causing him to stumble into the icy waters of the nearby beaver pond with a loud "KER-PLUSH"! As for Little Raven standing sideways to Gabriel, a simultaneously loud **SMACK!** from another arriving speeding lead ball meant that he had taken a solid hit! Down went Little Raven in a crumpled heap from the bullet's impact and soon he was rolling around on the bank of the beaver pond in pain! As Little Raven rolled around in pain, his three ambushers after shooting at the two nearby trappers, burst out from their hiding place of ambush within the aspens and with empty rifles hurriedly left behind, attacked the two trappers with upraised tomahawks!

Little Raven, seeing the three Indians running right at him with upraised tomahawks through pain-filled eyes after being hit with a rifle bullet, grabbed his burning side and stood up to defend himself. Quickly looking down, he smiled through his pain with typical Indian toughness. The rifle bullet fired at him and meant to kill him had only struck and dented the hell out of his sheath knife's blade! Grinning in pain over the fact that The

Great Spirit had allowed the bullet to hit his knife blade as it rested in his knife sheath, he staggered backwards in the fierce face of his attackers, drew his pistol that Ofer had purchased for him and shot the closest charging Indian right in his face! When he did, that face shot Indian and the one running right behind him with upraised tomahawk plowed into Little Raven with a heavy sounding "THUMP"! With that, into the nearby icy cold waters of the beaver pond all three men flew from the collision's impact! Thrusting the two Indians off him and struggling up out of the water, Little Raven was hit a glancing blow with the third charging Indian's tomahawk, knocking Little Raven to the bank and out cold! Realizing he could now kill his defenseless adversary, the Indian who had knocked Little Raven unconscious reached down and jerked his head up by one of his long braids to administer the killing tomahawk strike!

"SWISH" went Gabriel's sheath knife, as he in turn recovered from being knocked 'by the Indian's rifle bullet slamming the dead beaver tossed into the air' into the beaver pond! Gabriel grabbed Little Raven's attacker from behind and in the emotion of the moment, jerked him backwards and slammed his razor sharp sheath knife's blade so hard against the man's neck, that he completely severed Little Raven's attacker's head from his neck! Being that he had put so much force behind his knife thrust and having the man's head come off the neck so easily caused Gabriel to stumble once again and fall backwards into the beaver pond with a huge "SPLASH"! However, the icy cold water caused him to blow out all of the air from his lungs in shock when submerged, causing him to bolt upright out from the icy water and stagger back to the bank of the beaver pond.

"HI-YI-YI—HI-YI-YI-YI!" screamed two Indians bursting out from where they had been lying in ambush waiting for the beaver trap setters to get close enough to them so their attack would be a total surprise and successfully carried out! However, The Great Spirit did not smile on those two attacking Gros

Ventre... Hearing the rifle shot up on the distant bank where Jerimiah and Black Eagle had been sitting on their horses providing protection, was just the 'edge' needed in giving Ofer and Joshua adequate warning that all was not going well along the Musselshell that morning. As they scrambled out of the water where they had been retrieving several dead beaver from their traps, their running through the deep water had only been hastened when they heard the next quick and obviously coordinated series of shots being fired at Little Raven and Gabriel nearby!

Upon hearing and seeing their attackers, Ofer dropped the dead beaver he had been carrying and as he ran out from the deep water where he had been working, plowed right into one of the hard-charging Indians with an upraised tomahawk yelling at the top of his lungs! Quickly drawing his pistol from his waist band as he ran, Ofer shot the hard-charging and extremely near Indian in the belly with his one and only shot—**BOOM!** The closeness of the hard-charging Indian carried his now collapsing body right into Ofer and the two of them with a loud sounding "WHUMP" from their bodily impacts, sailed backwards into the deeper water with a loud "SPLASH"!

As for Joshua, his hard-charging and extremely close Indian was so near, all Joshua could do was slam his attacker in the face with the body of the dead beaver he had been carrying! That caused Joshua's attacker to stumble in the water and mud and fall right alongside the fur trapper with a loud "SPLASH"! Jumping right back up, the Indian with his tomahawk drew back his arm to strike Joshua, only to have the bones in his face busted all to hell when Joshua's tomahawk, swung with the full force of adrenaline, slammed just underneath the attacker's nose and sliced deeply into the upper jaw section of his skull! In fact, Joshua's tomahawk swing had such energy and force behind it that when he struck his attacker in his face with the blade, it broke the handle off his weapon, killing his attacker instantly!

With that, the beaver pond area was a whirlwind of yelling, charging horses, running Indians, shooting and an air full of loosed arrows! However, by now Black Eagle, earlier shot off his horse was back in the fight! The bullet meant for him earlier had hit him alright, but fortunately for Black Eagle the bullet had struck him in the lone pistol he was wearing that Ofer had purchased for him! The impact of that bullet striking him in the heavy horse pistol carried in his waist sash had cleared him from the saddle of his horse and in essence instead of being 'gutshot', had saved his life! When Black Eagle had been blown over the rump of his horse by the bullet's kinetic energy, a slew of arrows meant for him had sailed harmlessly over where he had once been sitting upright in the saddle! However, having been knocked from his saddle, the arrows meant for him passed harmlessly into the field beyond. Now Black Eagle was back in the fight, in extreme pain from the bullet's impact in the area of his stomach but back in the fight. Instantly realizing what had just occurred, Black Eagle quickly retrieved his dropped rifle from the ground and shot the first hard-charging Indian riding his horse right at him! The impact from that shot blew that attacker right over the rump of his horse and onto the ground behind his still running horse with a hard sounding "THUMP"! Running to his well-trained horse still standing where he had been left after Black Eagle had been blown from his saddle, he jerked out his reserve rifle from its scabbard and as he whirled around to face his next oncoming attacker, cocked it in the emergency of the moment. **BOOM!** Black Eagle shot the next hard-charging Indian off his horse with his reserve rifle, then dropped it and jerking his tomahawk out from his belt behind his back, managed just in time to get it free and swing it into a third Indian charging by on his horse just as he leapt off his steed and onto Black Eagle! "KER-THUMP" went the two men to the ground in a terrific collision! However, that hard-charging Indian had died in his own 'pew' when Black Eagle, swinging his tomahawk for all he was worth managed to strike his attacker in the man's throat while flying through the air! As for Black Eagle, he now laid under the Indian he had just killed, out cold from the man's bodily impact into him when he had bailed off his running horse at full speed and had slammed onto the 'gutty' fighter standing on the ground!

However, with Black Eagle now out of the fight, Jerimiah was back into the battle for his life with a vengeance after being dumped off his horse! He had been hit with an arrow right into his 'possibles' bag which had been full of extra rifle and pistol balls, jerky, wads, flints and the like. The closeness of the Indian who had shot such an arrow into him aiming for his torso, had fortunately only hit him in that heavy leather 'possibles' bag. However for the Indian shooting that arrow, Jerimiah's horse had run right over the top of him, killing him in the process! But right behind him ran the last two Indians on foot with their rifles in hand and at the ready to kill Jerimiah! **BOOM!** shot Jerimiah with his rifle killing the closest attacking Indian running right at him and "CRUNCH" went his swiftly swung rifle barrel into the other Indian's face, smashing it with a self-satisfying bone-smashing crunch! When that Indian hit the ground stunned over being struck into the face with such force, he then quickly discovered that all that warm flooding feeling over his body was his own blood, after Jerimiah had slit his throat as he lay there stunned for a moment on the ground after being struck in the face with the rifle barrel! Then upon hearing the ongoing battle 'swirling' over by the beaver ponds, Jerimiah ran to his horse. As he did, he broke off the arrow shaft protruding from his 'possibles' bag because it was in his way, grabbed his reserve rifle from his horse's scabbard and took off running for the closest beaver pond! As he did, he could see three Indians running for where Gabriel and Little Raven had been working skinning beaver when the shooting had started!

Having 40 yards to run to get to where his two friends were

locked in battle, Jerimiah found the wind lending speed to his flying feet. However, as he ran like the wind to help out, he could see the battle unfolding before his eyes and it almost froze his heart! Then his heart quickened when he saw Little Raven shoot the first of three Indians that had ganged up on him and were locked in battle. Then he saw the first Indian's head upon reaching Little Raven explode into a bright red spew! Then, miracle of miracles, the second Indian right in line attacking Little Raven had his head also exploded with Little Raven's initial single shot! It was then that Jerimiah realized when Little Raven had head shot his first and closest attacker in the head, that bullet had gone clear through the first attacker's head and into the head of the second attacker by sheer luck, killing him by accident! But the battle was not over! Still running like the wind and not close enough to shoot the third attacking Indian without hitting Little Raven, Jerimiah saw that third Indian grab Little Raven's long braid, jerk his head back and with his tomahawk, start to bring it down in a killing blow! With that, Jerimiah slid to a stop in order to take his shot and save his friend, only to have his feet slip out from under him on the dew-dampened grass and fall flat onto his back! Quickly rolling over and lunging back to his feet in order to shoot the Indian about to kill his friend, he saw the beaver pond nearby that struggle explode upward. Out from the pond's icy waters exploded Gabriel, who grabbed the Indian attacker about to strike Little Raven a mortal blow with his tomahawk. That was when Jerimiah saw a slew of blood erupt from the attacker! Gabriel had gotten there just in time, had grabbed the Indian attacker by one of his long braids, jerked his head back and with his sheath knife, sliced the man's head from his neck in one swift cut! Then Gabriel, because of the extreme emotional force he had used in killing his attacker and having his heavy head come off so easily, stumbled and fell backwards once again into the pond. Immediately up out from the cold water exploded Gabriel as he then tossed the Indian's head out into the water of the beaver pond. Then he scrambled out from the pond's waters, reached down and dragged Little Raven further up to safety on the bank.

Then Jerimiah saw Ofer and Joshua running out from the budding willows with tomahawks in hand as if to join the battle ongoing around Gabriel and Little Raven. Then running right up to where the battle had just been terminated with the head being cut clean off one Indian attacker by Gabriel and realizing the battle was over, Ofer and Joshua slid to a stop. Then Ofer could see Jerimiah running back to where he and Black Eagle had been ambushed and disappear. Within seconds, Ofer could see Jerimiah stand back up and he was holding up a staggering but very much alive Black Eagle!

Minutes later with all of the trappers safely together once again after being cleverly ambushed, Ofer took stock of what had happened. According to the men, they had been ambushed from three different places by ten different Indians as the trappers ran their trap line. All ten Indians had died in the attack and luckily, Black Eagle although sore as hell in the stomach area, had been hit in his pistol and had not suffered a mortal wound. Painful yes, and black, blue, purple and yellowish in color flesh where the pistol had been slammed back into his belly with such force that it had caused a surface wound, but he would live. Jerimiah on the other hand, had a sore shoulder from when he had been unhorsed and hit the ground after being hit with an arrow at close range in his 'possibles' bag. But other than being embarrassed over not being badly hurt, he would survive. Gabriel on the other hand had a painful bullet wound that had creased the flesh clear across his hand but in time would heal since he had no broken bones, would live and regain his functions as well. However, the beaver he had been holding now had a bullet hole in it and that would reduce its value once sold back at Fort Manuel… Other than being soaked to the skin, Gabriel, Little Raven with a sore head, Joshua and Ofer being soaked from their 'swims' in the cold beaver pond, all would live from their near deadly experiences that day. All would live because the good Lord had smiled on the trappers and The Great Spirit had not smiled upon the ten dead Indians...

Then the necessary work began. First of all, Black Eagle identified all of the Indian attackers as the much-dreaded Gros Ventre and thankfully not the Blackfeet hopefully still under a truce. After a bit of searching, the men discovered where the Gros Ventre had hidden their horses before springing their ambush on the unsuspecting trappers. Being that ten of the 20 Indian horses now captured were shod, Ofer decided to keep those. Those he was sure the Gros Ventre being a war party, had run across other trappers along the Musselshell and had killed them and taken their furs. That was later found to be the case when with a little more looking where all of the horses had been tied up prior to the attack, the trappers discovered an additional ten packs of beaver *Plus* 'which they would now keep for themselves! As for weapons, Ofer and company did not find any of the usual misused and often kept in poor condition, Indian trade rifles. As for the four rifles found in the hands of the Gros Ventre, all were good quality rifles, more than likely taken from the trappers they had killed and as a result, Ofer and company kept those as reserve weapons. Then without one ounce of regret, Ofer with the help of the other members of his party, scalped every dead Indian, tied their scalps to the manes of the ten Indians' unshod ponies, slapped with a bloody red handprint on their necks as a warning, removed their bridles so they could feed on the way home and turned them loose. Turned loose in the hopes some or all of them would return to their attacking Indian band's familiar site and be taken as a warning by the superstitious Gros Ventre to leave the white trappers trapping along the Musselshell country alone. After all, such scalping practices and red handprints on the horses' necks had worked on Chief Learning Bear's Band of Blackfeet, and it was hoped it would also work on the much more stubborn and deadly Gros Ventre eventually as well.

The rest of that morning was spent running the men's trap line in which 19 prime beaver were taken, including two that weighed around 70 pounds each! In fact, those two beaver carcasses were saved so the men would have some fresh meat for their supper that evening since their meat poles back at camp were once again empty. Then after having run the trap line, the men turned 'tail' for their cabin and slowly headed home since they were all slightly 'gowed' up from the fight, as well as herding an additional ten dead trappers' horses unfamiliar with the men. This they did considering they had just finished a hard day at work on the frontier, had survived and tomorrow was another hard, cold and wet day out on the frontier for six once again very lucky Mountain Men fur trappers...

For the rest of that spring beaver trapping season, the men ran their trap line until the fur on the beaver being trapped began showing signs of coming out of prime and slipping. With those signs of lesser quality in the beaver's fur being manifested, the men pulled their traps and turned to hunting buffalo. Those buffalo killed and butchered were used as everyday camp meat, and for making and replenishing their much-needed jerky supplies required for the soon to come long and dangerous trip down to Fort Manuel come the fast- approaching summertime. Soon the smoking fires were going under the meat smoking racks and within a week enough jerky had been rendered for the trip ahead if wild game could not be shot due to the closeness of hostile bands of Gros Ventre Indians hunting buffalo.

Since the men had not trapped out the Musselshell waters around their cabin, Ofer and company had decided to return to their current cabin for another trapping season on the Musselshell after the summer trip to Fort Manuel. With that in mind, the men located a sandy area in which to dig out a cache site and stored their gear and stores not needed for the trip to

Fort Manuel, the summer stay while there and for use on their return trip back to their cabin. With their duties completed around the cabin, the men arose way before sunrise the following week and began packing all of their horses and those recovered from the battle with the Gros Ventre with their bundles of furs and those supplies and cooking wares needed for the trip, their short stay at Fort Manuel and their return trip to their cabin on the Musselshell. Around noontime, the men had all of their animals saddled, packed and then headed out in a 20+ horse fur caravan to the southeast for the six- day trip to the fort. However prior to leaving, Ofer saw to it that the front door to their cabin was nailed shut as were the window's outer coverings in order to discourage any nearby grizzly bear looking for a comfortable new home other than a cold and damp cave in which to live...

Six days later of travel without incident, Ofer and company arrived at Fort Manuel. Along the way, Ofer and company had joined four other groups of trappers who had also trapped along the Musselshell and were heading for Fort Manuel at the same time to sell their furs and resupply as well. With the size of five groups of heavily armed trappers, every group of Indians encountered along the way shied away from such a large force of fur trappers and their heavily loaded fur caravans, figuring the risk of attack and losing too many of their warriors to the normally accurate shooting trappers was too great a risk.

Once again, as the caravan of fur trappers rode up to the front gate of Fort Manuel, they were greeted by a very happy Manuel Lisa over seeing such bounty coming to his fort to trade. Only this time when offered a place to stay in the clerks' sleeping quarters, Ofer politely declined, remembering all of the body lice his group had acquired staying that first summer in the clerks' sleeping quarters, and advised Lisa they wished to camp outside the fort in and among their other fur trapper friends for the camaraderie during that summer. Lisa was not offended with

Ofer's refusal but did take his caravan of trappers to the forefront of the fur grading and counting process, so they could be rid of all the associated packing and unpacking of their multi-herd of stock. Plus by showing such a favor of being first in line, Lisa, ever the shrewd businessman, was hoping for a return favor when it came to purchasing Ofer's extra horses acquired after the battle with the Gros Ventre at the beaver ponds, once they had been unloaded. Aware of what Lisa was angling for in horse sales, Ofer advised Lisa they wanted to have his black-smiths look the stock over and help him select the best ones to help offset the losses of some of his killed buckskins.

Once again, Ofer made sure his men watched the entire fur grading process and advised all that upon seeing any irregularities, they were to raise those issues right then and there. When all was said and done, Ofer and company had another good year. Counting all of their beaver furs, including those furs acquired right after the deadly battle with the ten Gros Ventre who had killed and stolen a number of bundles of furs from other white fur trappers, they had amassed 691 Made Beaver which brought the trappers $6 per pound. Additionally, they had amassed another 270 beaver smaller in size and of lesser quality which brought $4.50 per pound. Then they had 39 prime wolf skins that brought $35 each, 212 muskrat skins which brought 25¢ each, and 119 marten skins which brought $2 each, for a grand total amounting to $7,017.00! No matter how one looked at that figure for a year's worth of trapping, it was a fortune! Seeing that amount and quality of furs Ofer and his fellow trappers had brought into the fort to sell made Lisa's head just 'swim' with glee. No two ways about it, Ofer and his fellow trappers led everyone else in numbers and quality of furs of those who had previously reported to the fort with their annual catch of furs! Especially when one took into account the bundles of fur they had taken from the dead Gros Ventre, who had killed a number of trappers and taken their furs before they were killed in the most recent battle with Ofer's group of trappers. Unfortunately, Ofer and the rest of his fellow trappers failed to understand the cost of such fame among the 70 or so trappers already gathered at the fort and watching the ongoing grading and counting process with arriving trappers! Nor did they understand the meaning of so many inquiries made of Lisa's company sorters and graders as to the location in which Ofer and company had been doing all of their trapping with such success...

That afternoon after all the counting and grading of the Tal, Little Raven and Black Eagle's furs, Lisa wrote out a credit slip to Ofer for the amount of $7,017.00, and in so doing invited Ofer and his group of trappers to a very special supper cooked especially for them two days hence. Not wanting to embarrass Lisa over his previous generous offer for a place to stay in the clerks' sleeping quarters, Ofer went ahead and accepted for his group the offer of a special meal the following day. Then he and his group of men and horses exited the fort and headed for the cottonwood groves bordering the nearby Bighorn River to make their camp for the summer. There under the spreading leaves of several large cottonwood trees for the shade and to help in keeping off the afternoon rains from the many summer storms found in the area, Ofer and company pitched their camp. As Gabriel with his now pretty much healed-up hand and Little Raven began setting up their firepit area, the rest of the men scurried about gathering up dropped limbs and also cut some dry driftwood from along the Bighorn River's banks so they would have cooking fuels. Then the men finished unpacking and unloading their horses, hobbled them and let them out to water and graze along the river's banks under the watchful eyes of Jerimiah and Joshua so their herd would not mingle with other trappers' herds also feeding in the area. As that was happening, Ofer and Black Eagle gathered up their rifles and left their newly established campsite. Two hours later, both men returned with two medium-sized mule deer does laid over their saddles and now the hungry men would have fresh meat for their dinner being prepared by their two faithful camp cooks. Sleeping that first evening in their sleeping furs was uneventful except for the noisy great horned owl who selected one of the cottonwoods Ofer and company were sleeping under as his roost site. Then the great horned owl commenced 'hooting' back and forth most of the night at other nearby owls, keeping the men from sleeping soundly. Then to his chagrin, Ofer found a big splash of white liquid owl droppings spewed across his sleeping furs that stunk like all get-out. Then as if that owl poop had not caused enough embarrassment over the laughter among his group, a large owl pellet coughed up sometime during the night consisting of mouse bones and fur, had been dropped right next to his face where he had been sleeping! A pistol shot into the cottonwood's branches the following night by Ofer saw to it that the noisy owl went elsewhere and pooped on someone else...

The next day, Ofer and company met with a number of their friends looking to see who had made it back to the fort and discovering those of their friends who had 'gone under' during the previous trapping season due to Indian attacks, horse wrecks or drownings. Then come suppertime, Ofer and the rest of the family trooped over to Manuel Lisa's home within the fort. There they sat down to a set table of knives, forks and spoons along with expensive china plates for the men in which to eat from, for the first time in several years for the Tals. As for Black Eagle and Little Raven, the whole set-up around the table was new to them, so the brothers had to assist them on how to correctly dine when setting in front of a well-set table. As it turned out, supper was as fine as any of the men had ever had. There was roasted and stuffed mallard duck, hard-boiled duck eggs with sauce, fried potatoes mixed with onion slices from the fort's garden, homemade bread fresh from the fort's ovens, fresh peas in a cream sauce made from the fort's milk cows, real butter, coffee along with crystal glasses full of fine red wine and for dessert, all the homemade apple pie heavily dosed with brown sugar and cinnamon the men could stuff down their gullets! Afterwards, Lisa broke out a small keg of cigars and everyone sitting on the porch of Lisa's home turned the air gray in color and for once, there were no mosquitoes courageous enough to force their ways through the great gray clouds of cigar smoke for a 'meal' of fur trapper...

The next day, all the men in their group bathed in the Bighorn River and then shaved off their beard stubble while under the shade of spreading limbs and leaves of a cottonwood tree along the banks of the waterway. That was except for Little Raven and Black Eagle who had no beards to speak of, but they did take the time to re-braid their long hair after getting its first washing in two months. Sitting there under the shade of the cottonwood trees later in the day, Ofer broached the subject of making preparations for the return to the Musselshell to all of the men of his party of trappers. None of the men objected to making plans for what was to come, so Ofer proceeded with a lay-out of what he figured had to be done in order to be prepared for the coming fall and spring trapping seasons.

Firstly, he had Jerimiah and Joshua round up all of their horses including all ten of the horses previously belonging to the trappers who had been killed by the Gros Ventre in an earlier battle that, after that fight with the same Indians, they had subsequently acquired. With that, Ofer instructed that the two men were to select out five of the best ten horses once belonging to the dead trappers. Those were to be reshod, as well as their own buckskins for the year's coming trapping seasons. As for the remaining five dead trappers' horses not selected, they were to be sold to Lisa for whatever they would bring. That done, the brothers were to bring Ofer a credit letter from such sales back to him, which they would use to help pay off in part for the provisions they would need to acquire for the coming fall and spring trapping seasons.

244 | "FOUR SCALPS" OFER TAL, MOUNTAIN MAN

Next, Ofer advised that Black Eagle, Little Raven, Gabriel and he would be going shopping in the fort's warehouse now that they were all cleaned up and did not smell like a cow buffalo in heat, for their coming year's provisions. Figuring out loud, Ofer suggested that it might be best to make all of their provision acquisitions now while there were adequate supplies at the warehouse, instead of waiting until the end of summer when everything in the way of provisions had been pretty well picked over and as a result, might be in short supply.

The next morning after breakfast, Jerimiah and Joshua rounded up their herd of horses and drove them over to the location of the fort's blacksmith shops. There they instructed the smithies to reshoe all of the buckskin horses and the five now selected dead trappers' horses. They also instructed the smithies to check all of the horses' teeth to see if any of them needed to be 'floated' and if so, do it. Then they herded the dead trappers' five remaining horses over to where Lisa was overseeing the fur counting and grading operations, sold those horses and collected a credit slip from Lisa. Knowing the rest of their group would be over at the supply warehouse, Jerimiah and Joshua walked over to that log structure within the walls of the fort, entered and began looking for Ofer and the rest of their group among a number of other trappers also procuring their year's supply of provisions.

In the meantime, Ofer and company had previously walked over to the fort's warehouse, walked in and hailed over a company clerk in order to assist them with their provision selections. Once the selection group was all together in the warehouse, the selection of needed items began. First to select what was needed were Gabriel and Little Raven, the camp's designated cooks, who began making their choices based on known needs, likes and dislikes of the group's members. First off the bat, the 'cooks' made for the much-needed staples and began making their selections. High on their lists were sacks of flour (biscuits), tins of yeast (for making biscuits), sacks of beans, rice, dried fruit like apple slices, brown sugar cones, sacks of hard candy (a group favorite), sacks of raisins, bags of salt, pepper, red pepper flakes (to aid the trappers in their regular bowel movements needed as a result from having such a high meat diet and little fiber), sacks of dried green coffee beans, assorted cobbler-making spices, two one-gallon jugs of honey, three one-gallon jugs of rendered bear oil for use in the Dutch ovens for making biscuits, and on such selections went.

Then it was off to the clothing section of the warehouse where the group selected new capotes to replace worn out and lost ones, two dozen socks for each man, gloves, new wide brimmed hats to keep out the sun's rays, new blankets to replace those worn out or too smelly from body odors to continue using and new breechclouts and leggings for Ofer and Joshua, the group's main trappers. Then a number of tanned deerskins, buffalo robes, leather strapping, sewing needles, awls for sewing leather, spools of twine, a spool of cotton horse lead rope and the like were selected and piled up by the company clerk for later settlement.

Following those clothing selections, Joshua and Jerimiah re-joined the group of 'shoppers' so they could have their input as well on other selections. Off to the accessories section of the warehouse the trappers walked and first on their list of cooking accessories was another coffee pot. Another coffee pot to act as a reserve after their last one had been struck by a stray rifle bullet in the ambush back at their cabin when Coyote and his three fellow Blackfeet family members decided to kill the trappers and hopefully the one known as The Scalper as well. Then six whet-stones were added to help keep their knives, tomahawks and straight razors sharp. Next in the way of 'necessaries' were two more long-handled axes, five files, a two-pound hammer, another 25-pound keg of long nails to be used in any future cabin, table, chair and latrine repairs or construction, a half-dozen fire starters, several awls for leather repairs, a new needle sewing kit with additional thread for patching up wounds, and on it went.

Then when Ofer walked over to the section of the fort's warehouse holding assorted firearms, he got a number of questioning looks from his fellow trappers. Finally not able to stand himself, Gabriel said, "My Brother, why are you looking at the firearms? We have a passel of rifles that we have acquired after battles with the Blackfeet and Gros Ventre in addition to our own personal firearms, so why do we need any more?"

Ofer turned and said, "We need three more pistols. After that last battle with the Gros Ventre when we were ambushed, that battle was so 'close', I saw the need for everyone to be packing at least two pistols. Especially in light of Black Eagle's broken beyond repair pistol hit with that life-taking rifle bullet aimed for his body, and seeing Little Raven in action at such close range against overwhelming odds with just his one pistol, I just figured the lack of pistols among some of us was our one glaring weakness." With that, he beckoned Little Raven and Black Eagle over to the pistol section and gave one pistol to Little Raven and two to Black Eagle. "There," he said, "now both of you have two pistols each and hopefully if we are attacked ever again, the two of you can save not only your own lives but those of your 'brothers' as well." Then he beckoned the fort's clerk holding a wire shopping basket used for smaller items over to where he stood. Therein that wire basket Ofer quickly placed several more powder horns, bullet pullers, a number of spare rifle and pistol parts for repair if necessary, and several large bags of greased wadding so the rifles in use would shoot more accurately with less fouling from the black powder or the soft lead balls being used. Then into that basket also went three canvas sacks of precut flints for their rifles and pistols.

Then the entire group turned to the powder and lead pigs section of the warehouse and selected 100 pounds of lead pigs and numerous tins of rifle and pistol powder, as well as several more tins of priming powder (finer gained) for the flash pans on their rifles and pistols. Normally they would have selected even more because of the Indian country they were trapping in, but they still had good reserves of the above buried back in their cache at their cabin, so no more was selected in that section of the warehouse.

Lastly, off to the rum, whiskey and tobacco section of the warehouse went Ofer and Black Eagle who then selected eight flat kegs of the fiery rum the men loved so much and 12 'carrots' of tobacco, along with another dozen of the easily broken clay pipes the men loved smoking during their evening hours to help keep the mosquitoes at bay. As those men made those specific high-cost selections, the rest of the trappers headed over to the horse accessories section and procured six more panniers for use on the dead trappers' horses being reshod over at the blacksmith section of the fort.

Then as the fort's clerk compiled an accounting of all of the provisions selected, the rest of the group stacked all of their recent purchases in a corner of the warehouse for easy acquisition and packing once the horses were once again available after being reshod. Once the accounting had been done by the clerk, he handed Ofer a slip of paper with his tally. The bill came to $2,090.50 for all of those supplies so selected at of course, "Mountain Prices!" Later that afternoon, Ofer looked Lisa up on the fur grading line and handed him the slip of paper holding the tally of provisions he and his group had selected from the warehouse. Lisa, ever the astute businessman, took out his ledger, ran his finger down the tally page until he came to the Tal Brothers list of credit due for all of their furs. That credit due figure was $7,017.00! Without batting an eye, Lisa took out his stub of a lead pencil and after a few minutes of ciphering, showed his final figure to Ofer. Ofer nodded and then Lisa took out an official looking document from a leather pouch titled, "St. Louis

Missouri Fur Company Letter Of Credit." After filling in the blanks with his swan quill pen and ink from an inkwell on his business desk located alongside the fur grading line, Lisa handed the document to Ofer. When he did, Ofer looked down at the bottom line on the Letter Of Credit document showing the amount due from the St. Louis Missouri Fur Company as $4,926.50! With a smile over the small fortune he was now holding in his hand, Ofer shook Lisa's hand thanking him, whereupon Lisa said, "No, I thank you for your business. May you and your group's next trapping season up on the Musselshell be just as successful as this one has been and may none of your bunch end up 'going under'!" With that document in hand, Ofer walked back to his group's campsite. As he did, he failed to notice a nearby trapper intently listening and looking over his and Manuel Lisa's final transaction and conversation with more than just a casual interest...

Arriving back at their campsite and on the way noticing his herd of hobbled horses just back from the blacksmiths feeding nearby, Ofer smiled. Then walking over to his sleeping furs, Ofer placed his St. Louis Missouri Fur Company Letter Of Credit in his saddlebag right next to his previous year's fur company Letter Of Credit of $4,337.50, the two of which totaled $9,264.00! Ofer just shook his head over the Letters Of Credit math he had just done in his head. As a result of his ciphering, it was more than obvious that he, his brothers, Little Raven and Black Eagle were now wealthy men! Then Ofer just grinned, full-well knowing that with the "Good Lord a-Willing", he and his group would be able to duplicate their successes as beaver trappers in the coming year and become even richer... Little did Ofer realize what the "Good Lord" had in store waiting for him and his kind out on the beautiful frontier "He" had created...

CHAPTER 9 — TRAPPING ON THE "SMITH", THE DEATH OF "LEARNING BEAR"

TWO WEEKS LATER, OFER AWOKE WITH A START WHILE LYING quietly in his sleeping furs! Without moving anything other than his eyes in case a close at hand danger had been that which had abruptly awakened him, his eyes carefully searched all around looking at everything in view for what may have been a threat. Not seeing anything other than his brothers, Little Raven and Black Eagle still quietly sleeping in their sleeping furs, Ofer realized it was his sixth sense that was the culprit in what had suddenly awakened him from such a sound sleep... Lying there in his sleeping furs quietly, Ofer tried making sense of his sixth sense warning that heretofore had always been trustworthy and worth paying attention to. Since no thoughts of imminent danger came to mind and since he was now wide awake, Ofer arose, quietly dressed so as not to awaken the others and then headed over to the firepit to build a fire. As he did, he noticed several strings of trapper caravans even at that hour of the morning and early summer date, had arisen and were already heading back to their trapping grounds of choice. There was still another month of summer left but here they were moving out and heading for their trapping grounds of interest instead of staying at the fort and continuing to celebrate the summer months along with the rest of their trapper friends. Ofer thought that activity was a bit odd but soon erased such thoughts from his mind as the fire needed more wood. He would soon come to realize why some trappers were already on the move to their new trapping grounds of choice in the most personal of ways...

It was then that his earlier sixth sense awakening and meaning struck home within his inner being. Those trappers leaving early that morning and several other caravans he had observed days earlier leaving before the summer had run its course, were getting the jump on the other trappers as they headed out for the best trapping grounds known to them or discovered by word of mouth while at the fort. They had left earlier than normal in order to stake out the best beaver trapping territories and woe be it to any other trapper infringing on their beaver trapping claims of choice! Then he thought back to the number of trappers who had shown interest as to where he had trapped during the previous fall and spring beaver trapping seasons and then those simple questions reared their ugly heads for the real meaning of all of their interest...

Once again trusting his sixth sense and the insight it had given him that morning, Ofer woke up the rest of his group and soon their campsite was abuzz with their normal morning activities. Especially so when all present around the recently built campfire were told they were heading back to their Musselshell trapping grounds and their cabin the following morning! With those 'breaking camp' words, there were immediate questioning reactions as to why they couldn't stay longer and continue celebrating life in and among their many friends. Especially since the fall beaver trapping season was still several months away and they already had a built cabin waiting for them so they didn't have to build another one. Waiting until the whole chorus of questions stopped being asked by the group, Ofer replied, "I awoke this morning with a start when my sixth sense woke me up. I did not realize what 'it' was 'telling' me until I observed three large caravans of our fellow trappers already heading out towards the northwest. It then dawned on me that many a trapper had heard of our beaver trapping successes from the sorters and graders about the good beaver trapping luck we had over the past seasons while trapping up on the Musselshell. Then I remembered the number of trappers we saw last year on the lower reaches of the Musselshell. I then realized if they had good successes the same as us, the word will soon get out that the Musselshell is the place to be trapping if one wants to be successful. With that in mind and seeing these other fur trapping caravans leaving the fort early this morning, I halfway suspect they all may be heading for our beaver trapping grounds up on the Musselshell as well! If that is the case, we had best be staking out our fall and spring beaver trapping site if we want to hold it and not have any other trappers claiming our trapping area as theirs..."

The next morning after saying their 'Good-byes' to a number of their friends at the fort and in the trappers' campsites the day before, found the 'Tal' group strung out with their heavily loaded horse caravan heading back towards the northwest from Fort Manuel towards their cabin on the Musselshell. For the next six days of slow travel towards their cabin, Ofer could not get the nagging sixth sense concerns out from his head. Every day of travel no matter what beauty lay around the trappers as they traveled through the countryside, Ofer found his senses nagging him about something yet to come... It did not help in the concern department that every day of travel the Tals had been running across numerous shod horse tracks heading in the same direction as they were. In fact, for the last two days, they had been following a caravan of shod horses numbering over 20! A caravan of over 20 shod horses that had bypassed the lower reaches of the Musselshell because of the numbers of trappers now in that area, and seemed to be heading in the same direction of the Tals' old cabin on the upper reaches of some of the finest beaver trapping going on the Musselshell!

As Ofer continued leading his group of trappers towards their old cabin just off the Musselshell, his sixth sense of impending problems seemed to increase in its intensity as it whirled around in the depths of his soul. However, Ofer kept those warning senses to himself but did several times instruct his group to remain alert because they were now deep in the country of the dreaded Blackfeet, truce or not, and that of the Gros Ventre who were always spoiling for a fight. Finally arriving at the finger of trees leading up to their old cabin at the head of the meadow, Ofer finally realized what his sense had been 'telling' him all along... Rounding that finger of trees, Ofer realized the long string of shod horses they had been trailing for the last number of days had turned up into their meadow and were heading towards their cabin of use from the year before!

'Sure as shooting', when Ofer and his men turned into their meadow leading up into their cabin, they saw a large number of horses in their old corral and a number of unknown fur trappers busily working around their old cabin. Once those unknown men became aware of the Tals' caravan of men and horses quietly riding their way, all of them went for their nearby rifles and then took aggressive stances as they stared hard at the newly arriving fur trappers as if they were a bad case of the body lice! Riding right up to the men now standing around Ofer's old cabin in defiantly defensive positions, the meaning of his sixth sense that had been dogging him for the last week or so became clear.

"Good afternoon, may I help you men?" said Ofer Tal, in a very calm but questioning tone of voice. Then he sat there on his horse looking first at one man and then another, looking for the leader or spokesman for the group of trespassing trappers who could explain what they were doing at his cabin.

"Yeah, you and your motley crew can get the hell away from our cabin and off our trapping claim," bellowed out a rather tall fellow in a human's sallow yellowed skin from behind where Ofer sat upon his horse!

Turning in his saddle so he could face the booming 'voice' coming from the location of the horse corral, Ofer saw a very distinctive-looking, like a 'dead man standing' person that he remembered seeing earlier back at Fort Manuel. Then he remembered the 'death warmed over'-looking man as the one who had been standing by Lisa looking and listening to what had been said when Lisa had cut the rather large Letter Of Credit for their previous season's fur sales... The one and same man who appeared to be all ears when Lisa had mentioned to Ofer he expected to see the same quality and quantity of beaver furs at his fort from his next season's work up on the upper reaches of the Musselshell! It was then that Ofer realized the 'dead looking' man had purposely stood close to Lisa when he was talking to Ofer so he could learn the approximate location of Ofer's successful beaver trapping season. And now here he was!

Putting his judgment of the nosy man and now trespasser aside, Ofer once again calmly said, "Can I help you and your men before we unload all of our packs and put our provisions inside our old cabin?"

"What do you mean, your cabin? I and my men were here first and that makes it our cabin since I didn't see any of you "Johnny-come-latelies" getting here first! Now, what the hell can me and my men do for all of you before you leave us to getting our new cabin squared away and made ready for us to live in?" asked the 'death-warmed-over'-looking individual.

Looking over the man's nine armed and rough-looking men standing at the ready around the cabin, Ofer realized there was no way his group of six could take over their rightful property forcefully like he wanted to do. But he had quickly dismissed that thought, realizing they all would more than likely be killed in the process if he tried to take back what was rightfully theirs, so he backed off from that foolish idea. "Well, might I ask who I am having the pleasure of addressing?" asked Ofer in his softest tone of voice, not wanting to have anyone start shooting right off the bat.

"You be addressing one "Jack Thorn", the meanest son-of-a-bitch in the valley and one who has kilt over ten men for just looking the wrong way at me," said Thorn sharply.

When he mouthed out those words, Ofer had a tendency to believe some of what he had just said from all the steely looks he was getting from his men appearing to back up Thorn's words... Not wanting to get either himself or any of his group shot out from their saddles before they could swing into action, Ofer realizing their plight said, "OK, since you and your men were here first, Mr. Thorn, I would like to make a request."

"Go ahead but make it quick. Me and the boys here have to get that damn nailed-down door undone and get our packs unloaded and inside afore it rains, so state your piece," growled Thorn with a tone and tenor in his voice that was very menacing.

"Since we won't be living here anymore, we would like your permission to dig up our cache of goods and supplies we left behind when we rode out from here to go to Fort Manuel earlier in the summer, if you be so kind," said Ofer now really steaming under his collar, but realizing the futility of discussing the issue any further with the heavily armed bully and blowhards of Thorn's fellow trappers that he was now confronting.

"Sure, go ahead. That way me and my boys can quit this damn 'palavering' and get our business done," said Thorn, with a look like he had just fought and whipped the biggest kid in school and was looking for more. LITTLE DID THORN REALIZE THAT 'MORE' WAS COMING HIS WAY AND IT WAS 'RIDING A BLACK HORSE SNORTING FIRE AND FLAME'...

With that, Ofer and company rode out back behind their old cabin to their cache site and with a couple of shovels began digging up their earlier cached supplies. However, Ofer, with shovel in hand, had Black Eagle, Little Raven, Joshua and Jerimiah remain horsed and armed, watching to make sure Thorn and his men did not change their minds and try ambushing his family and friends once they saw the value of what lay in the cache. Then Ofer and Gabriel finished unearthing the cache and loading those supplies into the panniers on the extra horses recovered from the Gros Ventre who had ambushed the Tals earlier in the year. Once finished and without another word for fear of setting off a deadly shootout, Ofer and company silently rode out from their old campsite and then for the next two days, rode further to the northwest from their former campsite deeper into the Little Belt Mountains until they hit what Colter had told them would be the Smith River. That way they were far enough away from their old trapping grounds on the Musselshell so they would not 'cross swords' with Jack Thorn and his crew of nine rough-looking trappers while beaver trapping themselves. As for knowing about the Smith River and its beaver riches, Ofer and his group of trappers had hunted elk in that area the year before for camp meat, after hunting buffalo along the Musselshell had become problematic because of overshooting by the Indians and the other trappers in the area. And it was during that two-day elk hunting trip that the men had surveyed the beaver activity along the Smith River and decided they would trap that area after they had trapped out the beaver in their old location along the Musselshell.

Just about a day's ride northwest of where the Smith joined into the Musselshell; Ofer stopped his caravan of men and horses and quietly surveyed the lay of the land lying before him. Here the Smith traveled almost in a northerly direction through a number of small valleys totally surrounded by dense coniferous forests. Along the Smith were numerous groves of aspens, cottonwoods and dense patches of willows. Collateral with all of those varieties of excellent food sources for the beaver were numerous intersecting waterways as far as the eye could see. Intersecting waterways that were dotted with conical beaver houses, large beaver ponds, numerous stick and mud dams and throughout the Smith itself, extensive evidence of beaver activity in the way of swimming beaver, floating leaves and branches in the water. All of which were welcome signs and indicators in the eyes of the experienced Mountain Men trappers of extensive beaver population use and activity.

Turning in his saddle and looking to the west, Ofer spied a long meadow winding through the pines and firs with two vigorously flowing streams, one on each side of the meadow. Without another word, Ofer headed his steed up into the winding meadow until the long and densely grassed area opened up into a stand of timber from whence a spring vigorously bubbled out the waters of a third creek. In fact as Ofer had ridden his horse followed by his brother trappers up into the meadow and alongside one of the fast-flowing creeks, they had passed a lone beaver house and several ponded areas at the edge of the meadow. All of which were good omens of what was to come, to Ofer's way of thinking.

Stopping at the end of the northern fork of the winding meadow, Ofer quietly looked around as he could hear the hungry horses moving around behind him wanting to get unpacked so they could feed in the lush meadow. Smiling over their good fortune at what he considered a good-looking future homesite, he heard Black Eagle say, "This Indian likes what he is seeing and thinks this is our new homesite. Especially since The Great Spirit has blessed us with a beaver house in our stream right next to where we could build a cabin and make our home-site in this here meadow."

That potential location for a homesite and the fact that by the end of their second day of riding deeper into the Little Belt Mountains along the Smith River, the men had seen as much beaver sign as they had seen along the Musselshell the very first time they had ridden into that area! Turning in his saddle, Ofer asked, "I know what Black Eagle thinks but what do the rest of you think about making this area our new homesite?"

No one had anything to say when Gabriel and Little Raven, after handing their reins of their pack strings to one of the brothers, dismounted and began talking among themselves about where to construct their firepit and where would be the best place to build their next cabin. Then all of a sudden, Gabriel stopped, took a 'squinty look' at something that had caught his eyes, then took off running for a rocky bluff up at the head of the meadow. As he did, he yelled back to the rest of the trappers, "Follow me, Guys, I have an idea that the rest of you might really like to try on for size!"

Trying to figure out what Gabriel was doing, Ofer touched his horse in its flanks with his heels and began slowly riding up behind a running Gabriel. It was then that he saw what Gabriel was all excited about. Nestled in the bluff of rocks at the head of the meadow they were looking at for a new homesite was the opening to a cave. Without hesitation, Gabriel ran right up to its mouth, carefully peered in as if looking for a grizzly bear and then slowly walked inside. Soon all the rest of the men could hear Gabriel's muffled voice yelling excitedly from inside the newly discovered cave! Moments later out from the mouth of the cave he came at a dead run and running up to the rest of the men still sitting on their horses said, "That damn cave is dry as a bone, runs back quite a distance and is large enough for all of us to live in with lots of room and use as a storage area for all of our furs and provisions as well!"

Soon leaving Gabriel behind to watch over all the happy to be feeding horses in the meadow's lush grasses, the rest of the men walked inside of the cave to look around. In so doing, they discovered the cave was about 30 yards deep, the roof was about ten feet high and the width of the cave was about 20 feet! All in all, way more than large enough for all of the men, their packs full of provisions, was dry throughout and with a log front constructed in the entrance of the cave, that extra area could easily house a fireplace. And in so doing, the fireplace could be vented to the outside, yet could heat the inside of the cave and there would be ample room for a cooking and eating area in the cave's built-up extension! Additionally, it could easily be defended, not subject to Indians starting it afire and was nearby the spring from which flowed a vigorous, cold running stream. Also, it was near an area in the adjacent aspens where a horse corral could easily be built and the horses sheltered. A corral that was clean out of sight from being seen by anyone at the base of the meadow and yet was close enough to the front of the soon to be built "cave-cabin" for the rifle fire protection against horse theft that such a home could offer!

About then the men noticed an ominous-looking mass of blue-black clouds forming up and rolling high into the heavens off to the northwest indicating a possible violent summer thunderstorm was soon to be incoming. Seeing that, while Ofer and Gabriel quickly strung out a rope picket line in the nearby aspens and just as fast as a horse could be unpacked or unsaddled and the leather and provisions rushed inside the cave for the protection against the much-anticipated deluge of rains, that horse was led over to the aspens. There Ofer and Gabriel quickly tied up each horse to their makeshift picket line as fast as the horses arrived and by the time the last horse had been picketed, large and cold drops of incoming rain were heavily falling down upon the fast working men. Just as Ofer and Gabriel finally ducked into the mouth of their newfound cave-cabin site, a bright flash and loud "CRACK" followed by a thunderously loud "BOOM" was seen and heard, and then it seemed the heavens opened up and down with a passion fell a deluge of cold rains upon the area.

For the next 40 or so minutes, lightning sizzled across the darkened skies, the sounds of thunder boomed throughout the inside of the cave and the rain come down in proverbial buckets. Standing just inside the mouth of the cave watching Mother Nature in all of her glory washing down the land, Ofer took that as a good omen. Ofer took that as a good omen because falling rains to his way of thinking was a sign of new life. Here just hours earlier his entire pack string and fellow trappers would not have had anywhere to go if the storm had caught the trappers and their heavily loaded caravan of horses out in the open. But by finding the very livable cave in a timely manner, the men had managed to secure all of their valuable packs, provisions, horses and saddles, all the while remaining safe from the lightning and bone-dry from the rains. With that omen, Ofer was sure pleased both he and his group of trappers had just found their new home.

After the summer thunderstorm had passed and the rays of the sun began returning and warming the land, Ofer and the men dug out their horses' hobbles from one of the packs, hobbled their horses and let them out into the meadow to feed and become familiar with their new home. However as a precaution, Black Eagle and Little Raven accompanied the horses providing protection against any kind of attacks by man or beasts, as the rest of the men staked out their sleeping areas in the cave and laid out their sleeping furs and blankets on the cave's stone floor. With those chores completed, Ofer and Gabriel picked out an outdoor firepit area near the entrance to their new cave-cabin and with a couple of shovels began digging out the much-needed firepit, so coals could be accumulated in order to fire up the Dutch ovens for the much- loved biscuits, and on occasion a previously soaked, dried apple cobbler loaded with brown sugar, raisins and cinnamon from one of the Dutch ovens! In the meantime, aware of being in new and unknown Indian Territory the men carried their rifles everywhere they went, as they collectively looked for some dry firewood so Gabriel and Little Raven could begin creating their supper. A supper that was just before dark, augmented with the addition of a fat mule deer doe killed by Joshua in the next-over grove of aspens. A mule deer doe which had chosen the wrong time to come to the trappers' spring for a drink and ended its life where it stood looking curiously at the trapper with a rifle pointed at it! That night, the men slept soundly in their new cave-cabin, with full bellies of roasted venison, Dutch oven biscuits and hot coffee as only Gabriel and Little Raven could make.

The following morning as the steam rose from the wet soil from the previous afternoon's violent summer thunderstorm's soaking rains, found Gabriel and Little Raven hard at work around their newly established firepit. In just the short period of time they had been there, they had dug out their coal-making pit for Dutch oven use, hung their heavy cooking irons over the firepit, hauled over all of their pots and pans to the cooking area and had constructed a small log lean-to under which to store all of their cooking ware and implements during bad weather. Then as the water in the coffee pot hung on a cooking rod over the fire began boiling, they commenced butchering out the remains of the mule deer doe from the night before so they could make up a big pot of venison and beans for the rest of their clan in anticipation of the hard work being done that day. As they did, Ofer and company went into the surrounding woods and began cutting down a previously lightning-struck tree and cut it into long rounds with their single buck saw so the log sections could be used as sitting logs around the firepit. Then as the men hauled down their sitting logs, Gabriel and Little Raven put the finishing touches on the coffee, Dutch oven biscuits and roasted venison for the men's breakfast.

After breakfast, all the men except for Gabriel and Little

Raven headed once again into the nearby forest and began cutting down trees and sawing them into ten-foot sections for the planned front extension to their cave-cabin. As that work progressed, Gabriel and Little Raven paced off an extensive 'horseshoe'-shaped area in front of their cave. Once that area had been paced off and marked out, they began leveling the area and digging a two-foot deep trench in the shape of that 'horseshoe' out in front of their cave's entrance. That work was only interrupted when Gabriel had to stir the slow-cooking pot of beans and marinate the chunks of venison soaking in rum for the men's noonday meal. Then come the noonday meal, the hard-working 'lumberjacks' happily feasted on rum-soaked roasted chunks of venison, beans, Dutch oven biscuits and coffee.

Then it was back to the 'logging', noonday cleanup and finishing the digging of the 'horseshoe'-shaped trench in front of the cave's entrance. Come dusk, Gabriel brought in the horse herd from their day of feeding and watering in the adjacent meadow, as Little Raven put the finishing touches upon the same meal the men had feasted upon at noon, for their supper meal as well. After their supper meal, the men took out their pipes filled with tobacco and with cups of rum in hand, they relaxed around their evening campfire along with the resident hordes of mosquitoes found in the area. As they did, Ofer laid out the following day's plans for the start of building that portion of their cave-cabin in front of their new home. Finally finishing up their cups of rum and clay pipes full of sweet smelling and tasting James River tobacco, the men retreated to their sleeping area within the cave. With that, quiet descended upon the land around the trappers' new home except for the nervous shuffling of horses on their rope picket line in the aspen grove and the sounds of the nearby creek's rushing waters over the rocks and boulders. That and those sounds from a nearby wolf pack running an elk to ground for their 'dinner'...

After breakfast the following morning, all of the men

ascended onto the nearby timbered hillside and soon two teams of horses were dragging down the ten-foot sections of logs. By day's end, a pile of precut logs lay near the front of the cave as the tired men finished their supper and then one and all, headed for their sleeping furs for a much-earned rest. After breakfast the following morning found all of the men dragging and placing their larger base logs into the trenches for the stability that would long-time offer the front section of their 'horseshoe'-shaped log cabin entrance to their cave. This new way of building a cabin with a base of sunken logs was Ofer's idea. After seeing all of the beaver evidence in and around their living area, the group had decided they would make this a two-year beaver trapping work area because of the beaver riches in potential furs they had seen to date. With that in mind, the men wanted a fortress-like cabin front section placed in front of the entrance to their cave's living quarters. So with a very stout foundation of sunken larger logs for a base, the ten-foot sectioned logs just 'flew' up when it came to making the cabin's three-dimensional 'horseshoe'-shaped, log-wall structure.

Then with the walls' precut logs notched and firmly placed, the front of the cabin was quickly completed by the industry of six sets of willing hands. Then all of the men, mixing grasses and mud, 'chinked' the walls of the cabin-front to where it was now 'tighter than a wood tick'. With that chore finished, the 'loggers' went back to work on the nearby hillside, cutting the needed main and secondary timbers for the roof structure of their 'horseshoe'-shaped front to their cave-cabin. One afternoon was spent with the horses hauling down those timbers, as well as the next two days spent hoisting up those timbers on top of the log walls and then hewing, placing and then nailing them into place with long spikes. Following that, the smaller logs making up the secondary roof covering were laid, followed with cut brush and long grasses from the creeksides, and finally dirt hauled and dumped onto the roof making a roof covering that was two feet deep. That way, the front half of the cave-cabin was insulated, protected against leakage from the rains and snows, and resistant to any kind of fire from either attacking Indians or any forest fire either intentionally set or caused by lightning.

With the front of the cave-cabin completed, Joshua, the group's builder, finished cutting out the front door of their new home, lined it with split logs and built a one-foot thick front door hung on a series of heavy leather 'hinges', logs of which were meant to stop any arrows, bullets and grizzly bears from coming into the living quarters 'uninvited'. As Joshua completed those tasks, the rest of the men cut down insect-killed or lightning-struck pine and fir trees that were dry in nature and hauled them down the mountain with horse teams, made a winter log pile adjacent their cave-cabin for easy access and use during periods of deep snows come wintertime when travel would be difficult. Then as the men sawed those logs into rounds, Joshua cut out a side window on either side of their log addition cave-cabin. That way, the place could be defended from attack on each side of the cabin and through an open front door if necessary. Also, the side window facing the soon to be built horse corral could be used as defense against anyone caught trying to steal the men's valuable horses. Then Joshua split-log lined those window openings and using untanned deer hides that had been scraped razor-thin, placed them over the window openings to let in what soft light they could as well as keep outside cold, rains and snows from coming inside. Then as the rest of the trappers cut the needed timbers, dug the postholes and constructed the horse corral, Joshua constructed log tables, chairs and bedframes for inside use in the cave-cabin when the expected inclement winter weather arrived. Finally, all of the men assisted Joshua cutting another hole in the side of their cave-cabin's wall and constructing a fireplace with slab rocks from the two creeks, and mud, sticks and smaller stones for the chimney.

With that, their home was completed and then the men set

about building the very necessary meat pole structure near the campsite, making easy acquisition for the camp's cooks of its soon to be hanging meats and cave-cabin adjacent meat smoking racks for the making of the most necessary trappers' staple, that of jerky. Then the fun work began for the trappers, namely that of hunting for their daily supplies of camp meat and jerky meat making operations. Since only the occasional old, stringy and tough bull buffalo could be found in their current timbered areas, elk became their next meat making primary target. Soon the meat smoking racks hung heavy with strips of elk meat and the meat poles hung heavy with backstraps, hindquarters and racks of elk ribs. With the addition of numerous slabs of hanging elk meat, the trappers' campsite became a haven for every Northern chickadee, gray jay and Clark's nutcracker helping themselves to the fat and meat bounty swinging 'undefended' from the ropes tied to the meat poles. With that, life was not only good for the trappers but for the local winged critters as well...

Then with the onset of colder fall weather, the men took their leave from work around their campsite preparing it for the winter months to come, saddled up their horses and headed out one morning to travel the many numerous Smith River adjacent waterways and decide where they wanted to start their trap line with a two-year use of the area in mind. Heading almost due north, the men slowly rode along the waterways and Smith River, discussing what they were seeing and the bounty those beaver waters would provide once their trap line was in operation.

It was then about 30 miles south of what would in later days become Great Falls, Montana, that Ofer spotted a slight movement far ahead in the brush alongside the Smith River. With that movement, Ofer's frontier survival instincts went into high alert. Went into high alert because in the wilderness, any kind of movement could either be a critter moving along or an Indian sneaking up on one's person for a quick and easy kill. Stopping his horse and the otherwise 'chatter' coming from his fellow trappers about the potential beaver riches they were observing, Ofer just sat there and quietly watched the area where he had seen the suspicious movement.

It was then that Ofer spotted what appeared to be a small female gray wolf moving stealthily through the brush toward a small hillside. The wolf moved along steadily not seeing, smelling or hearing the six trappers who were all now quietly sitting on their horses and watching the wolf as well. Obviously on a 'mission' the female wolf carrying something heavy, awkward and brown in its mouth, trotted over to the small hillside and once there, was met by five tumbling and excited wolf pups quickly emerging from a den site. With her arrival, she immediately dropped the heavy-looking brown thing as two of her pups immediately began fighting over the object she had just dropped for her pups to eat. Then the female wolf began regurgitating up even more chunks of what she had killed or found as a food item for her hungry litter. Soon, all of the pups were gorging themselves and it was then that the female wolf spotted the trappers quietly sitting on their horses, watching her and her pups. Then the wolf obviously vocalized something because her pups immediately dropped what they were eating and scampered back under a log on the hillside into a den and disappeared. With that, the female with several looks backwards making sure she had not been followed to the den site, moved away and then disappeared into the forest and sagebrush background in a 'twinkling of an eye'.

Curious, the men rode over to the den site amidst the nervous prancing around their horses were doing over all of the wolf smells and took a look. When they did, they were shocked over what they saw! Lying there on the ground next to the den's opening were chunks of strong smelling rotting meat and the large brown thing the female had toted over to her den for her pups to feast upon was nothing more than a thigh and lower leg minus a foot of a dead Indian! As the men sat there in shock over what they were seeing and smelling, they could hear the wolf pups, still hungry, beginning to come out from their den. Then all of a sudden, a black wolf pup emerged from the hole under the log, lunged out making little snarling sounds, grabbed a large chunk of meat from the dead Indian and then ducked back into the den to the sounds of the other pups now fighting over the chunk of meat. Upon seeing what they were seeing and realizing some Indian had paid the ultimate price somewhere in battle, the men just looked at each other in shock!

Without a word, Ofer moved his nervous horse away from the grisly scene and the rest of his group of trappers quietly and without a single word over what they had just seen, moved away as well. However, their shock over what they had just seen was nothing like what they were about to witness. After traveling another mile upstream looking over the beaver trapping potential, Ofer stopped his horse and put his nose high into the air. Soon the other trappers were doing the same as all of them began smelling the very distinct smell of death! Then as they moved further and further north upstream, the sickly sweet smell of decaying human flesh became very distinct...

All of a sudden, the trappers found themselves 'dead-smack-dab' in the middle of an old Indian battlefield with numerous dead horses lying about, Indians lying bloated everywhere where they had fallen and scattered broken fighting equipment lying about in profusion! It was then that Black Eagle quietly said to the rest of the trappers, "Blackfeet and Crow fought here with many dead Indians from both sides." Carefully picking their ways with their horses amidst the numerous dead and decaying Indians and horses and careful to not step upon any of the decaying carcasses scattered about the Smith River, the men found themselves gagging with almost every breath! It was then that Ofer stopped his horse and looked at something lying on the ground that had more than obviously caught his eyes. Then leaning even further over the side of his horse for a closer look, Ofer all of a sudden shot straight up in his saddle with a look of disbelief spelled clear across his face!

"We are in trouble, Boys," said Ofer very slowly. Then shaking his head, he pointed to a clump of four dead Indians in a grisly pile where all four had obviously died in a vicious hand-to-hand battle saying, "That one with the tomahawk still stuck into the side of his head is none other than Chief Learning Bear! The one and same Blackfoot chief who we had a truce with some time back! Now with him dead, I wonder whoever replaces him as the Smith River Band of Blackfeet's new chief will be as forgiving with us and all the other white trappers as was Learning Bear. Because if the new chief isn't and as deeply as we are in Blackfoot country..."

With that revelation and Ofer's question hanging in the air, the trappers picked their ways carefully out from the deadly field of battle holding about 40 dead Indians from both tribes! In fact, Black Eagle and Little Raven, superstitious and fearful of the bad spirits on the battlefield, had already ridden away from the scene of death and were sitting on their horses a short distance away. That experience sent the trappers back downstream on the Smith River realizing they would be setting their beaver traps further downstream and far away from the deadly battlefield so as not to disturb the dead or bring on any bad spirits to the group as a whole. When the trappers returned to their campsite later that evening, all of them discovered their bodies and clothing still carried the sickly sweet smell of death. Come nightfall found all of the trappers in their creeks taking baths and washing out their clothing as best as they could with the strong lye soap they had made with the ashes from their own campfire and glycerin...

The next morning found all of the men quietly eating break-fast and still not over the grisly scene of death they had experienced the day before. That was when Ofer set his empty plate in the wash pan, took a drink of his coffee and said, "From now on, we must assume that the Blackfeet are now just as deadly an enemy as are their cousins the Gros Ventre. From now on, no one is to ever be very far from his rifle and when afield trapping beaver or hunting elk for our camp meat, every one of us must be wearing both of our pistols and make sure there are at least six extra loaded rifles in a quick at hand horse's pannier just in case the Blackfeet now come calling. I have a feeling that anyone who does any the less will soon find his scalp hanging from some 'Buck's' coup stick or battle lance..."

The next week, found the trappers out hunting more elk for camp meat and making it into jerky for when they were out on the trail trapping come the snows of winter. Additionally, they made sure all of their traps were duly smoked to rid them of the man smells. As for their old muskrat traps, they had been left behind in the hands of another trapper back at Fort Manuel who was high on trapping and the eating of muskrats. As for Ofer and the clan, they just didn't bring in enough money at the end of the trapping season for their tastes. That and running a muskrat trap line took too much time when they were also simultaneously running marten and wolf trap lines during the difficult to travel around in winter weather.

Stepping out from their cave-cabin one morning in late September, Ofer paused with his rifle in hand and looked all around their campsite as he always did. There just below him were Gabriel and Little Raven talking, laughing and cooking the men's breakfasts. Then looking over at the horse corral, he could see that all of their horses were present and accounted for, and over at the creekside stood Jerimiah and Joshua shaving and cleaning up. As for Black Eagle, he was sitting over the log-built latrine trying to get rid of the rich rice, brown sugar, raisins and a splash of rum supper dish made two nights previously in cele-bration of his 21st season of life. Walking around to the side of their cave-cabin, Ofer soon joined Black Eagle as both of them tried ridding their systems of the rich rice dish they had just discovered that their 'big and little' guts were unaccustomed to digesting without producing somewhat dire results... Especially dire results when one was riding a horse, setting traps in a beaver pond while wearing breechclouts and buckskin leggings and carrying two heavy horse pistols in a belt sash needing to be rid of quickly...

Then all of a sudden, Ofer grabbed up his rifle, quickly stepped away from the latrine seat and promptly fell face-first into the dirt, tripping over his buckskin pants still wrapped tightly around his ankles. Lunging back up and using his rifle as an aid, he staggered two steps to get his footing under him and then stared hard through the aspen grove holding the horse corral and beyond. When he did, Black Eagle, his liquid dribbling waste still running in rivulets from his 'tail-end' all over the latrine seat, realized Ofer did not make the move he just did without it being some sort of an emergency, grabbed up his rifle and prepared for the worst as well!

Realizing that Black Eagle was up off the latrine seat, alert and now looking as well, Ofer said through clenched teeth, "Down through the aspens by the old beaver pond with the washed-out dam. I am sure I saw an Indian peering up at our camp from behind that lightning-struck fir tree!" With his bodily waste still dribbling from his irritated intestinal system and onto his buckskins still lying down around his feet, Black Eagle's sharp eyes also caught what he felt was a slight movement of some sort but could not tell what it was from where he stood because it was so fleeting! Then nothing else was seen by the two half-naked men standing there with their rifles held at the ready. About then Joshua and Jerimiah saw what was happening back at the latrine and realizing that danger was at hand, simultaneously dropped their razors, grabbed up their nearby rifles, whirled and looked into the aspen grove of trees behind them as well! Upon seeing those two brothers' rapid arming movements over at the shaving tree caused Gabriel and Little Raven to drop what they were doing by the cooking fire, grab up their nearby rifles and look long and hard around them as well for any perceived danger. As all of the men so reacted to a man, everyone thought back to the Indian battlefield on the upper Smith, the face of dead Learning Bear and wondered if the truce once had was now long gone with his untimely death?

Seeing nothing else and suffering a great loss of dignity over their heavily soiled buckskin pants, both Ofer and Black Eagle 'crowhopped' for the nearby creek. Then with their rifles still in one hand helping them to steady themselves in a squatting position, attempted to rid themselves of the rice dinner's remnants into the fast flowing creek in which they now stood! However, as they did, Joshua and Jerimiah stood guard over the two men in the creek trying to regain some of their lost dignity, better smelling bodies and lowered clothing items with the use and aid of the creek's swift rushing waters running through their 'frontier laundry'. However by then four of the clan had outfitted themselves with 'possibles' bags, powder horns, both pistols and rifles as per Ofer's previous warnings about the possibility of the Blackfeet now being shed of the previous truce and with a new leader, on the warpath with all white trappers. Somewhat later with some dignity restored and wearing cleaner dry clothing, Ofer advised the others of what he thought he had seen, namely an unknown Indian slipping through the dense timber by the old beaver pond and as he did, looking up at the trappers' campsite and horse corral all the while with keen interest.

Shortly thereafter with keen-eyed Black Eagle and Little Raven in the lead and the four brothers providing protection while spread out and slowly walking from behind the two trackers, the men investigated the scene where Ofer thought he had seen an Indian skulking about. This he did because the last time he had observed such movement at their old campsite, he had not bothered to closely investigate and they had later been ambushed by Gros Ventre! Within moments of investigating what Ofer had thought he had seen, Little Raven discovered a faint set of moccasin tracks working their way through the timber and then down towards the Smith. Twenty minutes or so later, the men still following the faint and suspicious moccasin tracks, discovered them leading to where a horse with unshod hooves had stood tied to a tree! Then they could see where the horse had been ridden off towards the north, directly into the Smith River's shallows in order to shake anyone following them and then quickly lost to any further sight due to the rushing waters eliminating any kind of sign...

After breakfast that morning and a little 'unusual planning and preparation' by Ofer, the trappers streamed out from their campsite to begin their fall trapping season since the beaver were now coming into their prime and the men were more than ready to begin trapping. Ofer led the caravan with Joshua riding 'shotgun', followed by Gabriel and Little Raven leading three packhorses. Two of the packhorses being led carried panniers holding all of the men's needed beaver trapping accessories, and the third packhorse carried just two panniers and in those panniers were eight fully loaded rifles! Rifles that had been procured after their owners had been killed off in battle with the six trappers over almost a two-year period. Last in line rode Black Eagle and Jerimiah providing rearguard protection in case the trappers' caravan was ambushed from the rear by attacking Indians, a favorite method of attack. Upon closer examination, every trapper carried his own personal rifle in hand and sported two pistols in a belt sash and one extra rifle carried on a scabbard on his personal riding horse as well. It was very obvious that Ofer was now highly suspicious of the lasting ability of his previous truce executed with the now dead Learning Bear... That and he figured if the Blackfeet or Gros Ventre took the trappers on in a lopsided battle where the Indians outnumbered the trappers, it would be a 'very costly' attack for both sides... But this was the lifestyle the trappers had chosen and since Black Eagle and Little Raven now considered themselves fully fledged 'brothers' to their dear friends, the Tal Brothers, this was the current desired way of life for all concerned, come "hell or high water". **However, the trappers did not leave their campsite unobserved...**

Being that they had great beaver water right below their cave-cabin on the Smith, that was where Ofer had decided to set his first beaver traps of the fall trapping season. Then since they planned on trapping on the lengthy Smith River for two full seasons, they would just trap beaver further north during their second season from where they would start that day. That way they would have great beaver trapping throughout, they would not have to build another cabin or horse corral the next season, and with the six of them as heavily armed as they were, they would make a formidable force against any tribe's attackers, if given just half a chance in a fair fight. That being said, staying in one area for two years of beaver trapping was not unreasonable or out of line for such determined trappers and the amount of beaver resources in the trapping area, so the Tal trappers had decided that they would do so on the Smith.

After a short ride, Ofer and Joshua dismounted and after handing their riding horses' reins to Little Raven, partially disrobed and crawled into their breechclouts and buckskin leggings. Then with trapping gear in hand and Gabriel providing accessory support, the two trappers started doing what they did best, cold water, late summer mosquitoes and all. As they did, Black Eagle and Jerimiah stood guard closely at hand and in each of their belted pistols, the men now carried the very deadly at close range 'buck and ball' in case any attackers decided to fight a close-in battle from a planned ambush site.

By early afternoon, all of the men's 30 traps had been set and after a short rest out of sight in a cottonwood grove, the men returned and rechecked their previously set traps. Some 14 dead floating in the traps beaver were the trappers' rewards for their excellent previously set traps and after skinning out the same, they headed for the nearest grove of willows. There they gathered two panniers full of willow branches and then headed for their campsite. As they did, they once again formed up in an "Ofer suggested battle line" and headed for home, avoiding likely looking ambush sites where they could. On the way, they ran into a small herd of cow elk and killed a fat one who was not nursing and without a calf. After just butchering out the hindquarters and backstraps and loading those parts into several panniers, the men left the rest of the elk for the critters and then once again headed for home happy over their day's successes.

Rounding the fringe of trees at the bottom of their main meadow, the men turned their horses towards the corral and realizing 'their day was done', the horses eagerly picked up their pace under their riders 'realizing' they were soon to be unloaded and turned out to feed and water. That was when the returning men saw it! In front of their horse corral gate, a corral still holding a wealth of horses, lay a young Indian man in his teenage years! Smashed in an 'Ofer planning and preparation, previously hidden bear trap next to the corral gate', the young Indian lay with both leg bones crushed in the toothed jaws of the grizzly bear trap! As the not too surprised men, after Ofer had thought he had seen an Indian skulking around below their camp earlier in the day, rode up to the man in the trap, it was obvious the trapped Indian had died of shock and loss of blood because of his smashed and mangled legs! Without any words being spoken among the men other than Black Eagle saying, "Blackfoot" regarding the dead man's tribal affiliation, they dismounted and Gabriel went to their cave-cabin, making sure he carefully walked around its entranceway and went inside. Soon he emerged and once again carefully walking around the entrance way, brought the men standing around the corral gate the two clamps necessary to lower the springs holding the trap's jaws tightly clamped and in so doing, released the dead Indian's legs from the trap. Then without a single word being spoken, Gabriel loaded the young Indian man onto the back of a pack-horse now with removed panniers and tying him onto the back of the horse, began walking towards the Smith River. Once Gabriel arrived, he untied the Indian man and dragged him over to the river where there was a strong current. Therein he dumped the dead man and watched him float downstream and soon out of sight. Then Gabriel walked his horse back and it was soon released into their horse herd just let out to feed and water from the corral.

Just to make sure none of his trappers forgot and walked into the other bear trap previously set by Ofer, it was dug out from the entrance of the cave-cabin and laid off to one side of the entranceway. Then Ofer and Black Eagle backtracked the young Indian killed in the bear trap by the corral where he tried to enter and steal horses. About 100 yards from the trappers' camp-site, Ofer and Black Eagle discovered the young Indian's horse tied to a tree. There the two men untied the horse, removed its saddle, pulled its bridle and then slapped it on its rump and sent it on its way to wherever it wanted to go. Then the two men walked back to their campsite looking forward to whatever Gabriel and Little Raven were cooking up for the hungry men's supper that evening. After the group's supper that evening of biscuits, coffee and freshly roasted elk meat, the men adjourned to their cave-cabin and in the soft light from their beeswax candles and 'dancing' light from the blazing fire in their fire-place, defatted and hooped their first day's catch of beaver. It having been a long and exhausting day, the men shortly there-after headed for their sleeping furs and slept soundly that night knowing they had not had any of their horses stolen that day. As he lay there in his sleeping furs, Ofer was thankful for the fleeting glimpse of the Indian slipping through the trees earlier that morning. Never again would he mistrust his eyes and once again, he mentally thanked his old mentor Bear Trap Driessen, for everything that he had taught a young Ofer Tal about the beauty, majesty, life and death on the frontier and especially, his four grizzly bear traps...

******

Upon discovery of the young Blackfoot man's horse returning to its original horse herd three days later without the young man, there was soon much wailing within the new Chief Walks Fast's tipi of the Smith River Band of Blackfeet by his wife and three daughters... As the quickly summoned chief stood there looking at his young son's favorite horse, his dark eyes narrowed. Four days earlier, his young son not yet out of his teenage years had requested from his father the new chief, that he be allowed to go to the south as a solo warrior, where all of the white trappers were trapping along the Musselshell and count coup against them by either killing the 'hated ones', stealing their valuable horses or both, as other young warriors in their band had been allowed to do by their fathers. The "Little Chief" as he was known among the band's elders, had already proven himself in the recent battle between the hated Crow and members of his tribe when their old and much-respected Chief Learning Bear had recently been killed. Also eager to let his young and showing much promise son go forth and do battle with the much-hated white man trappers as a coming of age lone warrior, Chief Walks Fast, against the wishes of his wife and daughters, had allowed his son to do as he had so requested. Allowing his young son to go forth by himself and attempt to count coup against the white man as part of his coming of age ritual and in part, working to bring honor to the tribe and become a full-fledged warrior within the new chief's band, had concerned the new chief. Now as a result of giving his blessing to his 17-seasons-old son for such a trial of his manhood, he was now missing and presumed killed by the hated white man trappers flooding across the waters of the land! Walking over to his son's favorite horse, Chief Walks Fast closely examined the horse being held by another warrior. His saddle and bridle had obviously been removed since there were no injury marks on the horse's body or blood on its hide showing that his son had met a violent death. That was a deep mystery to the chief. Then if his son had been killed by another Indian or some white man trapper, why was there no blood on the side of the horse? Also, horses were very valuable out on the frontier and that being the case, why had whoever killed his young son just let his horse go back to the wild...?

With Chief Walks Fasts' dark eyes narrowing over the loss of his much-loved son and his heart now hardening like the flint on his arrows, he turned facing his group of warriors silently looking on saying, "The truce with the white man flooding across the lands of our ancestors never should have been declared by Chief Learning Bear and is now like him, no more! You men are released from our old chief's word of peace with the white man and can now go forward and kill and steal among him and his kind as you wish. However if you do, bring me the head of the man who killed my son and I will sing your praises to those in the "Cloud World" and The Great Spirit. And if my son was taken up to our "Cloud People" due to the hand of the one we call The Scalper, bring me not only his head but his heart in your hands as well. Do so, so I can eat his heart, gain his skill as a warrior and then know that he is forever walking among those others in the "Upper World" unable to join his own ancestors because he is missing having a whole body..."

As if he didn't have enough problems in just becoming the band's new chief following the reign of a very much-beloved chief, Chief Walks Fast turned to walk away in his deep sorrow over losing his son. Turned to walk away because he how had to return to his tipi and attempt to comfort his wife of many years and his three daughters. And in so doing explain to them as to why he had let him go by himself in the first place. Then thinking, he paused and turned once again to face some of his warriors. "To any of you, my young men, who wish to venture south to where the white man trappers are along the Musselshell remember this. Sub-Chief Coyote and a number of his family members as well as the great warrior Yellow Wolf and others of our band, went south many moons ago to the white trappers along the Musselshell who had the horses the color of our antelope they called "buckskins". If any of you warriors go south on a raid to steal horses from our enemy the Crow or the white men trappers, begin your raids with those who have the buckskin horses. I say that because those are the trappers who our old Chief Learning Bear in his wisdom started with when he went south to avenge the loss of his son. I think that is where I would look first, find and then kill the one we have come to call The Scalper. I say that based on Chief Learning Bear and the many others who we have lost over the years whose wisdom led them there first looking for The Scalper and those unique-looking horses and did not return. That tells me, find those uniquely colored horses called "buckskins" and I believe that is where you will find The Scalper."

Then turning once again, Chief Walks Fast headed for his tipi now even further saddened over the loss of his son who had gone south to count coup on the Crow and white man in the years of his youth hoping to gain recognition and respect among his band, only to meet his ancestors. That and to experience his wife and daughters cutting their arms with small cuts and wearing ash from their campfire as a sign of sorrow over losing a loved one.

As Chief Walks Fast walked away with stooped shoulders over his newfound sadness, warrior "Matchitehew" or "He Has an Evil Heart" gestured for his band of onlooking close friends and fellow warriors to gather around him. When he did, "Achak" or "Spirit", "Askook" or "Snake", "Hassun" or "Stone", "Samoset" or "He Walks over Much", "Nootau" or "Fire", "Sucki" or "Black", "Chogan" or "Blackbird", and "Segenam" or "Lazy" gathered around their 'firebrand' of a friend in order to hear what he had to say.

"I say we warriors make ready and ride south to the white man's Musselshell trapping grounds. There we do what the great Chief Learning Bear, other warriors and new Chief Walks Fast would like done in killing the hated white man who is stealing the animals from the land of our ancestors. Then we steal his horses, avenge the losses of two chiefs' sons and bring the head and heart of The Scalper back to our people and Chief Walks Fast. If we do, our people and those of other bands who hear of our deeds will sing our praises for many moons for our courage and honor us by calling us "Great Warriors of the Blackfeet People"! What do you say to that, My Friends?" asked He Has an Evil Heart, with a look upon his face and a feeling in his body that matched his namesake...

Two days later, warriors He Has an Evil Heart, Spirit, Snake, He Walks over Much, Stone, Blackbird, Fire, Lazy and Black sat upon their horses in front of Chief Walks Fast's tipi. They had gathered there that morning to let their chief know of their intentions and ask for his blessings for a safe and happy return. A safe and happy return bringing back many horses, Crow and white man's scalps, and the head and heart of the great killer who put his bloody red hand upon the necks of the horses of those he has killed in battle, namely the one known to his tribe as The Scalper...

Walking among his warriors and clasping each and every man's hand and forearm in a sign of great respect and support, Chief Walks Fast asked that The Great Spirit ride with his warriors in what they were about to do. He also advised he would be going with them but his wife and three daughters were still in such grief over the loss of the son and brother that he had to stay home and comfort them. With that and a yell of excitement and a wave of their arms, the nine warriors rode away in a cloud of dust from the Smith River Blackfeet Band's encampment amidst the supporting yells and waving of arms from a large number of their friends and kin seeing their war party happily off, led by warrior He Has an Evil Heart. Turning south, the nine-man war party was soon lost to sight, leaving only a slight dust cloud in the air from their horses' hooves. Chief Walks Fast stood there in front of his tipi until his warriors' fast disappearing sight and sounds were no more. However as he did, his 20,000 years of heritage began rising up in his being and somehow he knew before all was said and done, he himself would many moons from now be leading a like war party attempting to do what warrior He Has an Evil Heart was hoping to do. Little did Chief Walks Fast understand the greater oncoming ramifications and significance of what it meant for a race of peoples of superior numbers, hungry for free land to the west with a manifest destiny 'bent', to collide with a race of peoples of lesser numbers. And in so doing, leave a trail of tears that would eventually lead through many tribes of gentle peoples of the land, with their hearts and souls being destroyed and eventually succumbing to their inevitable losses of a gentle and meaningful way of life...

CHAPTER 10 — DEATH ON THE MUSSELSHELL, JACK THORN'S "REWARD"

FOR THE NEXT TWO MONTHS, OFER AND HIS GROUP OF trappers ran their beaver trap line north along the Smith and into its many adjacent waterways. Week by week, the trappers succeeded in adding numerous Made Beaver pelts to their panniers and eventually their bundles of dried beaver skins. Throughout that same period of time, they only had two run-ins with grizzly bears as their only major problems encountered and those 'problems' provided two bear rugs and many evening suppers of spitted bear meat. However, they were fortunate that they never did see a group of nine Blackfeet warriors passing their way on the Smith, in their desires to effectuate their 'war party' presence on those hated white men trapping along the Musselshell. Collaterally that same Blackfoot war party never did see the out of the way Smith River beaver trappers either in their haste to get to the Musselshell. Get to the Musselshell and see what damage they could do to the white American trappers and any roving bands of Crow Indians they could catch 'looking the other way' in inferior numbers and destroy them as well...

Come freeze-up, the trappers pulled their beaver traps to

avoid losing them in the mud under the soon to be arriving thick ice. Then they found themselves making preparations to trap wolves and marten in the high timber lying above their cave-cabin. In making those preparations for the winter trapping season, the Smith River trappers were unaware of a deadly band of nine Blackfoot Indians once again closely passing by their location. Blackfeet Indians who were trailing a long caravan of stolen Crow Indian and white trappers' horses all heavily loaded with bundles of beaver 'Plus', weapons, provisions and numerous scalps. Blackfeet Indians, who upon their arrival back in their Smith River Band of friends and family, were heralded as returning 'heroes' and the bravest of warriors! However, behind them as a result of their earlier deadly activities and depreda-tions, they left a number of burned out trappers' cabins, rotting bodies scattered around those burned-out cabins and in some cases, destroyed Crow tipis, leaving everyone around them rotting out in the waning late fall sun as well! With arrival of the bitter northern winters, those nine victorious warriors were celebrated throughout by their band's peoples as they waited for the season to turn so they could return and continue their mission of killing, stealing of valuable furs and the much-hated white man's provisions, burning and raping of their Crow enemies, as well as any of those they caught 'looking the other way' at the wrong time.

As for the Smith River trappers, far from the Musselshell and unaware of all of its previous summer's butchery committed by the Blackfoot war party of nine warriors against the trappers, they continued hunting the local elk and deer for their meat supplies, ran their wolf and marten trap lines and pelted out those animals so trapped. Then as the season changed into the warmer spring weather patterns, the Smith River trappers once again when the ice went out, began trapping beaver. And in so doing, added even larger numbers to their previous fall's catches in preparation for their summer trip to Fort Manuel. Fort

Manuel where they would sell those hard-won furs and celebrate the passing of another year of trapping successes with others of their own kind. And when in and among others of their own kind, quietly discuss the 'whereabouts' of some and acknowledge with a quiet drink of rum those friends and fellow trappers who had 'gone under' when their luck had run out on them...

******

With the season's change from the cold of winter into the warmth of spring, found war party leader He Has an Evil Heart with his other eight warriors quietly sitting once again on their horses in front of Chief Walks Fast's tipi. Once again they were asking for the chief's blessing in what they were about to do along the Musselshell to the white trappers and any roving bands of Crow Indians they stumbled across, ran to ground and killed. And once again, the chief and the band's Medicine Man asked for the blessings from The Great Spirit in what they were about to do and for their safe return with more stolen horses and furs, so they could be sold to the Hudson's Bay Fur Company for more rifles and whiskey. Products they could not purchase from Fort Manuel because Lisa would not sell them to the Blackfeet because of their historical constant warfare with the Crow Indians who were his most important fur traders, and their treachery among all white men caught roaming the lands of the Blackfeet.

In fact, a Canadian fur buyer with a long scar running across his face from a previous violent encounter of sorts at Fort Manuel, had just left the chief's village with all of the stolen furs taken by the nine warriors currently sitting before him from the fall before. As it turned out, that person was the same 'Scar Face' who had struck Black Eagle a year before at Fort Manuel and when Ofer had stepped in to defend his fellow trapper, found himself almost being killed by a rifle shot by the one with the scar running across his face! That uncalled-for action on the part of Scar Face caused him and his five henchmen to be expelled from Fort Manuel by Manuel Lisa because of that almost deadly incident and told never to return to his trading establishment on the Bighorn River. The one and same man who had tried killing Ofer, and had now since gone to work for the Hudson's Bay Fur Company from Canada as one of their fur buyers among the Blackfeet. A renegade who didn't care how he came by furs, stolen or not, just so he was able to purchase great lots of the valuable furs for his newfound company and trading partner and in so doing, keeping such fur riches from Manuel Lisa at Fort Manuel.

Once again Chief Walks Fast and the band's Medicine Man asked The Great Spirit to watch over and care for his group of nine aggressive warriors and provide for their safe return once again with much in the way from their spoils of battle with the Crow and white trappers in the way of horses and furs. Then amidst many shouts of support and encouragement from a number of the members of the chief's band, the nine warriors rode out from the chief's encampment and headed south with 'blood in their eyes'! Headed south with full intentions of starting along the Musselshell where they had left off from their killing spree the previous fall and continuing westward towards where the Musselshell eventually joined the Smith River... By so doing, they hoped they could kill off most of the trappers now crowding along the Musselshell trapping beaver and steal what valuables they might have in the way of horses, firearms, provisions and furs. War party leader He Has an Evil Heart had planned his trapper-killing mission well. In fact, his plan was to start killing where he and his band of Blackfeet had left off from the fall before, and end their killings along the Musselshell at the reported cabin and campsite holding the uniquely colored horses called 'buckskins' as old Chief Learning Bear had previously described. By so doing, he figured whoever the much-hated and unidentified Scalper of his people was, by killing every white trapper along the Musselshell, one way or the other they would manage to find, kill the mystery man and avenge all of his band's previous losses at his 'scalping' hand.

******

For the next three weeks, Ofer and company trapped beaver along the Smith and its many adjacent waterways, icy cold waters or not. As it turned out, after running their trap lines all day in the spring's icy cold waters of the Smith, Ofer and Joshua had to be helped into and out of their horses' saddles because the men had such near-frozen legs and feet from all the cold water immersions setting traps and retrieving dead beaver that they could hardly walk! Then when back at their cabin at the end of their day's work, the two men spent many an hour sitting either close by the outside campfire or by their blazing fireplace inside their cabin attempting to get bodily warmth back into their nearly frozen legs and feet. Then come morning, the two men, like most every other trapper in country that time of the year, could be found once again sitting in front of their fires vigorously rubbing their cold legs and feet for about an hour or so, so they could get the feeling back into their limbs and be able to safely walk and ride their horses. Then come nightfall, a repeat of the above ritual sitting by the heat from a fire and rubbing one's legs and feet became a requirement if one wanted to walk, ride or even be able to sleep with nearly frozen appendages! This they did until come late spring when the waters had warmed sufficiently enough, making those water immersions when setting traps or removing beaver from those traps more comfortable and less problematic. But the men considered it a small price to pay for the 291, almost all of them Made Beaver that they had caught just during the current spring beaver trapping season! Realizing they were up against "Father Time" and as the warming spring weather continued unabated thereby causing the beaver to begin going out of their prime, Ofer and company stayed at their trapping, adverse weather, icy water immersions or not. (Author's Note: Most research has shown that a majority of the fur trappers only lasted about 2.7 years in the outback before calling it quits due to a speeding bullet, zipping arrow, suffering injuries from a serious horse wreck, 'crossing swords' with a grizzly bear, drowning, starving, freezing to death in the winter weather, or being so stove up because of the onset of the early stages of rheumatism from the constant cold water immersions associated with running beaver trap lines! That they did essentially in the 'raw' because the invention of rubber and the making of rubber boots were still a few years distant from invention and industry.)

Once Ofer determined that the beaver they were catching were now starting to come out of 'prime', the men pulled their traps and began making preparations for their annual summer trip to Fort Manuel to sell their wolf, marten and beaver furs, reprovision their supplies and spend time safely relaxing in and among their old friends until the fall beaver trapping season called for their return to the wild. However, this time the men were ahead of the 'clock'. They had planned on trapping the Smith one more year and by so doing, they could return to a cave-cabin that was already built, a horse corral already constructed, meat poles and smoking racks already up and a known nearby woodpile supply handy for the saw, ax and horse teams to haul to their cave-cabin for use in their fireplace or outdoor firepit.

So with that, Ofer and company dug a cache site in some dry and sandy soil near their cave-cabin and stashed a large amount of their provisions, cooking implements, extra kegs of rum, airtight tins of powder and all of their heavy traps so they would not have to be hauled to Fort Manuel and then all the way back for no other purpose than just hauling them around. Then since the men still had some time before they had to leave, all of their furs were bundled up and made ready for transport, winter wood was cut in advance and stacked near their cave-cabin and

Gabriel checked all of the horses' hooves and reshod those needing a new or tightened shoe since he was the group's farrier. Then Ofer and Black Eagle tore down all of the men's firearms as well as their extra rifles gathered up after battles with the Indians from an earlier time, cleaned their mechanisms, had lead and black powder fouling removed, then reassembled them now that they had been made ready for use once again. Then for several nights running, the men cast more bullets in anticipation of the Fort Manuel trip soon to come and the potential dangers from the Blackfeet or Gros Ventre that may be lurking and possibly encountered along the trappers' known travel routes. Then there was always the possibility of running into an always hungry grizzly bear with a hunger for horsemeat and needing a .52 caliber round ball or two instead...

******

Near the current-day town of Cushman, Montana, on the Musselshell, trapper "One-Eyed" Jack Tatum had just removed a large beaver from one of his traps, turned around and found he was confronting the leering face of Blackfoot Indian war party leader He Who Has an Evil Heart! Freezing in surprise and then fear realizing the Indian had a fully drawn bow with arrow nocked and aimed right at him from just 30 feet away, his survival skills immediately kicked in as he then sprung into action! Holding up the dead beaver's carcass in front of him as a partial shield with his strong hand holding onto the tail, he dropped his weak hand to the pistol tucked under his sash. **TH-WHACK** went the steel-tipped arrow into the beaver's carcass being held in front of his chest by One-Eyed Jack. The speeding arrow hit the beaver's carcass with such force that it proceeded clear through its body and into Jack's stomach area, only stopping when it ripped into the trapper's liver! Jack all of a sudden felt a horrible burning pain that was so intense that he tried grabbing the shaft of the arrow and pulling it from his body. Then there was no more pain and the light in his eyes went out forever, as a result of the gushing of his blood from his arrow-ruptured hepatic artery! But before that light went out from his eyes, he saw another Indian bent over and scalping his partner "Muskrat" Johnson, who was supposed to be protecting Jack while he was setting or tending to the beaver caught in his traps… Both trappers were later discovered by a hungry grizzly bear and ended up as bear scat on the prairie.

Two days later, Peter "Bobcat" Chaplin was trapping further west of where One-Eyed Jack and his partner Muskrat had been ambushed, killed and scalped by Blackfoot Indians led by He Who Has an Evil Heart. Near the current-day town of Ryegate, Montana, on a beaver pond just off the Musselshell, Pete knelt near a freshly used beaver slide. That was the last beaver slide he ever saw, as he pitched into the spring's cold waters of the beaver pond upon being tomahawked in the head from behind by a sneaking Blackfoot Indian warrior named Fire! Pete never did figure out why his partners who were standing guard over his trapping operations failed to warn him of the close at hand danger. That was because all three trapping partners who were supposed to be watching over and protecting Pete were now lying back on the edge of the beaver pond! Lying dead at the edge of the beaver pond because they had just been filled full of arrows shot into them by Blackfoot Indian warriors Lazy, Stone, He Walks over Much, Spirit and Black when the trappers weren't as cautious or alert as they should have been! As it turned out, all three trappers had been so intent in watching their partner removing a live and mad as hell 90-pound beaver from his trap that they never even heard the five Blackfeet Indians sneaking up to within 20 feet of them before loosing their deadly arrows into the trappers' backs and heads!

That evening while back at their camp, trapper and designated cook Darrel "Swamp Water" Jenkins removed his Dutch oven from its bed of coals, turned and prepared to sit it onto a nearby sitting log so its contents could be removed and cooled.

That was when his head 'exploded' in pain as an arrow shot into him by a close at hand Blackfoot Indian warrior named Snake slammed into his right ear penetrating his brain case, killing him instantly! Hearing an unusual commotion out by the campfire when Darrel dropped his Dutch oven on the rocks surrounding his firepit with a loud metallic "CLANK", his three partners inside the cabin defatting beaver pelts arose to investigate. Those three partners streamed out from their cabin unarmed only to run into a furious flight of arrows shot at them by eight waiting in ambush Blackfoot Indians, who had arranged themselves on both sides of the cabin door waiting for the response reactions from those inside when they became aware of the trouble by the firepit! Those arrows fired from such close range all found their targets and as the men staggered forward in extreme pain, the eight Indians hurriedly dropped their bows and closed upon the three men with upraised tomahawks! Moments later, there were four dead trappers in camp cooling out along with a spilled Dutch oven full of freshly baked biscuits! After scalping all four of the now dead trappers, the Indians feasted on the now cooled biscuits originally meant for the four dead men's supper, as the nearby dead trappers' eyes stared coldly into the evening sky. Then they raided the trappers' cabin, and an hour later found all nine of the Blackfeet deeply into the dead trappers' 'rum cups' in celebration.

The next morning right at daylight, just off the Musselshell near the current-day town of Harlowtown, Montana, in a trappers' campsite eating breakfast sat "Buckskin" Jack Roberts, Calvin Wright, Randle Slooten and Harold "Tweet" Jackson. As they sat there quietly eating, Buckskin just happened to look up upon hearing a strange nearby sound, and saw He Who Has an Evil Heart rounding their nearby cabin at a dead run and heading right for him! Frozen in surprise with fear for just a split second that gave He Who Has an Evil Heart just enough time to close the distance and smash his tomahawk down upon Randle

Slooten's head so violently that his brains and blood shot forward and splattered all over Buckskin's face and plate! That deadly action awakened the more than stunned Buckskin to the danger at hand! Immediately, even with his face covered with blood and brain matter from his fellow and now dead trapper Randle Slooten, he dropped his plate full of food, grabbed his rifle off his sitting log, swung it from his sitting position to defend himself, and died with an arrow shot into his throat by fellow Indian Snake! By now, Calvin Wright and Harold Jackson, aware of the close at hand danger from the attacking Indians, jumped up only to be immediately filled with zipping arrows shot by the rest of the attackers sprinting into the scene of death! Soon the only sounds heard in that dead trappers' camp were those of nine hungry Indians eating the trappers' breakfast... Following that, those same nine Indians spent the rest of the morning packing the trappers' horses with stolen kegs of rum, gunpowder and their valuable bundles of beaver furs. Shortly thereafter, those same nine Indians streamed out from that trappers' campsite with all of their long string of riding and pack-horses in tow once belonging to a number of recently killed trappers along the length of the Musselshell. Trappers which the Blackfeet had now counted coup on the much-hated white trappers!

Two days later further west just off the Musselshell, nine staked-out Blackfoot Indians led by He Who Has an Evil Heart watched a trappers' cabin come to life right at daylight. Soon, ten rugged-looking individuals began flooding out from their cabin and began making breakfast, rounding up their horses from the meadow and bringing them back to their corral so they could be saddled for the day's trapping events. Then one or two at a time tended to their individual calls of nature. Being that the ten trappers always appeared to 'be ready for bear' with their rifles always in hand, He Who Has an Evil heart realized to make a frontal attack as he and his fellow warriors had done previously and so successfully with smaller groups of trappers since their return to the Musselshell, would not work with this large bunch. So with those thoughts in mind, he backed off. Then for the next four days, He Who Has an Evil Heart and his fellow warriors made it a point to quietly watch the ten trappers closely looking for a weakness in their daily routines and defenses which they could exploit once they decided to attack, kill the lot, steal their horses, furs and their remaining provisions. This they did because the horses, rum, provisions and a huge amount of beaver furs which those trappers were bringing in daily, made for a rich reward if they could safely pull off such an attack. He Who Has an Evil Heart also realized that if he were to lead his fellow warriors into a battle in which he lost a number of his men, that would not sit right with Chief Walks Fast or the rest of his people in their band. So like a hungry snake waiting patiently for a mouse to pass closely by, they waited, watched and learned from the trappers' activities they were now closely watching from hiding on a daily basis.

*****

With most of their work done before they headed down to Fort Manuel, Ofer suggested to the men that being low on their jerky supplies they augment the same. Later that day the men went elk hunting and killed two fat cows. Then after butchering them out, some meat was set aside for their coming meals and the rest was sliced thin, smoked and made into jerky for the coming trip to Fort Manuel. Then once the jerky was ready for eating, it was placed into tanned deerskin bags and hung from pegs driven into the cave-cabin's walls to prevent rodent and moisture damage. That and everyone had one of their saddlebags filled with the great-eating jerky in case finding good 'chow' sources along the trail was difficult to come by, either because of the lack of game or their inability to shoot any because of the close at hand nature of hostile Indians.

Once their supplies of jerky had been distributed, the men

began arranging all of their packs, saddles and the like for the morrow and the loading of all of their horses with the gear to be hauled down to Fort Manuel. Rising way before daylight, the six men labored long and hard loading and arranging the packs on their horses so they would not 'gow' or 'sore' up any of their valuable pack animals having to carry such heavy and many times awkward loads. Then with saddled horses, one and all left the confines of their campsite and cave-cabin around noon and headed out for Fort Manuel in a long string of riding and pack-horses. As was usual, Ofer and Black Eagle led the fur trappers' caravan with short pack strings trailing behind them so they could fight if surprised or intercepted by hostile Indians on the trail. Close behind came Gabriel and Little Raven with the longest pack strings since they were more or less protected by the riders in the front and rear of their caravan. Trailing the long fur caravan rode Joshua and Jerimiah with shorter pack strings as well, so they could provide quick protection if ambushed by hostile Indians from behind the fur caravan while all strung out en route Forth Manuel.

Two days of slow travel with such a heavily loaded pack string brought Ofer and his fellow trappers once again to a familiar trail. A once familiar route leading to that of the Musselshell to their south that they had finally given up on those waterways because of all the newly arriving trappers crowding in and wanting to trap in the same area. Newly arriving trappers who had heard through word of mouth back at Fort Manuel of Ofer and his group of trappers' many successes along the Musselshell and had now crowded into that area in order to share in the 'beaver' wealth! With that crowding and then being run out from their old cabin along that stretch of the Musselshell by Jack Thorn and his nine rough-looking compatriots at the start of the fall trapping season, Ofer and company had finally moved on further to the north. When they did, they moved into the wild reaches of the Smith River where they found no competition crowding into that beaver-rich area and made that country their current homesite for that coming year's fall and spring beaver trapping season.

However on this return trip down the Smith towards the junction of the Musselshell, Ofer and company as they had approached their old campsite, the one Jack Thorn and his wild-looking bunch of trappers had stolen away from them by arriving earlier and taking over a ready-made cabin, heard trouble brewing from a long distance off! Even over the sounds of the winds in the trees and the flowing waters nearby on the Smith, they heard the sporadic sounds of heavy rifle fire coming from the location of their old cabin! When they did, Ofer stopped his fur caravan immediately and for the longest time, the men just sat there at the ready as they listened to the rifle fire coming from their old cabin site trying to figure out what might be happening. With the Mountain Prices a trapper paid for powder and lead at Fort Manuel, Ofer and company damn well knew the cabin-stealing trappers were not just out and shooting off their rifles for the hell of it! From the sounds of the constant rifle fire, it immediately became apparent that the trappers at their old cabin site were under some sort of attack and a serious one at that!

Finally Ofer and Black Eagle after listening to the rifle fire and then hearing it slowly dying out and then stopping altogether, reasoned that whoever was in that battle, it was more than likely now over! And therein lay a dangerous situation. Because of the lay of the land, the easiest route of travel was along the waterways that ran right alongside their old cabin site where all of the shooting had been heard emanating from! That meant to continue along the easiest route of travel might expose them and their caravan to the same trouble they had just heard being settled moments earlier with heavy gunfire! Being that from the sounds of the earlier gunfire and there had been lots of it, it was a big battle involving numerous individual shooters, that caused Ofer and company grave concerns. That being said, Ofer was reluctant to just send one or two of their group into 'harm's' way' for a 'look-see' of the battle area. Send into harm's way in order to determine what was the scope and degree of the serious-sounding fighting that had just occurred, and if there was any danger remaining as to the battle's outcome to his small group of trappers if they were to pass by the earlier battle scene.

Drawing in his group of now very concerned trappers, Ofer said, "We need to continue following that lay of the land that leads us right by where all of that shooting took place earlier to avoid stressing our heavily loaded horses by fording the Smith and then having to climb over that nearby mountain ridge in order to avoid whatever has happened down there. Hell, even if we went over that ridgeline, what is to say we would not be discovered as we did, and then be drawn into a firefight with who was doing all of that shooting we heard earlier. That being said, I suggest with Little Raven and Black Eagle in the lead checking things out since they are our best trackers, the rest of us need to join in behind them as an extra layer of protection for them against any kind of an ambush and go see for ourselves what the hell was happening down there and determine if it is now safe to travel through that neck of the woods. But before we do that, we need to hide and tie off our stock so they are not encumbering us if we find ourselves drawn into some kind of battle."

Hearing no dissent from his fellow trappers as to his suggestions, the men tied off all of their riding and packhorses in the heavy timber after scouting around to make sure there were no grizzly bears or evidence of their immediate presence or fresh scat in the area. Then with Black Eagle and Little Raven in the lead on foot using their God-given native instincts and natural tracking abilities, the rest of the men followed closely behind and heavily armed with their extra rifles providing those two men protection from ambush. Keeping to the dense timber to avoid discovery, the men slowly stalked their ways towards the direction they last heard the heavy sounds of battle occurring.

Within minutes of their sneaking through the thick timber, the men came upon a surprising and hidden Indian encampment not far from their old cabin site! Therein that camp was definite evidence of nine Indian horses tied up awaiting the return of their masters, and 77 other shod horses tied on long picket ropes in the same area that had apparently belonged to what everyone now figured were long-dead trappers killed as they trapped along the lower reaches of the nearby Musselshell! Those concerns were attributed to the fact that from their hoofprints around where they stood tied to their picket lines, all 77 additional horses were not only shod but wore assorted white man-made brands on their rumps as well! Additionally, there were 32 bundles of beaver pelts strewn all around the recently used Indian encampment! Further careful looking around revealed numerous and obviously stolen kegs of rum and black powder, stacks of good quality rifles, 24 extra riding saddles, and a large number of packsaddles scattered and piled up around what appeared to be a very successful Indian raiders' camp! No two ways about it, from all indications and all of the white trappers' property strewn about the Indian raiders' campsite, it was deadly testimony as to what had happened over a period of time to a large number of white trappers working in the area...

With that absolute surprise under their belts over what they had just discovered, the men began moving stealthily through the timber towards where they knew their old campsite was located and from whence all the sounds of earlier shooting had more than likely occurred. As they did and as an added precaution, Ofer had Little Raven and Black Eagle follow the telltale signs of the Indians' moccasin prints from their camp to where they were heading in order to avoid a possible ambush from those same Indians. After about an hour of slowly sneaking through the dense timber heading towards their old campsite, Ofer and company could faintly hear a lot of Indians' voices excitedly talking and exulting in their excitement near their old cabin. Now really sneaking stealthily through the timber after the men had rechecked their firearms making sure they were ready to fire at a moment's notice, they dropped to the ground and began slowly crawling through the brush until they had reached the back side of their old horse corral undetected. From their laid-out positions in the brush, they could finally see and not be seen. Peering out from the cover of that brush around their old horse corral, the men were totally amazed at what they saw in front of them! There they saw nine heavily armed and fiercely painted Blackfeet Indians as identified by Little Raven, happily 'whooping it up' all around what appeared to be seven dead trappers' bodies strewn around the front of their group's old cabin. Then by the old campsite's outdoor firepit were three other trappers who had been obviously taken alive and were now tied up, looking miserable as hell from all of the physical abuse they had taken earlier as was evidenced from all of their bleeding facial and head wounds!

Then to the men's disgust and horror, the victorious nine Blackfeet Indians began shooting arrows from close range into the three tied-up live men on the ground in bodily areas that would not kill them but were engendered to cause the men even greater pain! With numerous arrows just shot into the captive men's hands, feet and lower legs, their blood-curdling screams could be heard from hundreds of yards away! It was then that Ofer and company recognized Jack Thorn, their old nemesis, as one of the three captive men now being tortured by the nine vicious and sadistic enjoying themselves, Blackfeet Indians!

Then horror of horrors, as three of the Blackfeet captors under command from what appeared to be the leader of the group, took out their sheath knives, grabbed their captives by their long hair, tilted their heads back and then began slowly scalping the three struggling and screaming men alive! That was when over the blood-curdling screams of the live white trappers being slowly scalped, Ofer quickly gathered unto him his five still-hidden men on the ground by the horse corral. Realizing they were outnumbered but from the looks in Ofer's narrowed eyes, the rest of the hidden trappers realized there was a killing soon to be on its way. A killing that would be equal to that being foisted onto the three live white men trappers now being tortured, regardless of who they were or their past differences! It was obvious from the looks in Ofer's eyes that regardless of whom the men and old enemies were now being tortured, what the Blackfeet were doing was obviously not 'Godly' and that was soon to be rectified by other than the hand of God! Little did the rest of the trappers realize what Ofer was now witnessing had just hardened his heart against the Blackfeet for all time! If they thought scalps fastened into their dead owners' horses' manes and a bloody red handprint slapped onto a horse's neck was bad before, they had best 'hang onto the willows' for what was coming next! Without a moment to spare and over the terrible screaming of those being horribly tortured, Ofer quickly whispered out a daring battle plan for his trappers to follow from their place of hiding by the horse corral.

About ten minutes later still amidst the horrifying moans of the men after being cruelly slow-scalped alive, the other Blackfeet began taking the three now scalped and badly bleeding men and began slowly skinning them alive, starting around their shoulder areas, amidst even more horribly rendering screams! As they did, Ofer and company began hurriedly executing their deadly battle plan soon to come before any more misery could be extracted from the three unfortunates by the cabin. With that, Ofer rose up into a crouch and took off running out of sight through the brush behind their old corral in order to get behind their cabin sight unseen. That he did while the rest of his trappers sneaked forward right to the very edge of the brush

298 | "FOUR SCALPS" OFER TAL, MOUNTAIN MAN

surrounding the corral without being seen and made ready for their deadly part in what was soon to come. Then everyone left behind hidden back at the corral cocked their rifles, took careful aim still realizing they were outnumbered and if they missed killing anyone soon to come, those missed would soon be shooting back at the trappers and possibly causing them deadly harm as well.

As He Who Has an Evil Heart continued cruelly skinning out a madly screaming and wiggling all over the place even though all tied-up, Jack Thorn, the rest of his Blackfeet compatriots continued laughing over the trapper's obvious terrible pain. Collectively, the Indians had identified in their minds Jack Thorn as the legendary Scalper! One who had killed so many of their kind previously, tied their scalps to the manes of their horses and then slapped a bloody handprint onto their horses' necks. Now it would be their turn to do the killing and scalping... Then all of a sudden, a Blackfoot warrior named Black, who was in the gruesome process of further skinning out another of the two remaining live trappers, had his head exploded into such a slew of blood, tissue and gray matter, that for just an instant there was a rainbow hew of colors from all of that once living matter being blasted into the air and sunlight!

Instantly upon hearing the sound of close at hand shooting in their direction from the very edge of the nearby trappers' cabin, the remaining eight Blackfeet whirled around in surprise! They then collectively looked directly over at the close at hand cabin from whence the sound of the deadly pistol shot had just come! When they did, they did so just in time to see a white cloud of black powder smoke streaming their way as Ofer fired his second pistol into the bunched-up Indians! When that happened, the huge .52 caliber soft lead ball blew the face clear off in a splash of flying tissue and bone from war party leader He Who Has an Evil Heart! In the next split second realizing the extreme danger at hand, the remaining seven Blackfeet charged towards

Ofer standing all alone by the side of the cabin and who was now the obvious target of the madly charging and revenge-minded Indians! When the Indians broke ranks and charged Ofer, discordant yells broke the remaining solemn stillness of the afternoon with several of the now hard-charging Blackfeet running right at Ofer singing their 'death songs'! Dropping his second pistol alongside the first one lying at his feet, Ofer calmly took up his rifle which had been laid earlier alongside the cabin's walls for quick retrieval when the Indians were distracted with their inhuman skinning activities. Calmly lifting the fully cocked rifle to his shoulder, Ofer shot a Blackfoot warrior named Fire right in the face, dropping him in front of the racing feet of the rest of the hard-charging Indians running behind him and thundering his way with 'blood in their eyes'!

Then the whole world next to the corral seemed to blow up! Rolling out from the brush by the horse corral streamed huge clouds of white black powder smoke fired from five rifles in unison from about 20 yards away into the horde of Indians now racing madly with a vengeance towards Ofer! Microseconds later, that fusillade of hot lead balls smashed into the chests, sides of faces and necks of the remaining six still charging Indians! In an instant only one Indian remained on his feet and not aware of the rest of his compatriots falling dying and dead behind him since he had been leading the Indians' charge, continued charging the lone white trapper to his front with tomahawk upraised, singing his 'death song' at the top of his lungs so The Great Spirit would hear his plea!

When he did, Ofer calmly dropped his rifle and drawing the third pistol from his sash that he had borrowed from Black Eagle back at the corral and loaded previously with buck and ball, completely blew off most of the entire head of the last attacking Blackfoot warrior! When Ofer took that shot, a stream of white black powder smoke enveloped the hard-charging Indian's head completely! That hard-charging Indian's inertia carried the man's body out from the stream of white smoke toward Ofer and when it exited, the dead Indian emerged momentarily still moving ahead without a head! The impact from all of that buck and ball fired from just a distance of six feet away into the man's head then instantly flipped the attacker's headless body backwards! Flipped the headless body over his heels and then onto the dark and bloody ground to only wiggle in his death throes as his essence drained away through the now open neck wounds! Then Ofer lowered his now empty pistol and surveyed the scene of death through cold eyes...

Then as their old friend and mentor Bear Trap had taught the Tal brothers, they calmly went to their 'possibles' bags and reloaded every rifle and pistol that had been carried and fired. Then with reloaded rifle in hand, Ofer calmly walked over to the firepit where the three barely alive fur trappers from Jack Thorn's original group lay squirming in agony around in the dirt partially skinned! As he did, the other five members of his party emerged from their hiding places in the brush near their old horse corral and watching all around for any other signs of Blackfeet Indians they had missed, they slowly walked over to the three Blackfeet-scalped and now partially skinned and barely alive fur trappers. Two of those trappers were in their last earthly moments. They said nothing as their bodies went into shock from being in such great pain and suffering from such tremendous losses of blood that they soon expired with only a last sigh as their lungs collapsed. However, Jack Thorn scalped as he was and with the upper part of his torso partially skinned and bleeding profusely looked up through pain-filled eyes at Ofer who was now staring down at him unable to do anything for the dying man. Then Thorn's pain-filled eyes flew open in wide amazement as they looked upon Ofer who was now kneeling at his bloody side. "YOU!" he gurgled out. Then his body gave a shudder, uttered a low sigh as his life left his body and then he lay still like the rest of his fur trapper comrades scattered around the cabin.

It was at that exact moment in time with the passing of Jack Thorn that Ofer had a revelation! Had he and the rest of his group been able to return to their old cabin instead of being thrown out by Thorn and his compatriots earlier in the fall, maybe they would be lying scattered around the campsite killed by the marauding Blackfeet, scalped and partially skinned instead! It was then that Ofer had another feeling almost like a sixth sense come over him, of realization that maybe his luck and that of his 'brothers" blessings were beginning to run out as fur trappers...

Rising to his feet and passing his revelation to the annals of his mind, Ofer looked all around to make sure there were no more Blackfeet lingering in the area and then said, "Men, we have a problem. As I see it, in light of all of the extra horses and bundles of valuable beaver fur scattered all about here and back at the Indians' encampment, we are now very rich men. However, do any one of you have a plan on how we are going to get all of those horses and a huge number of bundles of beaver fur all the way back to Fort Manuel without horse wrecks or getting ambushed and into fights with Indians? And in so doing, live long enough to be able to collect on all of these riches?"

For the longest moment in time, the only sound coming from the trappers' old campsite was the faraway sounds of a Clark's nutcracker hammering away on a dry limb in the top of a lightning-struck pine tree, as everyone looked around at each other for an easy or realistic answer to Ofer's question and the quandary it now posed. Then almost as if on cue, never having given it a thought, Gabriel, Joshua and Jerimiah broke out laughing over the situations they would be facing trying to herd all of those horses safely back to Fort Manuel. Then finally Gabriel with a big grin on his face said, "Well, Brother, you have found a way to lead this group through thick and thin before. I suggest you get your butt in gear and find us a way out of this mess as well." That was followed by more easy laughter all around the group as Ofer just smiled and shook his head over what his group was now facing. His group had faced more difficult issues in the past and like in the past they would just address them when they arrived, work through them and hope for the best. Besides, the good Lord had blessed all of them up to this point in their lives and all he could hope for were more blessings and less arrows, bullets, icy cold waters and grizzly bears in their lives in the future. However, in his earlier revelation, Ofer wondered just how many more beaver waters they could trap without ending up like Jack Thorn and his bunch of unfortunates...

That afternoon in their old trappers' campsite and later in the Indians' hidden campsite there was a flurry of activity. First Ofer scalped those Blackfeet who still had a head worth scalping, tied it to the Indians' horses' tails this time as a sign of even greater disrespect and with a bloody handprint on each horse's neck, sent those horses back to the Indians' horse herds from where they had come. That he did with his signature 'red-handed' warning for those 'foolish enough yet to come their way'. Then leaving Jack Thorn and the rest of his men were they fell for the time being, they went through the cabin looking for anything salvageable of Thorn's and that of his men that they could use themselves. After taking all of Jack Thorn's valuable beaver traps, tins of gunpowder, kegs of rum, weapons, lead pigs, bundles of furs, saddles, packsaddles and what cooking gear and food staples that Gabriel and Little Raven favored, they were removed and stacked over by the corral. Then they picked up Jack Thorn and the rest of all of the men's bodies, fur trapper and Indian alike, placed them inside the cabin, torched it and watched it burn to the ground...

Then after saddling all of Thorn's men's ten riding horses, the men packed all of the bundles of furs those trappers had trapped and loaded them up onto their 14 packhorses and walked all of them back to the Indians' old campsite hidden some distance away in the dense timber. Then unloading all of those horses and seeing that they were picketed along with all the other stock the Blackfeet had collected from the other dead trappers during their recent killing spree along the Musselshell, they walked back to where they had hidden their own saddle and packhorses. Shortly thereafter, those animals were brought into the Indians' old camp as well. That night, the men ate roasted elk taken from a meat pole in Jack Thorn's camp. Then they retired early knowing that the next day would be a long and wild one loading up all of the bundles of fur and herding such a large number of horses along the trail to Fort Manuel without losing any.

Starting around four o'clock the next morning, it took Ofer and company until around noon to load all 111 of their saddle and packhorses with 52 packs of beaver 'Plus' and all of their other gear! Seeing they had an almost impossible herd of animals already, Ofer made the decision and then released all ten of Thorn's trappers' riding horses to the wild in order to reduce the size of their herd. Then with Ofer and Black Eagle leading all of their loaded pack mares, the trappers headed for the nearby Musselshell so all of the horses could water. With Ofer and Black Eagle trailing ten mares each, they had the rest of their group just herd along the remaining horse herd behind the lead that Ofer and Black Eagle were setting. For the next ten days of slow travel along the Musselshell and then down through the Bull Mountains, Ofer and company labored along with their huge horse herd letting the heavily loaded horses almost graze themselves along the way on their trip to Fort Manuel. There were several 'horse wrecks' along the way, with the worst one involving a grizzly bear which caught and killed one of the heavily loaded packhorses who could not outrun the attacking predator! That evening after the run-in with the grizzly bear in the Bull Mountains, Ofer and company feasted on freshly roasted bear steaks… However, as Ofer and company traveled along the Musselshell and then into the Bull Mountains, they had a chance to observe the destruction wrought by the Blackfoot raiding party. There they discovered numerous burned-out trappers' cabins and in several instances, frightened off turkey vultures from around the bodies of a number of trappers killed by the Blackfeet warriors led earlier by He Who Has an Evil Heart. In several of the situations observed along the way, they discovered some trappers' bodies with their tongues removed and their man parts cut off and stuffed down the mouths of the dead! And in other cases, there were bodies tied to trees and used as target practice, as evidenced by being savagely filled with a dozen or so Blackfeet arrows! When viewing a number of those scenes of death, Ofer found his heart hardening even harder when it came to those marauding Blackfeet randomly killing every white man trapper they discovered and ran down while they were beaver trapping! Quietly to himself, Ofer decided the only way any Blackfeet would kill him, his brothers, Black Eagle or Little Raven would have to be through a hail of hot lead that he and company had sent their way first, so those doing all of the attacking could join their "Cloud People" or by catching them in an ambush and ending their great adventure out on the frontier as fur trappers…

Finally right at sunset on their last day of travel, Ofer and company with their huge horse herd hove into sight of Fort Manuel. Ofer sent Joshua on ahead in order to prepare Lisa for what was to be one of his largest windfalls ever in beaver pelts. That as well as acquiring a large number of horses for him to sell to his ever-increasing force of trappers arriving on his keelboats annually on the spring floods on the Yellowstone. Finally arriving, an amazed, happy and full of questions Lisa greeted a very tired Ofer and the rest of his worn-out men. When he did, he had his entire contingent of company men from the fort on hand to meet, greet and begin unloading all of the assembled packhorses as well as helping corral all of the horses so they did not wander off. As that was happening, Ofer gathered in his trappers and assigned each of them to watch where all the extra saddles, packsaddles, bundles of furs, weapons and extra provisions they had collected along the way ended up, so they didn't just up and 'walk off' in the hands of the many Indians now camping around Fort Manuel and looking on, or a number of light-fingered trappers now jealously watching on in wonder as well.

With that, Gabriel, just as fast as saddle broncs and packhorses were unloaded, other than their own, made a huge pile of saddles, bridles and packsaddles inside the fort for safekeeping. Joshua kept all the extra rifles and pistols gathered during their latest sojourn right alongside, where he sat on the steps of Lisa's home inside the fort for the safekeeping that offered as well. Then Ofer, Little Raven, Black Eagle and Jerimiah spent the rest of the night inside the fort under the lights from a number of nearby blazing campfires and whale oil lanterns, keeping their eyes on the company sorters and graders as they went through the 52 bundles of beaver skins. Bundles of beaver skins 24 now dead trappers along the Musselshell and Ofer's group had worked hard for during the fall and spring trapping season. By around ten o'clock the following morning after working all night at their counting, grading and sorting chores, Lisa's company clerks had finally finished! It was only then that Ofer settled up with Lisa after explaining in great detail how his group came across so many horses, bundles of beaver furs and firearms!

As it turned out, the 52 bundles of beaver furs totaled 3,320 'Plus'! Then Lisa set his pencil to paper figuring each pelt weighed in around 1½ pounds, which meant the beaver pelts weighed in at a total of 4,980 pounds. Then shaking his head realizing how much he would owe Ofer and his trappers at $4.50 per pound, Lisa once again put his pencil to paper and ran the figures twice just to make sure. When he did, those figures came to $22,410.00! Like Ofer had said earlier back at Thorn's camp, they were rich men if only they could get all of those horses and bundles of furs back to Fort Manuel to be sold... But Ofer and company were not yet done with Lisa, who still owed them $2,420 for all of their marten furs and an additional $1,200 for their wolf skins. That brought Ofer and company a total of $26,030.00 for their furs alone, which was an unheard of sum of money in those days! Then it came time to dicker for their horse herd which Lisa badly needed. Horses that Lisa badly needed in order to replace those horses his trappers had lost to horse wrecks, being eaten by grizzly bears and mountain lions, those stolen by the Gros Ventre, Crow and Blackfeet Indians, those needed by newly arriving trappers, and those killed inadvertently in battle with the Indians. Additionally, the friendly Indians who came to trade at Fort Manuel always had a healthy appetite for purchasing good horseflesh as well. After a lot of negotiation, Ofer finally settled up with Lisa for $50 per horse and he had 90 horses to sell after the grizzly bear had killed one. That figure came to an additional $4,500, and with that Ofer 'threw in' all of the extra saddles and packsaddles that came with those horses as part of the horse sale deal, in trade for their annual provisions and any blacksmithing work that needed doing. When 'all the smoke had cleared' and the ciphering was completed, Ofer and company were truly rich men with the $30,530.00 now owed them by Manuel Lisa's St. Louis Missouri Fur Company! With that figure before him, Lisa swallowed hard and advised Ofer he did not have that much money in the fort. He further advised Ofer that he would have to settle for a Letter of Credit good back at his company's main bank in St. Louis.

With that, Ofer settled for a Letter of Credit from the St. Louis Fur Company for the amount of $30,530.00! As Ofer had advised his fellow trappers earlier, they were looking at a fortune. Especially in light of the fact that the annual income for a working man in his day and age ran from $400-500 per year! With that, Ofer headed over to his saddle horse and deposited that Letter of Credit into his saddlebag along with his previous Letters of Credit received from Lisa. Then rounding up the rest of his crew and gathering up their remaining matched buckskin horses that hadn't been killed or eaten and all of their firearms from their many seizures, they headed for their old familiar grove of cottonwoods on the fort's grounds and made their camp. There they unpacked their horses and stacked all of their pack and riding saddles under the trees to protect them from any rain showers, laid out their sleeping furs, hobbled and turned out their stock so they could feed and water, and then slept straight through the next 14-hour period of time because they were so exhausted!

The next morning, the men awoke to old friends and visitors from times past who 'happened by'. While 'the fat was being chewed' among a number of those men, Gabriel and Little Raven set about making their campsite 'home' for the next few weeks of living, celebrations among old friends, reprovisioning for the fall and winter and spring trapping seasons to come, and managed their rather large horse herd to make sure they did not mingle with other trappers' horses or 'wander off' in the hands of the numerous friendly Crow Indians visiting the fort, trading and camping nearby.

That second week at the fort, Lisa came calling and while there with the men, suggested they head over to his warehouses and reprovision. He suggested so because a greater influx of Crow and Salish Indians than he had ever seen before with trading on their minds, had just arrived from their surrounding lands and he was fearful that he would run low on supplies for his main contingent of white trappers as a result. (Author's Note: In any given year during the heyday of the Mountain Men, historians figure no more than 1,000 white trappers were afield taking furbearers during the height of the fur trade. Historically speaking, the vast majority of fur trapping was done by the indigenous peoples throughout the land and not the Mountain

Men, as has become a latter-day belief among Americans! On another historic note, approximately 25% of the 1,000 or so Mountain Men afield in any given year disappeared annually due to horse wrecks, freezing to death, starving to death, being killed by grizzly bears, territorial battles among other trappers or the many battles with hostile Indians.)

Taking Lisa up on his helpful suggestion, Ofer and company shortly thereafter headed into the fort and visited Lisa's warehouse. Once there they were glad they had come when they did. 'Sure as shooting', Lisa was running low on some supplies and would not receive any more until the spring when the Yellowstone was at flood stage allowing the supply, deep-draft keelboats to leave the Missouri River and travel up the Yellowstone without running aground in the river's shallow waters.

Fortunately, some of the supplies that Lisa was running low on in his warehouse were cooking implements, pots, kettles and Dutch ovens, items which Ofer and company did not need. It seemed that the local Crow Indian women favored the white man's metal cooking implements rather than having to put fire-heated rocks into an empty buffalo's stomach filled with food and water and cooking that way. As a result of those desires, supplies of such metal items were low in numbers in Lisa's warehouse because of the great demand by the natives. However, Ofer and company were set when it came to all sorts of cooking implements because they had their own, plus what they had picked up at Jack Thorn's cabin before they had burned it down to the ground with all of the fur trappers' and Blackfeet Indians' bodies inside...

Mindful of the fact they were returning to the Smith to trap for another year because of all the remaining beaver, having their cave-cabin already built, their horse corral constructed and that area was also home to the dreaded Blackfeet, Ofer initially headed for the firearms section of Lisa's warehouse. There he selected 40 more one-pound tins of black powder, bags of flints, bags of greased precut wadding, 400 precast .52 caliber balls, bags of lead shot for the buck and ball combinations used in their pistols, two extra wooden rifle ramrods, spare rifle and pistol parts, 100 pounds of lead pigs so more bullets could be cast along the way, and two more .52 caliber horse pistols to go with those supplies they already had of the above items.

Then Ofer was off to the implements and knife sections section of the warehouse. There he selected 10 more fire steels for starting fires because they were easily lost, two more one-pound axes to be used when driving in anchor stakes when setting beaver traps because they were easily lost in the water and mud, three new scalper knives for cooking and skinning, six whetstones, three files, a new two-gallon coffee pot, three three-legged 16" cast iron frying pans, a six-pound wood splitting maul, new hanging iron, six roasting steels, six metal serving spoons, two more sets of knives, forks and spoons, 30 large beeswax candles and lastly two hay hooks to be used when moving hot Dutch oven lids off and on each other, as well as for moving hot frying pan lids off hot frying pans so contents being cooked inside could be tended to before they burned.

Following those selections, Ofer had Gabriel and Little Raven select the needed food and spice staples. Without hesitation, those two selected bags holding 300 pounds of dried green coffee beans, 400 pounds of flour, 20 tins of dried yeast, four jugs of honey, four jugs of rendered bear oil for Dutch oven cooking, 100 pounds of dried pinto beans, 100 pounds of rice, 50 pounds each of salt and black pepper, tins of cinnamon, nutmeg and red pepper flakes, 100 pounds of brown sugar cones, eight flat wooden kegs of rum (easier to pack), a keg of whiskey, 30 pounds of dried raisins, ten three-pound carrots of tobacco, and 30 pounds of dried apple slices for making Dutch oven apple cobblers.

Then it was off to the clothing section of the warehouse to replace those items worn out during the previous trapping seasons. There Ofer had the men replace their battered and old wide brimmed hats with new ones, selected two new capotes per man, two sets of gloves per man, two dozen socks per man, two pair of wool pants and shirts per man (Author's Note: Buckskin when worn in rainstorms will absorb 80 times its weight in rainwater, thereby reducing its body heating ability as a clothing item to zero! Wool pants and shirts, even when wet, will retain some of their ability to maintain one's body heat, hence their selections.), sewing needles and thread in order to mend torn clothing, awls for repairing leather goods, new breechclouts for Ofer and Joshua as well as new sets of buckskin leggings used when trapping beaver in water, one roll of tanned leather sufficient for making new moccasins, two rolls of gray cloth for making clothing repairs, and a roll of fine twine for repairing damaged wounds on the trappers or their horses.

As for supplies for the horses, Ofer had Gabriel, the group's farrier, select a small keg of horseshoes for replacements in the field, a 100' roll of one-inch cotton rope for making or replacing lead ropes or setting out a picket line, two rolls of tanned leather for repairing riding or pack gear, four tins of bag balm for the horses or injuries suffered by any of the trappers, and new bridles for all of the men's riding horses.

One day later, Ofer traded in all of their numerous assorted seized rifles and pistols taken by the Blackfeet during their raids against the trappers along the Musselshell for an even-up exchange for all of the new provisions they had selected in Lisa's warehouse. That and since Ofer had initially 'thrown in' all of the saddles and pack gear from all of the equipment they had seized from the Blackfeet during all of their depredations, Lisa called that exchange 'good' for the rest of the provisions they had selected for their upcoming fall and spring trapping season. Lastly, Ofer and company had a 'hodgepodge' of all kinds of assorted supplies they had gathered up at the Indians' encampment that they had taken off the dead trappers during their rampage. Then they still had some supplies removed from Jack Thorn's cabin before they had burned it and all of the Indians' and trappers' bodies to ash. So for once, Ofer and company had way more supplies on hand than they more than likely would need for the coming year, but on the frontier more was always better.

For the next month, Ofer and company spent the time doing what their fellow trappers did in celebration of the living at Fort Manuel. Horse races to see who had the fastest horse, shooting contests to establish who was the best rifle and pistol shooter in camp, and to the rest of the trappers in camp other than those of Ofer's group, spending personal 'time' with the Crow and Salish Indian women in trade for white man's goods and whiskey... Spending time in an Indian female's tipi in trade for white man's goods was not how Ofer and his brothers had been raised. And although they saw many very beautiful Indian women, they abstained as they had been taught as young men unless married. Many an evening was spent 'suppering' with other fellow trappers and friends, including several joint hunting trips with a number of trappers for the camp's always fast disappearing meat supplies. But as time went on, Ofer and company were found wondering what would be the beaver riches on the Smith that year, had any grizzly bears taken up refuge in their cave-cabin, had the Blackfeet discovered their campsite, and what would be the long-term consequences of their killing the nine Blackfeet Indians at Jack Thorn's campsite?

One evening around the supper campfire, Ofer broached the subject of when they should leave for their campsite back on the Smith River. For the longest time after that question had been asked, no one responded. Then Gabriel said, " 'Spect we best be getting back to our campsite up on the Smith afore another 'Jack Thorn' discovers it, takes a liking to it and throws us out on our 'last part over the fence' once again."

Around noon the following day, Ofer and company had

saddled and packed their 18 buckskins minus the one killed and eaten by a number of Indian horse thieves a year earlier and the one killed in battle. Then amidst many yelled "Good-byes, Good Luck, Keep Your Hair, Keep Your Powder Dry and Watch Your Backsides" from a number of trappers' campsites Ofer and company were passing, they left Fort Manuel. Left Fort Manuel for another year up on the Smith for the fall and spring beaver trapping seasons and what other blessings the good Lord had in store for all of them...

CHAPTER 11 — BLACKFEET TROUBLE ON THE "SMITH", RETURN OF "SCAR FACE"

SEVEN AND ONE-HALF DAYS LATER AFTER MAKING VERY good time heading back to their campsite up on the Smith from Fort Manuel, the men tiredly arrived. Fortunately no grizzly bears had taken up residence in the cave-cabin as their new home, and in short order the men had moved in all of their gear and had hobbled their horses so they could feed and water. Then Ofer and Black Eagle left the camp on their horses trailing one packhorse looking for an elk or deer so the men would have some camp meat. Three hours later, both men returned with their packhorse loaded heavily with a large, quartered-up cow elk. Another hour later found most of that elk hanging from one of their meat poles cooling and glazing out. As the elk cooled out, Gabriel and Little Raven tended to their cooking duties around a blazing campfire with their roasting steels loaded with spitted meat, their coffee pot was steaming away and two Dutch ovens were making biscuits, as they put the finishing touches on the trappers' supper.

The next day while most of the crew unearthed their previously hidden cache and retrieved all of their items, Ofer and

Black Eagle sawed down more dry timber in preparation for a subsequent wood gathering detail. The next day as a team of horses dragged down additional precut logs for the winter woodpile, Gabriel and Little Raven smoked their wolf, bear, marten and beaver traps in order to reduce the man smell. The following day all of the men went on an elk hunting trip, felling four elk and one mule deer which were subsequently brought back to camp. There as another elk was hung on the meat pole to cool out, the rest of the men cut up the remaining elk into thin strips of meat and hung it on the meat racks so the smoking process could begin making jerky. Three days later, the jerky had been smoked and bagged up into previously tanned deerskin bags and hung from pegs in their cave-cabin for use when the weather turned cold or while the men were out on the trail during long days of trapping beaver, marten or wolves.

By the time late September rolled around, Ofer had determined the beaver were in their prime and after a rather hearty breakfast of venison, beans, coffee and Dutch oven biscuits smothered in honey from one of their jugs of honey, the men set out for their beaver trapping waters to initiate their fall beaver trapping season. Following Ofer's beaver trapping plan established the year before, the men headed upriver in a northerly direction with their troop of horses. There at their next planned beaver trapping site, the men began setting out their beaver traps where they had left off at the end of the previous spring because most of the beaver had been trapped out for several miles closest to their campsite. For the next two weeks, Ofer and Joshua set out 40 traps daily. Thirty of those traps used were their old traps and the additional ten traps used that trapping season came from Jack Thorn's old camp. They just figured that since this would probably be their last year trapping on the Smith, they might just as well as trap it out and trap right up next to where they near as could figure the Canadian border began. That way if nothing else, they could reduce the competition by depleting the beaver waters on the Smith on the American side and in so doing, keep the Hudson's Bay men from coming down out of Canada along the Smith since there were no beaver remaining to be trapped in American waters.

Then following their old pattern of trapping and checking activity, the men found an out of the way place to rest, allow their horses to graze at the end of each morning of trapping and give the many beaver in the area time to find the traps and become casualties of the fur trade. Come early afternoon, they would check those traps previously set to see if they had any freshly caught beaver. If so, they were removed and while Gabriel and Little Raven skinned out the rodents, Ofer and Joshua reset the previously set traps in mostly new locations and then the men moved on their ways back to camp. Routinely back at camp, the men jointly fleshed out the previously caught beaver, defatted the pelts and hooped them so they would dry.

One afternoon when Ofer and Joshua were removing freshly caught beaver in just about every trap on their return trip, Ofer paused, looked up and then all around as if something was on his mind. He saw that Black Eagle and Jerimiah were still on guard duty alertly watching over the men, and that Gabriel and Little Raven were skinning beaver just as fast as they could. Continuing to look around, he saw Joshua intently watching him as he stood there looking all around like something was out of order. For some strange reason, Ofer was feeling that his sixth sense was kicking up once again. It had been a long time since he had felt that way and remembering times past when that had happened; usually some bad-happening was close at hand...

However, for once he was almost ready to disregard that morning's nagging sixth sense. They had seen no Indian activity the entire way from Fort Manuel to their arrival on the Smith. They had not crossed any unshod pony tracks since they had been back at their camp, the beaver catching was beyond compare, the weather was great and the men were functioning as a team like they had never done before. So with another good look all around, Ofer quashed those nagging thoughts in mind, but not entirely... With that, he waved Joshua back to the trap tending as he began cutting a pannier full of green willow branches to aid them in the hooping process to come that evening on the 19 beaver they had already caught just on their return trip.

Finishing with the running of their recently set 40 traps, Ofer waved the men in. Once all the men were together, Ofer and Joshua changed out of their wet breechclouts and leggings into a new set of their recently purchased woolen pants for the extra warmth they provided. After pausing for a quick bite of jerky and discussion as to the day's trapping events, the men mounted up. As they did and still not entirely disregarding his nagging concerns about something not being right, Ofer and the men headed for home. But in so doing being that they were deep in Blackfeet country, the men stayed alert to anything looking like it was out of place in the wilderness that could be a threat, as a matter of just good frontier common sense.

Rounding the lower end of their meadow leading to their cave-cabin, Ofer who was in the lead of the caravan reined his horse abruptly to a stop, almost causing the men trailing him to have a 'stack-up' horse wreck! When he did, Ofer went for his rifle lying across his lap and readied it into his arms as if expecting danger of some sort! All the rest of the trappers, always alert to each other's actions having lived together for so long, instantly mirrored Ofer's defensive movements! Without a word and only with a gesture with his left hand pointing down-ward at a large number of unshod horses' tracks in the moist spring soil, Ofer's eyes kept sweeping right and left across their encampment as if looking for any sign of danger close at hand. With Ofer's downward pointing hand movement signaling the group should take a look, the rest of the trappers paid heed. Looking downward and upon seeing all of the unfamiliar unshod horses' tracks, quickly flashed their eyes upward towards the end of their vast meadow searching their camp for any signs of danger as Ofer was doing!

Then the men saw that the door to their cave-cabin, previously closed, was now wide open! Then all of their eyes swept over to the now empty horse corral that when they had left to go beaver trapping that morning, had held 11 extra riding and packhorses! Instantly the men spread out making themselves harder to hit as targets as they spurred their horses into a slow walk as they entered the main encampment area. With their rifles at the ready and their eyes continually sweeping the area, especially the surrounding timber, the men moved forward in a line abreast defensive position.

Once in camp and seeing that all of the unshod as well as shod horse tracks led around behind their corral and disappeared down through the aspens, the men realized they had lost all of their life-giving horses to Indian thieves again! Quickly dismounting, Gabriel ran into their cave-cabin and moments later he walked back out and over to Ofer who was still sitting on his horse looking all around with his rifle in hand and at the ready.

"Ofer, they took all of our extra rifles, panniers, all of our gunpowder, all of our bundles of furs and our only keg of whiskey that we were saving for a celebration come the end of spring beaver trapping," said Gabriel through tightened lips.

Once again, Ofer just shook his head over the earlier sixth sense warnings he had and in so doing, bit his lower lip over being so damn dumb and not reacting to them! Now they had lost all of their reserve riding and packhorses save the ones they had used that morning as well as all of their gunpowder. That last loss meant the men only had enough fight left in them according to what they now carried in their 'possibles' bags! Then to make matters worse, it would soon be dark, making a pursuit of the horse thieves impossible at that moment in time!

Turning in his saddle, Ofer said to Gabriel, "You and Little Raven need to get a fire going and make us one hell of a supper. One hell of a supper because once we start tracking these horse-stealing Indians at first light tomorrow, it may be a long time between meals after that. In the meantime, Black Eagle, would you see to it that each man has at least one full saddlebag of jerky because that may be all we are eating for the next few days. And that is if we only can catch those bastards because it now looks like they will have at least a half-day head start over us and may get back to their home encampment before we can stop them."

With that, Ofer dismounted, unsaddled his horse and turned him loose so he could 'feed up' because it just might be his horse's last meal for a few days as well. Following that, the rest of the men dismounted, unsaddled and set their horses loose to feed and water realizing come daylight, they would be after the horse thieves 'come hell or high water' and forever how long it safely took. Safely took realizing if the Indian horse thieves made it back to their band of Indians and home encampment, the trappers would be outnumbered and as a result, their horses for all intents and purposes, would be long gone! That evening, the men ate spitted elk meat from off their meat pole, Dutch oven biscuits, boiled rice and a hurriedly thrown together apple cobbler made in a Dutch oven with raisins, dried apple slices and mounds of brown sugar. Like Ofer had instructed Gabriel and Little Raven, "feed um up for the long trip ahead" and the two cooks did as they were instructed...

That night, sleep came fleetingly for the trappers who realized they were going to be cold tracking dangerous Indian horse thieves. They also realized that they most likely would be outnumbered if they caught the thieves based on the numbers of unshod horse hoofprints they had left behind. Lastly, they also realized that if the thieves made it back to their own encampment, they would have no chance of recovering their life-giving stock or the rest of their supplies! Daylight the next morning found the desperate men eating their breakfast in the saddle consisting of cold biscuits from the night before and jerky. They also quickly came to the realization that from all the unshod horse tracks, they could be facing at least 20 Indians and from the looks of the trail, those Indians were in a big hurry to put as much distance as they could between themselves and the trappers sure to follow. For the rest of that day, the men put their heels to their horses' flanks in an attempt to close the distance between the horse thieves and themselves. That they did in the open country but when it came to pursuit through timbered areas, the trappers slowed down to avoid being chance-ambushed by the thieves and shot out of their saddles for being so careless and reckless in their pursuit.

Come nightfall that first day of pursuit, the pursuing trappers had yet to see 'hide nor hair' of the fleeing Indians and the horse droppings from their mounts although fresh, were not warm to the touch when the trappers came across such evidence. That first night of pursuit, the men huddled under several spruce trees and did so without any fire for fear of maybe tipping their hand if the Indians were watching their back trail and by some stroke of luck, the trappers were anywhere close at hand to their targets. The next morning before daylight, found the trappers already mounted and waiting for the first light of day to come along so they could continue tracking their quarry. However that day, they had Black Eagle and Little Raven out in front because of their uncanny tracking abilities with the four Tal Brothers close behind providing protection against any kind of ambush. Then their luck changed when about noonday, the two trackers noticed that the Indian thieves had now slowed their pace figuring pursuit was now not forthcoming, or so far behind them that the thieves could relax and not stress their horses any longer but allow them to just move along at a natural but constant pace.

Just as the trappers were getting ready to shut down their

pursuit on their second day at dusk because of the oncoming darkness which made tracking impossible, the men got another break. Topping a ridgeline still on the very evident trail of shod and unshod horse tracks, the men got just a faint whiff of pinewood smoke! Quickly dropping into a dense copse of timber below the ridgeline, the trappers dismounted and began leading their horses and following the old trail from a distance and off to one side with their eyes. Then with darkness, they began using their noses more and more as their tracking aid in pursuit of their horse thieves. Following the now stronger and stronger smell of pinewood smoke, the trappers continued down the ridgeline into another heavy stand of timber leading to a creek. All of a sudden, **BOOM!** went a single shot below the trappers' position, causing the men to scatter like a covey of mountain quail as if the shot had been taken at them! However, no more shooting accompanied that first shot and the trappers finally figured the Indian horse thieves had just killed a deer or elk for their supper and so they relaxed, but just a bit…

By then darkness had covered the land so the trappers tied off their horses so they would not give the approaching trappers away when they smelled other horses and whinnied out a recognition call. With the horses left behind, the trappers began a very slow and stealthy sneak towards the still getting stronger smell of pinewood smoke from a campfire below. This amount of caution they used figuring they were outnumbered by at least three to one, and knew it would be pure and deadly foolishness just to bust into the Indians' encampment and start shooting. For to do so by attacking the horse thieves frontally would surely cost some of the pursuing trappers their lives before all of the black powder smoke had cleared in the air, not to mention allowing a number of the horse thieves to escape off into the darkened timber. Then if that were to occur, the trappers would be facing the possibility of the horse thieves regrouping, turning back around so they could sneak back under the cover of darkness and then in turn, ambush the fur trappers' depleted ranks after the initial shootout.

Then the trappers got a third break in what happened next. As they continued sneaking the last 100 yards towards the strong smell of wood smoke, cooking meat and now very happy chatter among their Indian horse thieves, Ofer stopped their advance by stopping himself and standing there dead-still. Standing there quietly, Ofer carefully listened to all the happy chatter now forthcoming from the Indians' encampment and then turning whispered, "I think those Indians have gotten into that keg of whiskey they stole from the cabin and are now celebrating. I say we sit down right here and wait them out. Wait them out because if they get very deeply into that keg of 100 proof whiskey as Indians are inclined to do, by late tonight many of them will be 'loop de clook' on that firewater and it will make our attack a whole lot safer if about half of them are in no condition to fight back."

For the next three hours, the trappers sat patiently out of sight of the Indian encampment as the revelry got louder and louder as the level of whiskey in the keg went down lower and lower... Around midnight, no further noise came from the Indian encampment now lit up by two large campfires. Taking that as their cue, Ofer had the men check their weapons and make sure their pistols were ready for action as well, and then in a line abreast the trappers moved slowly up to the very edge of the Indians' encampment and peered at the scene lying before them. By the grace of God, every Indian was strewn about their sleeping furs and campfires, drunker than skunks, 'dead to the world' and oblivious to the danger now at hand with the heavily armed and pissed-off trappers slowly moving into their camp!

Slowly the trappers with their rifles held at the ready, walked into the firelight of the Indians' encampment and sure as shooting, there lay 23 Indians drunk to the world and sleeping soundly! The other trappers looked over at Ofer for a command on what to do and it was then that he held up his right hand and gestured for the men to gather around him. With whispered instructions, the trappers melted off into the darkness and walking over to the picket line holding all of the horses, untied all of the Indians' horses. Then after removing all of their bridles so they could feed more easily, let those horses quietly walk away. Then after Black Eagle and Little Raven had quietly moved through the Indians' encampment now identified as Blackfeet, they collected up every rifle and pistol possessed by the horse thieves. Those weapons were then quietly brought over to the picket line and placed into the panniers the Indians had stolen from the trappers along with all of their tins of powder, bundles of beaver fur and other provisions. As for the keg of whiskey, well, it was empty and left behind...

Then gathering around Ofer one more time, he whispered out new instructions and once again, Black Eagle and Little Raven entered the arena of the Indians sleeping off their drunk, and gently removed every pair of their moccasins that they were wearing. This they did under the now leveled rifles from the remaining four trappers just in case someone woke up and needed killing. Those just-removed moccasins were then thrown into the campfires as were all of the Indians' saddles, and as the campfires burned higher and higher, Black Eagle and Little Raven quietly left the Indians' encampment as quietly as they had entered. As they did, they found the rest of the horses that had been stolen were in the process of being now quietly bridled, packsaddled, loaded and being led away from the still sleeping off their dead-drunk, Indians... An hour later, the trappers mounted up onto their previously tied-off horses and letting the horses have their heads since they could see fairly well in the darkness, moved out of the area and headed for the trappers' distant encampment without having to fire a single shot.

With the arrival of daylight the next morning, found the trappers moving across country right smartly as they continued heading for their campsite. During one of their many stops to let the horses and trappers rest a bit, Jerimiah asked Ofer why they didn't kill and scalp the Indians who had stolen their horses. Without any hesitation in his response, Ofer said, "I never have killed a defenseless man nor will I ever do so. True, they needed killing but there is no way I will ever kill a man who does not have a fair chance of defending himself. Now let us continue hitting the trail because we still have a trap line to run and a mess of pelts to process before this day is done. Besides, I am hungry for some of Gabriel and Little Raven's biscuits slopped over with some of our honey, so I suggest we get moving afore I starve to death..."

Come dusk, the trappers had run their trap line, retrieved all of their dead beaver, skinned out the same and were now just turning into the lower end of their meadow. With that, the horse herd was unsaddled and let out to feed and water while the rest of the men, other than Gabriel and Little Raven, processed all of their fresh beaver hides. That evening for supper, the men only had Dutch oven biscuits slathered in honey, spitted elk meat from off their meat pole and hot coffee. Then as Gabriel and Little Raven cleaned up after supper, all of the men had a cup of rum and then headed off to their sleeping furs for some much needed rest after experiencing a rather few exciting days... However just in case, three kegs of rum were stacked in front of the door of their cabin on the inside just in case any other Indians came by wanting to steal some fine horses and whatever was else contained inside the trappers' cabin.

*****

Meanwhile back at the horse stealing Blackfoot Indians' encampment, all awoke to throbbing heads, dry mouths and... cold feet! Once everyone had finally figured out what had happened, war party leader "Deer Who Moves Fast" was so embarrassed over letting everyone, himself included, drink the stolen whiskey that he could hardly face or talk to any of his equally as well embarrassed compatriots. Compatriots were equally embarrassed over losing all of their stolen horses, their own riding stock, all of their firearms, the trappers' furs and even their footwear, not to mention 'face'... One week later, 23 almost starving and footsore Blackfeet Indians walked into Chief Walks Fast's camp to the embarrassing laughter and jeers from their fellow campmates! When Chief Walks Fast heard the whole sad and embarrassing story from a number of his footsore warriors about their losses, he called war party leader Deer Who Moves Fast to the Blackfeet Council and had him stripped of any further war party leadership roles, much to that man's shame. Shame not only when around his chief but in and among a number of his peers and a number of the rest of his band's members as well! Those kinds of stinging rebukes coming from his own kind did nothing but leave a fuming Deer Who Moves Fast thirsting for revenge! Little did he realize that ultimately it would be one 'thirst' he would wish he had not tried to 'quench'...

However, Deer Who Moves Fast wasn't the only warrior embarrassed. Chief Walks Fast had appointed Deer Who Moves Fast as the leader of the war party and now he had to share some of the embarrassment and blame in and among the members of his tribe and the Tribal Elders as well for making such a poor selection. Embarrassing Chief Walks Fast was not what one did and in so doing, made for a vengeful chief with a long and deadly memory as well. Then to make those embarrassing matters even worse, Chief Walks Fast had previously arranged for the Hudson's Bay Fur Company to send one of their fur buyers bringing whiskey and firearms to the chief's village in anticipation of Deer Who Moves Fast's return with a number of stolen horses and furs to trade for that expensive whiskey and those much-needed guns for a number of his warriors who still lacked such weaponry.

Two days later, the Hudson's Bay Fur Company's man

arrived to arrange for the trade of whiskey and firearms for the beaver furs and horses brought back to the chief's encampment as had been requested. When the Canadian representative arrived, Chief Walks Fast was notably embarrassed over the arrangement he had made which had just fallen through. However, when told of the haul of furs and buckskin horses that were lost, the Hudson's Bay Fur Company man's eyes lit up evilly! Then that Canadian fur buyer, a man named "Scar Face" Griffin, the one and same man who had physically accosted Black Eagle and Ofer back at Fort Manuel during an earlier altercation a year earlier, sat back upon his rest in the chief's tipi saying, "Chief, me and my men have a few days in our schedule that are open. What say you assign one of your men familiar with where these American fur trappers live who have those valuable buckskin horses and have him lead us there. I ask that favor of you because that type of horse would be very valuable to my company for resale to any number of our trappers. That and not to mention those bundles of valuable beaver 'Plus" that were lost as well. If you were to do that for me and my men, we would go down there and bring back all of those horses and furs. Then as a favor to you and your people, we would arrange very favor-able trades with you for the escort provided us. And of course, that would also mean all of those rifles and kegs of whiskey we brought down from our trading post in the Land of the Queen Mother could be purchased at a much-reduced price as well."

Upon hearing those words, Chief Walks Fast got an idea. Shortly thereafter, he had disgraced war party leader Deer Who Moves Fast summoned to his tipi. Once the disgraced war party leader had arrived, Chief Walks Fast ordered him to prepare himself for a trip back to where he had located the valuable buckskin horses. Additionally, he was to lead his Canadian friends there so they could take the horses and furs away from the American white fur trappers and bring them back to his band. There they would be traded for the whiskey and firearms his friends the Canadians had brought down to originally trade for the stolen goods his war party was supposed to have brought back the first time.

Upon hearing those words and seeing a chance to redeem his name, Deer Who Moves Fast could not accept his chief's offer for redemption in the eyes of his friends and those in the rest of his band fast enough! With those arrangements made, Deer Who Moves Fast and the Canadian fur buyer from the Hudson's Bay Fur Company with the scarred face agreed to leave the following morning. In the meantime, they would attend a welcoming ceremony arranged by Chief Walks Fast that evening. As previously arranged, come daylight the following morning, Deer Who Walks Fast led Scar Face and his five men out from the Smith River Band's encampment and headed south...

******

As the first of November loomed large, Ofer and company were deeply involved with their beaver trapping in an effort to trap all they could before the arrival of the freezing temperatures and thick ice. One late morning after their newest set of traps had been placed out on their new trap line, Ofer and company relaxed in a grove of aspen trees that were rapidly losing their leaves. As the men let their horses graze under the weak November sun's warmth, the trappers in turn after a hard morning's work sat around under the rustling aspen trees branches, discussed the morning's events and feasted on jerky. Then as the sun's weak rays warmed the men as they rested in the deep bed of fallen aspen leaves' comfortable duff, sleep finally overcame them one by one. Lying back against the trunks of several aspen trees, the men at first rested and then one by one, fell asleep with the soft rustling of falling leaves swirling around them.

ALL OF A SUDDEN, OFER'S EYES FLEW WIDE OPEN IN ALARM! When they did, Ofer's wilderness training set in and he moved not a muscle fearing what had awakened him if it was some form of danger like a hungry grizzly bear, it may be just feet away... So at first, all Ofer did was just move his eyes all around looking for what had awakened him so suddenly and violently. Seeing or hearing nothing other than rustling and falling aspen leaves, he began slowly moving his head from side to side looking for what had awakened him. All he saw were the sleeping forms of his fellow trappers nearby and no other signs of danger in the form of man or beast. However, his sixth sense was roiling around inside of his body something fierce! So much so that those feelings of warning were almost physical-like in nature!

Remembering back to what had happened several weeks earlier when he had 'suffered' those same sixth sense warnings he had neglected to heed and had suffered the consequences. Finally, Ofer rose up onto his elbows and carefully looked all around once again for any signs of danger. Seeing none and feeling his sixth sense really letting him know that to neglect the warnings this time was in essence pure folly, he quietly awakened the rest of the men. When he did, Ofer clued in the men as to why he had awakened them. When he did, Gabriel, his only brother who also occasionally had sixth sense warnings, said, "Brother, I suggest we head back to our encampment. If those damn Blackfeet robbed us once, there is nothing that says they won't try it again. As we all well know, those damn Blackfeet and Gros Ventre have a tendency to roam far and wide, and they are always in the market for someone else's horses! And if they are successful this time and we lose all of our stock as we did last time, we may not be so lucky and get them back like we did last time. And if that happens, we are in real danger when it comes to survival out here in the wilderness or even making it back to Fort Manuel so we can once again purchase the horses that we would need to continue."

Those concerns voiced by his brother, a fellow sufferer of occasional sixth sense warnings, was all that it took to build a fire under Ofer's feet. "Let us get our rears in gear and head back to our encampment. I am getting that same damn feeling like I had last time, when those 20 or so Blackfeet discovered our camp and helped themselves to our horses, supplies and furs. I say we head back and just let our traps work their magic and not check them on our return this time. That way we can get back to our camp more quickly and by so doing, can make sure everything is alright and not in the hands of some damn Blackfoot." With that, the men scrambled around, gathered up any of their gear and mounted up. So much was their urgency and trust in Ofer's warning senses by then that Joshua and Ofer did not even change into their warmer woolen pants but just saddled up and headed back to their camp at a pretty good 'clip'!

About two hours later, Ofer drew up his following men into a small group saying, "This time, I suggest we head into that stand of conifers and tie off our horses so they are well hidden. Then we sneak back through those timbers and come into our camp from the back side by our corral. That way we will have the brush around our corral to use as cover and if my senses are correct, that should give us the ability we need to look around our campsite for any signs of trouble and yet not be seen." With that, the men dismounted, led their horses into deep cover in the timber and tied them off. Then every man checked the priming on their rifles and pistols like they would just before going into battle. Additionally, each man helped himself to an extra fully loaded rifle carried in their third horse's panniers. With Ofer leading the way, the men in single file led by Ofer and Black Eagle sneaked up through the dense timber into the larger stand of aspens surrounding their horse corral some 400 yards distant. Being that it was now November, many of the covering leaves from the brush in the aspen grove had previously dropped off making sneaking close much more difficult. However, the trappers being experienced Mountain Men, found they could move through the terrain almost as fast on all fours once they got closer to the corral than they could standing up and ultimately did so safely.

By the time the trappers had sneaked into the remaining brush surrounding their horse corral, THEY DISCOVERED THEY DID HAVE COMPANY! Right next to the corral were seven unfamiliar horses tied off onto the corral's rails! Then from their prone positions lying in the brush and leaf litter, Ofer and company could see four strange white men quickly moving bundles of furs out from their cave-cabin and running with those bundles over to where they were lying hidden next to the horse's corral. There they dumped the fur bundles into a pile and then ran back to the cave-cabin for more of the same. In the meantime, two other unfamiliar white men were hurriedly packing their removed from the corral buckskin horses with the stolen bundles of beaver furs, totally oblivious to the danger from the six hidden trappers lying close at hand! Then Ofer froze from where he was hiding in the brush when a large man with a badly scarred face dropped off a bundle of furs and then ran back to the cave-cabin for more. It was then that Ofer recognized Scar Face as the man who had almost shot him in the head after knocking Black Eagle down because he was intolerant of being near an Indian in the free 'rum line' back at Fort Manuel! As near as the men could tell, there were six white men stealing their furs and horses, as well as one Indian standing guard over by the entrance to their meadow watching the lower end, as if looking for the returning trappers so he could warn the other thieves of the trappers' arrival if they returned to their encampment earlier than suspected.

Crawling back away from the horse corral as the six white men thieves were emptying out their cave-cabin to avoid being inadvertently discovered and gathering back in the gloom of the aspen trees was when Black Eagle spoke. "Four Scalps, that lone Indian watching out for the six white men as they steal our furs and horses is one of the same Indians we let live who took our horses and supplies last month and then got drunk on our whiskey. I recognized him as one of the Indians that I took moccasins from and tossed into the fire! I am sure of that and I would bet he is the one who is leading the rest of those bad white men to our camp who are now stealing our things. This time we must not let him live or he will be back once again and with more help if we do not do something about it this time. I say that because this time he brought the white man with the scar on his face and next time it will be more warriors who will not get drunk."

With those wise words, Ofer's eyes narrowed and he found his heart hardening once again over what was occurring and Black Eagle's words. With that, he realized what was required of them this time and coming next in the form of a deadly action on the part of his trappers when it came to dealing with such persistent and deadly thieves. Without another word, Ofer quietly laid out a plan by taking a stick and drawing out the layout of their camp in the dirt and what each man was to do when the shooting started. Then with everyone briefed on what they had to do, the men split up and silently melted off into the surroundings for the deadly action that was yet to come. Black Eagle had the longest distance to go, so he left first in order to get into position in order to complete his deadly task and then shortly thereafter, the rest of the men followed on their deadly missions as well.

For the longest time thereafter, the thieves kept removing all of the bundled beaver furs from the cave-cabin with the utmost haste. This they did hurriedly, then packing them onto the 11 buckskins they had previously removed from the corral and were now loading, unaware of the creeping danger at hand! As the thieves led by Scar Face removed every valuable item they could get their hands on, there was much laughter over the little 'funny' they were pulling on the trappers. Trappers that they thought were still afield running their trap line unaware of what was happening to them back at their camp. As for Deer Who Moves Fast, it was all he could do to keep his happy, now revenge-satisfied feelings from surfacing from his lone position at the lower end of the meadow watching for the early return of the trappers being once again cleaned out of their valuables. He knew once they had robbed the trappers of all of their valuable livestock and provisions and had returned to his Smith River Band of Blackfeet, he would once again be held in high esteem as the superior warrior that he felt himself to be. Then he changed his position of observation so he could see clearly if the being-robbed trappers were returning.

That was the last earthly thought he had, as Little Raven had slipped up from behind Blackfoot warrior Deer Who Moves Fast, all wrapped up in his vengeful thoughts and not watching and listening like he should have been. That was when Little Raven shoved his long-bladed sheath knife into Deer Who Moves Fast's rib cage from behind and sliced his heart open! With a loud 'whoosh' of air from his dying lungs and a kick with his feet outward as Little Raven tilted Deer Who Moves Fast's body back in his arms and carried him back deeper into the brush from where he had emerged just seconds earlier! The first part of Ofer's deadly attack had just been successfully carried out...

Just about then, Scar Face exited the cave-cabin with another bundle of valuable beaver fur and walked over to the corral where he dropped it for his two men hard at work to place onto a packsaddle. Then looking down the meadow, he wondered why he did not see their Indian guide standing guard. About then his guts growled over the tainted earlier breakfast he and his men had eaten back at their last camp before arriving at the trappers' homesite. Then remembering the presence of a latrine behind the cave-cabin, Scar Face beat a hasty retreat for that convenience before he had a wreck and soiled his buckskins! Racing over to the seat over the latrine, Scar Face hurriedly loosened his leather pants' belt-tie, dropped his pants and bottom at the same time upon the bench seat and heard the gusher of excrement leave his body just in time. Glad he had not been a step or two too late arriving at the latrine, Scar Face turned and saw an unfamiliar Indian materialize out from behind a large nearby pine tree and now standing just some 20 feet away quietly watching him! Taking a double look at the Indian standing there just off to one side of the latrine, he all of a sudden recognized the face on that Indian! It was the same Indian he had knocked down and shoved out from the free cup of rum line at Fort Manuel a year or so back! "What the hell!" Scar Face bellowed, as he rose to his feet with his breakfast remains still dribbling from his behind, just in time to see a glint of metal from a rapidly spinning through the air tomahawk coming his way! "WHACK" went the tomahawk's blade deeply into the top of the forehead of Scar Face and with only a loud 'groan', he fell over backwards and into the bottom of the latrine pit on top of his previously deposited breakfast!

Hearing their leader yell out and then seeing him rise up off the latrine seat and then fall over backwards into the pit, his two men loading fur bundles onto the packsaddles a distance away just stood there in surprise over what they had just seen. Then not having seen the tomahawk strike, and just figuring their boss had just fallen into the crap hole, they both broke out in loud roars of laughter over their leader's bad case of smelly misfortune. However, their loud roars of laughter did not override the loud roars of two .52 caliber flintlocks firing at the two men from just a few feet away! Had those two men had a choice of falling into the crap hole over at the latrine or in their particular cases, having their heads blasted open with soft lead, high speed balls, they may have taken falling into the crap hole over what actually happened to the both of them...

The loud roars of two rifles being fired just 30 yards away over by the corral by Gabriel and Joshua loudly reverberated within the cave, where the remaining three thieves were hurriedly stealing more bundles of beaver furs so they could be run over to the horse corral for packing onto the buckskin horses the men were stealing. "WHAT THE HELL?" yelled Peter Schmidt. With the sounds of those two rifles being fired in such close proximity, the cave-cabin seconds later emptied out three thieves in a stream like they had been 'puked' out the opening all at once! When the three men erupted from the cave-cabin's front door, they were immediately enveloped with white clouds of black powder smoke to such a degree that all of them disappeared in the white 'froth'! Emerging from the smoke came one man, a large man named Russell Roman, sporting two pistols, one in each hand and bellowing in surprise like a gored oxen bull! Unfortunately for Russell, he caught another white cloud of black powder smoke from just six feet away from Ofer's second pistol shot and with it, a .52 caliber hot, speeding lead ball directly into his right ear and then blowing itself out the far side of his head in a bright red and gray matter gusher of bodily essence! As for his two compatriots running close behind him previously, they had been enveloped in the first white cloud of black powder smoke from just four feet away, causing both to now lay bleeding out their bodily essence from being head shot as well by Ofer and Jerimiah, who had been standing just outside the doorway in ambush when they pulled their pistols' triggers...

Then quietly one by one, the killers of the horse and fur thieves melted out from their places of hiding and walked over to the front of their cave-cabin. When they did, there were six smiles all around from close 'brothers-at-arms' over seeing all of their 'kin' alive, and their bloody targets 'well served' as well... The rest of that afternoon was spent hauling all of the bodies of the dead white men fur and horse thieves down to the Smith and dumped into its icy waters. As for Deer Who Moves Fast, he was scalped, his scalp tied to his horse's tail, a bloody red handprint slapped onto its neck, had its bridle removed, and then slapped across its rear and let go as a sign to all that The Scalper was still alive and well. As for the thieves' horses, they were all kept by Ofer and company because they would be needed come summer to help haul to Fort Manuel their huge catch of beaver furs for sale. Then once again as Gabriel and Little Raven went about their duties as camp cooks, the rest of the men hauled back into their cave all of their furs, the saddles from the horses of the men just killed as well as all of their firearms. Later that night in celebration over paying heed to Ofer's unique warning senses and the men's safety in carrying out their battle plan, the men feasted on spitted elk meat from their meat pole, a rice dish cooked in a Dutch oven loaded with apple slices, raisins, brown sugar and loads of cinnamon, Dutch oven biscuits slathered in honey and baked with raisins, coffee and later several cups of rum celebrating the day's events, all in the absence of their normal clouds of hard-biting mountain mosquitoes due to the advent of cooler weather.

******

It had now been a full month of absence from the date they had left the Smith River Indian Village for the six Hudson's Bay Fur Company men and their Blackfoot warrior escort Deer Who Moves Fast. Chief Walks Fast, with the arrival of Deer Who Moves Fast's horse with the now signature scalp tied to the horse's tail as a sign of disrespect and a faded but sure as hell bloody handprint on the animal's neck, figured his warrior and the fur company men were now with the "Cloud People"! With that, the chief went into the vacant tipi where all of the Canadians' supplies had been stored waiting for their return on the horse and fur stealing trip, and soon a number of his warriors were no longer armed with just bows and arrows but new rifles as well. Additionally, there were several celebrations held over the next few months using the remaining supplies of whiskey that had been brought down for trade as well, once the buckskin horses and the Smith River trappers' furs had been brought back and figured into the settlement costs of the Canadians' whiskey and firearms...

But with the return of Deer Who Moves Fast's horse with the signature scalp tied to it and the bloody red handprint affixed to the horse's neck, Chief Walks Fast now figured he knew where The Scalper resided! The chief figured come warmer weather when travel would be easier, he and some of his best warriors would pay the trappers' encampment on the Smith River a visit and once and for all, see to it that the trapper known as The Scalper and the rest of his fellow trappers were no more...

WITH THE FIERCE arrival of the winter in such northern latitudes, the trappers' activities were curtailed and relegated to care of their horses, hunting for camp meat, running their wolf and marten traps, cutting of firewood and more hunting for the camp's daily meat needs. Even though the trappers knew that because of the deep snows and routinely adverse weather, that most Indians kept their travel to a minimum, they still maintained a very high level of readiness because of all the previous Blackfeet troubles they had experienced. And true to form regarding Indian travel during the deepest aspects of winter, quiet reigned throughout the trappers' world on the Smith River during those snowiest of months...

CHAPTER 12 — A "SIXTH SENSE", BLACKFEET AND "BEAR TRAPS"

STEPPING OUT FROM THEIR CAVE-CABIN ONE WARM SPRING morning, Ofer took a look skyward to be able to 'read' the weather for that day. Seeing nothing but blue sky and feeling a warm breeze coming out from the south, he yelled over to the camp's cooks hard at work around their outside cooking firepit. "Boys, best set your best 'table' this morning. I am feeling it is time to begin our spring beaver trapping season and since I am planning a longer day with us running a more extended trap line than usual, feed us up good!" said Ofer with an anticipatory smile on his face.

Then he headed off to their latrine to take care of a call of nature and following that, a trip to their creekside shaving and cleaning up area where after several long moments, was made presentable with washed hands, a cleanly shaven face and combed locks. However as he performed those tasks, he found his mind racing all the while. For much of the night he had lain awake with new thoughts spinning through his head on the men's futures as beaver trappers. Finally in the early hours of the morning, he had come to a conclusion on his thoughts and figured now was as good a time as any to share with the men what he had been mulling over regarding their coming year as fur trappers. About then Joshua and Jerimiah came over to their 'cleanup' section alongside the creek and he said, "Before the two of you get all gussied up, I need you to go to the back of the cave and bring out the rest of Jack Thorn's beaver traps. We are going to start using all of them so if you would, bring the rest of them out and leave them over by the corral so they can be loaded into a pannier for today's trap setting efforts." With an affirmative nod of their heads and no questions as to why they were going to extend their already long trap line, off went the two brothers to bring forth the extra traps as had been requested.

Come breakfast time and figuring what was coming next, Gabriel used up a mess of his dried yeast in a special bowl of dough and soon the heavenly smells of an apple and raisin cobbler rent the air around the cooking fire. That along with the smell of spitted and roasting venison, Dutch oven biscuits, hot coffee and the cobbler soon to be, had all of the men eagerly sitting on their sitting logs, more than ready for whatever Gabriel and Little Raven served that morning. Upon finishing their main course somewhat later, as Gabriel and Little Raven began serving up their apple cobbler hot out from one of his Dutch ovens into each man's now empty and quickly proffered coffee cup, Ofer began with what he had to say after mulling it over most of the previous night while lying in bed.

"As most of you have realized by now because of my quiet actions lately, I have had something serious on my mind for several days now. Something that I felt we all needed to discuss and now is as good a time as any to do that, so here goes. The way I figure it, this is our last year on the Smith. It has been more than good to us and even this year, we will be going to Fort Manuel with over 700 beaver pelts to our name to sell! Never have we done as well and in so doing as most of you know, we will more than likely trap out the best portions of the Smith that are safely open to us by the end of this spring trapping season. That said we need to move on to a different trapping location and that is what I have been mulling over for the last few days. Sure, we could continue trapping further north on the Smith all the way up to Canada. But in order to do that, we will need to trap even deeper into the home territory of the Smith River Band of the Blackfoot and I don't think they will take too kindly to that if we did, since that is one area they are beaver trapping as well would be what I am thinking."

Then taking in several mouthfuls of the sweet tasting apple cobbler and marveling over Gabriel's flaky crust, Ofer began once again. "Additionally, we have had a number of run-ins with them damn Blackfeet and I don't see them slacking off in the future. In fact, after the deadly hands we have dealt those we have previously come into contact with, I figure it is about time we start thinking about not always coming out ahead in those battles as we have in the past. The way I figure, it is just about time we begin thinking about the fact that it is just a matter of time before one or more of us will feel the speeding arrow or lead ball entering our carcasses for the first and last time here on this earth and that is a fact. The Blackfeet far outnumber us and it is just a matter of time before they confront us with really superior numbers. When they do and that will happen, I don't 'cotton' to the idea of losing any one of you, my 'brothers', to them murdering damn Blackfeet nor do I want to be one of their casualties either. Plus, they haven't taken the hint with returning horses carrying their warriors' scalps like the Gros Ventre and just left us alone. They just seem more determined than ever in running us out of this area. With that in mind, I say after this trapping season, we pull up our stakes and move on to another area of the country with less Blackfeet roaming around but still holds good beaver trapping for us. In fact, the way I see it, we want one more good beaver trapping season and then all of us can return to Missouri rich men, settle down, find some good women to marry and no longer worry about catching an arrow, speeding lead ball or becoming a meal for some damn ole hungry grizzly bear. And since they have no one to go home to and are as close to us as we are to them, I would hope that Black Eagle and Little Raven, who also share equally in our riches, move down to Missouri with us and make that their new home as well. Besides, I told mother I would bring as many of you home as I could and I mean to keep that promise. Now I have said enough. What do the rest of you have to say about my feelings and suggestions?" asked Ofer, as he held out his coffee cup for Gabriel to refill with some more of his damn good apple and raisin cobbler heavily laced with brown sugar and cinnamon...

For the longest time, no one said a word regarding Ofer's suggestions but kept their attentions riveted on consuming their share of the great tasting and fast disappearing apple cobbler. Then it was like a dam had broken. Gabriel said, "I am more than ready to move on. Like you, I figure it is just a matter of time before these damn Blackfeet get an angle on our number and wipe us out or cripple a number of us up. I originally came west to see the "Elephant" and I have, but I sure did not figure on every time I did, 'it' was covered with angry Blackfeet or Gros Ventre warriors looking to lift my hair!" (Author's Note: Seeing the "Elephant" was a commonly used phrase in that day and age when one wanted to venture forth to see and experience something fantastic that one had never seen before.)

Joshua and Jerimiah at the same time said, "Let's move on." Then Jerimiah said, "I too came west to see what all the folks who had already done so and upon their return to civilization, spoke so highly of and in such glowing terms about their recent experiences in the wilderness. But I am not a dummy. Like you, Ofer, I feel it is just a matter of time before members of this family will be staring death in the eye once again and to be quite frank, we have gotten off pretty damn lucky so far by only losing Daniel to that damn old grizzly bear."

Then Black Eagle after looking over at Little Raven to see what his eyes 'read', rose from his sitting log and said, "Four Scalps, Little Raven and me have no one but you brothers as our only family. If you all decide to go to live in that place you call 'Missouri', we would like to go with our brothers as well. That is all I have to say." With that, Black Eagle sat back down and continued eating his favorite part of the breakfast, namely his share of the Dutch oven apple cobbler... Following those statements, all was quiet around the men's campfire as they enjoyed their morning's Dutch oven apple cobbler treat and did so until the 'Dutch' had been eagerly emptied.

"Then it is settled. If all of us can survive this trapping season here on the Smith in the heart of Blackfoot country, then we are out of here and will go somewhere else for another year. Then we will give up this beaver trapping thing since we have made our fortunes. This I feel we can do since we all have seen and experienced living in the wilderness and love it to this day, especially me. Then when we 'pull the trigger', we can head for home as a family, enjoy some good home cooking from our family's cook and quit dodging bullets, arrows, grizzly bears, cold water and cold weather," said Ofer with an even bigger smile now on his face. But as Ofer said those words, they rang somewhat hollow because like his old friend Bear Trap had said, "the wilderness grabs ahold of some men and never lets them go"...

An hour later, Ofer and company with their usual three packhorse string left their campsite for the start of their spring beaver trapping season on the Smith. And as usual, the third horse in the string of packhorses carried two panniers with five extra loaded rifles in each pannier just in case the local 'neighbors' started a squabble over who the beaver belonged to and wanted to do something about it... And that morning, the other two packhorses found themselves carrying even heavier loads of weight in the form of all of the trappers' extra beaver traps.

Heading north up along the Smith once again, the trappers

rode until they came to where they had quit trapping during the previous fall's trapping season. Then their daily work began. As usual Ofer and Joshua did all of the trapping while the rest of the group did all of the skinning or provided protection for those doing the actual trapping that were pretty much defenseless against a surprise attack. Changing into their trapping apparel, Ofer led the way as Joshua followed with the next trap to be set. Only today there was a difference in their trapping activities. Today they not only carried their usual complement of 30 beaver traps but the extra 20 beaver traps they had taken from Jack Thorn's place after he and all his cohorts had either been killed or in several cases, scalped and then continued to be tortured as they were partially skinned alive by the Blackfeet who had surprised and captured them at their campsite.

(Author's Note: In the days of the Mountain Men, 6-8 traps per trapper was the normal number of traps used. That was because such traps weighed around five pounds each, were expensive to purchase at Mountain Prices at the trading posts or Rendezvous (around $9 each) and then because there were so many beaver, most traps set by an experienced trapper would be filled daily. Then there were still the same-day duties of skinning the beaver, defatting and removing any further meat from the pelt and hooping the same so they could dry. All in all, more than a good day's work for a trapper running just 6-8 traps a day. However, where there were larger groups of men working together, more traps would be set because there were more hands to do all the pelt finishing work as well as accomplishing the other required duties around the camp. Plus with larger groups of trappers, more traps would have to be run in order to be able to finance their everyday existence. An existence which was provided for at the trading posts or at latter-day Rendezvous sites at what were called by the trappers 'Mountain Prices', which ran from 700-1,000% over what it would have cost to purchase the same item back in St. Louis!)

With 50 beaver traps to set, the men were not finished with setting out their trap line until the early afternoon. Then instead of resting under some budding aspens for a short while, they turned right around and began checking their traps on the way back to their campsite. That they did because since beaver were so territorial and smelling the castoreum being used on the lure sticks, there would already be a number of the curious rodents lured to and into the men's traps. That plus the fact they did so because they knew they would have extra beaver to skin and hoop and lastly, if there were any Blackfeet lurking about hoping to steal a trapper's horse, by changing their rhythm of activity, they would surprise them and 'ruin their day'. As expected in the beaver-rich waters in and around the Smith, the trappers had caught a number of beaver shortly after their traps had been set. True to a beaver's strong natural territoriality, great ability to smell and the penetrating essence of the castoreum used as a lure to the traps, the men had 27 dead beaver already hanging from their traps on that first return trip!

That first day, trappers arrived around five in the late afternoon with their panniers bulging with beaver pelts, fresh green willow branches for hooping and the hindquarters from two mule deer bucks killed on the way back and quickly butchered out for camp meat. Like Ofer had advised earlier, their day would be a long one and he was right. Then as Gabriel and Little Raven finished skinning out the mule deer quarters, hung them from the meat poles to cool out and form a glaze and begin their supper preparations, Ofer, Joshua, Black Eagle and Jerimiah attended to the defatting and hooping duties in the cave-cabin under the light from six beeswax candles and the dancing light from their fire in their fireplace. Suffice to say, right after supper and a cup of rum in celebration of the successful start of the spring beaver trapping season, the men went to their sleeping furs early with their hind ends dragging from such a long and busy day...

******

Sitting on their horses early one morning, three Blackfoot warriors respectfully waited in silence in front of Chief Walks Fast's tipi. Moments later the chief emerged from his tipi and after a brief discussion as to what he wanted his warriors to do, they departed with just a nod of their heads acknowledging their chief's instructions. As they did, Chief Walks Fast watched his warriors as they headed in a southerly direction towards the white trappers he wanted 'visited'...

******

For the next week of their spring beaver trapping season, it just seemed that the beaver waters being trapped were full of beaver just waiting to find themselves in the trap! Every day they ran their traps, the Tal group of trappers brought in an average of 20 beaver a day! However on several of those days, the trappers had their suspicions aroused and cautions increased... The first being when Black Eagle spotted what appeared to be the back end of a horse moving in the shadows through a dense stand of pines one afternoon, and the other was when Gabriel spied another horse-like movement in another stand of dark timber three days later! Collaterally, both Ofer and Gabriel began having slight sixth sense feelings of 'danger warnings' 'winging' through their inner beings during those same two occasions! However, Gabriel upon seeing his 'movement' in the dark timber mounted his horse and quickly went over to investigate. But before he arrived at his spot of suspicious movement, he spooked a young bull moose out from the same deep stand of timber. He then shot that moose for camp meat and figured that had been the mystery movement seen earlier and 'wrote off' his earlier observed curious movement. Gabriel's sharing those feelings with Ofer that same day allowed Ofer to disregard his sixth sense feelings stirring within him as well, by blaming his 'unusual movement' concerns on the ill-fated but damn good tasting moose steaks served for supper that same evening.

******

A week later, the same three previously dispatched Smith River Band of warriors reported their findings on the Smith River trappers and homesite location of the one possibly known to them as The Scalper back to Chief Walks Fast. After a short discussion, Chief Walks Fast had those warriors select seven more members from their band and report back to him. Later that afternoon, Chief Walks Fast solemnly addressed his ten warriors. The following morning, the chief and his ten men assembled and then left the Smith River Band for a certain trappers' campsite reportedly located further south along the Smith River above its junction with the Musselshell. To the chief's way of thinking, he and his fellow warriors would see to it that previous Blackfoot deaths that had been attributed to the one they called The Scalper were soon going to be avenged. Then the chief and his ten warriors would be riding back into their encampment with the reported beautiful buckskin horses and none of them would have a bloody handprint on any of their necks, if Chief Walks Fast and his ten warriors had anything to say about it...

******

Stepping out from the cave-cabin one morning during the height of the spring beaver trapping season, a tired looking Ofer looked around his campsite as he always did to 'scent' the daily weather and look for any signs of danger. Looking around, Ofer first observed their corral full of beautiful-looking buckskins and the six horses once belonging to the ill-fated Scar Face-led Hudson's Bay men who had come looking for trouble. Then his eyes swept over to Gabriel and Little Raven busily cooking breakfast and then Joshua over by the creek shaving. Lastly, his eyes looked off to the west where he saw that Jerimiah and Black Eagle were 'busy' over at their latrine. However, none of those tranquil scenes around him made him relax because of the warning senses he still had once again surging through his physical being! All night long he had tossed and turned in his sleeping furs in the cool darkness of their cave-cabin over such warnings, and finally just lay there trying to interpret their 'dark' meanings so he and the rest of his group of trappers could be prepared for what was coming. He was also getting tired of every time that he seemed to be 'turning around', he was getting these kind of sensory warnings lately and began thinking maybe it was time he gave up his much-loved life in the wilderness for that of a much tamer existence back on his family farm without danger at every turn in the trail...

Looking around his campsite one more time did nothing to make him relax over what he was still feeling inside and then his eyes met those of his brother Gabriel. Gabriel was looking right back at him with an equally unusual look. Without saying a word, Ofer headed over to the creek, shaved, washed up, combed his hair as best as he could and then walked over to the firepit and was handed a steaming cup of hot coffee by Gabriel. When that happened and he looked up to tell his brother 'Thank You', he found himself looking into a set of piercing dark eyes like he too knew that something was coming that was out of 'kilter' and could mean danger was in the air and coming their way...

"Care to tell me why you are looking at me like that?" asked Ofer, as he took a drink of the piping hot coffee and not paying attention to what he was doing, burned the hell out of his lip by taking too deep a sip.

"I am looking at you just like you were looking at me when you left our cave, and in so doing checked all around as if you were looking for some very apparent signs of danger nearby," replied Gabriel quietly, still looking intently at his older brother.

"I am sorry I was looking that way at you earlier. I didn't sleep very well last night and I guess it is showing," replied Ofer as he now more carefully took another sip of the strong trapper's coffee.

"I didn't sleep very well last night either," replied Gabriel, his dark eyes never leaving his brother's as if he was looking for something in his brother's eyes that was telling as to why both of them were having such feelings of foreboding at the same time.

"I don't know what is bothering me but I just feel for some reason that we are being watched by someone who has evil intentions or bringing such intentions to 'our table'. I have had these nagging feelings ever since you saw some unusual movement in the dark timber recently, went over to investigate and ended up killing that poor damn ole moose storming out from the timber and almost running right into you. For the last several days I have questioned why that moose was spooked and almost ran over you. As you know, they are so damn tough and this time of the year with their antlers full of blood, sensitive and growing, they don't usually take off through the antler-damaging brush and timber unless something has really spooked the hell out of them like a hungry grizzly bear or such. And being so damn big, I have never found moose spooking easily unless something is really bothering them. Yet you didn't find anything out of the ordinary and to me that spells trouble in the form of 'Blackfeet'. I say that because they are so damn cagy and surreptitious when they want to be...," and with that, Ofer's voice trailed off into a very telling silence as he kept looking at his brother as if looking for answers as to their concerns as well.

"I have never had the sixth sense 'gift' as well-developed as you do, my brother. I think you got it from our father, Yossef. To his credit, he was always able to read his innermost senses and as a result, was able to avoid trouble in its many forms like when to pull a baby horse when the birthing mare was struggling and the like. But like you, I have been bothered recently by some of my inner feelings as well. I am not sure what they mean but they are there and if you noticed, for the first time since I became a camp cook that I am cooking breakfast while wearing both of my pistols," said Gabriel quietly, as he pointed downward towards his sash carrying two horse pistols.

"Well, since neither of us can put our fingers on what is bothering us, let us get on with breakfast because we have a long trap line to run today and if I am worth a damn on this trapping thing, I will bet you a cup of rum we have a pannier or two full of beaver pelts to process when we get back to camp. Anyways, let me think about what we should be doing in light of both of our concerns and see what I can come up with," continued Ofer, this time taking a bigger sip of his coffee now that it had cooled somewhat. Then sitting there on his sitting log in deep thought, the memory of his mentor and old friend Jan "Bear Trap" Driessen mysteriously drifted through his mind and with that came a helpful idea as if 'intentionally planted' there by his old Mountain Man friend and Man of the Mountains in so many aspects of his life. Aspects of life that also included his uncanny ability to 'read the weather and many things that were not of the world'...

Once breakfast was done, Ofer told the group that he needed to speak to all of them. As the group sat back down on their sitting logs Ofer began by saying, "I am not sure of my innermost self but lately I have been having stirrings from within that I feel are warnings of something bad to come. In times past when I have had these same almost nagging feelings, I have ignored some of them and then have been involved in a horse wreck, gotten washed off my horse while crossing a river or even been poked in the head by a low hanging limb when we were traveling back to camp late at night on horseback and worse. For the last two days these feelings have never left me, which tells me whatever is going to happen is going to happen to me or us as a group and I feel pretty damn soon."

Then Ofer paused as if trying to read in the rest of the men's faces what they were feeling upon hearing his words of concern. Ofer didn't have long to wait for a response.

"My Brother, your earlier concerns of warning have pretty well panned out in the past so I suggest we follow up on those concerns. What do you suggest we do to counter those very real feelings of dread you are having?" asked Jerimiah. "I ask because I remember our talk about your concerns and the odds about some of us taking an arrow or speeding lead ball in the future."

"I am not sure which way to turn but in the past, we have always had 'warning' troubles of some sort that is related to theft of our valuable livestock or having to fight our ways clear of a mess of mad Indians. If I were a gambling man and I guess I am since I chose to live a life out here in the wilderness, I would say something is going to happen to our rather unique horses and their overall numbers pretty soon. And I would guess if my concerns are horse-related, I would also suspect trouble coming from the Blackfeet or the Gros Ventre because of their past histories with us, especially when we are out in the field trapping. That being said and remembering the luck we had with Bear Trap Driessen's grizzly bear traps, what say we have a go with them once again and set a trap or two just in case. Then by doing so, if someone is after our horses and they fall into one or a number of our bear traps, we will at least know who they are and slow them down a bit from what they are trying to do. And if Indians are our horse stealing culprits, getting caught in a bear trap ought to spook the hell out of them and maybe even run them off because of their concerns over what they call the 'evil spirits'. And it would sure seem like an 'evil spirit' if I was an Indian and all of a sudden had a giant bear trap leap from out of the ground and grab one or more of my brothers and crush their legs! Those are my thoughts because I don't have anything else to suggest. However, if we set those bear traps this time, we need to be very careful when working around them so they don't catch one of us or have one of our horses step into them. If that happens and it is one of us stepping into one of those monster-toothed bastards, it more than likely will be our death sentence. The same would go for any of our horses as well."

Then Ofer paused for a moment as if getting his thoughts

350 | "FOUR SCALPS" OFER TAL, MOUNTAIN MAN

together for the best plan and then said, "Here is what we are going to do. I want to set two bear traps around one side of the gate by our horse corral. That way we can still remove our horses one by one and put them back into the corral one by one by just walking them over by the side of the corral where the traps are not lurking. I also suggest we do the same over by the front entrance to our cave-cabin with the remaining two bear traps. That way, knowing where those monsters are set, we can avoid them, still get our work done and carry on just like we normally would, especially if someone is watching us and hoping to catch us unawares or when we are afield running our trap line."

Those words had no more than left Ofer's mouth when Jerimiah and Joshua got up without being asked and headed over to the cave-cabin wherein the monster bear traps were kept in the back of their cave. Moments later, the two men came over to the corral each lugging one of the monster-toothed giants in hand. Then while Black Eagle and Ofer dug a pit in which to conceal the traps just off to one side of the corral gate opening, but in such a position that it would catch someone 'with a black heart' who was unwary and trying to open the corral gate so he could steal the horseflesh inside, Jerimiah and Joshua each lugged out the remaining two bear traps from their cave. Those they set down outside the entrance to their cave-cabin. Then those two brothers began digging a pit in which to conceal the two traps just off to one side of the entrance to their cave-cabin as well. That way by being just slightly offset from the entrances of the cave-cabin and their horse corral, they would catch anyone unaware of their locations by being in the immediate vicinity of those two access points, aiming for provision thievery or just plain old damn horse stealing. And if any of that was to occur, those up to no good would soon be 'riding a black horse along with the devil'...

Somewhat later that morning, Ofer and company trooped

out from their campsite en route their trap line just like they always did in the mornings. However, cleverly concealed with dirt, grasses and horse manure lurked two giant grizzly bear traps capable of smashing the legs of man, horse or grizzly bear once stepped into by the horse corral still holding a number of buckskin horses not in use, as well as the six horses taken from the dead Hudson's Bay men. The same concealing acts had been performed by the entrance of their cave-cabin with the remaining two traps as well. In fact, Black Eagle and Little Raven put the finishing touches on the ground covering both sets of traps with human footprints all around the pans of the traps so it would look like everyday traffic by the horse handlers and users of the cave-cabin entrance. Following those efforts, the men departed for their trap line just like they had done every day since they began their busy spring beaver trapping activities.

For the rest of that day, Ofer found his inner senses seemed to be less active but still there almost as an afterthought. However he quickly found his beaver trapping activity was such that he soon forgot all about the four bear traps, with his inner feelings being replaced with the hard beaver trapping work required and attention-getting cold water immersions. That afternoon with 29 beaver pelts in their panniers and more willows cut for the hooping process to follow, the men tiredly rode back to their compound. Once there, they discovered that nothing had been touched and with lots of repeated warnings among themselves about the exact locations of the traps so no one would run afoul of the steel-jawed monsters, the camp's activities soon returned to normal. However, Ofer's internal nagging concerns returned once all the hard work involving their beaver trapping and pelt processing had faded into the daylight's long hours, causing Ofer to begin worrying all over again. And once again, Ofer began wondering if he had covered all of his concerns with just the four bear traps being strategically placed around their cave-cabin and horse corral. That evening after all of their work was done for the day, Ofer once again found sleep hard to come by as he lay there in his sleeping furs tossing and turning. All he had were his brothers, Black Eagle and Little Raven in a country that was historically harsh on maintaining one's health, life and lifestyle. To lose any of those 'brothers' would break his heart, and once again he found himself wondering if he had thought through all of the possible dangers that could be facing his little group of trappers. Then sleep finally came to Ofer, the oldest 'brother' and the one most concerned over what might be coming their way. For the next two days, the trappers found their work swirling about them in such volumes, especially the hooping and defatting duties, that soon Ofer's earlier conversation with all of the men about his inner feelings began fading. Began fading like such issues do with most human animals when they are facing other problems of life...

******

For two days after their arrival in the area of the Smith River trappers' campsite, Chief Walks Fast, somewhat spooked over The Scalper's historical 'evil spirit' powers of destruction over his people and reportedly the Gros Ventre, made their hidden camp a goodly distance from the trappers' campsite. This he did hoping to avoid detection by the trappers or having The Scalper's 'evil spirits' find them and do them harm. Then each day, the chief and his men from deep seclusion in the forest watched the trappers running their trap line, and soon had the timing down when the trappers awoke, made breakfast, went trapping, returned to their camp, processed their beaver hides and went to bed. As a result of the chief and his men's careful observations of the trappers' daily activities, Chief Walks Fast was soon able to plan a deadly ambush of the much-hated and at the same time, feared trappers. Plan an ambush when the trappers were most vulnerable and in so doing, get around any 'evil spirit powers' that The Scalper might possess. By so doing, that would allow for the taking of The Scalper's life and that of his fellow trappers and not result in losing any of his warriors in the ensuing battle.

As a result of their careful observations, the wise old chief, a veteran of many battles with the Crow Indian Nation and many white trappers, figured the best time to lay an ambush would be at the end of the day when the trappers were tiredly returning from their daily activities. With that decision made, the chief would soon close his trap upon the trappers, kill off all of them including the dreaded one named The Scalper, whichever trapper he was, steal their horses, provisions and furs and return to the Smith River Band victorious in the eyes of his people. Then he would call down the traders from the Land of the Queen Mother and have many horses, guns and furs to trade for more whiskey, powder, lead and even more modern firearms. Yes, the trap was soon to be laid and the deed done...

Two days later, the chief and his warriors were up early. After watching the trappers leave on their daily trapping activities, the chief and his men slowly trailed the trappers from their places of hiding, making sure they were busy on their usual beaver trapping grounds. For several hours the Indians watched the activities of the trappers making sure they were deep into their work. Then the chief and his men slowly travelled back through the timber, making sure they were staying concealed from the eyes of the trappers. As Chief Walks Fast and his fellow warriors moved silently through the timber on their way back to the trappers' campsite, they disturbed a nesting colony of crows, filling the air above the riders with their concerned overflights. Then later they spooked out a small herd of cow and calf elk from the deep timber as their horses moved along. When they did, no elk were taken as food because they still had part of a large mule deer doe hanging in a tree back at their camp as their camp meat. Then just before they got to the back side of the trappers' campsite, they spooked a cow and calf moose out from the deep timber and once again no attempt was made to take the cow for camp meat. They just sat on their horses and watched the largest member of the deer family blow through the timber and speed away from the disturbance they had inadvertently created with their presence. Then dismounting, the chief began leading his men on foot the last quarter-mile through the timber to the trappers' campsite so they would leave no telltale signs of unshod hoofprints at the bottom of the trappers' meadow to warn the trappers of the presence of Chief Walks Fast and his ten warriors if they decided to delay their attack. To Chief Walks Fast's way of thinking, his careful trap was almost set and so far, the 'evil spirits' that he figured were surrounding and protecting The Scalper had not been aroused...

******

Ofer and company arrived at the southern end of their trap line later in the morning and after stopping and changing into their trapping breechclouts and leggings, Ofer and Joshua began removing dead beaver hanging in their traps. These they brought to land and turned over to Gabriel and Little Raven to skin. They then returned to walking along their trap line pulling other dead beaver from their traps and resetting those traps still in beaver-rich areas. As Ofer and Joshua performed the trap checking and resetting duties, Black Eagle and Jerimiah continued their oversight and protection duties from atop their horses watching the trappers, skinners and surrounding countryside for any signs of danger.

Long about late morning, Black Eagle's keen eyes observed a large flock of nesting crows fleeing their nesting and roosting sites in alarm high up in the distant surrounding timber. He watched the noisy display of the birds circling above their nesting and roosting area with interest born of his 20,000 years of Native American heritage manifesting itself. About half an hour later, Black Eagle's sharp eyes noticed a small herd of cow and calf elk erupt from their cover in the dark timber along the trappers' back trail and noisily splash across the beaver ponds adjacent the Smith to the far side and then disappear into the timber. By now, both events involving the noisy crows and highly disturbed cow and calf elk herd had caught Black Eagle and Jerimiah's keen attentions. Not so much for the danger warnings it could have represented but for the unusual animal behaviors exhibited in their wilderness surroundings of beauty. That was until a highly disturbed cow and calf moose erupted from their hiding place in the deep timber along the same line of travel where the noisy crows and disturbed elk had been observed! Especially when the larger animals burst forth at a dead run from the trees far back on the trappers' back trail and headed directly for what they deemed the safety of the brushy watered areas in the nearby beaver ponds, then disappearing out of sight into a large patch of willows...

By now, Black Eagle was standing up in his stirrups so he could see better in order to try and figure out why three separate instances of different species of wildlife were disturbed along different locations of the trappers' back trail. As Black Eagle carefully scanned their back trail from his place standing up in his stirrups, Jerimiah kept carefully scanning the surrounding countryside for any other signs of danger that might be associated with the three groups of animals' unusual behavior along their back trail as well. However, neither man saw anything more of interest that might lead the men to believe that any form of danger might be close at hand. As those two men relaxed and just wrote off the three events as maybe grizzly bear induced, they chanced a look back at the two men still running the trap line and setting the traps.

When they did, they saw Ofer standing alongside a beaver pond holding an empty beaver trap in his hands. As he did, he intently watched the behavior of his two men assigned guard duties for the four defenseless men on the ground running the trap line and doing all of the skinning of dead beaver. Moments later, they saw Ofer and Joshua heading their way and signaling with a wave of Ofer's right arm for them to come in from their place of observation. When they had gathered all together, the rest of the group could see Ofer and Joshua hurriedly stripping down from their breechclouts and buckskin leggings and quickly crawling back into their warmer woolen pants! The rest of the men thought that strange behavior since they still had more traps to run. Then when Ofer and Joshua began retrieving from their riding mounts all of their pistols and placing them under their sashes around their waists, Black Eagle and Jerimiah began looking all around at the group of men figuring Ofer and Joshua had damn good reason for such activity in arming themselves before all of their work was finished! Once again seeing nothing of danger around them, Jerimiah asked, "What the hell is going on? We still have at least 30 more traps to check and set before we are anywhere near done for the day. What the hell is going on?"

As Ofer and Joshua, without a word being uttered continued hastily checking to make sure they had plenty of priming powder in their pistols and rifles, the remaining four trappers sensing danger of some sort, went into even higher alert. That was when Ofer said, "Something is bad wrong. My warning senses are getting the best of me. I can't hardly set a trap or pull a dead beaver from one without almost feeling physically ill. Something is happening and I just can't put my finger on it but I think it must have something to do back at our camp. Maybe there is a fire starting in our cave-cabin from our fireplace. If that was to occur, we stand to lose everything and maybe even our horses if a fire gets loose and starts burning everything up around our camp, including our horses. I say we haul our backsides back to camp and make sure everything is alright!"

That was when Black Eagle spoke up about the oddity of the three different animal-alarm events he had witnessed at different locations in the timber along the trail back to their camp over the last hour or so. Upon hearing those words, Ofer's back went straight as a rifle's ramrod as he stood there stone silent for a few long moments looking at Black Eagle as if something had just occurred to him. Then Ofer quietly and slowly said, "That is it! I have had a feeling for the last several days that we were being watched. I even wondered if someone was watching us this morning. And if so and they are in the process of riding back to our campsite through the timber, is that what is alarming those critters and spooking them out from the animals' usual hiding places? If that is the case and there are mystery riders in the timber, we need to get back to camp! I knew it! I knew it! It has to be our horses! Those damn Blackfeet or Gros Ventre have located us and our camp and are now making a raid on our supplies and horses! Check your priming, Boys, we may find ourselves once we get back to camp in a shootout for our very own lives!" said Ofer as he hurriedly mounted up into his saddle. Then turning, he instructed Gabriel to tie off the two packhorses carrying all of their fresh pelts and trapping gear to some nearby willows. "We will leave those packhorses behind because they will just slow us down. The rest of you boys gather up those reserve rifles we have been carrying on that third packhorse. Check them to make sure your priming powder is still good and then hurry up and place them back into their extra scabbards and get those tied onto your horses for easy access in case we need them. That way if we are outnumbered back at camp, each of us will have four shots from our two rifles and pistols that we will be carrying before we have to go to our tomahawks and knives!" barked out Ofer.

Following those instructions, there was a mad scramble to the third packhorse carrying all the extra firearms, where they were checked for adequate priming powder and then their scabbards were tied on everyone's riding mount, giving each man two rifles in his possession. Then that third packhorse was tied off and left behind with the other two packhorses as well. With

Black Eagle and his sharp eyes in the lead, the trappers, keeping to the edge of the timber along the way to avoid early detection of their movement, moved back towards their campsite. Not at a gallop mind you, but at a trot which still allowed the trappers to be on the alert and prepared for any ambush along the way in case there were Indians laying for them when they headed back to their campsite...

******

Still cautious of The Scalper's powers and his favorable 'evil spirits' to his way of thinking, Chief Walks Fast stopped a good 100 yards from the back side of the trappers' horse corral to avoid detection of any kind. Then he had his men spread out leaving even less evidence in the form of footprints as they cautiously made their way quietly on foot just in case some trappers had come back early and were now watching over things. Arriving at the back side of the trappers' corral, the chief held up his men as they carefully looked all around, checking for any signs of danger. Seeing none, the chief still took the precaution of sending in two of his warriors to quietly scout out the trappers' campsite just to make sure there was no existing danger while the rest of his warriors stayed hidden out of sight. Somewhat later, those two scouts returned with big grins on their faces as they told their chief that the trappers were all gone and the way was open for them to do what they came to do. The chief then had several of his men return to where they had quietly tied off all of their horses back in the forest and bring them into the trappers' camp. Shortly thereafter those men returned leading all of the Indians' horses and they were then tied off along the back side of the trappers' horse corral for safekeeping. That way the chief figured their horses would be available for a quick and easy getaway if circumstances such as the arrival of The Scalper's 'evil spirits' so dictated.

Leaving one man behind by the horse corral as a lookout for any arriving back early trappers and with a grin of anticipation,

Chief Walks Fast led the remaining nine men toward the trappers' cave-cabin and the white man's riches inside of furs, firearms, powder, pig lead, whiskey, rum and packsaddles to be used to pack off all of the trappers' items he and his men deemed valuable. Walking up to the trappers' front door with a big smile of victory, the chief led all of his anxious men single file JUST MISSING THE TWO BEAR TRAPS and into the cool of the cave-cabin. The white man's riches that greeted all of the Indians' eyes were beyond compare and soon the mad ransacking of the cave-cabin began amid numerous hoops and yells of exultation, victory and discovery!

Twenty minutes into the ransacking of the trappers' cave-cabin and over all the noise the thieves were happily making, WAS INSTANTLY QUIETED UPON HEARING A WARNING YELL FROM THE MAN LEFT AS A LOOKOUT BACK DOWN BY THE TRAPPERS' HORSE CORRAL! THE INDIAN LOOKOUT, UPON SEEING THROUGH THE TREES AT THE BOTTOM OF THE MEADOW THE TRAPPERS' HORSES SLOWLY COMING HIS WAY AND THEN UPON HEARING AN ONCOMING HORSE'S RECOGNITION WHINNY OF THE CAMPSITE, REACTED! YELLING AT THE TOP OF HIS LUNGS WITH A WARNING THAT THE TRAPPERS WERE COMING BACK UNEXPECTEDLY, THE LOOKOUT THEN RAN AROUND THE CORRAL TO THE CORRAL'S FRONT GATE IN ORDER TO LET THE VALUABLE HORSES OUT SO THEY COULD BE QUICKLY ROUNDED UP AND HERDED AWAY BY HIS COMPANIONS OUT THE FAR WESTERN SIDE OF THE MEADOW!

That second warning yell from the Indian lookout now starting to open up the corral gate so he could herd out the horses was instantly followed by a blood-curdling scream as he stepped into one of the hidden grizzly bear traps! "WHOOOMP" went the bear trap's powerful toothed jaws, crushing the Indian's legs beyond salvage, followed by his screams of intense agony before he passed out in pain!

Inside the trappers' cave-cabin, upon hearing the first warning yell and then short moments later the second warning yell, followed by a horrendous scream from the lookout, created intense panic among the looters in the cave-cabin! Out the door streamed the contingent of cabin robbers with their few rifles and bows and arrows in hand to do battle! When they did led by their chief, he was the first of his kind at the cabin to discover one of the hidden bear traps, quickly followed by a bone-crushing "WHOOOMP" AND A LOUD SCREAM OF INTENSE PAIN! A SCREAM OF INTENSE PAIN WHICH WAS QUICKLY SILENCED WHEN THE CHIEF PASSED OUT IN HIS AGONY OF HAVING BOTH OF HIS LEGS CRUSHED BY THE MASSIVE JAWS OF THE BEAR TRAP! A SECOND "WHOOOMP" QUICKLY FOLLOWED, AS ANOTHER INDIAN, FALLING AFTER BEING PUSHED FROM BEHIND BY AN EAGER INDIAN IN HIS HURRY TO EXIT THE CABIN, FELL FACE-FIRST INTO THE REMAINING BEAR TRAP AND WAS INSTANTLY CRUSHED TO DEATH WITH A BONE-CRUNCHING "WHOOOMP" OF THE TRAP'S JAWS ACROSS HIS HEAD!

The remaining eight Indians, now in a panic over having the ground around them 'leaping up and "eating" them', by what they figured were The Scalper's now aroused 'evil spirits', streamed down from the cave-cabin towards their horses tied up at the back of the corral at a dead run! Without the leadership and direction from their chief, now with his legs crushed in the jaws of a bear trap back at the cave-cabin and forgetting their original mission, nothing but absolute panic reigned! Especially with one Indian named Buffalo Calf. His brother had been the lookout who had stepped into the bear trap down by the horse corral and now lay moaning with both of his legs crushed in the jaws of the monster grizzly bear trap! Running with all due speed to aid his brother not knowing what had happened to him, just that he lay on the ground moaning out in agony, Buffalo Calf's luck ran out as he raced into disaster as well! Running up to his brother, Buffalo Calf with another Indian named Black Elk, both had the misfortune to simultaneously run across the remaining unsprung bear trap in front of the corral! "WHOOOMP" went the jaws of that bear trap, crushing a leg each of Buffalo Calf and Black Elk in a microsecond, all to the 'tune' of two more blood-curdling screams of agony and pain from the two horribly leg-crushed men!

Upon seeing the 'ground jumping up and grabbing' some of the legs of their comrades, the remaining six untrapped Black-feet Indians from Chief Walks Fast's group quickly gathered at the horse corral now in a total and utter panic over what they were experiencing! Then if the 'evil spirits' in the ground jumping up and crushing the legs of some of their comrades didn't add a sense of panic among the highly superstitious Indi-ans, seeing the oncoming trappers rounding the edge of the trees at the bottom of the meadow and coming their way now at a gallop 'was the final straw that set the hair on their collective asses'! Finally regaining a small sense of mission and survival, the remaining Indians up and fired a blizzard of arrows at the now oncoming racing men, just as fast as they could put arrow nock to bow string! Then upon realizing the futility of loosing a mess of arrows at such a number of determined and oncoming hard riding, heavily armed men, those remaining six Indians broke and ran for the back of the horse corral where they had all of their horses tied off!

However, horses being horses, seeing six madly fleeing Indians running right at them did like most horses are apt to do when now panicked out of their minds. Instantly, they all reared back in extreme fright over seeing six madly onrushing men, broke free from their reins and attempted to whirl and run off through the nearby aspens. When they did, two of the six

Indians scrambling for their horses got trampled in the melee and were left stomped and lying pretty much senseless on the ground! The remaining four managed to grab the reins from their panicked horses and in a mad scramble, mounted up and tried to ride off down through the aspens and make their escape before the 'evil spirits' or the onrushing trappers got them!

******

Rounding the edge of trees leading into their meadow and cabin site, the trappers saw a number of Indians scrambling down from their cave-cabin and sprinting to their horse corral! Then the next thing the trappers saw was a blizzard of arrows streaking through the heavens coming their way! Those who were doing the shooting with such a primitive weapon were no slackers when it came to knowing what they were doing and doing it well! Within seconds the oncoming now at a gallop trappers were quickly enveloped with the deadly arriving projectiles! With Black Eagle and Ofer in the lead they made the first contact with the arriving arrow storm! Black Eagle's horse whinnied pitifully and went down with an arrow through its right eye and into its brain case, killing it and tossing Black Eagle head over heels! Ofer fared somewhat better being hit twice by arrows. One arrow was driven clear through his 'possibles' bag and stuck into his stomach's muscle tissue, while the other was driven superficially through the side of his thigh! Little Raven also in the lead, had his horse killed out from under him, launching him into the air over the head of his horse, only to have his dead horse roll over him in a cloud of dust and flailing feet and hooves! Jerimiah took an arrow on the top of his right foot! Not a crippling wound but painful as hell later on, especially when its steel arrow point had to be cut away from the small bones in his foot! Gabriel took a flint arrow into the right shin of his leg, which shattered the stone arrowhead upon impact! However, wounded or not, Ofer, Gabriel, Joshua and Jerimiah rode hellbent for leather toward the horse corral like their lives depended on it and they did! There were four Indians still trying to mount up on their panicking and wildly bucking horses and in so doing, were not shooting any more arrows toward the hard-charging and oncoming trappers riding hell-bent for leather right at them! With that, the four trappers rode right into the aspens, further panicking horses and Indians alike trying to flee. Realizing that if any of the Indians escaped back to their band there would be hell to pay in the form of more attacks, Ofer, the first to arrive, shot one Indian down through the top of his head with his rifle! Then as he rode by another who had managed to mount his horse just in time, only to have his face crushed in by Ofer's now empty rifle barrel as he rode by and in the process, swung it hard and unhorsed the Indian with his crushed face! Jerimiah and Joshua combined with two shots from their rifles, killing another Indian who had just mounted up on his horse as well! That left Gabriel who rode right up to the last of the four Indians trying to escape and in so doing, took a swiping blow across his left shoulder from the man's toma-hawk for his trouble! The tomahawk-wielding Indian then began riding off down through the aspens, only to be back shot by a now very pissed-off Gabriel and then the killing of the escaping Indians in the aspens was over...

Black Eagle, limping and bent over with a damaged back from his horse wreck, had managed to stagger over to the horse corral where he dispatched with his tomahawk the three living but badly injured Indians who had befallen the two bear traps earlier! Then Ofer and Joshua seeing an Indian barely wiggling up by their cabin, rode their horses up to take a look. Looking down from their horses, they saw Chief Walks Fast writhing around in agony with both legs caught in one of the bear traps. Ofer shot him from his horse with his pistol and put him out of his misery! Then still living in the emotion of the moment from all of the killing and almost being killed, Ofer felt the almost physical feeling of his sixth sense warning of danger peeling away from his innermost being and now dissipating. No longer did he feel that an evil energy was filling his body with warning signs of danger and his soul with dread...

That afternoon, Little Raven and Ofer returned to their trap line in order to complete its 'run'. In so doing, they cleaned out the 19 dead beaver hanging in the traps and reset them. Since Ofer's stomach wound was only an inch deep into his muscles having first penetrated his 'possibles' bag, he could still function even with the painful gash left in his thigh left by an arrow. However, all the bending over setting the traps and removing dead beaver caused his stomach and thigh wounds to bleed so much that he soon found his buckskin leggings becoming soaked with his blood. Then he discovered that in light of the blood-soaked clothing, everywhere he walked in the beaver waters attending to his trap line he had a swarm of leeches following him swimming through the water as they sensed his blood in the beaver pond. Then with Little Raven doing all of the skinning and Black Eagle now sitting atop one of the Hudson's Bay men's horses, somewhat stooped over from his horse wreck standing guard duty, the three trappers finally finished, picked up their three packhorses tied off in the willows and headed for their campsite slightly worse for wear, but alive!

In the interim, Jerimiah, Joshua and Gabriel managed to toss a loop around each dead Indian, drag their bodies to the Smith River and leave them floating away to who knew where. Then when Ofer and company returned, it took all of them using their trap setting tools to depress the springs releasing the jaws of the traps so they could remove the broken bodies of the bear trap victims so they could be hauled off and deposited into the Smith as well. When the body haulers arrived the second time, they discovered that a sow grizzly and her two sub-adult cubs had already discovered several of the previously dumped bodies and were making short work of them...

That night without any supper found the men in their cave-cabin after they had let their horses out to feed and water, in the messy and painful process of patching each other up. After two cups of rum, Ofer had Jerimiah slosh some rum through the arrow cut in his thigh. Then with a liberal dose of bag balm pushed into the tear in his thigh, it was sewn up with needle and thread and then wrapped with gray cloth. As for the arrow hole in his gut muscle, a dose of rum and a mess of bag balm pushed into the wound and six stitches filled that bill. As for Black Eagle, he just had to gimp around for about a week after his arrow-induced horse wreck. Well, that and a couple cups of rum helped fill that 'bill' as well. Gabriel was a fairly easy fix as far as his arrow wound in the shinbone went. All it took was a cup of rum and Ofer with the tip of his knife digging out the chips of flint that had shattered and stuck in the shinbone! Then a liberal dose of bag balm and Gabriel was ready to go. As for Little Raven, even after being dumped off his horse and having it roll over the top of him, he was surprisingly alright. A little stiff and sore but no broken bones and with a cup of rum, he too discovered that he would also live. Jerimiah was a different story however, with a now bent steel-tipped arrow point still lodged firmly into the top of his foot! Under the light of two beeswax candles, Ofer, using the tip of his candle-flame cauterized sheath knife blade, carefully dug out the bent over steel arrow head. Upon hitting the foot, the arrow point had bent over after hitting the bones and then had stubbornly dug itself under a number of tendons. However after careful digging with his knife tip, pulling, tugging and teasing the arrow point away from one stubborn last tendon, the point was finally removed. Then after several more rounds of rum per trapper, the men then made sure that all of their weapons were reloaded in case more Blackfeet came along. Then with three bundles of furs placed in behind the front door as added protection in case Indians tried entering the cabin at night, the men staggered off to their sleeping furs for some much earned and needed rest.

The following morning, Black Eagle and Little Raven brought in all of the men's buckskins which along with the six Hudson's Bay men's horses, had fed all night. They were then allowed to water and put back into their corral. Then taking all nine of the Indians' horses (two had run off and escaped), the walking wounded double hobbled them and let them out from the corral to graze as well, since they were going to be kept by the trappers. Kept because with the men leaving the Smith come summer and moving on to another area with less Blackfeet, they figured they would keep those nine Indian horses to pack out all the leftover provisions, cooking implements, numbers of bundles of furs and such. That, plus they needed two additional riding horses since two of the trappers' horses had been killed in the "bear trap" battle.

Then the two buckskin horses killed in the battle were quartered up and since they were now bloated and not fit to eat, were hauled off and left along the Smith for the critters to enjoy. Since the men had been wounded to the degrees they were, time was not taken to scalp the dead Indians and tie their scalps to their horses' manes because the decision had been made to keep and use their horses in the future. Besides, the grizzly bears eating the dead Indians did not seem to mind having a little hair in their food...

For the next two weeks, Ofer and company of trappers gimped along with their recent wounds and ran their trap line. However just in case they had more uninvited visitors, all of the very effective and deadly bear traps were reset by the corral and cave-cabin once again and left in place with a lot of daily warnings among the trappers to be careful where they were stepping. The same care was taken by the horse corral by only bringing one horse out at a time and walking it on the far side of the open corral gate away from where the deadly devices had been set so there would not be an accident. As for Little Raven and Black Eagle, since they had their buckskin riding horses killed in battle, they each chose a Hudson's Bay horse as their replacements. That they did since both of those horses had been previously shod and up to the rocky riding they were facing.

Right up until Ofer decided to remove all of their beaver traps because the beaver were losing their prime and putting on their lighter summer coats, the men worked hard at removing every beaver they could. Soon their daily returns had dwindled down to less than 10 beaver being caught because most had been trapped off the Smith in their current trapping area. Finally all of their traps were pulled and the men made ready to pack up all of their belongings and head southeast towards Fort Manuel for the usual summer get-together with other trappers and friends, sell their furs, reprovision and head to a new trapping area yet to be determined. However, with all of their friends flung to the far corners of the wilderness, Ofer was sure he could, through conversations with his fellow trappers, find a reliable beaver trapping location for what he figured would be their last year afield as trappers. Then they would take their Letters of Credit back to St. Louis in order to redeem them at the main St. Louis Missouri Fur Company warehouse and office. Then the brothers, Black Eagle and Little Raven would return to the Tal Ranch and having 'seen the Elephant' would settle down, hopefully marry and continue in his father's horse raising and farming business. A business and a lifestyle Ofer was beginning not to look forward to...

So with that, the 'brothers' began making their final preparations for departure to Fort Manuel. All of their over 900 beaver furs were bundled and covered with deerskin coverings to protect them during transport by packhorse the many miles to Fort Manuel. Then the men worked together patching up all of their much-needed leather packing and saddle gear for the long trip. Finally, Ofer and company tore down all of their weapons, removed the lead and black powder fouling and reassembled the lot. That they did in case they ran into any number of roving

Blackfeet or Gros Ventre raiding parties on the lookout for returning trapper caravans, so they could make a good accounting of themselves as shooters. Then one evening, the men melted a number of their pigs of lead and cast several small mountains of bullets for both of their pistols and rifles just in case after killing off a number of Blackfeet they ran into more. Then the men killed four elk and made most of those animals into jerky for the trip ahead in case game along the way was scarce. That and they found themselves unable to hunt any game on the way back to Fort Manuel due to the closeness of hostile Indians on the lookout for trappers and easy 'pickin's' who were on their way back to the fort.

Finally the day of departure from the bountiful Smith River's beaver trapping grounds arrived to find the men up way before daylight because of all of the packing duties that lay ahead of them. Finally by noon the entire fur trapper caravan had been loaded and made ready for departure. Sitting there quietly on their horses, the men looked over what had been their home for the past two years with mixed feelings. True, they had caught a bounty of beaver but it seemed they had to fight the bloody Blackfeet for almost every one of them... Leaving the door to their cabin ajar for whoever wanted to call the cave-cabin 'home', the men slowly rode out from that area of their lives without looking back. They were grateful to be alive but to a man, it seemed in that dark and bloody ground they had called home for the last two years they had to fight for every breath taken and bore the scars to prove it...

CHAPTER 13 — A MAN CALLED "EUSTACE", TRAPPING THE "ROSEBUD"

BECAUSE OF SEVERAL VIOLENT SUMMER THUNDERSTORMS experienced along the way and one close call when over 50 Gros Ventre Indians passed by without seeing the trappers' fur caravan cleverly hidden in a river bottom, the men finally arrived safely at the front gate of Fort Manuel. Arriving around mid-morning, there they were happily greeted by Manuel Lisa with a 'whoop and a holler' when he recognized his old friends, the Tal Brothers and their two Crow Indian adopted brothers. Well, that and a fully packed and heavily loaded pack train with many bundles of valuable furs in evidence for businessman Manuel Lisa and his coffers in the fort...

Being that they were early arrivals that summer, Lisa was able to get their fur train into his fort and put his company men right onto their counting, grading and sorting duties. Soon the 'fur' was literally flying as Ofer and company carefully watched the process making sure the work was fair, aboveboard and honest. By day's end, Lisa's men had counted out 973 beaver 'Plus', 39 wolf pelts and 81 marten pelts! That year there was such a demand both nationally and internationally for beaver fur for the beaver hat trade, that the price had shot up once again to $6 per pound! That being said, with 973 beaver being submitted for sale at 1½ pounds per pelt meant there were 1,459½ pounds of beaver presented by Ofer and his group! With the going rate being $6 per pound, Lisa was facing having to pay out for the beaver just brought in by Ofer and company a princely sum of $8,757.00! Then Lisa paid Ofer and company $35 per wolf pelt which brought in another $1,365. Lastly, the marten were also highly priced that year, costing Lisa and his fur company $3.30 per pelt. With 81 marten pelts on the grading table, Lisa was looking at another $267.30, for a total of $10,389.30 in proceeds for Ofer and company's year to date trapping efforts! Once again, a small fortune in that day and age! There was lots of 'whooping' and dancing around by Ofer and company upon seeing such a final tally for a year's hard and oftentimes dangerous work as trappers in the wilderness along the boun- tiful Smith River!

With that, Lisa, as was his customary practice, wrote out a chit for the above amount so when the men once again reprovi- sioned at his fort's warehouse, his company clerks could have such a figure from whence to work from as the trappers shopped along knowing the bill at Mountain Prices would be paid. Then when all the reprovisioning and any blacksmith work including shoeing the nine captured Indian horses, was subtracted from that total, Lisa would then personally issue a Letter of Credit from the St. Louis Missouri Fur Company good at the First National Bank of St. Louis located on 3rd and Front Street for that amount remaining due. (That Letter of Credit subsequently issued a month later amounted to $9,549.00, which Ofer once again placed into his saddlebag along with his other Letters of Credit.)

With that chit firmly placed in his shirt pocket, Ofer led his men out from the fort and over to their familiar cottonwood grove of trees by the creek. Being that they were there pretty early in the summer for the usual gathering of trappers, they found that once again they had that spot all to themselves except for one lone and raggedy-looking trapper camping nearby. But even with that trapper camped off to one side, Ofer and company were still able to move into their old campsite from years before and settle in. Then the scramble was on because of the oncoming lateness of the day. While Gabriel and Little Raven began preparing a firepit, the rest of the men scrounged around their grove of cottonwoods and several nearby tree groves for any limb wood or downed trees they could cut up and use back at their firepit. Then as Ofer and Black Eagle unloaded their pack animals carrying all of their sleeping and cooking gear, Jerimiah and Joshua arranged the now empty pack and saddle gear under the cottonwood trees' canopy to preclude any afternoon soakings from summer thunderstorms. There they also arranged everyone's sleeping furs so each man would have his own space also under the cottonwood trees' canopy for the shade and protection once again from afternoon thunderstorms. Then their horses were all watered at the side of the small creek near their camp, hobbled and let out to graze on the nearby grassy flats.

By then, Gabriel and Little Raven had the firepit dug, a roaring fire ongoing making Dutch oven coals, with the hanging irons set up and over the fire ready for use. Hanging from one of the hanging irons was a happily boiling pot of water soon to be ready for the several handfuls of crushed green coffee beans to follow. Sitting on a saddle near the fire, Little Raven was busily mixing up his flour, water, salt and dried yeast so he could make the men a batch of their favorite, namely Dutch oven biscuits. Since they had no meat for supper that evening, Little Raven was planning on adding a mess of raisins into the biscuit dough along with healthy helpings of brown sugar so the hardworking men would have some kind of a treat come suppertime. Then the plan was for Little Raven and

Gabriel to sally forth the next day and come that suppertime, see to it that the men would have healthy slabs of venison or antelope meat to 'worry over' once suppertime rolled around again.

Once supper was done, the men went into the nearby field and brought back all of their horses now numbering 32 in number, counting their remaining buckskins and those from the Hudson's Bay men and the Blackfeet recently defeated at their old campsite! Then a long cotton rope line was unrolled from a coil of rope carried in a pannier and strung through the cottonwoods. so a picket line could be established and all of their horses tied thereon. Then it was back to the firepit, the usual gathering place for the men as their last flat keg of rum was opened and the men happily sat there around their fire smoking their pipes, drinking rum and visiting, while warding off the hordes of summer mosquitoes found in that area next to the Bighorn River and its several adjacent shallow waterways.

However as they did, Gabriel kept looking over at the rather shabby-looking trapper quietly sitting alone by his small campfire. Standing there for a moment, Gabriel kept looking at the rather lonely looking trapper who had hardly moved from his small fire ever since they had arrived and did not appear to be eating anything for his supper. That was when Gabriel, ever the brother with the biggest heart among all of the Tal Brothers, walked over to one of his Dutch ovens sitting by their fire, loaded it up with the last of his bread dough and set it to baking over the coals with a Christian 'mission' in mind.

Then without saying where he was going, Gabriel walked over to where the lone trapper was sitting by his campfire. "Hey, Old Timer, my name is Gabriel Tal and I am one of our designated camp cooks. As such, I have a Dutch oven baking away some of my favorite brand of biscuits and everyone in my camp has already eaten all they wanted for supper. If you have a 'likin'' for Dutch oven biscuits, come on over to our camp, help yourself to my baking, sit a spell and meet the rest of my gang of brothers and close friends."

For the longest moment in time, the old trapper just looked up at Gabriel and then slowly extended a weathered hand saying, "They call me "Eustace", young fella. By 'damn it', if you have Dutch oven biscuits, I could sure use some. I haven't 'et' in two days since I ran out of grub. You lead the way and I would be happy to meet the rest of your clan, not to mention putting a 'hurt' on that Dutch oven full of biscuits," said Eustace, as he rose and then quietly followed Gabriel over to the Tal campsite.

"Guys, I want all of you to meet my new friend Eustace," said Gabriel, as he then commenced introducing everyone to the lone trapper. After introductions had been made all around, Eustace looked over at Gabriel saying, "Now, young fella, where be them damn Dutch oven biscuits you was a-braggin' about over at my camp?"

Getting out a metal plate, Gabriel loaded it with piping hot biscuits fresh out from his Dutch oven and handed it to his newfound friend, who without a word, began gobbling down the biscuits, hot or not, like he hadn't eaten in days, which he hadn't. In fact, Eustace said not a word until he had emptied out the entire Dutch oven 'empty as a hound's tooth' of biscuits! Then with a loud 'belch', he accepted a seat upon a saddle that Ofer had brought over to the campfire and arranged so the man could at least sit in comfort and visit with the rest of the group.

Then looking all around at the rest of the men sitting around the campfire looking at him, Eustace finally said, "I suppose all of you are a-wondering why I am all alone when most trappers in this sometimes Godforsaken wilderness run in pairs or even in larger brigades. Never used to be that-a-way a year or so back. Me, my four brothers and a cousin used to work the docks in New Orleans when we got the bug to come this a-way in the lands of the Louisiana Purchase, to try our hands at trapping them damn beaver everyone was a-talking about and shipping across that big pond everyone calls "The Atlantic" to all those beaver-hungry folks in Europe. Seemed like the thing to do after me and my kin loaded hundreds of Indian-caught bundles of valuable beaver pelts onto oceangoing boats all headed for that place they called Europe. Then according to all of them fur shippers, them beaver were going across the Atlantic to be made into beaver hats which are all the rage with the men about town. And according to them fur shippers, them beaver skins were each worth more than me and my kin could make in a week of hard work on them damn hot and sweaty boat docks loading 'um'. So we pooled what little money we had and came upriver to St. Louis. Then we all got jobs on the boat docks here in St. Louis and loaded more of them damn beaver skins all over once again as we all saved our money. After a year of hard work and a-savin' our money, we all got all fired-up once again when them Lewis and Clark fellas returned from that long trip they took clear across this land of ours to those waters of the Pacific. When they got back to St. Louis, all they could talk about was how many of those damn beaver were in every drop of water clear across this land of ours all the way to the Pacific and back."

About then Black Eagle handed Eustace a cup of rum and in a twinkling of an eye, he had drained it dry! Then handing his empty cup back to Black Eagle with a look on his face 'asking', "Is there any more of that damn good rum where that came from?" the old trapper continued with his story. A story that was going somewhere and at that moment in time had everyone's attention. "Anyways, where was I before I was handed that cup of damn good rum? Oh yes, after them Lewis and Clark fellas left, me and my kin, we met an upriver Indian trader named Manuel Lisa who wanted to go into the wilderness, make a fort and trading post and have his men trap beaver. When we heard that, we all spoke up and soon the six of us and a man who knew how to trap named Del Garrison formed ourselves into a group of fur trappers. Then pooling all of our money and getting some credit from Manuel Lisa, we provisioned up and headed up the Missouri River trailing several of his keelboats as they headed for his fort located in this here beaver trapping country where we are a-sitting."

Then Eustace seemed to run down on his storytelling until he got a second wind. Then continuing, he said, "Right off the bat, we all should have knowed it were a fool's mission. Del Garrison, our leader, got himself 'kilt' right off the bat by them damn Arikara Indians when our keelboat went by one of their damn villages located right on the Missouri River! Seems a stray arrow had his name on it and that was that! Seems them damn Arikara hate every white man they run across. I hear tell that several years ago one of their greatest chiefs was invited to Washington to meet the President and get a 'look-see' at how great our country is. The thinkin' was we would baffle that there chief with our country's greatness, humble him and then send him back to convince the rest of his ornery damn people to let the white man have at it on their lands. Well as that story goes, that Arikara chief up and died from some white man's disease and was buried in a Potter's Field somewhere. Then no one in the government took the time to tell the Arikara people how their great chief died until about a year later. Upon hearing that and how their beloved chief had died, them damn Arikara went on the warpath and have been on one ever since. So my word to all of you is to stay away from them damn Arikara as much as you can unless you want to invite a speeding lead ball or arrow slammed into your carcass and your hair lifted and hung on some 'Buck's' tipi pole."

Black Eagle, all wrapped up in Eustace's storytelling, finally got the message when Eustace kept coughing like he had a dry throat as he continued telling his story of life and woe. With that, Black Eagle brought him another cup of rum to 'wet his whistle'. Once again, that cup of rum disappeared as quickly as a falling star across the vast prairie sky and then he commenced with his story which by now had everyone's rapt attention…

"Let's see, where was I?" said Eustace. "Oh yes, after Del up and got 'his self' 'kilt', we six all kin continued on to Fort Manuel and then moved out into the country of the trapping waters not far from here to a place called the "Rosebud" after a trapper around the fort showed us how to trap. Talk about beaver on that there water, hell man, there were so many in those waters that we just kept trippin' over the damn things! Realizing what we had, we set down our roots in a small draw not far from the Rosebud near a crystal clear spring. There we built one hell of a stout cabin for the lot of us and a horse corral to make anyone proud. Then we began trapping all serious-like and soon we had more damn beaver pelts than you could shake a stick at!" Then Eustace paused, looked at Black Eagle and handed him his empty cup with a hopeful look spelled clear across his heavily whiskered face…

Moments later, Eustace was into his third cup of rum, only this time he sipped it all slowly like as he continued gathering in his thoughts. Then he said, "Me and my kin did right fine and then it seemed that the good Lord above stopped takin' a likin' to us for some damn reason. One fine day when we were running our trap lines, a huge thunderstorm rolled upon us. Well, we had six more traps to run so we kept at it and then 'wham'! Out from one of the blackest damn rain clouds I ever saw come a bolt of lightning striking Cousin Albert and the horse upon which he was riding! We buried Albert back at our cabin that afternoon and he were a mess. Not much left except a mass of burned flesh and snot… Same went for his nag which we left for the wolves back out on the prairie. Then two weeks later my Brother Clem walked up behind our cabin hunting deer for our camp meat and come dark, he had not returned. The next day we went looking for him and had to kill the grizzly bear that had 'kilt' my brother and was sleeping next to what was left of his body after he had eaten most of it! Once again, we buried what was left of Clem alongside Albert so the two of them would have something to talk about as they went through the heavens. Then after the spring trapping season, me and my remaining brothers were coming to Fort Manuel to trade in our furs and got jumped by a mess of them damn Northern Cheyenne and afore all was said and done, they had 'kilt' my Brother Isaac! Well, we turned around and went back to our cabin where we buried Isaac alongside the rest of his kin. Now I bet the bunch of them are a-trappin' beaver up in heaven. We hadn't made enough money by the time we paid Lisa for what we had borrowed on credit, so me and my remaining brothers returned to the Rosebud and continued fall trapping and did right good. Come spring, we continued doing right good in the beaver trapping but with just the few of us, it were wearing us down with the trapping, skinning, hooping, hunting, woodcutting and all. Then trouble reared its ugly head once again when my oldest brother Walbert stepped into a deep muskrat hole while setting a beaver trap! He wrenched his hip so badly all he could do was stay back at our cabin and try not moving so much. However, he kept getting worser and worser until we could see his hip was infected all terrible like and so much so, my brother smelled something awful and putrid! That turned out to be 'the smell of death' when the infection took him. He was laid along with the others out behind our cabin. Having had enough, my younger brother Calvin and I headed for Fort Manuel to trade in our furs and call it quits. However, we got jumped by a pair of them damn Northern Cheyenne as we started down the trail and they got a rifle ball into Cal's guts before I 'kilt' the two of them damn savages! I took Cal back to our cabin and three days later he swelled up, stunk to high heaven and died. I buried him alongside the others and then went on a drunk that lasted for three days. On day three of my drunk I kept hearing my horses acting all nervous-like and walked outside just in time to see three

Northern Cheyenne 'Bucks' running off all of my horses out from the corral with the exception of my riding horse and one packhorse! I did manage to kill one of them damn 'Bucks' but the other two made off with the rest of my horses. That being said, the next day I dug a cache and buried everything I had of value in my cabin and loading what I could and one bundle of my furs so I could have something to sell for food, left everything and headed for Fort Manuel. That I did because I couldn't bring out my provisions or furs because I had no horses to haul everything that I owned except the one I was riding and one packhorse. Besides, what was I to do? There was only one of me and I couldn't do all the beaver trapping by myself and watch out for the dangers in that area, so here I am." Then with those words, he drained his cup of rum and then quietly turned on his sitting saddle and stared into the men's fire as if he was finished talking and now into deep thinking. When he did, no one else made a sound after hearing a story of such great loss that was so encompassing that no one felt like breaking the silence out of reverence over what they had just heard and respect for the old trapper who had such bad luck...

As Eustace slowly nodded off to sleep while sitting on the saddle with his belly filled with Gabriel's Dutch oven biscuits and probably having imbibed too much rum, the rest of the men seeing him sleeping, quietly got up and headed for their sleeping furs. They left Eustace sleeping quietly by himself next to the fire out of respect for a man who had lost almost everything he ever had. However, just before Gabriel went to his sleeping furs, he grabbed up a sweaty old horse blanket and gently placed it over the old sleeping trapper's shoulders so he wouldn't be so cold once the fire went out and then headed for his sleeping furs as well.

The next morning when Gabriel and Little Raven rolled out from their sleeping furs so they could start a fire and begin making breakfast for the rest of the men, they spotted Eustace still sitting there sleeping under the smelly old horse blanket. Careful not to wake him, the two cooks made as little noise as they could out of respect for the old trapper who had gone through so much misery in his life. However, when Little Raven dropped a coffee pot lid on one of the rocks alongside the firepit, Eustace awoke with a start.

Then realizing where he was and looking over at Gabriel, Eustace said, "Gabriel, are you going to make some more of those damn fine biscuits like you made for me last night? Because if you are, I will trade you one of my Made Beaver pelts for some if that be a fair trade in your book. And if not, I will throw in two Made Beaver 'Plus' but no more than that."

Gabriel walked over to the weathered old trapper and handed him a cup of steaming hot coffee and said, "Eustace, we are fixing some spitted buffalo meat that Manuel Lisa brought over to us last evening, coffee and Dutch oven biscuits for our breakfast. If you have the time and inclination, we would be honored to have you share some breakfast with the six of us."

Eustace just beamed over being included with others of his kind saying, "Is there anything I can do to help since I will be mooching off you fellas this morning?"

Gabriel just beamed and said, "Yes there is. You being our guest can just sit there and warm up and when the rest of this lazy bunch gets up, join us for breakfast."

Upon hearing those words, Eustace just beamed once again and then settled back down and enjoyed his newfound friends and his very welcome steaming hot cup of coffee... Standing over by the creek, Ofer just smiled over hearing Gabriel's warming words and observing his brother's kind treatment of the old trapper. However, he had slept little the previous evening. That was not because he was having another sixth sense warning sensation after mulling over a possible opportunity that could serve his camp and that of Eustace as well. Finishing up with his shaving, Ofer combed his hair and then wandered over to the morning's activity swirling around the firepit.

"Good morning, Eustace. How the hell did you sleep all wrapped up in that smelly old horse blanket?" Ofer said with an easy teasing smile.

"Ofer, good morning to you as well," replied Eustace right back at him with a big ole whiskered grin. "I slept pretty damn well. In fact, that was the first real night's sleep that I have had since I buried my last brother and got the hell out of that burial grounds neck of the woods in the Rosebud. But you know something? I miss my ole cabin, the goodness of the water in the spring by the cabin, the quietness of the mornings in that neck of the woods and all the many birds we used to have around our cabin. But I guess that is the way it has to be," Eustace quietly replied with a very audible sigh.

"Well, the way I see it, it doesn't have to be that way unless that is what you want," quietly replied Ofer, as he watched the old man carefully to see how his just spoken words with a hidden question in among them were received by the old trapper.

With those words, Eustace's head swiveled around like a shot and his dark eyes just stared hard at Ofer as his quick-thinking mind realized Ofer had asked him a kind of a hidden question, before he said, "What did you say, Ofer?"

Those weren't the only heads that swiveled around that morning either, as Gabriel and Little Raven's heads spun around upon hearing Ofer's hidden words signifying he had a serious thought in mind and 'was now on the hunt'! And knowing Ofer as they did, they damn well knew there was something important in the 'wind' and it wasn't the smell of their campfire or Dutch oven biscuits baking away either...

"Well, Eustace, I have been thinking most of last night while lying in my sleeping furs listening to the rest of you folks snoring away. And when I let my mind and ideas wander along with me regarding my actions in the future, most of the time it is for the good. With that said, I have a proposal for you, Eustace. If you would care to hear what I have to say, let me know what your thinking is and I will proceed, or I will just sit here and enjoy my coffee."

"Hellfire, Ofer, nothing that you have said since we met last night has caused me any worry. So I say, let it all hang out and let's hear what is sticking in your craw," said Eustace with a big grin, as Gabriel refilled his coffee cup knowing the old man could be long-winded.

"Well here it is since you asked for it. As you heard last night, the boys and I are through trapping up on the Smith. No beaver left and them damn Blackfeet are just getting too friendly with trying to run off with our horses all of the time. And it appears you got run out of the Rosebud after losing all of your kin, plus the Northern Cheyenne were getting a bit too nosy as well. So here is what I would like to suggest for your consideration. What say you and the rest of us couple up and form a trapping team and go back to the Rosebud? You say you have a brand new cabin all built that could from the sounds of it hold our entire gang. You already have a ready-built horse corral that could hold all of our horses and you have a spring near your cabin with all the fresh water we or our horses would require. Lastly, you mentioned that the adjacent waterways around your cabin are full of beaver with at last count no one around up there to trap them. If you did decide to throw in with us and share, we would have enough guns to keep the Northern Cheyenne at bay, we all could make a damn good living on all them beaver you purport to say are in those waters and we would be more than willing to split the profits right down the middle with you. Especially since you would be supplying the cabin, horse corral and the directions to that location, not to mention you would be helping us with all of the trapping as well. What do you have to say about that proposal, Eustace?" asked Ofer.

For the longest time, Eustace just stared hard at Ofer after hearing what he had to say as if he could hardly believe his ears! He wasn't the only one staring hard as well, since he had caught the attention of Little Raven and Gabriel, as well as Joshua, Black Eagle and Jerimiah who had just arrived at the fire site and had overheard most of what Ofer had just proposed to the old trapper they hardly even knew...

Then the old man's eyes welled up with tears and he freely let them rain down upon the front of his raggedy ole buckskin shirt. Then taking his weathered old hands, he unashamedly wiped them roughly across his eyes as if mad at himself over showing such emotion in front of a number of strangers. Then Eustace quietly said, "Ain't no one ever offered such a hand to me since I have been alive. I have always had to scratch shit with the chickens ever since I was just a small lad. No one has ever made such an offer to me to help as you just have. You good folks hardly even know me, yet you have taken me in and now are offering me a chance to go back to where I have laid all of my living kin, so's I can follow the dream all of us had afore they all got kilt. All my life I have worked hard for everything I have ever gotten and now my dreams of returning to the Rosebud with help and finally doing what I set out to do are finally coming true! Ofer, if what you are offering me is true and comes from your heart, I say YES! But wait! What does the rest of your party of trappers have to say about such a generous offer to someone all of you hardly even know?"

For the longest moment in time, the Tals, Black Eagle and Little Raven just stood stock-still thinking over what had been offered and the possible future events now whirling around them. Then Ofer stood up, offered his hand saying, "Welcome to our 'family', Eustace!" Then Eustace was surrounded by the rest of the men all backslapping the old man, shaking his hand, even giving him a hug as only Gabriel could do, as they welcomed him to their 'clan' and the adventures to come with trapping back on the Rosebud. Only this time instead of being alone, he would be a member of the Tal Clan...

That morning the men feasted on spitted buffalo meat, Dutch oven biscuits, beans, coffee and afterwards, a number of cups of rum in celebration for the adventures soon to come on the Rosebud. Then the entire group herded all of their horses over to the fort's blacksmith shops, selected out the best of their 32 horses and then had them shoed for the year ahead of beaver trapping. The surplus 12 horses out of the bunch were then sold to Lisa and a credit chit was received for $1,200, which went into Ofer's shirt pocket for later redemption after they had provisioned up. As for Eustace's two horses, he kept those as a reminder of his earlier days as a Free Trapper on the Rosebud before misery overtook him.

Then the men headed for Lisa's nearby warehouse on foot to reprovision while their horses were being shoed by Lisa's three blacksmiths. Once at the warehouse and shopping for what the group would need for the coming year, Eustace traded in his .50 caliber rifle for one that was a .52 caliber so his would match what the others were carrying for ease in using the same size balls. Then Ofer had Lisa's company clerks set aside 50 one-pound, watertight tins of powder for their rifles and pistols and ten one-pound tins of priming powder to go with the powder they already possessed. Those selections were then followed up with bags of precut flints for their rifles and pistols, sacks of greased wads, 100 pounds of lead pigs, additional spare rifle and pistol parts that fitted all of the men's rifles and pistols, two spare rifle ramrods in case any were broken in use, extra bullet pullers, gun grease and two more cast iron bullet casting kettles.

Then since Eustace had cached most of his equipment before he left the Rosebud and not wanting to chance the cache still being there, not dug up by wolves or bears, raided by Indians or ruined by moisture or rodents, Ofer had everyone totally outfitted with capotes, gloves, new wide brimmed hats, socks, woolen pants, woolen shirts and for those doing the trapping, new breechclouts and buckskin leggings for all the immersion in water work that lay ahead in a year of trapping beaver.

Then since the group was more than adequately supplied between the two camps with traps, cooking gear, shovels and such and since they did not have to build a cabin or horse corral this time, no further purchases were made of those kinds of items. But Gabriel, Eustace and Little Raven sure went to town when it came to selecting sacks of flour, tins of dried yeast, bags of salt, black pepper, red pepper flakes, cinnamon, dried raisins, dried apple slices, beans, rice, brown sugar, sacks of hard candy, bag balm, light gun oil, nine kegs of rum and the like. In fact, those three men were selecting items so fast, it took three heavily sweating company clerks just to stay ahead of the men and their many and varied selections! But since there were now seven men in the trapping group, the designated cooks made sure there were adequate foodstuffs to last the men all known to be eager eaters through the fall and spring beaver trapping seasons. Plus there once again arose the question of such supplies that still existed in Eustace's cache being edible and not ruined that could be used as well.

Then at the end of that exhausting day of provision selections, the men returned and after waiting a period of time, returned with their herd of horses fully and newly shod by the fort's blacksmiths. Then it was back to their campsite where their horses were hobbled and let out to feed and water except for Gabriel and Little Raven's riding horses and a single packhorse. That afternoon, those two trappers went hunting for camp meat and returned right at dusk with their packhorse carrying a rolling fat mule deer doe and buck. While the crew of men set about skinning and butchering out the two deer, Gabriel and Little Raven commenced making fires so there would be adequate cooking and baking coals, biscuit dough so it could rise, set another pot of beans to slow cook on the cooking rods and fired up the always-present coffee pot. Meanwhile while supper was being prepared, Black Eagle, Ofer and Eustace moved his camping site over to where the rest of the group now occupied their own campsite and now the group was under one set of cottonwood trees and complete...

For the rest of that month, the men gathered in more firewood, cared for their livestock, hunted several times a week for camp meat, visited with a number of their trapper friends arriving on a daily basis, traded with some of the arriving Indians for fancy beaded shirts and moccasins, took part in other trappers' celebrations and got even better acquainted with the 'man only called Eustace'. As they did, the Tals, Little Raven and Black Eagle came to love the old trapper they had taken in, and soon he was treated and became almost like a much-loved and very welcome 'grandfather' to all of the men...

By the second week in August, both Ofer and Eustace were showing signs of itching to be on the road and heading southeasterly towards Eustace's previous Rosebud trapping grounds to see what might still be standing. Then after a week of summer thunderstorm after thunderstorm, Ofer and Eustace were tired of living out in the open at Fort Manuel and preferred that they were inside a nice dry cabin instead of being under a constantly dripping cottonwood tree. Two days later found that group of trappers saying their 'Good-byes' to their friends and wishing them well, then heading out to the Rosebud. Ofer and Eustace led the way and the rest of the men followed trailing their heavily loaded extra riding and packhorses. Three days of travel later found Eustace getting excited as he began recognizing different landmarks that signaled he was getting closer to his cabin and old stomping grounds. By the evening of the third day of travel, the men rounded a long sagebrush-covered ridgeline and then angled slightly northerly into a long draw between two long and low ridges. To their east lay the Rosebud and at the end of the long draw sat a perfectly good and brand new-looking cabin that had been built 'hell-for-stout' and appeared to be roomy enough for all seven of their party if its large outside dimensions spoke to its living space inside.

Upon seeing his cabin, Eustace gave out a yell of joy, spurred his riding horse and galloped right up to the hanging all crooked-like open front door. Bailing off his horse and just dropping the reins, he hobbled right up to the cabin like a kid with a bag of hard candy, moved through the open doorway and disappeared inside. This he did as the rest of the trappers' pack string ambled up to the cabin with grins on their faces over seeing Eustace being so happy to be home and especially on all of their faces upon seeing such a nice roomy cabin in which to live for the coming year.

All of a sudden, the men heard Eustace yell and then moments later he staggered out from the open doorway rubbing his eyes, gagging and coughing! Then being partially blinded from whatever had happened to him while inside the cabin, Eustace staggered out the open doorway, stumbled and fell flat on his face in a cloud of dust! By now upon seeing Eustace in trouble, caused the rest of the men to go into high alert and go for their rifles looking for any signs of danger that had caused such an unexpected ruckus from inside the cabin! About then, out from the open doorway trotted a large striped skunk! A large skunk, who upon seeing all the other trappers right outside the open front doorway of the cabin sitting on a mess of horses, ran right up to the mounted men and their curious and onlooking horses. With that, the skunk stopped, stomped its front feet in warning and then swung its backside around in order to face the trappers with his 'best side'!

What happened next had to make God laugh until he cried! In an instant, the irritated and very disturbed skunk filled the air with a cloud of its natural defense, which in the sunlight turned into a rainbow of colors and a mountain of acrid bad smells! Instantly, horses out of curiosity over the little critter had all dropped their noses down checking the little animal out. When they did, they too got a blinding spray spewed into their noses and faces which were now almost touching the critter out of curiosity! When the horses got 'rewarded' for being so curious and nosy, they immediately commenced bucking off their riders, as they tried getting the hell out of the way of the foul smelling spray continuing to be spewed into their faces! Then it was the trailing packhorses rearing back on their reins to get out of the way and in so doing, pulling their surprised handlers over the backs of their riding horses and onto the ground and into the 'gun-zone' of the now REALLY pissed-off skunk! A skunk who took umbrage with the perceived 'attack' by the bodies falling off the horses and in so doing, took advantage of the close at hand targets lying on the ground and saw to it that they got more than a whiff of his perfumed essence as well! Soon the meadow near the cabin was full of running and milling horses, coughing and gagging trappers, and packhorses trying to buck off their loads so they could flee the smelly scene! So it was that Eustace was 'welcomed home' and the rest of the trappers got a close look at their new 'digs' and that of a surprised inhabitant who had walked through the cabin's open door and made himself right at home! Oh by the way, the striped skunk, now empty of his 'fire-power', managed to make a clean getaway...

For the next week, the trappers who had left Fort Manuel because it was time and they were tired of sleeping outside under summer thunderstorms, got to continue sleeping outside at their new homesite as well. And their bad luck did not end there. When Eustace went to dig up his cache site and retrieve a mess of his goods, he discovered that a pack of wolves had sniffed out his cache site and had dug their ways into it. What they didn't eat or urinate on setting up their territorial sign posts, the ground squirrels chewed up and then the grizzly bear after the chance for a ground squirrel dinner, made a mess of what was left! Then the local Northern Cheyenne Indians subsequently looting the remains of the cache site pretty much ruined any chance of using anything else so stashed! In fact, the only items that were worthy of retrieval were a few pigs of lead and cast iron cooking implements left by Eustace. Shortly thereafter, the cache site was filled up with dirt to preclude any of the trappers' horses from falling into the hole and injuring themselves. It was then the wisdom and experience of Ofer Tal, Mountain Man, in his decision making to ensure everyone was outfitted from head to toe and a full ration of supplies were purchased while there at Fort Manuel just in case Eustache's cache turned out to be ruined, more than bore fruit of the best kind...

After a week of sleeping outside and letting their new cabin air out from all of the smells of skunk spray after Eustace had surprised and pissed off the skunk, then gotten 'blasted', the trappers finally got to move into their still slightly smelly new home. It was just as Eustace had predicted back at Fort Manuel, the cabin was more than roomy enough for all seven of the men and all the rest of their gear. Then the work began in light of the rapidly oncoming fall beaver trapping season. Since Eustace and his kin had hardly lived long enough at their new cabin before all had been killed, there was still plenty of work to be done at the new homesite.

Right off the bat, Gabriel and Little Raven saw to it that two meat poles were constructed in the timber near the horse corral and their firepit. Then Ofer and Black Eagle built a set of smoking racks so they could smoke all of their traps and use the same to smoke their buffalo meat from the now numerous buffalo herds in the area in order to make jerky. At the same time, Joshua and Jerimiah saw to it that chairs and tables were constructed for indoor use during inclement weather. Additionally, they split a number of logs and made a latrine complete with bench seats behind the cabin not far from the gravesites. Then for five days, the small wooded area behind the cabin rang to the sounds of a single buck saw and several axes along with two teams of horses hauling down dry logs to be 'decked' and used as firewood during the winter months. Additionally, a number of those logs were bucked up into sitting 'rounds' and placed near the outdoor firepit for the trappers to use during good weather. Then a number of the logs hauled off the hillside were also cut into rounds, split into usable firewood and then stacked up near the front door opening of their cabin for easy access during winter weather. Lastly the firepit and spring by the side of the cabin were rocked in, so Dutch ovens could be more easily used in the firepit and the livestock would have easier access to water at the spring head during the winter weather as well.

Finally the men got to do some of the kind of work they dearly loved. Small herds of buffalo were located and sneaked up on, and six cow buffalo were soon dropped by the excellent-shooting trappers. Those animals were butchered out and the meat hauled back in panniers to the outdoor firepit. Then as Gabriel and Little Raven saw to it that a mess of the meat was spitted for the men's suppers, the rest was either hoisted up onto a meat pole to cool out for later consumption or cut into thin strips for the making of jerky. Then after supper, the thin strips of meat were placed on the smoking racks and low burning smoky fires started for the making of jerky. Following that, the men adjourned to their sitting logs and enjoyed several cups of rum and smoked their clay pipes stoked full of sweet tasting James River tobacco, which helped to keep the evening's hordes of mosquitoes at bay. Then while five of the men headed for their sleeping furs inside the cabin, the remaining two tended the smoking fires making sure they did not get too hot and over-cook the meat on the smoking racks. Six hours later the first two men watching the smoking fires were sent to bed and the next two trappers took over the jerky-making process, and that regimen continued until the jerky was hanging in tanned deerskin bags from pegs in the cabin several days later for use while out on the trail.

Come the last week in September following a long cold snap in the weather, Eustace and Ofer were sitting outside on their sitting logs by the firepit watching Gabriel and Little Raven work their magic in making the men a hearty breakfast of spitted buffalo meat, beans, Dutch oven biscuits, coffee and a rice dish full of raisins, brown sugar and cinnamon. The reason for such a celebratory breakfast was that the men had decided today would be their first day of fall beaver trapping season. A week prior, the entire group of heavily armed trappers had ridden along the Rosebud and marveled at the numbers and sizes of the beaver in the waters. It was as Eustace had previously advised, there would be beaver at every turn in the river and in every adjacent beaver pond and he was right.

Being that Eustace was a little 'down in his right hip', the group had decided he would remain horsed and sitting with Jerimiah and Black Eagle as protectors of the almost defenseless remaining four trappers running the trap line. Then once again, Gabriel and Little Raven would do the assisting and skinning of the men's catches and Ofer and Joshua would do all of the actual trap setting and tending. With those individual work assignments in mind, the now much-experienced trappers sallied forth from their encampment that first day of the fall beaver trapping season with Ofer and Eustace leading the way. They were followed by Gabriel and Little Raven leading their normal three packhorses carrying all of the anchor poles, traps, extra rifles and the like, trailed by Jerimiah, Black Eagle and Joshua protecting the rear of the caravan of trappers.

Riding to a location just below their camp where the men had previously selected a long string of beaver ponds dotted with conical beaver houses and 'stitched' in numerous places with the beaver's characteristic mud and stick dams to start the fall beaver trapping season, the men doing the trapping dismounted.

The plan for the day was to run a string of 40 beaver traps and after changing into their breechclouts and buckskin leggings, Ofer and Joshua set out searching for the freshest beaver slides and once located, began setting their traps. With Gabriel assisting in the carrying of the anchor poles and extra traps, the trap setting went along just 'slicker than cow slobbers' until a low whistle during late morning was heard coming from where Black Eagle was sitting on his horse near Jerimiah and Eustace watching over the trappers below.

Looking up from what they were doing Ofer and Joshua observed Black Eagle and Jerimiah standing up in their stirrups and pointing towards the east. Looking over a series of rolling sagebrush and grass-covered hills to the east, Ofer and Joshua observed a lone Indian sitting on his horse on a distant ridge top watching the men running their trap line. Then the Indian was there one moment and gone the next once he realized he had been discovered... Once again, Black Eagle's 'lynx-eyes' had paid off, as Bear Trap had once explained to Ofer about the greatness of an Indian's eyesight.

The three men serving as lookouts for the trappers running the trap line below them watched the suspect ridgeline for the rest of that morning and never again saw that Indian or any others watching them. But now forewarned that they had been spotted by an Indian, the men on guard duty remained extremely vigilant watching over the trappers, as did Little Raven and Gabriel who were next to the packhorse carrying all the extra rifles. However, around noontime, all 40 of their traps had been set and like in past instances, the men headed for a patch of aspens along the Rosebud, dismounted once out of sight deep in the grove of trees and let their horses feed. Then as the men relaxed and chewed on some of their buffalo jerky, they visited over how pleased they were over the great amount of beaver sign they had seen during the morning's trap setting activities.

After about an hour of lounging around in the aspen grove hidden from sight and letting their horses graze nearby, the men once again mounted their horses and headed back along their newest previously set trap line. Right off the bat the men discovered a good omen. Floating in their last set trap of the day was a Made Beaver weighing about 90 pounds! Seeing that, Ofer said with a big grin on his face, "Gabriel, save that horse of a beaver and a couple more big ones that we find in our traps this day as we work our ways back to our cabin. We can have them spitted and roasted tonight as a celebration of our first day's bounty while trapping on the Rosebud for the good luck that will bring us." Then for the next two hours, the men removed another 20 beaver from their previously set traps! Now fully loaded with beaver carcasses, pelts and two panniers full of freshly cut willow limbs for hooping the day's pelts, the men turned for home, the lone Indian seen earlier was not seen again and now was mostly forgotten...

That evening while Gabriel and Little Raven prepared the men's supper of 'spitted' beaver, Dutch oven biscuits, beans and coffee, the rest of the men spent their time in the cabin under beeswax candles and light from their fireplace defatting and hooping their 21 freshly caught beaver pelts. By the time they had finished those chores, Gabriel's familiar ringing voice announcing that supper was almost ready rang out. With that, the beaver 'hoopers' made their way to their spring box, washed up with soap and water to get the beaver grease and smell off their hands, then ambled their ways over to the outdoor firepit for what was smelling like a great supper to come. However as they did, every man carried their rifles casually in their arms and at least one pistol in their sashes... This they did because they were now in the land of the fierce Northern Cheyenne who were an unknown entity to the newly arrived trappers.

For the next few weeks of the fall beaver trapping season, the men trapped the Rosebud hard and were duly rewarded with huge numbers of almost all Made Beavers being caught in their traps. Then with his gimpy hip not seeming to bother him anymore, even with the onset of the cooler weather, Eustace's 'not being able to get involved with the beaver trapping' impatience got the best of him. That evening during supper, Eustace advised everyone that on the morrow, he would relieve Joshua of his cold beaver trapping duties and would join Ofer as one of the two men doing all of the trapping. There were grins all around over hearing those words of Eustace's hip recovery, especially from Joshua who was nursing a set of the sniffles and did not really favor wading around in the damn cold and getting colder by the day, beaver trapping waters.

The next day right at daylight as the men sat around the outdoor cooking fire waiting for their breakfast to be ready, they noticed that in addition to the colder beaver trapping waters they now faced, an ominous dark and low hanging set of storm clouds was moving in from the northwest. Quickly finishing their breakfast, the seven men mounted up their previously saddled horses and leading their usual three packhorses, exited their homesite and headed for where they had left off on the Rosebud trapping the previous day. Once on-site, Ofer and Eustace changed into their trapping gear and off they went with Joshua acting as their close at hand assistant. It did not take long for Joshua, Little Raven and Gabriel to realize that Eustace, even as old as he was, was an outstanding trapper! Cold water and onsetting colder winds from the oncoming storm did not seem to deter or dampen the old man's spirits as he sped along, expertly setting trap after trap. Even Ofer had to pause in his trap setting routine in order to watch and learn from Eustace's trap setting techniques. It wasn't long before the two trap setting experts had every trap set in new locations, had mounted up and retreated to a dense stand of aspens in order to get out of the now very cold winds blowing down from the northwest.

Letting their horses 'put on the feed bag', the men rested in the deep duff of fallen aspen leaves, ate some jerky and happily discussed their morning's activities. Then feeling some rains spitting down from the heavens, the men hurriedly remounted, headed for their previously set trap line and began checking their traps as they worked their ways back to their cabin and a chance to warm up. As expected, a number of their traps already contained the highly territorial beaver, who smelling the strange castoreum smells associated with each trap's lure stick, chose to investigate who else might be in their territory. When they did, they were trapped, drowned and then hung there in the trap waiting for the successful trap setter to remove them so they could be pelted out and added to the horde of beaver pelts previously trapped and now being stored in bundles in the trappers' cabin.

Walking out into the deeper water of a beaver pond to remove a dead beaver hanging in his previously set trap, Eustace removed the dead beaver from the trap and it being a very large in size animal weighing about 70 pounds, turned and yelled at Ofer so he would look at the magnificent specimen. When he did and as he turned, Eustace promptly stepped into a deep unseen muskrat hole! "OOOWWIE!" yelled Eustace, as he immediately fell into the deeper water and dropped his dead beaver in the process as he grabbed an injured knee on his bad hip side! Immediately upon hearing Eustace screaming out in pain, Joshua dropped the dead beaver he was bringing back to Gabriel to skin, turned and just in time saw Eustace's head disappear into the deeper water! Sprinting over to where he had last seen Eustace disappear under water, Joshua plunged into the cold waters and rapidly walked out into the waist-deep water to where he could see in the deeper water where the old trapper was struggling underwater with his leg trapped in the deep muskrat hole!

Finally arriving where he could see Eustace struggling under water, Joshua reached down, grabbed him by his long hair and started pulling him upward out from the water. When he did, he discovered that Eustace was hung up in the deep muskrat hole and had to be pulled with great force in order to get the old man's head above the water! When he pulled, Eustace let out another scream of pain! Finally grabbing the old trapper and holding him up and out from the water so he could breathe, Eustace let out a loud "OOOOPH", as he sucked in some life-giving fresh air! Then Joshua dragged him to shore and sat him down on the beaver pond's bank so he could get his wind and come down emotionally from stepping into the muskrat hole and twisting a knee badly. It was then that Joshua and an arriving Ofer, Gabriel and Little Raven saw the old trapper's left leg was twisted in a funny-looking way...

"Goddamn, Boys, I really did it now. When I stepped into that damn ole muskrat hole, I really twisted my leg and hip badly. I now hurt so badly that I can hardly move that damned ole leg. Help me up, Boys, so I can see if there is any way that I can stand," said Eustace through gritted teeth evidencing his great pain. However, when he was helped to his feet, the pain was so intense that Eustace screamed out in agony and collapsed straight away! However when he did, he hit the ground in such a manner that his disjointed knee luckily popped right back into place. Moments later when he came back around after passing out in pain, Eustace found that he could now carefully stand on his bad leg and with a bad hobble and an assist from Joshua, he could get to his horse. And then with an assist from Ofer and Joshua, Eustace was able to mount his horse and sit in the saddle without too much pain, providing the horse did not jiggle his bad leg too much. With that issue somewhat under control, Joshua changed into his trapping clothes and finished out Eustace's portion of running the trap line checking for and retrieving any trapped beaver.

After their trap line had been checked for any more dead beaver of which they found 23 hanging in the traps, the men after the beaver had been skinned turned to a nearby grove of willows. There all the men except Eustace cut more willow limbs so they would have enough hooping materials for the beaver just trapped. Then they headed for their cabin as small snowflakes began silently falling. Once back at their cabin, Little Raven and Gabriel helped Eustace from his horse and assisted the old trapper inside the cabin so he could dry out and warm up. There he was seated by their fireplace, given a cup of rum and as he sat there nursing the drink and his sore knee, Gabriel started a roaring fire in the fireplace. That he did so the old man could dry out and get some heat on the damaged area of his leg and hip as well.

Then the rest of the trappers scurried around the campsite bringing in more wood for their fireplace, released all of their hobbled horses so they could feed and water, cut out a chunk of buffalo from a quarter hanging on their meat pole for their supper and then scurried back inside the cabin as the snow began falling around them in a serious manner. Once all the men were inside, they changed out of their wet clothing into something dryer and warmer and began defatting and hooping all of their fresh pelts, while Gabriel and Little Raven brought forth a hot supper and coffee for the men from their fireplace. Then not forgetting his hurting friend and fellow trapper, Gabriel poured him a fresh cup of rum to help him with the pain and discomfort he was still feeling in his damaged leg and now sore once again, hip.

The next morning when Ofer stepped out from the cabin, he was 'greeted' with a fresh six inches of snow on the ground and a day with not a cloud in the sky. However, the air temperature was a cold 20 degrees and a cold wind was blowing out from the northwest. Taking that as an omen of more bad weather on its way, Ofer helped the rest of the men in saddling their riding horses and filling the panniers with the needed gear on their packhorses. In so doing, Ofer had decided today after they had pulled any trapped beaver from their traps, they would also pull their traps to preclude them from being frozen into the mud and possibly lost with the oncoming of the deeper part of winter. Additionally, today they were going to leave Eustace home so he could continue to nurse his bum leg and help it heal more quickly by him resting and keeping his weight off the damaged limb. At first Eustace did a lot of grumbling about being left behind but soon a very sore knee 'advised' he best listen to Ofer and his suggestion over staying home and nursing his knee. A cup of rum helped with that decision.

As the trappers now reduced to six in number exited the campsite to check and then pull their traps, they waved 'Good-bye' to Eustace, who was standing by the cabin door using his rifle as a crutch in order to take the weight off his bad leg. However, as they left, Ofer began feeling those same old nagging feelings of warning from within. But right off the bat, one pack-horse went on one side of a tree and the other one trailing close from behind went on the opposite of the tree and a horse wreck and 'rodeo' occurred! Finally getting the 'knot-headed' horses under control after they had 'amped' up thinking 'a tree was going to eat them', the trappers continued on their way. Within the hour, Ofer and Joshua were tending their traps and pulling the near frozen dead beaver from them and pulling their traps as well. It was then that Ofer had pushed his nagging thoughts to the back of his mind over their great trapping successes, icy cold waters hitting the areas of his crotch causing him to 'suck wind' and struggling through the deeper than normal mud in one beaver pond. Since they were now far south of their cabin, they did not stop to rest but just kept going so they could finish as soon as they could and get the hell back into some warmer clothing. Then opportunity reared its head and soon they had a cow buffalo down and were butchering out the same. Following those welcome endeavors, it was over to a nearby patch of willows where they harvested a pannier full of green willow limbs in order to be able to hoop out their recent and last catch of beaver during the fall beaver trapping season. Once the willow limbs had been harvested, the trappers headed for the warmth of their cabin since the sun was now in the process of setting behind the ridgeline. And once the sun had set, riding a horse during the winter was nothing more than a rather cold and not a delightful experience…

******

"Blue-Eyed-Antelope" of the Rosebud Band of Northern Cheyenne, smiled over the fact that the trappers he had observed months earlier were camped right where he suspected, by the spring near the low ridge that was always home to a covey of greater sage grouse. Riding into the suspect area, he observed the trappers' cabin with a corral full of unattended horses. Upon seeing that, he turned in his saddle facing his three friends, "Black Wolf", "Big Buffalo" and "Afraid-Of-His-Horse", and waved them forward towards the horse corral. Riding line abreast up to the corral knowing the trappers were afield running their trap line, the Indians stopped and happily looked over their valuable find. In the corral were 12 buckskin horses and six other horses. And just as Blue-Eyed-Antelope had suspected, the trappers were out running their trap line and without them being around, the horses were easy prey. Smiling, the four Indians dismounted and began removing the sets of bridles arrayed over a corral post, unlocked the gate and began bridling all of the horses so they could be led off and eventually taken back to the Indians' encampment. As they did, Big Buffalo advised that they needed to hurry so they would be out of reach once the trappers returned later in the day to avoid any kind of meaningful pursuit looking for those who had stolen their valuable horses.

Then with all of the horses rounded up, bridled, tied to lead ropes and then tied off on the corral, the four Indians headed for the cabin to see what else they could find of value that they could use and take, such as any left-behind firearms, whiskey, gunpowder, knives, axes and the like. Opening up the cabin's door, the four Indians happily streamed into the darkened interior only to be met with a bright flash and a loud **BOOM!** from that of a pistol being fired from close range! Not suspecting anyone would be there, Blue-Eyed-Antelope died from a head shot from a very surprised man just awakened, who had been lying in his sleeping furs at the end of the cabin nursing a very sore leg and hip. Freezing for a moment over the unanticipated occupant in the trappers' cabin, Big Buffalo quickly recovered, turned, grabbed his tomahawk and stepped over to the dark moving form of a trapper initially discovered sleeping and now trying to rise awkwardly from his sleeping furs. Grabbing the trapper by his long hair and jerking him to his feet, Big Buffalo reared back his arm holding the tomahawk to strike a killing blow, only to feel the blast of fire and the crushing impact from a pistol ball in his face from a second fired pistol from just one foot away! Understandably, Big Buffalo never heard the following **BOOM!** since the lead ball had already killed him! But that was where the surprised bed-ridden trapper died when Black Wolf and Afraid-Of-His-Horse, recovering from their surprise at finding a trapper in the cabin, ran over and chopped the trapper to death with their tomahawks! Then forgetting why they were there in the cabin in the first place, the remaining two Indians realizing their two friends were already dead, bolted from the cabin and ran for their horses. There they hurriedly gathered up the roped-together horses and led them out from the trappers' encampment. That they did moving as fast as they could, even though they were trailing 18 rather unwieldy horses on long lead lines, as they headed for their distant encampment some two days distant. In the meantime, Eustace, Blue-Eyed-Antelope and Big Buffalo quietly bled out their bodily essence onto the floor of the trappers' cabin as their bodies quivered their last...

******

With panniers full of trapping equipment, fresh buffalo meat and willow limbs, Ofer happily headed his fellow trappers for home now that the sun had set and they were riding in the cold winter twilight. About an hour later, the six trappers now riding in darkness rode into their encampment only to surprisingly find the gate to their corral open and every animal normally contained therein, missing! Then a cold-blooded shout from Gabriel, who had dismounted and hurriedly walked over to their cabin wondering why Eustace did not have a candle burning for them and a fire going in the fireplace, made the rest of the surprised trappers dismount and run to their cabin in alarm! Bursting through the open doorway just in time to see Gabriel light several candles as Ofer took a quick look around, then froze in mid-stride and heartbeat!

"Eustace," yelled Ofer, as he stumbled over to the old trapper lying on the floor of the cabin with his head split wide open! Then just standing there by two freshly obviously head shot Indians, Ofer just shook his head. *Here Eustace had lived a very hard life and teaming up with his brothers and cousin, had left for the wilderness in order to make their fortunes. In turn, Eustace's four brothers and cousin had all died dramatic deaths and now so had he,* thought Ofer sadly, as the emotion of the moment welled up in his body shaking it uncontrollably. It was then that Ofer remembered the earlier feelings of dread and uneasiness that had struck him just as the two packhorses had tangled with a tree and started a 'rodeo'. A feeling of unease that had left him shortly thereafter over the hard work of the day and more than likely after the deed had been done, leaving his dear friend dead on their cabin floor...

Later that evening, the two dead Indians that Eustace had killed in defense of his life were dragged outside and left for the time being. Then with the rest of their stock placed into the now empty corral, the men sadly headed for their cabin. There Ofer saw to it that their rum was opened and every trapper was soon nursing a cup of the fiery liquid. However, there was still work to do and after wrapping Eustace back into his sleeping furs, the beaver pelts were quietly dragged out, defatted and hooped for drying. Then without any supper since everyone was no longer hungry, the men adjourned to their own sleeping furs and slept a rather restless night. Slept restlessly, now fully realizing, because of the closeness of the deadly event in their cabin, in their simple innocence for the first real time that the wilderness in all its beauty could be a 'savage mother'. Especially if tomorrow's 'hunt' was successfully carried out and the killing horse thieves and "Sons of the Prairies" were run to ground…!

Rising before dawn, Ofer and company by the dancing light of a fire, dug a grave for Eustace right alongside those mounds representing the frontier lives cut short of his much-loved brothers and cousin. Then lowering Eustace into the dark and cold ground wrapped up in his bloody sleeping furs so the last moment's agony could not be seen in the remains of his head, the dirt was shoveled back into the hole. By then it was getting light as the men quietly but with cold determination, saddled their riding horses, loaded their saddlebags full of jerky and with Black Eagle and Little Raven in the lead doing the tracking, the trappers began the very deadly business of cold tracking their horse thieves and the ones who had savagely killed their friend.

Being that it was now light enough for tracking in the six inches of freshly fallen snows, the trappers determinedly hustled their horses right along as 'hunters of men' on a mission were wont to do. In so doing, they could now tell from the spacing of the 'escaping' horses' hooves that the Indians leading the horses were having difficulty in making good their hurried escape. Being that the horses were loosely tied together with a long rope, there were numerous times the trailing trappers saw where one portion of the horse string would go alongside one tree and the rest of the string the other side! Then from all of the tracks in the snow, the trappers could tell the Indians were having trouble untangling the two sets of horses on one lead rope with horses on both sides of a particular tree. That became even more evident when the Indians trying to make pursuing them difficult went through patches of dense horse rope-tangling timber.

Because of those struggles with strange animals and the Indians' reluctance to let any of their valuable horses go, the trappers made good time in their cold tracking efforts, closing in on their horse thieves and killers. However, the Indians had a good lead and because of that, that found the trappers camping out alone under a number of fir trees come nightfall that first evening. Jerky made due for supper that evening and with that, the trappers huddled together for the body warmth each man supplied to keep from freezing. Daylight the following morning found the half-frozen trappers already in their saddles and once again, even more determined in cold tracking their horse thieves and killers of their friend Eustace. Long about noontime that second day, the men following Black Eagle drew up when he signaled all should stop. Then riding back to the rest of the trappers while Little Raven continued watching what Black Eagle had spotted, the men conferred.

"Four Scalps, at the foot of that long ridgeline in the timber, I saw a wisp of smoke coming up through the treetops from what had to be a small campfire. I believe it is from those who stole our horses and killed Eustace. I say that because all of those horse tracks we have been following lead across that ridgeline and down into that stand of timber. There they disappeared into the timber and it is there that Little Raven and I spotted that small wisp of smoke coming from a small campfire like that an Indian and not a white man would make," said Black Eagle, whose flashing and cold-looking dark eyes said it all for what was coming...

"Did you see any way possible where we can sneak up on that campfire without being seen coming across all of this open country?" asked Ofer, whose tone and tenor of voice clearly spelled out into the cold winter air the essence of violence as he saw it that was also soon to come...

"Yes, Four Scalps. We can drop behind the back side of this ridgeline we now are on and ride right up to the very edge of that timber from where that smoke is now coming. Then we would have to dismount to avoid being heard coming through the trees and then sneak through that timber on foot. The fresh snow should cover any sounds we would be making as men on foot when sneaking that last distance to our suspects' camp," said Black Eagle with a stark, killing coldness in the tone of his voice.

"Good, now let's get going because we are burning daylight and I don't know how much further it will be before those thieves and killers make it to where they are going and the safety of their band of Indians. If they do make it home, then we are out of luck because we would be badly outnumbered and would have to turn around and go back without our horses or the revenge we are seeking for what they did to Eustace. And to be quite frank, I do not intend to let those bastards get away, especially after they killed a crippled old man," said Ofer quietly, and in such a tone of voice that once again spoke to a reckoning soon to come if he had his 'druthers' for the Indians they had been cold tracking...

About an hour later found the trappers slowly moving through the heavy timber in the direction from whence had come the earlier wisp of campfire smoke. Additionally, the men could now not only smell wood burning they were so close, but could even hear the agitated shuffling of the horses who had not been fed or watered for two days. Led by Ofer and followed closely by Black Eagle, the trappers quietly moved through the last few feet of covering timber towards what they suspected was the pursued Indians' campsite. Finally quietly emerging out from the dense stand of timber into a small clearing, the trappers became keenly aware that the horses had stopped their hungry stomping around where they were tied up along a picket line and just silently and curiously watched the oncoming trappers. A line of oncoming trappers slowly and quietly advancing towards two blanket-covered mounds of exhausted Indians, obviously sleeping alongside their small fire impervious to the danger near at hand... That was, providing the changing behavior of the nearby horses and the noises they were making did not alert the sleeping horse thieves.

Then one of the blanket-covered mounds, upon hearing the changes in sounds of the horses' 'hoof-shuffling' behavior, rolled over and looked up at the now quietly standing there horses and then looked over and saw the line of trappers standing there watching the two earlier sleeping figures from just 20 feet away with his now wildly opened eyes! At first Black Wolf could hardly believe what he was seeing! Then springing to his feet with his rifle in hand in one fluid motion and shouting out a warning of the impending danger to his friend, he died when Gabriel shot him squarely between the eyes as a 'reward' for killing his dear friend Eustace! Afraid-Of-His-Horse, upon hearing his friend's verbal warning and coming out from a much-welcomed deep sleep, sprung groggily upward from his blankets! Then swinging his rifle upwards to defend himself at what he now saw in the way of danger, had his face splattered thickly with blood and gray matter the very instant Gabriel shot his friend Black Wolf between his eyes! When that happened, Afraid-Of-His-Horse was partially blinded with his friend's flying essence. Quickly wiping his eyes clear so he could see to defend himself, he once again went to aim his rifle, just in time to see a metallic glint flying through the air of Black Eagle's quickly thrown tomahawk. In that next instant in time, Afraid-Of-His-Horse died in the same manner and with the same kind of instrument he had used when he had killed Eustace... Leaving the dead where they fell for the critters of the forest to enjoy after Ofer had scalped the two Indians, the men gathered up their horses and those from the Indians and walked them back to where they had left their riding stock. Mounting up and with each man trailing a short string of horses, the trappers arrived back at their campsite around midnight that same deadly day. As they herded their livestock into their corral and then headed for their cabin, the very hungry trappers noticed with satisfaction that a heavy snow was now falling. That was good because if anyone tried following them from the Indians' kill site, that would now be almost impossible because of those now newly falling snows. Especially when the trappers awoke to discover another foot of freshly fallen snow the following day...

Right after breakfast the next day, Ofer adjourned to the corral where he retrieved from his saddlebag two frozen scalps from Afraid-Of-His-Horse and Black Wolf. Without a word, he retrieved a shovel from the side of the corral and walked over behind their cabin to where six similar burial mounds poked up through the snow. Shoveling the snow from the top of the freshest mound covering his friend Eustace's gravesite, Ofer carefully laid the two fresh but frozen scalps on top of Eustace's burial mound saying, "There you go, Old Timer. The same two bastards' scalps who took a tomahawk to you when you could hardly walk are now lying atop your grave. They didn't get far, Eustace, and now you have the proof of their bloody demise. Now you can rest more easily, My Friend. Thank You for being my friend. I only wish I had been there for you in your moment of eternity. But at least today I am at least in thought and deed by your side wherever you may be." Standing there for a few more moments by the old trapper's grave lost in his personal emotions over the loss of his friend, Ofer finally turned away from the gravesite and was surprised over what he saw! There standing quietly by the side of their cabin stood the rest of his group of trappers looking on at Ofer's ritual of saying 'Good-bye'. They too keenly felt the absence of their friend Eustace and the frustration of not being there for him in his time of need. They all knew that life made no promises, especially when living out on the frontier and that in the end there were no words, just peace... But in those moments of peace, a transformation of sorts was manifesting itself in the emotions and spirits of Gabriel, Joshua and Jerimiah that would have far-lasting effects regarding their lives and living out on the frontier as Free Trappers and Mountain Men!

With that fleeting moment in time now part of the ages, the trappers let their hungry horses out from the corral so they could paw down through the newly fallen snows to the rich grasses lying beneath and fill their empty stomachs. More wood was cut for the fireplace, as Gabriel and Little Raven set about making preparations for their evening meal of beans, buffalo steak, biscuits and their 'trapper's brew' known to one and all as coffee. Then Jerimiah and Joshua bundled up in their heavy winter clothing, grabbed up their rifles and spent the rest of the day watching over their feeding horse herd in case other Indians had a hunger for the trappers' horseflesh. Collaterally, Ofer and Black Eagle bundled up a number of their beaver furs for summer transport to Fort Manuel back at the cabin. After all, life out on the frontier was harsh and dangerous, but one had to go on if one wanted to survive in order to enjoy the next sunrise...

That winter up on the Rosebud proved to be a harsh, long and very cold one. Snows fell almost weekly and the daily temperature hardly rose above the freezing mark! However, the trapping of wolves became easier as the very hungry wolves fell in high numbers to the men's traps. And because of the freezing temperatures and deep snows, the men had to take their horses out daily to the numerous windswept prairie ridges so they could feed alongside the hungry buffalo trying to get enough to eat. But the trappers had come well-prepared with a more than sufficient woodpile gathered next to their cabin, a well-developed spring box fed by a warm water spring that never froze when it came to supplying their needs for water as well as for their horses, and plenty of buffalo near at hand that more than kept their meat poles loaded. Then while some of the men dressed their more than 50 trapped wolf skins, others cast bullets for their rifles and pistols, disassembled their firearms, cleaned them of their black powder and lead fouling and then reassembled them for the safety such procedures guaranteed. Then during more heavy snow days, the men busied themselves in their cabin making new moccasins, repairing ripped or torn clothing and conducting the required inspections and associated leather repair work on the packsaddles and riding saddles. Lastly on the worst of the winter days when temperatures plunged many degrees below zero and blizzards raged outside, the men slept, ate and carved figurines of animals from wood, bone and antler to be used in trade with the Indians come summertime back at Fort Manuel. However, during those quiet kind of days, Ofer, Black Eagle and Little Raven observed that Gabriel, Joshua and Jerimiah many times were lost in numerous quiet conversations among themselves. Especially in those days after they had lost Eustace and Ofer had ritually placed the scalps of the two Indians who had killed their friend upon his grave's burial mound... During those many quiet moments when Gabriel, Jerimiah and Joshua were in what appeared to be serious conversations among themselves, Ofer could see a change occurring in his younger brothers. A change that he could not put his finger on, but a serious change nonetheless.

After a very harsh and cold winter, spring came earlier than normal that year as did 'ice-out'. Emerging from their cabin one morning, Ofer with cradled rifle in his right arm surveyed the campsite as he always did having been taught to do so by his now deceased friend and mentor, Jan "Bear Trap" Driessen. To his front Little Raven and Gabriel were hard at work making breakfast, all of their horses had been rounded up from their all night feeding binge and were now back into the corral, Jerimiah was over at the spring box shaving and washing up and Joshua was back at the latrine 'seeing a man about a horse'...

"Boys, best double up on the biscuits and spitted buffalo this morning. I have a feeling that today our spring beaver trapping afield may make for a long day," said Ofer with a lightness in his command. Gabriel gave a wave of his arm in recognition as to what his older brother had commanded and Little Raven, in true non-committal Indian style, said nothing. He just headed for the meat pole with a long-bladed knife in hand, where swinging high in the air away from land predators swung half of a buffalo. Soon he had butchered out about a ten-pound chunk of back-strap and was now heading back towards his cooking fire with the meat in hand. Soon the smell of spitted buffalo meat swept around the cook site and in so doing, began drawing the men to the firepit like 'moths to the flame' realizing what was coming next and medium rare as they all liked it cooked.

Later when breakfast had been served, the sounds around the outside firepit were none other than those made by hungry men doing what they loved with a large piece of medium rare buffalo meat between their teeth and gums. After breakfast while Gabriel and Little Raven prepared several pots of rice and beans for soaking to be later cooked for supper, the rest of the men saddled up their riding horses and packhorses for the first day of spring beaver trapping.

Heading out from their campsite led by Ofer and Black Eagle, the men headed for that portion of the Rosebud they had yet to trap within easy riding distance from camp. However as they silently rode along the Rosebud looking over its many adjacent waterways that normally held all kinds of beaver, they observed something that did not look right. Many beaver houses they rode by appeared to be abandoned or in disrepair, a number of the mud and stick dams appeared to be neglected and not a single beaver swimming in the waters was observed, as the men rode along the many waterways en route to where they wanted to begin their spring trapping!

Finally arriving where they wanted to begin trapping, the

men stopped and just sat there on their horses in silence looking over at Ofer. As they did, Ofer himself kept critically looking over the beaver waters to be trapped in their spring beaver trapping endeavors. Finally Ofer said, "Boys, we may have a hard go this spring when it comes to trapping beaver. I would say the winter was as hard on the beaver as it was on us. I don't see any remaining beaver food cache sites, what few beaver we have seen swimming appear to be in an almost starved state and from the looks of the structures associated with a healthy beaver population, they all appear to be run down, neglected and in a state of disrepair. If I had to guess, I would say the hard winter has killed many of the beaver we planned on catching this spring! And the beaver I have seen all looked like they were half-starved and of poor quality furs when it came to their appearance. We may be glad we have over 600 beaver 'Plus' already bundled up for sale at Fort Manuel come this summer that we took during the excellent fall trapping season. But who knows, Mother Nature may prove me wrong and the only way we will be able to tell is to get looking some more and maybe then some trapping."

With that and a little more looking along the beaver waters, the men aside from Black Eagle and Jerimiah dismounted and began making preparations to start running their spring beaver trapping line. Around noon, the men had set out their 40 traps and all of the men were more than discouraged. None of the men had seen a single swimming beaver and it was very difficult to locate very many beaver slides that looked like they were being utilized at all! Following their usual pattern of activity, after setting all of their traps, the men 'holed up' in an aspen grove where they were in the sunlight, let their horses 'put on the feed bag', ate some jerky and discussed what they had discouragingly observed during that morning. Bottom line was that none of them had ever seen such a dearth of fresh beaver sign in all of the years they had been trapping! In short, they had a disaster in the making when it came to being able to successfully trap any beaver!

However, after spending a few hours resting and visiting, the men remounted their horses and with renewed energy, hopefully set out to run their previously set trap line. They did so not expecting the surprise that was waiting for them at the end of the day! THEY HAD ONLY CAUGHT ONE BEAVER IN ALL OF THEIR 40 TRAPS AND IT APPEARED TO BE OF POOR QUALITY AND STARVING! It was then that Ofer realized the hard winter they had just experienced had just about wiped out all the beaver along that portion of the Rosebud! Running their trap line the following day was more of the same. As they quickly discovered, they had only caught two beaver for all of their efforts on that second day! With that, Ofer pulled all 40 of their traps and they moved their trap line even further down the Rosebud and were now many miles away from their campsite and old trapping grounds when they began trapping once again.

For the next week, the men trapped beaver waters even further from their campsite than they ever had, but everywhere they trapped all along the Rosebud, it was the same. There were very few beaver and those trapped were of poor fur quality and most showed evidence of being starved! It was then that Ofer and the men realized that the hard winter in their neck of the woods had pretty much wiped out the beaver populations because of the extra thick ice and the rodents' inability to get to their underwater food caches! Realizing the futility of spending any more of their time attempting to trap beaver in waterways that appeared to be destitute of any viable populations of beaver, Ofer finally came to the realization of what needed to be done. To his way of thinking, his group needed to pull up their stakes and head for Fort Manuel early and sell their over 600 furs they had trapped during their outstanding previous fall trapping season.

And as "Hell Would Have It", Gabriel, Jerimiah and Joshua

were now making noises and voicing their desires to return home. This they wanted to do in order to see their folks once again and see if by working on the horse ranch and farm, that is what they wanted to do instead of beaver trapping out on the frontier. They voiced those concerns because they indicated they were tired of having to always be looking over their shoulders at every turn in the trail... Ofer figured that with the death of Eustace and the spring's poor beaver trapping results, his brothers had lost their feelings, heart and longings for 'the lure of the west' in their souls. And with homesickness now setting in, were so discouraged that they needed a trip back to their home place in order to 'gather up what was in their souls' and look at the next episode in their lives...

Those concerns from the three brothers really came to a head one evening after supper when the men had gathered around their campfire with cups of rum in hand and the usual evening's noises had dwindled away into quiet nothingness other than the sounds of wood crackling in their outdoor firepit. Then Gabriel said, "Ofer, we three younger brothers would like to return home. Mother and father were old when we left and we three sense that we need to return and see if they need us back home to help with the ranch and farm. They had us late in life after they had conquered their portion of what was then the frontier and now we think since they are getting older, they could use our stout backs and strong hands back home once again."

Quietly sitting there after Gabriel had uttered those 'frontier world-changing words', Ofer let his inner senses wander over what had just been said. He had been the last of the brothers wanting to go west and see what the wilderness had to offer the young men over that of living on a farm years earlier. However, his younger brothers had finally convinced him what a great adventure it would be if as a family of brothers they were to go forth and explore the largely unexplored western frontier and get involved in that much talked about 'beaver trapping' thing.

Ofer found that he had finally relented after many family conversations among the brothers had occurred. And now, here they were on the frontier and had been for several years. And during those years, they had prospered if the Letters of Credit in his saddlebags said anything as to the successes the brothers had achieved during many trying and 'growing up' adventures to date.

Now as he saw it, their group of trappers was at a crossroads. If they left now, Ofer was in a quandary. He had fallen in love with the wilderness, its beauty, unexplored corners and yes, the numerous unseen dangers at many turns in the mostly untraveled trails... Yet, he was the oldest brother and responsible for the lives and well-being of his three younger brothers and that family 'draw' was very strong as well. That was when the main issue of life and ultimate responsibility dawned on Ofer loud and clearly. He was the oldest brother and clearly responsible for what happened to his remaining three younger brothers, as his Father, Yossef, had always taught him. That family responsibility of watching out for his brothers directed earlier by Yossef was now clearly fixed in his mind, even overriding his strong desire to remain in the wilderness for a few more years so he could enjoy its excitement, beauty and grace. That in mind, Ofer over his own feelings and strong love for that of the wilderness, made a family decision that saddened him on one hand and yet addressed his family responsibility on the other...

Then before Ofer could reply to Gabriel, an unseen and ultimately fatal decision was made for him... "Ofer, we want to leave now since the beaver trapping is no good! We have talked it over and would like to take our money waiting for us in our Letters of Credit, return home and see mother and father once again before they pass. And we want to do it in style. What say, since none of us have ever ridden on a keelboat, we get back to Fort Manuel and make arrangements with Lisa to pay our way back home by riding on one of his returning keelboats when they take all the furs and hides back to St. Louis? That way we won't have to work our ways back on land with all the hazards along the way. And when we do, we take Black Eagle and Little Raven with us because in all reality they are just like brothers to all of us, we are all they have, they have indicated numerous times that where we go they would like to go also, and we can share the rest of our lives with them back on the farm."

Looking over at Black Eagle and Little Raven, Ofer could see the smiles and looks of excitement on their faces over their thoughts of going to this magical place called 'St. Louis' with the rest of their 'family' and having a chance to see what the brothers thought so highly of. Pushing away his desire to remain in the wilderness for the foreseeable future and see even more of what it had to offer in the ways of adventures, Ofer finally relented, saying, "Alright, if that is what the five of you want to do, let me hear all of you say it."

The next few seconds, all Ofer heard were the cheers and excitement being expressed over the new adventure of being able to ride a keelboat home and returning to their family farm. As for Black Eagle and Little Raven, the huge smiles on their faces over the new coming adventure made it very plain as to their exact wishes as well...

"Alright, the decision has been made and we will make plans for our departure back to Fort Manuel and our trip home to St. Louis," said Ofer, as he once again pushed his desires and feelings to the back of his mind, and as he did he found that once again and all of a sudden, his sixth sense began stirring within... For the next few moments, Ofer mulled over in his mind what the sixth sense might mean. As he did, all he could think of was they were pulling up their stakes, returning to the safety of Fort Manuel, taking an easy ride downriver on a keelboat and then returning home. *What the hell could go wrong with that?* he asked himself.

CHAPTER 14 — THE ARIKARA AND GOING HOME

FOR THE NEXT WEEK, THE TRAPPERS MADE READY FOR WHAT they considered their last trip to Fort Manuel. The horses' shoes were checked to make sure they could make the long trip without losing one while traveling back to Fort Manuel. More bullets were cast in case they ran into Indian trouble along the way and the last of all of their furs were bundled up, bound with tanned deerskins and made ready for transport on the pack-horses. Then one afternoon the men went forth, shot a cow buffalo and butchered out the same. Upon their return to their camp, the buffalo meat was immediately cut into thin strips suitable for making jerky and hung on the meat smoking racks. Then the smoking fires were started as the men began the jerky making process so they would have 'standby' food along the trail in case hunting successes were lean or hostile Indians were close at hand, limiting any kind of shooting to preclude discovery and the possibility of a fatal attack upon the trappers.

Two days later, the men and their heavily loaded packhorses streamed out from their encampment for the last time carrying everything they owned. Looking back at the excited looking faces of his brothers to finally be on their way home and those of Black Eagle and Little Raven, Ofer quietly said his 'Good-byes' to his two friends he was 'leaving behind in the frontier soil'. Leaving behind his friend and mentor, Jan "Bear Trap" Driessen, buried under a rock pile, and the quiet old trapper and man who had nothing in his life but hard luck and a violent ending, who just went by the name of "Eustace" and was buried under Mother Earth with two scalps laid across his dirt mound...

For the next four days, the men labored long and hard bringing such a heavily loaded pack string into Fort Manuel. But finally on the morning of the fifth day of travel, the log palisades of Fort Manuel hove into view much to the relief of the men. As they approached the front gate of the fort, the men noticed there at anchor in the river were two keelboats which had come upriver during the flood stage so they could navigate through the shallower portions of the Missouri and Yellowstone Rivers. Seeing those two keelboats lying at anchor visibly ignited even more excitement among Gabriel, Joshua and Jerimiah, realizing they were just one step closer to going home, as well as that of Black Eagle and Little Raven!

However, after meeting and conferring with Manuel Lisa, 'storm clouds quickly formed on the men's horizons'... In talking with Lisa, one of his keelboats had been ambushed and destroyed by the fierce Arikara Indians close by one of their villages while poling upriver on the Missouri! As such, all of that boat's supplies heading for Fort Manuel were lost, as were all of their boat crew except for one man! As it turned out, during the height of the battle and upon seeing his boat was doomed, that man had jumped overboard and swam to another keelboat still coming upriver. That keelboat upon hearing of the devastating and deadly attack wisely waited out of reach in the middle of the Missouri until the wee hours of the next morning when the Arikara were deeply asleep in their village. Then that boat's captain raised anchor and they quietly slipped by the sleeping

Indians in the Arikara village located alongside the river and escaped upriver to Fort Manuel.

Additionally, when Ofer inquired about the prices that year per pound of beaver fur, he got surprised! Beaver prices that year being offered by Lisa were only $2.50 per pound to offset his total loss of one of the three keelboats to the Arikara and one-third of his annual supplies! Therefore to offset his losses, instead of $6 per pound of beaver fur which would have been the going rate that year, Lisa was only offering $2.50! And he was still charging Mountain Prices for all of his supplies and goods being offered to all of the trappers at his fort!

Lastly, when asked about transport of the six trappers down the Yellowstone and Missouri back to St. Louis, Lisa advised that because he was short of space to carry all the pelts, hides and furs he had accrued for shipment to St. Louis that year and now only having two boats to take everything back instead of the usual three, deck space was extremely limited. Hence and only because Ofer and his crew were long-time and original travelers and trappers, he would allow three of them to ride back on his already overloaded keelboat and that was it!

With that problematic information coming from Lisa, Ofer halted his pack train from entering the fort, much to the surprise of everyone! Then while his horse herd grazed outside of the fort's protective walls, Ofer held a 'council of war' with the rest of his trappers! Once all of the men were gathered together, Ofer advised them as to what Lisa had said and offered. There was a fair amount of grumbling among the men, especially since they had been original members of Lisa's trappers to take the dangerous gamble, journey forth, help build his fort and then trap for him all the subsequent years. But the realization of what they were facing under the circumstances also slowly settled in among the men.

Ofer seeing the disappointment and frustration upon all of his men's faces, thought for a moment and then offered an option to the situation they found themselves now facing. "Hear me out on what we might be able to do," said Ofer quietly. Seeing he now had the men's attention, he continued saying, "Here is what I propose we do. Lisa would only offer deck space for three of us and that means whoever goes will be sleeping out on the open deck the whole way back to St. Louis come rain or shine. So I want all of you to think about that first of all. Secondly, I don't want to sell our hard-won furs for just $2.50 per pound. To me, offering just $2.50 per pound is nothing more than 'Frontier robbery'! With those two things in mind and knowing how badly you three brothers in particular would like to vacate the wilderness for something less dangerous, I say we draw straws and the three winners get to ride home on one of the keelboats. For those who draw the long straws, we take our pack string across the Yellowstone when the floodwaters go down and head down to St. Louis with our valuable horses, sell our furs there at the fur houses for much higher prices, and then the three of us meet the other three who sailed down on the keelboat back at the farm. What say the five of you to those suggestions?" asked Ofer, with a devious plan already forming in his mind on how to partially address the situation.

For the longest time there was lots of discussion among the three brothers with hardly a word being uttered by Black Eagle or Little Raven who just listened. As the three brothers 'cussed and discussed' among themselves the suggestion 'on the table', Ofer leaned over and picked three long straws and three short straws in case the brothers bought into his rather stark group-separating suggestion. Finally the brothers agreed to Ofer's suggestion as Black Eagle and Little Raven just gave a half-hearted nod in going along with the majority. Making a show of mixing up and arranging the straws in his hand because he was the oldest and that was his responsibility, Ofer made sure all the exposed ends were even and then before anyone could say or do anything, he drew the first straw. Upon seeing everyone's looks of surprise over what Ofer had just done, he advised since he was the oldest, he got to draw first. That he did making sure he drew one of the long straws that he had purposely placed on the end of the line of straws between his thumb and index finger...

"Damn," said Ofer, making it sound like he was surprised over drawing a long straw and disappointed, "I drew a long one so it looks like I get to take the horse herd to St. Louis. Who wants to draw next?" he quickly said, so no one would figure out what he had just done to 'rig the game of chance'...

For the longest time, there was much hesitation among the brothers, as Ofer watched closely as to what would be the actions of Black Eagle and Little Raven. And sure as he figured knowing how the two Crow men felt about him after he had rescued them from certain death at the hands of the Gros Ventre or at least a life of slavery among another tribe, Black Eagle after looking over at his 'brother' said, "We both go with you, Four Scalps! We three will take the horses and our bundles of beaver fur to this place you call St. Louis."

For the longest moment in time, Gabriel, Joshua and Jerimiah just looked over at Black Eagle, Little Raven and Ofer and then grabbing each other, they began dancing around in obvious delight at being the ones to be able to just ride down the two great rivers and enjoy not only themselves but the magnificent scenery along the way as well...

"Then it is decided. You three will take the boat and Black Eagle, Little Raven and I will take our valuable buckskin horses and ford our ways across the Yellowstone. That we will do when the spring runoff waters go down so we can safely cross the river and then travel down along the Missouri to St. Louis. Then as I said earlier, we will sell our furs for a better price, cash in our other Letters of Credit and then meet the three of you back on the farm. Then we six can decide what we want to do with the rest of our lives," said Ofer, making sure he sounded very happy with the outcome. That he did knowing full well the dangerous challenges lying ahead of the three men trailing a valuable horse herd for several thousand miles during a multi-month trip, all the while traveling through dangerous Indian country occupied by the hostile Arikara and Lakota tribes...

With those decisions 'made', Ofer approached Lisa and advised him that his whole clan would be leaving the frontier and going home to the St. Louis area. He further advised his three brothers would be the ones going downriver on the keelboats and that he, Black Eagle and Little Raven would be trailing their packhorses all the way down to St. Louis. Then after their arrival, they would sell their hard-won furs, cash in all of their Letters of Credit for the money owed them by the St. Louis Missouri Fur Company, and then return to their mother and father's farm, raise horses for sale and become gentlemen farmers.

Upon hearing those words, it was obvious Lisa was very disappointed in not being able to buy all of the Tals' furs at his self-imposed cheaper price but said he understood. Then he volunteered that if he had purchased all of their furs, he more than likely could not have sent them downriver that year anyway because he was one keelboat shy from the three he needed to transport all of the pelts, furs and hides he now possessed in his fort's warehouses. Much less purchasing and shipping any others from the expected arriving trappers later that summer... "However," continued Lisa, "Your brothers will be expected to help the other men if poling and pushing is required, especially if the keelboat runs aground on the Yellowstone or Missouri Rivers," he coyly added, "to help in paying for their costs in the food they will eat along the way." Ofer just grinned over hearing those words and nodded, remembering what his father had told him years earlier about Lisa being a very shrewd merchant and businessman...

That afternoon, the men headed their tired pack string over to their same old camping spot under the grove of cottonwood trees and set up their camp. But first their riding horses were unsaddled, hobbled and turned loose to graze along the nearby stream bank's tall grasses. Next came the unloading of all their pack string animals and placing their packs under the protective leaves of the cottonwoods in case they were subjected to a summer thunderstorm. Then those horses were all curried down, hobbled and turned loose among their other horses so they could graze and water as well. Since the remnants of their old firepit still existed, Gabriel and Little Raven set to cleaning up the area and carrying their ridding saddles over to the camp-fire location to act as 'chairs' when the men ate their suppers. Then as Ofer and Black Eagle arranged all of the men's sleeping furs under the shade of the grove of trees, Joshua and Jerimiah went about the area and brought back armloads of limbs and other larger chunks of wood for their campfire. As they went about their chores like a well-oiled machine, Ofer felt a lot of pride over what his group of men had developed into, as well as a pang of remorse over breaking up the industrious and depend-able men soon to come in the near future. He then also noticed as he stood there watching all of the men working, a slight twinge of his sixth sense kick in once again. A sixth sense that had started up its roiling around from within, once the decision had been made way back in camp the evening the men had decided on going home and leaving the dangers of the frontier behind. However, there was work to be done around camp and Ofer passed off his sixth sense warnings as maybe just hunger, since they had been eating so much jerky instead of fresh meat on their trip to Fort Manuel.

For the next three weeks, the trappers lounged around their campsite, gathered in more wood, cared for their horses, hunted for the much-needed camp meat and visited with the few other trappers straggling onto the camping grounds at Fort Manuel. Trappers who had also basically given up the spring beaver trap-ping on their trapping sites because the hard and long winter had wiped out their beaver trapping populations and prospects for the spring season on their trapping grounds as well.

Finally came the day when Lisa had unloaded his two keel-boats of all the fort's supplies and had reloaded those boats to the brim with all the buffalo and deer hides, wolf and bear pelts, and beaver and other soft furs he had purchased from the Indians and trappers in the area. That evening as the men supped on their usual hot coffee, Dutch oven biscuits and spitted elk meat, Lisa arrived as a visitor. After being welcomed and handed a cup of coffee, he advised the men that his two keel-boats would be leaving the very next day! He further advised that both boats were so heavily loaded with valuable hides, pelts and furs, that they needed to leave during the highest spring snowmelt runoff waters so they could make it all the way down the treacherous Yellowstone and Missouri Rivers without running aground. He further advised they would be leaving at first light so if his brothers still wanted to go, they had best be on board because the boat captains were not waiting for anyone who arrived late at the docks.

For the rest of that evening, there was a mad scramble by the three brothers riding down on the keelboats to get all they wanted to carry with them gathered up and ready to go. That included casting more bullets for their rifles and pistols, making sure all of their powder horns were filled with fresh powder, and making sure their 'possibles' bags were full of flints and greased wadding in case they were needed along the way since they would be passing through hostile Indian territories. Knives and tomahawks were then put to the whetstones for better edges and anything not really needed was distributed back to the three men who were staying behind while waiting for the Yellowstone's waters to recede. There they would wait for the Yellowstone's spring runoff to recede so the trappers' horse string could be safely forded across the river. Then they would start their long journey down along the Yellowstone and

Missouri Rivers and on to St. Louis, a trip requiring several months of dangerous travel. Then their last supplies of rum were broken out and everybody celebrated the coming day's events after supper. But that last frontier celebration did not really happily develop, as everyone began thinking about the dangers to be faced while floating down the river or traveling many months with a long and valuable pack string through Indian Territory. Soon the rum was finished and everyone adjourned to their sleeping furs because tomorrow's events would come early...

The next morning Gabriel and Little Raven finished their last breakfast-making together rather quietly, breakfast was served and then the men saddled up their riding horses and headed for the fort's boat dock. Upon their arrival those last minute preparations were being made and both boat captains hustled everyone aboard. In fact, the boarding came so fast the six men hardly had the time to say their 'Good-Byes' and then the three brothers were aboard, the boats were cast off and the boatmen began poling their ways out into the fast-flowing Yellowstone and soon they were gone... But not gone was Ofer's sixth sense still roiling around inside him as he quietly watched the two boats slowly disappear from view carrying his three brothers...

******

Standing on the stern of their keelboat heading down the Yellowstone towards where that river joined the mighty Missouri River further to the east, Gabriel, Joshua and Jerimiah watched Ofer, Black Eagle and Little Raven slowly disappear from view. Upon their final view of their brother and friends, Gabriel felt a slight twinge from what he considered his sixth sense. Then a command from the boatman manning the steering tiller for the brothers to move so he could better see and 'read' the river's waters ahead, that sixth sense was quickly forgotten in the excitement. Moving towards the bow of the keelboat as they had been commanded, the brothers moved forward and sat upon bundles of beaver furs and began watching the sights along the river as they slowly passed on by.

For the next six days, the three brothers had a grandstand seat atop the bundles of beaver furs, looking at the wonders of the frontier. They passed numerous herds of buffalo, some of which were swimming the river in huge brown 'carpets' numbering tens of thousands of animals. Animals that were more than likely swimming across the river to get to better grazing on the far side! Then there were the grand herds of bull elk with developing antlers, along with huge numbers of cows and calves herded up in just about every grassy meadow the keelboats serenely drifted by. Then more herds of buffalo were passed feeding along the rivers and grassy areas or rolling around in buffalo wallows to rid themselves of skin parasites and the perennial clouds of biting flies that routinely followed the herds. Dotted throughout roaming the riverbanks were feeding black and grizzly bears, many of which were shot at by some members of the boat crews just for the hell of it. Merganser and mallard ducks abounded along many of the quiet pools of the river or were seen feeding in the river's adjacent marshy areas in such numbers so as to become boring to watch. The areas along the river were alive with bald eagles and the noble osprey, many with occupied nests in tall dead trees along the waterways as well. Then there were the dark, ten-foot long sinister-looking shadows of white sturgeon passing alongside the quietly moving keelboat that drew amazed looks from everyone who had never before seen such thousand-pound riverine monsters! Then the brothers got to see all of what the keelboat men called 'the little people'. River otter, beaver, mink, muskrat and giant carp were observed rolling or swimming in the warmer and shallower waters and in marshes adjacent the river. It seemed that every day was something of a new adventure to the brothers and they were very happy they had chosen such a means of travel going back to their home in Missouri!

Then as the days passed and the boats slowly drifted or were poled along, more and more bunches of Indian hunting parties were seen moving along the river. And when the boats had to follow the river's channel which took it close to the shore and when Indians were seen in those circumstances, a shout would be given and the two swivel cannons mounted on top of the 65'-long keelboat's upper deckhouse would be manned and made ready to fire in the case of being attacked. Several times, the brothers had to scramble off their bundles of furs when hostile Indians would fire their arrows or rifles at the boats passing close by and then the swivel guns would be unlimbered and fired. Twice the brothers saw times when Indians firing upon the keelboats would be fired back upon with the swivel guns loaded with pounds of deadly flying lead balls! During both occasions when this occurred, they saw firsthand the effects of the cannons firing upon hostiles who did not truly understand the fury a single cannon shooting handfuls of killing lead balls could unleash on the uneducated. Upon hearing the cannons blasting forth, the brothers saw unhorsed Indians flying through the air, horses being splattered all to hell with broken limbs and intestines flying through the air, small trees in the background being splintered into bits and pieces, and always a horde of leaves being blown from their limbs and scattered down among the foolish Indian shooters as well!

Finally, it was onto the mighty Missouri after days on the smaller Yellowstone with the keelboats. And once again, hordes of buffalo could be seen throughout the countryside along the river and swimming therein to get to the far side for only they knew the reason why. Also, more and more Indians and their tipis or earthen lodges could be seen dotted along the river as the keelboats slowly passed by. However, now the brothers saw a different demeanor occurring among the boatmen. Especially when the river channel took the boats very close to the shore where hostile rifle fire and that of arrows could be deadly! Now they observed that the boats' cannons were manned every hour of the day until the boats were moored far out into the middle of the river away from the harm of the Indians come nightfall. And now the boatmen spoke in hushed terms about the Assiniboine, Lakota and Arikara Indians with a slight tone of fear in their voices. Additionally, the boat captains now stationed lookouts on the bows of their boats to be wary and alert for any signs of hostile Indians waiting to ambush the boats in hiding along the riverbanks as they drifted by.

Daylight one morning after a breakfast of beans and biscuits, the two keelboats moored out in the middle of the Missouri River lifted their anchors and with swivel guns manned and ready, began drifting down the river towards an Indian village located right along the river inhabited by the much dreaded Arikara! Now the boatmen each carried a pistol and had their rifles always near at hand as well. Sensing such a high degree of danger, the Tal Brothers made sure both of the pistols each man carried were ready in case trouble popped its head up and double-checked their rifles as well. Then sitting on their bundles of furs, the Tal Brothers closely watched the countryside slowly drifting by for the much talked about Arikara, just in case they tried ambushing the keelboats so they could steal their valuable furs and kill off the much-hated white men manning the oars or poles.

As they did, they found themselves that day the second boat in line slowly floating down the Missouri. By noon, the warm sun had made keeping awake problematic, especially sitting on the soft bundles of beaver furs, so that found the brothers drifting off as the boatmen slowly and quietly poled their ways downstream. About then was when sleep finally overcame the Tal Brothers, as they stretched out on their bundles of soft furs above the boat's deck. As they slept, the warm sun beat down upon the men, and the coolness found on the river, the quiet of drifting boats and soft breezes soon had the men snoring quietly as if not to disturb the serenity of the area as they slowly drifted downstream.

BOOM—BOOM—BOOM—BOOM—BOOM! went five quick shots from ambush by Indians hiding in the dense brush fields located along the river, as the first keelboat slid by the nearby riverbank in a channel close to the river's shoreline! In an instant a blizzard of arrows filled the air and accurately dropped upon the first keelboat with deadly and telling effect. Over half of the men guiding the boat down the narrow channel right next to the bank of the river were swept overboard, many with three or more arrows in their bodies! **BOOM—BOOM!** went both of that keelboat's swivel cannons into the still unseen Indians in the river's brush-lined banks, blowing great gaping holes in the brush and blasting and scattering a number of Indians out the back side of the brush field in bits and pieces! Then the first keelboat was free from the narrow channel alongside the Missouri River's bank and drifted out into the safety of the width of the river away from the deadly ambush site. However, the boat now drifted wildly around and around because it had lost so many men poling and controlling the boat that it was in danger of running aground onto the river's many sandbars! However, the man manning the keelboat's tiller finally managed to gain control and the boat was moored out into the center of the river out from harm's way along the riverbanks!

Then it was the second keelboat's turn floating close-in behind the first boat, now being dragged by the river's swift current into the narrow river channel near the site of the previous ambush! Not being able to break free of the current and find deeper water out further in the middle of the river away from the deadly ambush site, it too drifted into the dangerous channel's killing zone! As luck would have it, the swivel cannon man, in his nervous excitement, fired his gun too soon and in so doing, did little damage to the dense brush patch on the river-bank overlooking the narrow and close at hand channel and its ambushers hidden behind... And as the gods would have it, the second swivel cannon on the upper boathouse deck misfired! Realizing what had happened, hundreds of Arikara Indians now swarmed out from their covering brush field and loosed a blizzard of arrows into the keelboat, now located not 20 yards from the riverbank in the middle of the narrow channel! That was also followed with streams of white black powder smoke flowing from the riverbank by a line of armed and rifle-shooting Arikara, which covered the entire 65'-long keelboat in its acrid cloud! Then at least two dozen rifle-armed riverbank Indian shooters killed every man on that side of the boat and in addition, now dozens of fire arrows rained down upon the boat from just a few yards away! Realizing they had killed every man on their side of the boat, the Arikara raced along the riverbank in plain view shooting their rifles and hordes of arrows into anything that even resembled a boatman trying to defend their boat or pole their getaway out into the now widening river channel!

Gabriel, standing up from behind the deckhouse on the river side of the keelboat, shot and killed a particularly large Indian reloading his rifle and standing out in plain view. However, for his effort in defending his boat, Gabriel fell overboard after having been hit in the face, neck and chest by three different and deadly arrows! When he did, he disappeared under the boat never to be seen again... Joshua, seeing his brother dropped with three arrows overboard, out of hatred and frustration shot and killed one Indian standing out on the riverbank with his rifle, then jumping up onto the top of the wheelhouse roof in plain view, drew both of his pistols loaded with buck and ball and killed two Indians trying to leap aboard his boat! When he exposed himself, he also fell to a flurry of well-aimed arrows including two fire arrows! Mortally wounded with five arrows in his body, Joshua turned in terror and pain to his brother Jerimiah saying, "Jerimiah, help me!" Reaching for his brother's extended hand, Jerimiah took a fire arrow directly into his right eye socket and when hit, instinctively reached for the arrow only to have Joshua's body fall upon him from atop the higher wheel-house deck! When that occurred, the falling weight of Joshua's body landing upon Jerimiah drove the arrow even deeper into Jerimiah's brain case killing him instantly. With that impact of both bodies colliding into each other, the two men then fell overboard, never to be seen again! By then the boat was a mass of flame and in order not to get burned alive, the living men on the far side of the boat began jumping off and into the water trying to escape. There they were all killed as they floated in the water by the Indians on the close at hand riverbank shooting down upon them with their rifles and bows and arrows! The last thing observed by the first boat that had basically escaped the ambush being first in line, was the second keelboat running aground on a sandbar. Then hordes of Arikara Indians began swimming out to it and throwing the bundles of fur overboard to their compatriots. That they did until the fire got too hot and eventually to the horror of the first keelboat now anchored out in the middle of the Missouri River out of harm's way, that second boat furiously burned itself to its waterline without any survivors! All that eventually remained were the 12 bodies of arrow-riddled boatmen slowly drifting by on the Missouri River...

******

Quietly and sadly Ofer, Black Eagle and Little Raven rode back to their campsite that last morning leading the much-prized for their gentleness and spirit, riding horses belonging to Gabriel, Joshua and Jerimiah. There they were unsaddled, hobbled and turned loose so they could graze and now roam as packhorses with the rest of the herd. Nine days later one after-noon, Ofer was gathering wood for their campfire when all of a sudden he stood straight up as if shot out from a gun! He then realized his sixth sense was roiling around in his body so violently that it made him physically ill, so much so that he began violently vomiting! Black Eagle picking up limb wood nearby, upon seeing his dear friend Four Scalps vomiting, ran over to Ofer to see if he could help! Black Eagle could see nothing wrong with Ofer except that he was violently ill for no apparent reason! Finally dropping to his knees, Ofer kept vomiting until all he could do was dry heave. Finally, the physical feeling left Ofer's body like a gush of water being thrown from a pail and then he found himself standing up and trembling like an aspen leaf in a violent November winter wind...

Finally getting his breath back, Ofer stood there for a few more moments until the uncontrollable shaking had ceased. Ofer had never had such a feeling like that before, and then a calm feeling now overcame him that was not of his world... It was then that a realization came over him that a great loss in the family had just occurred and a light had just gone from his life! Then a clearness of vision came over him and he saw his four brothers together, including Daniel, laughing, having a good time and then turning and waving 'Good-bye' to him! Then that vision slowly faded into nothingness... Black Eagle held his breath as he saw his dear friend, mentor and father figure drift into the "Upper World" of the "Cloud People" in front of his very own eyes for a few moments and then slowly return! This he realized because of his 20,000 years of Native American heritage and being a 'Mystic Warrior of the Plains', that what had just occurred was centered in the 'other world's' mysteries of life. Sensing what had just happened in that mystic world, Black Eagle asked Ofer no questions as to what had just happened and Ofer offered no explanations...

For the next month, the three trappers quietly made do around their campsite as they waited for the Yellowstone River to rid itself of the high water caused by all the snowmelt from the surrounding distant mountains. Weekly, the three trappers would ride down to the Yellowstone and check out the water levels to see if they could cross the river and finally begin their long trip to St. Louis. And weekly, the high runoff continued until Ofer thought it would never end! Finally on one of their weekly trips to the riverside checking the water levels, Ofer finally decided the water was now low enough for safe fording. Somewhat later, they rode their horses over to a place on the river that was normally used by the trappers in the area in which to ford. Looking the ford over carefully one more time, Ofer cautioned Black Eagle and Little Raven to make sure their saddle cinches were tight and then he slipped his horse into the shallow waters of the ford and shortly thereafter, he was safely across! Riding back across the Yellowstone with gusto, Ofer rode out of the river and yelled, "Let's go, Boys! We need to head back to our camp and make ready for fording this damn river on the morrow and be on our way!"

The next morning way before daylight because Ofer could not sleep, he got Little Raven and Black Eagle up and as Little Raven made breakfast, Ofer and Black Eagle began putting all the beaver '*Plus*' bundles onto the packsaddles and packing all of their packhorses. After a breakfast of just Dutch oven biscuits and coffee because they had no more camp meat, all three men then finished loading the rest of the packhorses. By noontime and eager to be on their way, only jerky was had for lunch and then the men rode by the fort and bid Manuel 'Good-Day'. They then headed for the Yellowstone River and one of its shallow water fords amid Lisa's final pleading for them to sell their furs to him and remain one of his trappers. Those pleadings fell on deaf ears as Ofer now for some reason felt a strong and mysterious inner calling for him to come home...

Arriving somewhat later with their valuable pack string, Ofer and company safely crossed the Yellowstone and headed to the southeast knowing the mighty Missouri River lay in that direction and once along its banks, they would head southerly until they met the junction of the Missouri and the Mississippi Rivers.

From there it would be a few more days of travel to St. Louis and the end of their journey on the frontier as Mountain Men.

For the next two months the men traveled in a southeasterly direction until they came upon the Missouri. Then for the next month of careful travel, some of it at night to avoid obvious encampments of first the dreaded Arikara and then the mighty Lakota Nation of peoples, the men quietly continued on their journey. As they did, they were careful to keep any shooting of their firearms for camp meat to a minimum to avoid garnering attention from any nearby wandering bands of Indians. Additionally, their night camps were kept only in secluded river or creek bottoms or brushy draws to avoid attention, regardless of the associated dense clouds of mosquitoes. As for campfires, they were kept minimal as well to avoid anyone noticing a 'white man's size of fire' and associated smoke column and then coming to investigate. Being that there were only three of them pushing a very valuable herd of horses carrying bundles of furred riches, the men were now very much aware that making any mistakes of discovery more than likely would be their last because of being outnumbered by the attacking Indians. However, if an attack was to occur, the attackers would pay dearly because each man rode with a rifle across his lap, an extra rifle on his riding horse in a scabbard, two pistols in each man's sash and an extra rifle in a scabbard on the first packhorse in every man's trailing pack string!

One evening after experiencing a tremendous summer afternoon thunderstorm while out on the open prairie, Ofer and company managed to kill a cow buffalo near a brushy draw. Quickly dismounting and hoping their rifle's report would be 'read' by any nearby Indians as just more distant thunder, Black Eagle quickly stripped off the two backstraps from the cow and then remounting, the men rode about another mile to get away from the sound of their rifle shot and the carcass of a freshly killed buffalo, and then moved their pack strings deep into a creek bottom and set up their evening's camp. There they unpacked their mounts, hobbled them and let them forage within the creek's brushy bottom under the watchful eyes of Black Eagle. While the horses foraged, Ofer arranged all of their packs in a defensive circle under some trees for protection in the case of an attack. This he did while Little Raven spitted the buffalo's backstraps over a small 'Indian's type of fire' that he had built. Then as Ofer strung a long cotton rope in and among the creek bottom's trees, Black Eagle herded the horses back to their camp and after letting the horses have a long drink of water from a runoff stream, tied all of them onto the long picket line for the evening. Then after arranging their sleeping furs under several white ash trees, Ofer and Black Eagle headed for their most welcome campfire and the smell of spitted buffalo meat smelling up the creek bottom with roasting buffalo meat smells.

As they settled down next to the meat sizzling on the metal spits, Little Raven asked Ofer to watch the meat because he had to 'go see a man about a horse'... When he did, it was about then that Ofer's sixth sense began rattling around in his carcass. But having gone hungry for the entire day and in much anticipation of eating all the buffalo backstrap that evening for their supper that he could hold, he wrote off the sensation. He figured it was just 'his big guts trying to eat his little guts' and continued watching and smelling the spitted buffalo meat with much anticipation of what was soon to come...

As Little Raven disappeared off into the creek bottom's brush to take care of a call of nature, Ofer adjusted the metal skewers holding the chunks of buffalo meat so they would cook to just medium rare and then be removed for eating. Sitting back down on a saddle placed next to the fire used as a 'chair' and looking over at Black Eagle with a happy look on his face over how the cooking was progressing and how much of the delicious meat he was going to personally eat himself, Ofer's heart froze! Black Eagle had a look on his face that read plainly and simply, "Danger!" Realizing he was looking past Ofer, Ofer turned and found he was looking down the business ends of four rifles! Four rifles held by four serious-looking Indian men who had silently sneaked right into their camp on the rain-dampened soil and now were not four feet away and holding them captive!

For what seemed like an eternity of time and expecting to first see flame then smoke erupting from the ends of those rifle barrels and then feeling hot lead tearing through his body, Ofer tried to only breathe shallowly for fear of setting off those Indians and then their rifles! Then he was aware of Black Eagle standing up and 'talking' in sign to the four impassive-looking Indians. Knowing sign, Ofer could tell that Black Eagle was welcoming his Indian brothers and asking them if they were hungry and if so, would they like to 'supper' with the trappers.

When Black Eagle had finished 'speaking' in sign, not a sound was heard from their Indian captors or any movement made except for the sounds of raindrops from the recent thunderstorm still dripping off the white ash trees' leaves. The four Indians 'holding down on them' appeared to be unimpressed with what Black Eagle had to 'say'. Then two of them spotted all of the valuable horses back in the trees tied to a picket line. That broke the silence! All of a sudden two of the Indians said something to the other two Indians, who quickly looked into the trees a short distance away at the long string of valuable horses. Then those two quickly locked their eyes back onto the two men by the fire and never let their serious killing expressions leave their faces for even just a moment!

However, the other two Indians broke ranks and after saying something to the two still holding their rifles on Black Eagle and Ofer, headed down to look over all of the valuable horseflesh just waiting to be taken back to some Indians' encampment and bragged about. About then Ofer could smell the buffalo meat beginning to burn. Pointing to the meat spitted around the fire and pointing to his nose and making a face about smelling burning meat, Ofer took a gamble, slowly moved off his saddle and began adjusting the spitted buffalo back a bit from the flames. As he did, his mind was racing on how to get out of this situation without being killed or wounded! In the meantime, his move to the fire had confused the two men still holding their rifles on Ofer and Black Eagle. In so doing, they hurriedly stepped back from the trapper tending the meat by the fire and then readjusted their rifles once again on Ofer!

Ofer soon discovered that his mental question about what to do under the circumstances was violently solved. **BOOM— BOOM!** went two quick shots down by the horse picket line where the other two Indians were standing looking over the horses! Ofer figured the other two Indians had just discovered Little Raven taking a dump and had shot him where he 'squatted'! Ofer immediately saw 'red' over the other two Indians killing Little Raven whom he considered almost like a son and went crazy! With that, Ofer lunged forward just as the two Indians guarding both him and Black Eagle, took their eyes off the two of them for a moment upon hearing the two quick shots fired down by the horses and the other two members of their party! Seeing their attentions diverted for just for a second was all Ofer needed as he lunged for the end of the closest rifle barrel next to him being held by a big and hugely fat Indian! Catching that Indian unawares, Ofer pulled on the end of his rifle barrel causing the Indian holding that rifle to inadvertently pull the trigger! **BOOM!** went that rifle and the shot sailed harmlessly into the dirt at Ofer's feet! But when Ofer pulled on the end of that rifle barrel, it caused the big fat Indian to stumble forward and land squarely on top of Ofer. That Indian died in his own 'pew', as Ofer's quickly drawn sheath knife was buried up to its handle into the man's guts, gushing a 'spew' of warm blood all over Ofer's hands, forearm and chest area!

That was when Ofer heard another close at hand gun going off and tossing his dying Indian from off him and still holding his knife in hand, he looked wildly around for the other Indian who had been holding the rifle on Black Eagle and himself! When he did, he was surprised to see that Indian wiggling his last after being shot in the stomach by Black Eagle's quickly drawn pistol when Ofer had made his move to disarm the other Indian! Then Ofer looked down by the horses to see what the other two Indians were doing as he dropped his knife and went for one of the pistols in his sash, still figuring they had already killed Little Raven. That was when he saw Little Raven coming toward the campfire still holding two pistols in each hand. As Ofer discovered, Little Raven had drawn his two pistols when he had observed the two strange- looking Indians coming down to look at the horses from his place in the brush taking a dump. They had not seen him but he had seen them, and when they were greedily looking over the horses, he had risen up, slinked in behind the two horse-distracted Indians and had head shot both of them with his pistols! Now here he came up to the campfire and without a word being spoken, handed both empty pistols to Ofer to be reloaded as Bear Trap had always counseled when on the frontier for one's safety, and then turned and quietly tended to the spitted buffalo to keep it from burning like it was an everyday event...

After a supper of spitted buffalo meat, medium rare of course, and some coffee, the four dead Indians were dragged further down into the brushy ravine and left for the critters of the land to discover and ultimately feast upon. As for the four Indians' horses, they were found tied off a short distance away from the trappers' campsite. There they were unsaddled, unbridled and slapped on the ass to go wherever they wanted since the trappers already had almost more horses than they could handle. The rest of that night the three trappers slept rather lightly out of concern there might be more Indians lounging around who had heard all of the shooting in their camp and were now coming their way to investigate. That being said, the three trappers were up way before daylight the next morning. By noon all the packhorses and riding stock had been loaded and saddled and the men were once again on the trail continuing to head to the south and east. As they rode however, they were even more cautious than usual. The night before, being sneaked up on without warning by those four Indians, had a surprising effect on those who had that happen to them and were still deep in Indian country and lucky to be alive...

But the 'stain' from the night before was far from being over. The next day was a repeat of the day before. The men had once again been caught out on the wide open prairie during a terrific summer thunderstorm as can only roll across the prairies during the heat of the day. Once again, the men were forced to seek shelter in a deep and brushy ravine to avoid the many close at hand dancing bolts of lightning smashing down onto anything sticking up from off the prairie! And once again after the characteristic following high winds and torrential downpour, the men found themselves wet, cold and yet blessed once again. The ravine they used while seeking shelter was filled with buffalo and one shot by Black Eagle dropped a cow deep in the brush of the gully right during a long and loud rolling clap of thunder. For once Ofer figured they were safe from wandering eyes and listening ears, so they made camp early and unpacked all of their horses for the night.

The horses were let loose to graze in the lush grasses of the ravine and with rainwater now running down through the normally dry creek bottom, their livestock was able to water as well. Once again, the men prepared for the night and a rope picket line was strung in among the dense white ash timber and the horses tied up. Then as Ofer and Black Eagle butchered out their dead cow buffalo, Little Raven not 40 feet from the dead animal made a small 'Indian's fire' and once again, spitted buffalo backstrap was merrily sizzling away on the metal spits and the coffee pot was later boiling away over a nice bed of coals. That evening, Ofer was not blessed with another sixth sense over uninvited arriving guests with ill thoughts and loaded rifles, not at least during that moment in time anyway...

After an excellent supper of spitted buffalo backstrap, the tired men retired to their damp sleeping furs from the summer's earlier rains and soon a deep sleep overcame all of them. ALL OF A SUDDEN IN THE DEEP OF THE NIGHT, OFER'S EYES SHOT WIDE AWAKE, AND AS BEAR TRAP DRIESSEN HAD TAUGHT HIM WHAT TO DO UNDER SUCH CIRCUMSTANCES WHILE OUT ON THE DANGEROUS FRONTIER, HE DID NOT MOVE ANYTHING BUT HIS EYES IN CASE THERE WAS DANGER NEARBY! Hearing Black Eagle and Little Raven still deep in sleep, Ofer frantically let his eyes roll all around in the deep darkness of the tree-covered ravine looking for what had caused him to 'fly' into a wide-awake mode! As he did, he saw or heard nothing of any sort indicating danger was nearby, OTHER THAN HIS SIXTH SENSE LETTING HIM KNOW THERE WAS A PROBLEM! Then he began shaking uncontrollably just like he had when he had sensed a problem back at Fort Manuel and then moments later had seen his four brothers in a very clear vision waving to him... Sinking deeper into his warm sleeping furs, Ofer let his senses take over and trying to breathe normally and not waken the others, his body violently shook like that of a 'dog passing peach pits'! THEN AS CLEAR AS A BELL, OFER HEARD HIS FATHER'S VOICE FROM DEEP IN THE BACK OF HIS HEAD CALLING HIS SONS HOME! Then the shaking slowly died away, he heard no more voices in his head and then a fit of exhaustion took over in his body and he slept soundly the rest of the night...

The next thing Ofer remembered was being shaken awake by Black Eagle in the pre-dawn light telling him to get up so they could pack and saddle the horses and then be on their way. As he rose and the cold rain-dampened air enveloped his warm body, he felt a shudder go through him as he once again remembered hearing his father's voice clear as a bell calling 'all of his sons home'... Then kneeling down by the still rapidly flowing rain-filled creek, he washed his face in the cold water, steeled himself internally over hearing such an ethereal call the evening before, and walked over and began quietly packing the many packhorses with their loaded packs. However, he now found himself eager to get to St. Louis and explore the depths of his latest sixth sense 'call' for all of the sons to return home.

Thirty-three days later found the three trappers tiredly reining up in front of the St. Louis Missouri Fur Company's main fur house. They had safely made it home and now they were going to sell their furs at the price of $6 per pound, St. Louis prices, instead of the $2.50 per pound offered at Fort Manuel, and cash in their Letters of Credit in Ofer's saddlebags from previous years. Then as Ofer waited out front of the fur house for the company's graders to unpack all of their furs, sort them out and then settle up on a final price, he saw a gathering of fur company officials talking quietly over by the edge of the warehouse. As they did, Ofer kept noticing they kept looking over at him and when he caught them looking at him and his pack string, they would hurriedly turn away and pretend they had not been looking at him with unusual interest.

That was when Ofer began having those sixth sense feelings of dread creeping back into his body for some reason once again... Finally one of those company officials walked over to Ofer, Black Eagle and Little Raven. He introduced himself as Robert Oates, Chief Buyer for the St. Louis Missouri Fur Company and asked if Ofer was one Ofer Tal. Ofer sensing bad news about falling beaver fur prices replied that he was Ofer Tal and asked, "Why, what is the problem?"

"We need to talk over by our warehouse," said Oates, where-upon he gently took Ofer by the elbow and walked him over to the side of the warehouse where they could have some privacy. There Oates said, "Mr. Tal, there is no easy way to say this. Your three brothers were killed by the Arikara on the Missouri when their keelboat was attacked and burned to its waterline as they were bringing down a load of furs from Fort Manuel earlier this spring!"

Upon hearing those words, Ofer felt his heart 'chill' and then he found it hard to breathe. If he hadn't been standing and able to grab the side of the warehouse, he would have fallen to the ground over hearing of the deaths of his last three brothers! Then he realized what the vision of his four brothers laughing and waving 'Good-bye' to him back at Fort Manuel had really meant when he had such a violent sixth sense reaction causing him to uncontrollably shake and then vomit over the amazing moment at hand...

About then Black Eagle and Little Raven ran up and surrounded Ofer with concerned looks on their faces after seeing him moments earlier turn as white as a sheet. "Four Scalps, what is the matter? We saw your legs buckle when this man talked to you and figuring you needed some help, came over to see what we could do," said Little Raven with concern spelled clear across his face over what he now considered his 'father figure'!

Ofer, emotionally distraught and with the realization of his deep loss of his last three brothers, still knew he had to carry on as the oldest brother and that his parents, the farm, Black Eagle and Little Raven all depended on him now more than ever. As the tears rolled down his cheeks and stained his buckskin shirt with dark blotches, he found the emotional strength to tell Black Eagle and Little Raven of the loss of their three 'brothers' and dear friends! However, that moment in time proved too much and emotional for all concerned and soon found all three Mountain Men in each other's arms crying like small children over their losses! When that happened, Oates moved away and let the men share their obvious deep sorrow in and among just themselves...

After having a good cry among themselves and finally gathering up their emotions, the men realized they still had a year's business to attend to, and moments later three very sober and quiet Mountain Men walked back to the fur buyers and oversaw their grading, sorting and counting actions with hardly a word being spoken among them. Finally all 603 of their fall trapped beaver '*Plus*' had been counted and graded by the company men. Being that those beaver skins weighed in around 904½ pounds and at the going rate of $6 per pound, that equated out to $5,427.00! With that amount in mind, Ofer walked over to his riding horse and withdrew his four previous Letters of Credit owed to him and his fellow trappers by the St. Louis Missouri Fur Company. Those four Letters of Credit came to $49,343.00! Then adding their most recent fur sale to those previous Letters of Credit figures and the final amount amounted to $54,770.00, or a fortune in that day and age! It was all Ofer, Black Eagle and Little Raven could do to contain each other over that unbelievable figure, even in light of the recent horrible news regarding the loss of the three brothers.

It was then that Ofer realized as the remaining brother, he would just have to internalize the great loss of his last three brothers and still continue on for the sake of Black Eagle and Little Raven, who had been his trusted brothers in arms throughout. Besides, this was their first trip to a white man's city and there was so much for them to see and learn when they arrived that it appeared their heads were on swivels they were turning and looking around in amazement so much at so many new and unbelievable sights, smells and sounds discovered at almost every street corner and behind every store window!

That was when Ofer decided he would not ruin Black Eagle and Little Raven's newfound joys at finally arriving safely in the white man's city of St. Louis, and their looking to the start of a new life after they had lost all of the living relatives a number of years earlier when the Gros Ventre had attacked their encampment. He would just have to live with what had happened and see to it that his parents were able to live out the rest of their lives in peace and that Black Eagle and Little Raven would have a wonderful start in their new lives as well.

With those determinations solidly in mind, Ofer decided they would go to the nearest bank with their final and consolidated Letter of Credit in hand from the St. Louis Missouri Fur Company and deposit such a large amount of funds into a bank account. Then withdrawing a certain amount needed for what he planned next, they would proceed on to what he had now planned and try setting their emotional losses aside. First, they were going to get their horses housed in a livery then have a big meal at a local eatery in celebration of their safe arrival. Then sleep in a bed far from the dangers out on the frontier but before that, take a hot bath. Then Ofer had decided they would head to a local emporium the next day, throw away their old buckskins and clothe themselves in the dress of the day. Then they would head to Ofer's home where he would introduce Black Eagle and Little Raven to his parents and their family's cook, Emily, who Ofer had missed so very much. With those plans in mind, Ofer accepted his final Letter of Credit from the fur company's main office and then with directions to the First National Bank of St. Louis located on 3rd and Front Street, off the three ex-fur trappers rode with their large horse herd.

For the next two days, Ofer acted as a 'big brother' and showed Black Eagle and Little Raven what a small slice of the white man's world looked like. Then eager to see his parents and get back to the horse ranch and farm, the three men pulled their horse herd out from the livery and headed for 'home', a family reunion and new life that was soon going to follow for the three of them after Ofer had shared with his parents the news about the loss of four of their sons.

CHAPTER 15 — THE CALL OF THE WILDERNESS

HERDING THEIR LARGE HERD OF BUCKSKINS ALONG THE road leading to his home, Ofer could not wait to make the turn in the road and then ride into view of his parents' grand house sitting off in a grove of giant oak trees. As he did, he found his heart racing over finally coming home, seeing his parents once again, advising them of their great family losses and then taking a look to see if a quiet life of ranching and farming was what he wanted after the exciting and rewarding life he had just experienced as a Mountain Man. Looking over at Black Eagle and Little Raven riding alongside, all he could see were their big grins of anticipation at finally coming to a place where they could start a new life in a white man's world without all of the dangers found swirling around them while out on the frontier.

Turning onto his home road after rounding a long timbered area, OFER WAS SHOCKED TO SEE THAT HIS PARENTS' HOME WAS MISSING! Stopping in the middle of the road in shock, Ofer just stared at what amounted to a large pile of darkened ash, bricks, burned timbers and chimney remains starkly sticking nakedly into the sky of what had once been a large, white-colored, Southern-style plantation home! Of what had once been, Ofer could see nothing left but a large heap of ashes, burned timbers and two brick chimneys sticking into the air! "NO!" Ofer yelled, as he spurred his horse down the road leading to what had once been his family's home. Riding up to the burned ruins of what had once been a rather palatial home, Ofer bailed off his horse and ran over to the ash heap in disbelief as if that would change what he was seeing! For the longest time he just stood there and stared and then he saw the family's house mistress, Miss Emily, walking towards him from where she had been living in the family's nearby carriage house which had not burned.

"EMILY, WHAT HAS HAPPENED? WHERE ARE MOTHER AND FATHER?" yelled Ofer, with a sinking and now breaking heart over what he was seeing.

Emily continued walking over to Ofer who was now crying his heart out, and like when he was younger as a child, the old black woman who had basically raised him as his parents struggled in putting together a life on the horse ranch and farm, gathered him into her arms and tried comforting him. Finally when Ofer had regained himself sufficiently enough, Emily explained what had happened. "Ofer, when your mother found out about the loss of her other sons, she went into shock and became bedridden. Then one evening when your father was tending to her and had left her side to get her a drink of water, she got out from bed, knocked over a whale oil lamp and set the house afire! When your father saw what was happening, he ran back into the burning home to rescue her and never came out... They both died in the fire and the other slaves and I have been waiting here praying for your return. It is so good that you are now home. Absalom and Jericho have been managing the ranch and farm but we are now in trouble. Because they are still slaves and have no legal right to anything on your father's property, we have been unable to borrow any money to keep the place running. So we have been selling off your father's horses and some crops in order to keep functioning as a family unit like your parents would have wished. Now that you are back and the legal owner of the ranch and the adjoining 1,000-acre farm, we can all relax and you can now manage the affairs of the homesite," said Emily quietly with eyes filled with tears.

It was then Ofer saw Emily looking at Black Eagle and Little Raven, obviously of Indian stock and then Ofer realized in his hurt and surprise of the moment he had forgotten his two very close friends. Turning, Ofer said, "Emily, this is Black Eagle and Little Raven who are my two very dear and close friends. A long time ago I managed to rescue them from sure death or a life of slavery and we have been very close ever since. Fellas, this is the woman who basically raised not only me but my brothers as well when my parents were wresting the wild land from the forests and turning it into our ranch and farm. Emily, Black Eagle and Little Raven have been through thick and thin with me while I lived out on the frontier and the three of us now are as close as I was with any of my brothers. In fact, I now consider them to be my brothers or even, my sons!"

Then holding Emily in his arms and still looking around, Ofer said, "Well, it looks like I came home at the right time. From the looks of the place, I have a lot of hard work to do to bring the home place back to where it should be. Thanks to Absalom and Jericho, they held her together until I got back here to take care of the much-needed legal affairs."

Throughout that winter and following spring of 1811, Ofer, Black Eagle and Little Raven set about setting the home place's affairs in order. The first thing Ofer did was call in a local family-known judge and with sanctioned and legally registered documents, freed all of the family's slaves! Then using the remaining buckskin horses he had brought back from his days as a Mountain Man trapping on the frontier, Ofer used them to once again begin building up their horse farm's breeding stock.

In the meantime, the now freed slaves built a smaller home place in which for Emily and the boys to live. Following that, Ofer got the farming program up and going once again and using some of his money derived from his earlier trapping ventures, bankrolled the purchasing of new farm equipment, as well as the purchasing of newer and younger draft horses for the heavy and strenuous farming work. By the following spring of 1812, the ranch and farm was once again back in the black and making a profit for not only Ofer and his two new 'brothers', but for all the now 'Freedmen' tilling the land and raising their special breed of buckskin horses. Horses that were being sold to all the newly arriving immigrants arriving in the St. Louis area, just starting to explore the undeveloped and largely unexplored lands lying further to the west being sold for $1 per acre by the United States Government in order to help pay off the War of Independence debt.

But in so doing, many a night after the work of the day was done found Ofer, Black Eagle and Little Raven sitting around the supper table visiting about their earlier days out on the largely unexplored frontier and their wonderful days of extreme freedom as Free Trappers and Mountain Men... And no matter what had happened involving the work of the day on the ranch or farm, their conversation always seemed to return to their wondrous days as trappers... And in so doing, bringing back such memories as the extreme freedom experienced as Mountain Men, the raw beauty found out on the sometimes dangerous frontier, killing and eating buffalo, especially the warm liver right from the side of the animal just killed, fighting Indians, trapping wolves, easy summers at Fort Manuel, visiting with other fellow trappers and friends, Dutch oven biscuits every morning, happily finding beaver in most every trap and enjoying cups of rum when the day's work was done among the brotherhood. And yes, the hordes of mosquitoes found around their campfire when the day was done or in their plates of food...

One evening after Emily had served the men their supper after a hard day planting corn, the talk around the table once again went back to the good times they had spent together out on the frontier. Tales then began flying back and forth about happier times, funny things that happened out by the latrine, good rifle or pistol shots made on Indians, huge beaver caught in traps, finding leeches covering one's body after trapping on a particular beaver pond, and soon the men were laughing so loudly over funny events that had happened to each of them that Emily, over hearing such loud laughter, came back into the kitchen to make sure everything was alright!

After a particularly funny session one evening when the men were enjoying tales from their past days as trappers, it got very quiet around the table as the men then individually paused and then quietly remembered some of the better times they had out on the frontier. It was then when Ofer broke that silence around the supper table with the words, "Man, how I miss some of those days with you guys and all of my brothers…" Then even more deep silence followed his words, as one could now tell that all of the men were thinking back to some of their better days as Men of the Mountains, who were free as the wind that blew daily across the prairies and through the tops of the tall trees… Then more silence followed as each man found himself lost even more deeply in memories of their past. Memories of when they were younger, free as a golden eagle circling in a thermal and listening to the wind moving through the trees, along with being able to hear one's heartbeat while out in the utter stillness of the wilderness…

"Do any of you ever think about going back and facing the odds of life back in the wilderness?" asked Ofer quietly, clear out of the blue…

For the longest time, no one said anything in response to Ofer's question. No one said anything because they didn't have to! Looking around the table, Ofer saw in the faces of Black

Eagle and Little Raven the desire to return to those days when they were as free as the wind. In fact, if Ofer had looked in a mirror at that very moment in time, he would have seen the same introspective look on his face that he was seeing on the faces of his two 'brothers' sitting across the table from him! Then all at once, each man sitting around the table that evening found himself quietly and deeply looking into each other's eyes at the same instant! And when they did, each could almost see into the other's soul and read what each of them were feeling but not daring to say…

"Want to give this up and go back?" asked Ofer quietly, with searching eyes scanning the faces of Black Eagle and Little Raven. For the longest time, not one of the three men moved or even hardly dared to breathe. Then the looks on the men's faces followed by grins of anticipation simultaneously said it all! With that moment in time captured in the three men's souls, all realizing that "memory is the scribe to the soul"! With that revelation, Ofer rose and walked over to their storeroom just off the kitchen, opened the door and quietly examined everything stacked about in organized disarray from their days as Mountain Men trappers. Without thinking past what he was seeing, Ofer quietly said, "In order to make use of our cast iron once again, we will need to throw all of it back into a roaring fire, cook it off and then re-season it, and that may take some time." With those words, Ofer turned around and discovered himself facing Black Eagle and Little Raven eagerly looking at him and then over his shoulder at the many stacked implements from their days as Mountain Men. Days spent as free as a golden eagle riding the thermals and surveying its world below…

For the next week around the Tal ranch and farm, there was a flurry of activity by everyone realizing the souls of Ofer, Black Eagle and Little Raven had been captured by what was called and known as "The Wilderness"! And from the looks in those three men's eyes and their lightness of step, they were going to respond! Additionally, Ofer spent several long hours in with the judge and county recorder once again before coming home late one evening. The next day, Ofer gathered around him the 30 recently Freedmen and their families from the farm and ranch. There he deeded half the horse ranch to Absalom and the other half of the ranch to Jericho. Then he deeded the entire farm to all the rest of the men and women who had so faithfully served the Tal family over the years... Later that day in the quiet of her new kitchen in her new home, Ofer deeded the immediate home ranch grounds over to Emily, and advised her that a rather large sum of money derived from Ofer's fur trapping was in the local bank in her name for her remaining years so she could live in comfort. Upon hearing those words of 'life', Emily and then Ofer shed many tears while wrapped in each other's arms over a previous life lost to the ages and another one beginning once again...

The following day, Ofer, Black Eagle and Little Raven selected 14 buckskin riding and packhorses and had all of them reshod and an additional set of shoes set aside for each horse. Then Ofer made sure he remembered how to shoe horses by spending a day with the ranch's blacksmiths, and assembled a complete set of farrier's tools so he could re-shoe their horses once afield on an as-needed basis. Then the following day was spent re-seasoning all of their cast iron pots, frying pans and Dutch ovens. Then as the rest of the ranch hands made ready all of the pack and riding saddles, Ofer, Black Eagle and Little Raven visited Manuel Lisa's emporium and purchased an allotment of food supplies and other clothing accessories needed for a year afield as Mountain Men trappers. However, since they still had a goodly supply of firearms, traps, tools, repair equipment and the like from their previous days as trappers, those types of items were not purchased in any quantities. But the men did purchase a goodly supply of flints, greased wads for their pistols and rifles, rifle and pistol powders in watertight tins and 100 pounds of lead pigs for the making of balls for their rifles and handguns.

Two days later, Ofer gathered all of the ranch and farm hands together and their families for a last time together family dinner. Later the following morning, Ofer thanked all of them for serving his family so faithfully over the years, as Black Eagle and Little Raven sat on their horses trailing all of their heavily loaded packhorses. Then Ofer scooped up Emily in his arms and whirled her around and around in the joy of loving a very special kind of person until she had him put her down in embarrassment over the attention she was individually receiving. Then Ofer wrapped her up in his arms one more time, gave her a kiss and then holding her hand, walked over to his mother and father's gravesite where they had been buried near the carriage house. There he silently said his 'Good-byes' and thanked them for being such loving parents. Then he 'told them' he was now going off to be with his brothers..., turned and never looked back.

Four months later, Ofer, Black Eagle and Little Raven tiredly rode onto the grounds of Fort Manuel. Sitting on his horse and looking all around at old and familiar sights, Ofer thought, *There was the love of adventure so natural to the heart of every Mountain Man that it led him to the wilderness and kept him there clinging to it and now, here they were...* About then they met an old friend walking out to meet arriving fur trappers, one very surprised Manuel Lisa. "Well, what brings you three back to my neck of the woods?" Lisa asked with a big grin on his face.

"Well, Manuel, we missed your smiling face and being invited to one of your famous dinners that you set for some of your arriving trappers," said Ofer with a smile.

"Well, after you men get your camp set up, come back for dinner tomorrow night and I will see to it that the three of you are welcomed back in typical style," said Lisa, as he reached out and warmly shook the hands of all three Mountain Men and now and forever, Men of the Mountains...

Shortly thereafter some questions on how the beaver trapping was going more than started Lisa off on a surprising rant! "Ofer, you and the boys may be in for a rough trapping season. Oh, we have beaver in great numbers and big ones too, but it is those damn British. According to my keelboat crews with the latest news from St. Louis, ever since Lewis and Clark went to the Pacific Ocean and built their fort and flew the American flag over it, the British have been on the warpath. It seems they have been stopping and boarding our ships, taking their cargos including all of the beaver furs we are shipping to Europe, taking our sailors and impressing them into the British navy because they are short-handed sailors for their own naval fleets. Hell, according to the news in St. Louis, the British have even emptied out their prisons just to get enough men to man their ships! Then because the British are concerned the Americans' expansion into the frontier will cost them the very lucrative fur trade found out west, they are once again stirring up trouble among all of the Indian tribes along the Canadian border. Near as I can tell, the Hudson's Bay Fur Company and their British agents are arming the border tribes like the Blackfeet and Gros Ventre, filling their guts with whiskey and turning them against the American trappers. Right now many of my trappers are telling me that those British agents are assisting the Indians as they come way south of Canada's border, steal our traps, trap our beaver and are running off my trappers! So it behooves you men to be on the lookout for them stirred-up Indians anywhere you might be interested in beaver trapping. Keep a sharp peeled eye in whatever you do because those killing Indians are really on the warpath now that they have buyers for every fur that is brought to them, plus all the whiskey they can drink, and powder, guns and lead they can use in moving the Americans out from the beaver trapping grounds in this country. I also hear tell there are war clouds in the air between the United States and those damn British over this and them doing what they are doing to our ships and the Americans who man them. In fact, if this keeps up, I may have to move my trading post further south in order not to be attacked by them damn British and their Indian allies!" (Author's Note: The following year because of the War of 1812 and the British stirring up the Indian tribes along the Canadian border, Manuel Lisa did in fact close down his Fort Manuel in current-day Montana along the Bighorn and Yellowstone Rivers and moved his fur buying and trading business further south into the current-day State of Nebraska where he set up another trading post.)

"Well, that certainly is not good news, Manuel. Me and the boys here will just have to keep a sharp eye peeled and our powder dry if we want to trap any beaver," said Ofer quietly. "But we are here to make a living on the frontier and trap beaver until they or we are all gone, so them damn British and their allies as you are calling them best keep their distance. Last time I looked, me and the boys were damn good shooters and just given half a chance, should be able to take care of ourselves," said Ofer with his characteristic smile, as Black Eagle and Little Raven with big grins, shook their heads in support of what Ofer had just said.

"Well for your sakes, I hope so. Anyway, welcome back and good beaver trapping to the three of you. If you need any supplies my warehouses are full so make yourselves at home and get what you might need. In the meantime, get your camp set up and don't forget my supper invite for tomorrow night," said Manuel with a meaningful smile on his face.

With that, Ofer and company headed over to their favorite camping spot outside the fort's walls in their old cottonwood grove near a creek. Arriving there a short time later, the men dismounted and unloaded their horses so they could graze and water in the area. Then after stacking up their packs and arranging their sleeping furs under the cottonwood trees so if it rained they could stay dry, they set about gathering up wood for their fire. As they did, Ofer found himself going back in his memories of previous times when all of the brothers were present at that campsite and then shook his head as he found his eyes misting up over better times in his life. Then looking over at Black Eagle, he saw him staring off into the prairie's vastness more than likely thinking about better times in his life as well. Then heading for their old firepit with an armload of firewood, Ofer saw Little Raven standing there looking down at the firepit like he was also thinking back on better times when he had his cooking partner Gabriel there with him to give him a hand...

Then Ofer said, "Thinking about Gabriel, Little Raven?"

That was when Little Raven caught himself and turning, Ofer could see tears in his eyes as well. Then thinking to himself, Ofer thought, *It will take some time before all the old memories and better times 'scar' over and we can begin living our lives once again...* Ofer then dropped his bundle of firewood and to break the somber mood said, "Little Raven, what is for supper?" That evening, because they had no camp meat, supper consisted of Dutch oven biscuits and just coffee. However, the next night's supper over at the big house of Manuel Lisa consisted of fried spuds and onions from the fort's garden, roasted buffalo backstrap, Dutch oven biscuits and apple cobbler. Then afterwards, the men smoked some of Lisa's cigars and drank his very special Fourth Proof rum while sitting out on his front porch. Then they walked back to their campsite and after a long day filled with many memories from times past, the men drifted off to sleep under the cotton-woods in their sleeping furs.

Two days later and anxious to check out some beaver trapping areas not occupied by other trappers, the men headed towards the Musselshell to see what beaver riches it still might hold. And 'sure as shooting', they found evidence that the beaver had recovered their numbers from a couple of previous hard winters. In fact so much so, Ofer, Black Eagle and Little Raven thought they would swing by their old cave-cabin up on the Smith River and see if it was still there and possibly livable. As they rode in that direction, they saw that the Musselshell was once again more than populated with good beaver numbers and that got their hopes up, meaning maybe they would trap that area once again after looking the Smith over first. So they left the Musselshell, turned and traveled up along the Smith looking those beaver waters over. When they did, they were encouraged to see so much sign. In fact, Ofer thought the waters looked a lot like they did the first time he and his brothers had ventured into such country as trappers.

One day later they arrived back at their old cave-cabin and upon examination, other than needing a front door's leather hinges replaced and new deerskins spread over their window frames, their old cave-cabin was very livable. There the men decided they would use that cave-cabin and trap the upper reaches of the Smith once again for their fall and coming spring beaver trapping seasons. With that decision made, their horses were unpacked and their supplies were hauled into and stored in their cave-cabin so they would be out from the summer thunderstorms. Then the horses were hobbled and let out to graze and water while the men arranged all of their items in their old home, making it homey once again. Finishing, as Little Raven sat about rebuilding his firepit area, Black Eagle and Ofer scouted out around their old cabin for some firewood so Little Raven would have cooking fuels.

Then once the firewood issue was solved, Ofer and Black Eagle grabbed up their rifles and headed out back to see if they could find and kill a deer for camp meat. Within the hour, the two men had each fired one shot and had killed two doe mule deer for their camp meat. Dragging their deer back to the cave-cabin for Little Raven to work his cooking magic upon them and then hang the remains from their old meat poles, the men noisily laughing and talking rounded the side of their cave-cabin and immediately stood stock-still! LYING IN HIS FIREPIT SMOKING AWAY IN THE FIRE'S FLAMES LAY LITTLE RAVEN WHOSE BODY WAS FILLED WITH FOUR OR FIVE ARROWS! DROPPING THEIR DEER IN ALARM, BOTH MEN SHOULDERED THEIR RIFLES LOOKING FOR THE DANGER THAT HAD CLAIMED LITTLE RAVEN'S LIFE! SEEING NONE AROUND THE FIREPIT AREA, A LOUD NOISE WAS HEARD OVER BY THE CORRAL AND BOTH MEN IMMEDIATELY LOOKED IN THAT DIRECTION. WHEN THEY DID, THEY SAW NINE INDIANS WITH RIFLES AND BOWS AND ARROWS AIMED THEIR WAY FROM JUST A FEW YARDS DISTANT! IT WAS AT THAT VERY DANGEROUS MOMENT IN TIME THAT OFER IMMEDIATELY FELT HIS BODY'S SIXTH SENSE COME ALIVE! THEN HE FOUND HIMSELF ALMOST MAGICALLY DRIFTING OFF INTO THE "UPPER WORLD" AND WHEN HE DID, HE WAS AMAZED TO SEE HIS FATHER, MOTHER AND FOUR BROTHERS STANDING THERE QUIETLY WATCHING HIM! HE THEN REALIZED HIS ENTIRE FAMILY WAS SMILING AND NOW BECKONING TO HIM...

THE FIRST TWO FIRED RIFLE BALLS STRUCK OFER, ONE IN THE FACE AND THE OTHER IN THE CHEST, KILLING HIM INSTANTLY! BLACK EAGLE DIED HARDER JUST MOMENTS LATER! TWO BULLETS STRUCK HIM IN THE CHEST AND STOMACH, IMMEDIATELY DROPPING HIM TO THE GROUND! HOWEVER, FROM HIS LYING POSITION, HE GOT OFF ONE SHOT WITH HIS RIFLE, KILLING A BLACKFOOT WARRIOR HURRIEDLY RELOADING HIS RIFLE AFTER SHOOTING AND KILLING HIS DEAR FRIEND AND FATHER FIGURE, FOUR SCALPS! BUT ALL OF THAT WAS TO NO AVAIL, AS THREE OTHER INDIANS COLLECTIVELY SHOT BLACK EAGLE THREE MORE TIMES, KILLING HIM...

That evening the remaining eight Blackfoot Indians and their two British agents from the Hudson's Bay Fur Company who had been quietly watching and then trailing Ofer, Black Eagle and Little Raven as they rode into the cave-cabin area, feasted on the freshly killed mule deer previously killed by Ofer and Black Eagle. Then the Blackfeet and Hudson's Bay Fur Company British agents got roaring drunk on the trappers' rum supply over their victory killing the American fur trappers and Mountain Men. The next day, the eight remaining Blackfeet and two British agents with ringing heads from the many cups of rum imbibed the evening before, loaded up all 14 of Ofer's prize buckskins and all of the trappers' supplies, as finally the Smith River Band of Blackfeet got their hands on the much sought after and prized buckskins. Little did they realize that they had also finally killed the one their band over the previous three years had come to know and fear called The Scalper! As the Blackfeet and British agents left the trappers' now empty cave-cabin and horse corral, off in the distance a lone Clark's nutcracker could be heard hammering away on a limb on a dead lightning-struck pine tree... That was a new species of bird named by famed explorer William Clark during his heroic 1803-1806 new continent-establishing journey from St. Louis to the Pacific Ocean and return. An epic journey of discovery that generated the intense interest in the Tal Brothers years earlier to come and explore the new frontier themselves as Mountain Men fur trappers, a 'time' that ended years later in the deadly ambush at the cave-cabin by the Blackfeet and their British allies...

For those so called "Mountain Men", all were equal and shared the toil of the day and the rest of night with their fellows. And for many, they shared the wilderness with bravery, hope, love, awe, and many times also with their 'brothers' in kind, in unmarked graves or as bleached bones in the forests, or as bear scat lying out on the prairie... As Ofer had wished, he was once again with his brothers Daniel, Gabriel, Joshua, Jerimiah, Black

Eagle and Little Raven. Men who all had shared the adventures of a lifetime in a short period of time with him, as well as many times their associated laughter until the arrival of their untimely deaths...

THE "WILDERNESS" HAD BECOME OFER'S, DANIEL'S, GABRIEL'S, JOSHUA'S, JERIMIAH'S, BLACK EAGLE'S AND LITTLE RAVEN'S "MOTHER". NOW SHE HELD ALL OF THEM FIRMLY TO HER BREAST...

A LOOK AT CROSSED ARROWS

BY TERRY GROSZ

In 1829, Jacob and Martin left Kentucky to become Mountain Men, trappers of the Rocky Mountains. The rugged mountains that lay beyond America's frontier remained mostly unexplored. In those days, when beaver were plentiful and the buffalo roamed freely, the killing was good. The two young men would also find that life would be hardscrabble in the high frontier. They would face grizzly bears and hostile Indians. And they would risk horse wrecks and mountain storms to trade their furs each year at "rendezvous." Crossed Arrows is the story of two adventurers who lived hard in the earliest days of the Wild West.

AVAILABLE NOW FROM TERRY GROSZ AND WOLFPACK PUBLISHING

ABOUT THE AUTHOR

Terry Grosz was born in June of 1941, in Toppenish, Washington. He graduated from Quincy High School in 1959, and attended Humboldt State College where he earned his Bachelor of Science Degree in Wildlife Management in 1964, and his Master of Science Degree in Wildlife Management in 1966. He was a California State Fish and Game Warden from 1966 until 1970, based first in Eureka, California, and then in Colusa, California, in the Northern Sacramento Valley. He then joined the U.S. Fish and Wildlife Service in 1970, first serving in California as a U.S. Game Management Agent and later as a Special Agent until 1974. In 1974, he was promoted to a Senior Resident Agent position over the States of North and South Dakota where he served until 1976. In 1976, he was promoted to a Senior Special Agent position and was transferred to Washington, DC, where he served as the Endangered Species Desk Officer and Foreign Liaison Officer until 1979. In 1979, he was transferred to Minneapolis, Minnesota, where he served as the Assistant Special Agent in Charge until 1981. In 1981, Terry was promoted and transferred to Denver, Colorado, as the Special Agent in Charge over the wildlife resource-rich eight-state region of the Service's Region 6, encompassing over 750,000 square miles in the States of North Dakota, South Dakota, Nebraska, Kansas, Montana, Wyoming, Colorado and Utah. He retired from the U.S. Fish and Wildlife Service in 1998, after a 32-year career in state and federal wildlife law enforcement.

In 1999, Terry began his second career as a writer, with the publishing of his first wildlife law enforcement true-life adventures book titled, "WILDLIFE WARS", which won him a National Outdoor Book Award in the Nature and Environment category. He has since had 13 additional wildlife law enforcement adventure books published, titled, *For Love Of Wildness, Defending Our Wildlife Heritage, A Sword For Mother Nature, No Safe Refuge, The Thin Green Line, Genesis Of A Duck Cop, Slaughter In The Sacramento Valley, Wildlife's Quiet War, Wildlife Heritage On The Edge, Wildlife Dies Without Making A Sound (volumes 1 and 2),* and *Flowers And Tombstones Of A Conservation Officer (volumes 1 and 2).*

In addition to this current book titled, "FOUR SCALPS" OFER TAL, MOUNTAIN MAN, Terry has written ten additional Mountain Man and Western historical novels titled, *Crossed Arrows; Curse Of The Spanish Gold; The Saga Of Harlan Waugh, Mountain Man; The Adventures Of The Brothers Dent, Mountain Men; The Adventures Of Hatchet Jack, Mountain Man; The Adventurous Life Of Tom "Iron Hand" Warren, Mountain Man; Josiah Pike; Hell Or High Water; Elliott "Bear Scat" Sutta, Mountain Man;* and *The Saga Of The Barnes Clan, Mountain Men.*

Additionally, Terry has a two-hour movie film credit on the reality-based TV series of "Animal Planet" titled, "WILDLIFE WARS", filmed in 2003 and released nationwide, based on a number of Terry's true-life wildlife law enforcement adventures involving his very active career as a state and federal wildlife officer.

Terry has earned many awards and honors during his lengthy career, including the U.S. Fish and Wildlife Service's Meritorious Service Award in 1996—Recognized as one of the "Top Ten" employees of the U.S. Fish and Wildlife Service under Service Director Frank Dunkle, for which he received a $5,000 bonus— The first federal employee to be honored with the "Guy Bradley Award" presented by the National Fish and Wildlife Foundation in 1989 for outstanding excellence in the field of wildlife law enforcement—Colorado Conservationist of the Year Award in 1984—The Conservation Achievement Award for Law Enforcement from the National Wildlife Federation in 1995 (the first such law enforcement officer so honored by that organization)—Special Achievement Award for Law Enforcement Excellence from the U.S. Department of Justice in 1998—Distinguished Alumnus Award, College of Natural Resources, Humboldt State University, 1995—Humboldt State University Distinguished Alumnus Award, 2008—Distinguished Achievement Award from the Native American Fish and Wildlife Society, 1992—Received the U.S. Fish and Wildlife Service's highest Annual Performance Ratings under five different senior level supervisors from 1983-1998—Unity College in Maine awarded Terry an Honorary Doctorate Degree in Environmental Stewardship in 2002.

Terry resides in Evergreen, Colorado, with the Co-Author of his life, Donna, whose heart he won and was his high school Sweetheart and now Bride of 55 years and counting...

Lightning Source UK Ltd.
Milton Keynes UK
UKHW04f1517170918
329048UK00001B/203/P